more . . .

"Entertaining . . . a real page turner . . . one of those books you just can't put down . . . a wonderful plot with loads of suspense, intriguing characters, and a bit of humor."
—BestsellersWorld.com

"As always, Kate White brings us a charming and down-to-earth heroine, and one adventure after another. This is an easy and pleasurable read with plenty of well-paced suspense to keep you turning those pages!"
—BookReporter.com

"Spicy . . . seamless and tightly woven . . . a well-crafted murder mystery that's clever, interesting, and compelling."
—EdgeBoston.com

"A winner . . . a page-turner with a great cast of characters."
—FreshFiction.com

"A fast-paced, action-packed gossip-fest, with all the guilty pleasure of a celeb gossip magazine."
—NightsandWeekends.com

"A fun mystery . . . Bailey Weggins is quickly becoming a favorite crime solver."
—TheBookHaven.net

"Great . . . stellar . . . a perfect read . . . A new Kate White novel is always a treat."
—The RomanceReadersConnection.com

'TIL DEATH DO US PART

"White's slick tale is as fun as nabbing a couture gown at a sample sale."
—Entertainment Weekly

"Wonderful . . . packed with insider stuff about the magazine business."
—Connecticut Post

"Juicy . . . cleverly plotted . . . funny . . . positively suspenseful."
—Publishers Weekly

A BODY TO DIE FOR

"Nancy Drew turned *Cosmo* girl . . . Best served with a side dish of sex and the city."
—People

"A breezy . . . fine read."
—Boston Globe

"A hot page-turner."
—Redbook

IF LOOKS COULD KILL

"*Sex and the City* meets the murder mystery, and Bailey Weggins is a sleuth a girl could love . . . What wicked fun!"
—Lisa Scottoline, author of *Courting Trouble*

"A page-turner . . . keeps the reader guessing."
—Chicago Sun-Times

"White is scathingly observant, capturing the mood at a glossy magazine with a verisimilitude some of her peers might recognize."
—New York Times

OVER HER DEAD BODY

KATE WHITE

WARNER BOOKS

NEW YORK   BOSTON

Copyright © 2005 by Kate White
Excerpts from *How to Set His Thighs on Fire* copyright © 2006 by Kate White
All rights reserved.

Warner Books
Hachette Book Group USA
1271 Avenue of the Americas
New York, NY 10020

Visit our Web site at www.HachetteBookGroupUSA.com.

Printed in the United States of America
Originally published in hardcover by Warner Books

First Trade Edition: June 2006
10 9 8 7 6 5 4 3 2 1

The Warner Books name and logo are trademarks of Time Inc. Used under license.

The Library of Congress has cataloged the hardover edition as follows:

White, Kate
   Over her dead body / Kate White. — 1st ed.
       p. cm.
    ISBN 0-446-53176-6
   1. Periodicals—Publishing—Fiction. 2. Women journalists—Fiction. I. Title.
   PS3623.H578O95   2005
   813'.6—dc22

2005000376

ISBN-13: 978-0-446-69770-5 (pbk.)
ISBN-10: 0-446-69770-2 (pbk.)

To the fabulous
Miriam Friedman

ACKNOWLEDGMENTS

Thank you to those who so generously helped me with my research: Paul Paganelli, M.D., chief of emergency medicine, Milton Hospital, Milton, PA; Barbara A. Butcher, director of investigations for the office of the chief medical examiner, New York City; former FBI profiler Candace deLong; attorney Daniel Kenneally; photo editor Robert Conway; writer Sheila Weller.

And a big thank you to my wonderful editor, Kristen Weber.

CHAPTER 1

What you see isn't always what you get.

The trouble with clichés is that they're so downright tedious, you fail to pay any attention to the message they're meant to convey. And sometimes you really should. I know because during a very hot and muggy summer in New York City, that particular cliché jumped up more than once and took a large, hard bite out of my butt.

On the initial occasion, before summer even started, I was an idiot to have been blindsided. It was the last week in May and Cat Jones, my boss at *Gloss* magazine, had invited me out to dinner. Now, there was nothing inherently odd in Cat treating me to a meal—despite our work arrangement, we'd always been friends in a weird sort of way. But she'd suggested that we meet at six forty-five at a kind of out-of-the-way place in the Village, and that's when the warning bells should have sounded. As a friend of mine once pointed out, when a guy suggests dinner at an untrendy restaurant before seven o'clock, you can be damn sure that he's going to announce he's in love with another chick and he's hoping for a fast escape before you start to sob and lunge for his ankles. My mistake was not realizing that the same warning applied to bosses, too.

I *did* suspect that the dinner was going to be more work related than personal. For the past few years I've been under contract with *Gloss* to write eight to ten crime or human-interest stories a year. Cat had worked out the arrangement herself when she'd first arrived at *Gloss* and was in the process of turning it from a bland-as-boiled-ham women's service magazine into a kind of *Cosmo* for married chicks. I'd always pitched my own story ideas, and they were green-lighted pretty quickly. But lately I'd been batting zero, and I didn't know why. Perfect example: Two weeks ago I'd suggested a piece on a young mother who'd disappeared without a trace while jogging. The husband had become the main suspect, though interestingly it was she, not he, who'd been having an affair. Cat had nixed the idea with the comment "Missing wives just feel *sooo* tired to me." Tell that to the Laci Peterson family, I'd been tempted to say—but hadn't. My hunch was that Cat had suggested dinner together so she could offer me insight into what kind of crime *didn't* put her to sleep these days.

I arrived at the restaurant first, which is typical when dealing with Cat, but at least it gave me a chance to catch my breath. It was a small, French country–style restaurant on Mac-Dougal Street in the Village, and I ordered a glass of rosé in honor of the weather and the ambience. As each group of new diners strolled through the door, they brought a delicious late spring breeze with them.

Let this be a hint of how delicious the summer will be, I prayed. I was thirsty for a summer to end all summers. In January, I'd broken up with a guy I'd really cared about, and though I wasn't eager for another serious relationship right now, I was hoping for *some* kind of romantic adventure. I'd had a brief fling in late winter with a male model in his early twenties, ten years younger than me, but then he'd relocated to Los Angeles. After that it had been slim pickings unless you count four or five booty calls with an old beau from Brown who had become so stuffy that I practically had to ask him not to talk. I'm pretty, I guess, in a kind of sporty way—five six, fairly slim, with brownish blond hair just below my chin—and generally I'd never had trouble rustling up dates. I was banking on the fact that my dry spell might end now that we were in the season of nearly effortless seductions.

Cat sauntered in about ten minutes late, and heads swiveled in her direction. She's in her late thirties, gorgeous, with long, buttery blond hair, blue eyes, and full lips that never leave the house unless they're stained a brick red or dusky pink. She was wearing slim turquoise pants and an exotic gold-and-turquoise embroidered top that made her look as if she'd just come from the casbah.

"Sorry I'm late," she said, slipping into her seat. "Minor crisis."

"Diverted, I hope."

"Unfortunately, no. I'm having a huge problem with the new beauty editor. Her copy is about as exciting as the instructions that come with a DVD recorder, and her judgment sucks."

"What did she do this time?"

"She signed up for a junket to Paris without clearing it with anyone."

"*Really?*" I said, feigning interest just to be polite. I felt about as much concern as I would have if Cat had announced she could feel a fever blister coming on. "What else is going on?"

Before she could answer, the waiter scurried over. Cat ordered a glass of Chardonnay and asked for the menus ASAP. Hmm, I thought. She seemed in a hurry, almost on edge. I wondered if something might be the matter.

"So, where were we?" she asked as the waiter departed.

"I was asking what else was new."

"Oh, the usual," she said distractedly. "It's been kind of crazy lately."

"How's Tyler?" I inquired, referring to her little boy.

"Good, good. He managed to graduate from nursery school even though he bit two of his classmates during the last month. I thought the parents were going to ask that we have him checked for rabies. How about you? Are you going up to your mother's place on Cape Cod this summer?"

"I'll go up a couple of times, but just for weekends. Both my brothers will be around with their wives and I end up feeling like a fifth wheel with them—though they try their darnedest to be inclusive."

"So you're not madly in love with someone these days?"

"No, and that's okay. All I would love this summer is a fabulous fling with someone."

"Sounds good. You're still in your early thirties and you've got plenty of time to get into something more serious. Shall we look at the menus?"

Oh boy. Something was definitely up. She was moving things along so quickly that the next thing I knew she'd be asking the waiter to connect me to a feeding tube. As soon as we'd ordered, I decided to take the bull by the horns.

"Is everything okay, Cat?" I asked. "I have the feeling that something is on your mind."

Cat studied the tablecloth with her blue eyes, saying nothing. I could see now that she was nervous as hell.

"Cat, what's up?" I urged. "Are you in some kind of trouble?"

"No, not exactly. Bailey, I've got bad news, and it's so hard for me to say." As she raised her head, I saw a half tear form in the corner of her left eye.

"Are you having *marriage* problems again?" I asked.

"No, it doesn't involve me," she said. "It involves you."

"*Me?*" I said, thunderstruck. I couldn't imagine what she was talking about, though I felt a wave of irrational panic, the kind I always experienced when an airline clerk asked me if I'd packed my own bags. "Why? What's going on?"

"Let me start at the beginning," she said after taking a deep breath and straightening her already straight utensils. "You're aware, I'm sure, from some things I've said over the past year, that *Gloss* has been *challenged* on the newsstand. At first I blamed my entertainment editor for not being able to book me the right people for covers. Then I began to see that it was something more fundamental than that. My whole vision for *Gloss* when I first arrived there was to make it fun and sexy and juicy, full of the most important news in a young married woman's life. I wanted the magazine to generate buzz. And it worked brilliantly—for a while."

She paused and took a long sip of her wine. I had a bad feeling about where this was headed.

"Well, I've been doing some research—focus groups, phone surveys. It's the most fucking draining experience in the world, but in the end it's been worth it. I feel I have some answers. And it's clear to me that the world is changing, women are changing, and I'm going to have to change directions with the magazine."

"How do you mean?" I asked. It came out in the form of a squeak, like the sound a teakettle makes after you've turned it off but it's filled with enough leftover steam for one last desperate peep.

"I think that these days *Gloss* needs to be less about buzz and more about bliss," she said.

"*Bliss?*" I said, almost choking on the word. "Are you talking about things like, uh, aromatherapy and savoring the sunrise?"

"Believe it or not, yes. Women are stressed, and they want relief from that stress. We need to create features in the magazine that help them deal with all of that. Look, Bailey, it's not my cup of tea. I think you know me well enough to know that my bullshit meter goes off the minute I hear words like 'feng shui.' But I'm fighting for my survival here."

"So where do I fit into all of this?" I could feel my dread ballooning like one of those pop-up sponges that has just been submerged in water.

"This is so hard for me to tell you, Bailey. You know how much I care about you—and you also know that I think you're an amazing writer. But I've come to realize that I need to seriously pull back on the crime stories for the magazine. I've rejected a bunch of your ideas lately, and it's not because there's anything wrong with them. I just look at each one and I can't picture it in the new mix I've got in mind. You can't have page after page on how to live a serene life and then jam in a story about a woman whose husband has smashed in her skull with a claw hammer and dumped her body in Lake Michigan."

I'd done some discreet snooping over the past year, and I was aware that circulation numbers at *Gloss* had become less than stellar, that Cat was probably under a ton of pressure. I'd even considered the idea that she might lose her job down the road and I'd be out of the best of my freelance arrangements. But I'd never entertained this particular permutation—or thought that anything would happen so soon.

"But what about my human-interest stories?" I asked, floundering.

"I wish I could include them," she said, looking at me almost plaintively. "And I've thought over and over about whether there's a way to fit them in. But they're just not on the same page with what we'll be doing. I need to make *Gloss* very *visual*. In some ways, pictures are the new words today. I'm not saying that we'll have only photos in *Gloss*, but the articles we run will be shorter—and *gentler*."

Her words stupefied me. It was as if she'd just announced that she had written an op-ed-page article for the *Times* in favor of creationism. I was too dumbfounded even to offer a reply.

"But don't worry," she continued with a wan smile. "You

have five articles left on your contract, and of course I'm going to pay you the entire amount."

"And then that's it?"

"Bailey, this is killing me to say it. Yes, that's it. *Gloss* is in trouble and I need to fix it—or they'll hire someone who will."

For a few seconds my anger found a foothold, but it didn't get very far. What was the point in being furious with Cat? I could tell she was being honest and that she believed her job was on the line. But that didn't make it any better for me. I felt hurt, disappointed, even, to my surprise, humiliated, as if I'd been handed a pink slip and told to clear out my desk within the hour.

The dinner came and we picked at our food. Cat tried to praise my writing some more, and I suggested we move on to other topics, which turned out to be as easy to find as the Lost City of Petra. Neither one of us bothered with coffee, and when she offered me a lift home, I lied and said I had to make a stop nearby.

"Here's a thought," she said, lingering on the sidewalk beside her black town car. "Would you be open to writing a different kind of piece for me?"

I smirked involuntarily. "You mean like 'How to Optimize Your Chi'? No, I don't think so. But thanks for asking."

"Bailey, I'm sorry, truly sorry," she said.

"I know," I told her. "And I'm sorry if I sounded sarcastic just then. It's just that you've really thrown me for a loop."

The driver, perhaps trained to run intervention at awkward moments, leapt out of the car and opened the door. Cat slid in and waved good-bye soberly. As the car moved soundlessly down MacDougal Street, I thought: Of course she doesn't want to jeopardize her job at *Gloss*. God forbid she should ever be forced to take a taxi instead of a Lincoln Town Car.

I slunk home on foot through the Village, like a little kid who had just been banished from the playground for having cooties. It took only fifteen minutes for me to make it to my apartment building on the corner of 9th Street and Broadway, but the short walk gave me a chance to assess my new lot in life.

Financially the situation was in no way a disaster. Ever since my ex-husband, the Gamblers Anonymous dropout, had run through much of our mutual savings and hawked some of my jewelry, money matters had made me extremely anxious. But I was really going to be okay. I wrote for other magazines besides *Gloss,* and my relationship with most of them was good. And luckily I also had a backup source of income. My father died when I was twelve, leaving me a small trust fund that provides a regular income each year. Nothing that puts me in the league with the Hilton sisters, but it helps pay for basic expenses, like the maintenance on my one-bedroom apartment in the Village and a garage for my Jeep.

What I was going to have to kiss good-bye, however, were all the extra niceties I'd been enjoying thanks to my generous *Gloss* contract—everything from cute shoes to *el grande* cappuccinos to the occasional Saturday afternoon massage. I'd gotten used to them, spoiled, like one of those women who can have an orgasm only with a Mr. Blue vibrator.

I'd also miss having an office to go to, someplace to mingle with other human beings. And there was something else, I suddenly realized to my horror. In the fall, a collection of my crime articles was being published by a small book company, and now I wouldn't have the *Gloss* affiliation to leverage. What would the jacket say? "Bailey Weggins is a freelancer who works out of her own home. When she isn't writing, she enjoys going through her coat pockets looking for spare change." Cat had even promised to help with PR, since so many of the articles in my book had first appeared in *Gloss*. Now I'd have to rely on the book company's tiny, and reputedly weak, publicity department. I'd heard from another writer that the last time they'd gotten someone on the *Today* show was for a book on the negative charisma factor of Michael Dukakis.

After letting myself into my apartment, I helped myself to the last cold beer in the fridge and checked the calendar on my BlackBerry. I had a fairly busy week ahead, but I'd have to make time to talk to editors and see if there was the potential for another contributing-editor gig someplace else. I'd forgotten that tomorrow night I was having drinks with Robby Hart, an old pal from *Get,* the magazine I'd worked at before *Gloss*— and where I'd first met Cat. Robby was a great networker and the perfect person for me to brainstorm with.

As it turned out, my drink with Robby was the only step I ever had to take in my job search.

The spot he'd chosen for us to meet on Thursday night was a wine bar on the Lower East Side. Robby was already at a table when I arrived, dressed as usual in a cotton plaid button-down shirt with a white undershirt peeking out from underneath. I guess you can take the boy out of Ohio, but you can't take Ohio out of the boy. As soon as he spotted me, he stood up to greet me and offer one of his big toothy Robby smiles. He'd never been Mr. Svelte, but I realized as we hugged each other that he'd put on some weight since I'd seen him last.

"Wow, it's so good to see you," he said. "It's been too long."

"I know. I've been so looking forward to this."

The waiter strolled by just as I was sitting down, and I asked for a glass of Cabernet.

"Nice 'do," Robby said, pointing with his chin toward my hair. "I almost didn't recognize you."

"Thanks, I decided to grow it out. But just watch—once it's finally long enough to pull into a sloppy bun, they'll be out of style."

"Well, at least you've got some to grow," he said. Robby was my age but totally bald.

"So tell me—how's the new gig?" I demanded. "I'm dying to hear."

Robby had stayed at *Get* until it folded, then gone in desperation to *Ladies' Home Journal,* where he'd assigned and written celebrity pieces for several years. Three months ago he'd bagged a job as a senior editor for *Buzz*, the very hot celebrity gossip magazine. Circulation at *Buzz* had languished until the top job was taken over about a year ago by Mona Hodges, the genius—and notorious—editor known for resuscitating ailing magazines. Sales had since skyrocketed, and in a recent profile, Mona had claimed that forty-nine percent of her readers would choose an evening reading *Buzz* over sex with their husbands.

"Well, I've got to admit, it's awesome to be at such a *buzzy* magazine," he said. "When people used to find out I worked at *LHJ*, all they'd do was ask if I had a recipe for chicken chili or knew how to get ink stains out of clothes. But when someone finds out I work at *Buzz*, their eyes bug out."

"That's fabulous, Robby," I said, but as soon as I said it I saw his eyes flicker with uncertainty. "*What?*"

He squeezed his lips together hard. "On the other hand, it's been a tough learning curve," he conceded. "They expect your writing to be very cute and snappy, and I'm not so experienced with that. The chick in the office next to me wrote this line about Hugh Grant the other day—she said he had the kind of blue eyes you could see from outer space—and all I could think was why can't I write something like that? Though I think I'm finally starting to get the hang of it."

"Do you work late most nights? I heard someone say that there were sweatshops in Cambodia that have better hours than *Buzz*."

"Mondays are the worst because we close that night," he admitted. "Sometimes I'm there till five a.m. Tuesdays are the one early night 'cause things are just gearing up again. The other nights—it all depends. They say it's going to get better now that Mona has finally settled in."

"And you're covering TV?" I said.

"Mainly *reality* TV. Behind-the-scenes stuff. Are the bitches really as bitchy as they seem? Who's bonking who? The head of the West Coast office says we should just change the name of the magazine to *Who You Fucking?* I guess it's pretty dumbed-down stuff from what I used to be doing, but what difference does it make?"

"What do you mean?"

"Well, we tried to make the celeb stuff at *LHJ* more *journalistic,* but it was wasted effort considering who we were dealing with. I suggested to a celebrity's publicist once that we could approach someone like Maya Angelou to do the interview, and you know what he said to me? He asked to see her clips."

I laughed out loud.

"So you see," he continued, "there's a watermark you can never rise above, anyway."

"*Buzz* can get pretty nasty, though—right?"

"It's mainly this one gossip section that's down and dirty. It's called 'Juice Bar.' You don't want to get on their radar if you can help it. The rest of the magazine is cheeky but not nearly so bitchy."

"Well, are you happy you made the switch?" I asked skeptically as the waiter set our drinks down in front of us.

"Overall, yes. It's great experience and the pay is certainly better. I got a twenty-thousand-dollar bump in my salary— which I need right now. I wanted to tell you this in person— though it's still hush-hush: Brock and I are applying to adopt a kid."

"Oh, Robby, that's fabulous," I said, giving his hand a squeeze. "You'll be a fantastic parent." And I meant it. Robby was one of the kindest, most thoughtful guys I'd ever worked with, and I knew that he'd always felt frustrated that as a gay man he couldn't have a child.

"Thanks," he said, beaming. "I'm dying to be a dad. The problem is Brock's business has been hit or miss lately, and if our application is going to be accepted, I must have a well-paying job. So I just need to grin and bear it and hope I can get on top of things."

"Wait—I thought you said you were on the other side of the learning curve."

"Sort of. I mean, I think I've started to get the hang of the *style,* but the weekly pace is still a problem for me. If I had more time, I could do a better job of polishing my copy, but I don't—and then later it gets tossed back to me for endless revisions."

"Is she really as bad to work for as people say?" I asked. I was referring to Mona Hodges. Though editor in chiefs could be tough, Mona's reputation made her unique in the pain-in-the-ass-to-work-for category. She was reportedly cold, demanding, arbitrary, and at times even abusive. Some people believed that Mona had been spurred to be this way so she could stand out from the pack by generating press about her antics—the all-publicity-even-bad-publicity-is-good-publicity theory. She supposedly was insanely jealous of Bonnie Fuller, the editorial director of a rival publication. Bonnie had a more illustrious track record in juicing up magazines and causing circulation to skyrocket. Though Bonnie had the advantage of having a longer tenure in the business and therefore more time to make her mark, it still galled Mona, who was impatient to get recognized. The "I be bad" strategy apparently was meant to gain Mona recognition faster, even if *hers* was all negative.

Robby rolled his hazel eyes. "Well, she can come on strong if she doesn't like what she sees. I heard her verbally bitch-slap the poor mail guy the other day because he'd left a package in the wrong place. But she's a genius at what she does, and our sales are through the roof. There's a lot to learn from someone like her. I just wish I could get the hang of the copy."

"You feeling pretty stressed?"

"Yeah. And the worst part is I've been using Cheetos and chocolate as my stress reducers of choice. I'm so fat now that I have *man* tits. When Brock and I start telling the world we're becoming parents, people will think that *I'm* the one giving birth. But enough about me. How's your life, anyway?"

"Not so great." I told him the whole story and described how much of a curveball it had thrown me.

As I was speaking, Robby's eyes widened and his jaw went slack. With his elbows resting on the table, he stretched out both arms and flipped his hands over.

"Omigod, I just thought of something," he said. "I know the perfect job for you."

"Where?"

"*Buzz* magazine."

"Huh?"

"Wait till you hear this. They've decided to treat celebrity crimes in a more journalistic way, rather than just write them up as gossip stories. And they're looking for some really great journalist types to do them—people they can offer contracts to. I never once thought of you because I knew your contract with *Gloss* ran through the end of the year."

"But is there really enough celebrity crime out there to make it worth their while?"

"Absolutely! I mean, every week some celebrity tries to leave Saks with a Fendi purse stuffed down her bra or shoots his wife with a Magnum. God, you'd be perfect for this. Needless to say, for selfish reasons it would be so great for me to have you there."

"But we just finished talking about how tough it is there."

"But it would be different for you," Robby declared. "Mona is secretly intimidated by anything truly journalistic. She wouldn't micromanage you because she doesn't see that as her strength. And it wouldn't be expected for your copy to be all cute and perky. You'd be in the power position. And from what I've heard, the crime stuff is going to be overseen by the number two guy, Nash Nolan. He looks like a bully, but he's perfectly decent. Please, let me set up the interview."

My mind was racing. I'd never once imagined myself at a

magazine like *Buzz,* yet I had to admit I was intrigued. The magazine had become a must-read in the last year, and people would get to know my name—just in time for the launch of my book. That advantage could end up outweighing any negatives.

"But I don't really follow celebrities that much," I said, playing devil's advocate.

"You'll find out everything you need to know the first week on the job. There are only about thirty celebrities who matter anyway, and you don't even have to know their last names. Have you ever met Mona, by the way?"

"No. I've seen her picture in the *Post,* but I've never had the pleasure of a face-to-face."

"Look, there's no harm in just talking to her, is there?"

No, there didn't seem to be any harm in talking.

"Okay, I'd be open to an interview," I told him.

Robby beamed when he heard my reply. "She'll love you," he said. "And she'll turn on the charm in the interview—within limits, of course, because it's Mona we're talking about. There are two things you need to watch out for. When she's talking to you, she'll lean in and stare at you really intently. The first time I met her, I thought she was checking out my pores and I half expected her to prescribe an exfoliant before I left. And she's wall-eyed—in just one eye. Always look straight at her face. Don't make the mistake of following the bad eye—it drives her insane when people do that."

I let Robby go ahead and set it up.

My appointment with Mona ended up being on the Wednesday after my drink with Robby. The *Buzz* office, to my surprise, was only a few blocks south from *Gloss*'s, at Broadway and 50th. It took up half of the sixteenth floor of the building; the other portion was occupied by *Track,* an upstart music magazine owned by the same company. Robby had once told me that *Buzz* staffers sometimes bumped into people like Justin Timberlake in the reception area.

There were plenty of people bustling around in the large open offices when I arrived. Their blasé expressions remained unchanged as I was led through by Mona's assistant, yet I could sense some of them following me with their eyes. Perhaps a few were wondering if I was a potential replacement for them.

The front wall of Mona's office was made entirely of glass, but the blinds were drawn today. Her assistant asked me to wait outside, and through the half-open door I could hear a woman and a man in conversation.

"Take a few days to review it, but then we need to get moving on it," said the man, his voice moving closer toward the door. "Try to give Stan a call as soon as you can."

A second later, a fiftyish, dark blond man, dressed in a dark suit, charged by me. I recognized him as Tom Dicker, the owner of the company. His picture appeared in "Page Six," in the *New York Post,* almost as often as Mona's did. I barely had a chance to give him a thought when Mona herself stepped outside, dressed in too tight black pants and a sleeveless neon yellow top, and ushered me into her office.

Robby was right about the fact that she'd attempt to be charming. Mona smiled pleasantly as we shook hands, though her voice was oddly flat, with a slight midwestern accent. Robby was also right about the wall-eyed thing. As Mona's left eye drifted off, I had to fight the urge to follow it—or worse, turn my head, because it created the illusion that someone had snuck into the room and was standing just behind my shoulder.

I'd heard people make fun of her looks, but her face wasn't unattractive, especially for someone in her early forties. It's just that the wandering eye kept her from being pretty. And at around five six she was slightly pudgy, a fact exaggerated by the pants she'd chosen. Her best feature was probably her hair. It was auburn colored and glossy as a movie stallion's—though she was wearing it in an unfortunate new shag cut with loads of layers heaped on her head. Her hair was just too thick for that kind of style, and it made her look as though she might be distantly related to a Wookie.

Without bothering to tell me to take a seat, Mona plunked down into the chair behind her desk, so I slipped into one facing her. She glanced at the package of material I'd sent over by messenger and then back up at me.

"So what's wrong with this deal you've got with *Gloss*?" she asked bluntly.

"Nothing at all," I said. "But *Gloss* may be going in a slightly different direction, so I've been keeping my ears open for other opportunities."

"You read *Buzz*?"

"Not religiously," I confessed. Something told me it was smarter not to bullshit Mona. "But it's definitely a guilty pleasure I indulge in at times."

"I see you were in newspapers once. Why'd you switch to magazines?"

"I loved the pace of newspapers—and that wonderful sense of urgency that goes with it," I told her. "But you're limited stylewise. I decided what I'd do was get experience covering news, but then move into magazine journalism, where I had more freedom as a writer."

Well, aren't you special? I felt like screaming to myself as soon as the words were out of my mouth. I've always had a hard time finding that fine line between talking up myself the right amount and not sounding obnoxious.

Mona didn't seem to mind, however, and my comment led to a discussion of my background. Then she briskly described what the job would entail. She envisioned the person both writing stories and editing filed stories from other reporters. Through the whole discussion she leaned forward, staring at my face too intently—again, just as Robby had warned. She even stared when *she* was talking, as if she had never been informed of that unwritten rule dictating that when you're the one speaking during a conversation, you should glance away periodically so that you don't appear to be boring into the other person.

"Your stuff's pretty good," Mona said finally, leaning back in her chair. "And on one level you're the right type to do these stories for the magazine. But you've got absolutely no experience covering celebrities. Tell me why I should hire you."

"Actually, I think that my lack of experience with celebrities would be an advantage," I told her. "Cops and experts would take me far more seriously than someone who's usually covering the MTV Music Video Awards. I could also help you give stories the right context. For instance, let's say you have a situation like you did lately where a male star gets slugged by his wife because she caught him at a strip club and the wife ends up in jail. *Buzz* reported it in this wide-eyed way, as if no one had ever heard of a *wife* slugging her husband. But there's research these days suggesting that plenty of wives assault their husbands and that it's a much bigger problem than anyone ever realized. That info could make your story more interesting.

"Plus," I added, "if I needed contacts in the celebrity world, you've got a ton of people on staff who could help me."

Clearly thinking it over, she stared at me from behind her desk—or at least one eye did. I forced myself to look straight at her nose and not seem too eager. She stood up finally and told me she would let me know.

Two days later I got the call from Nash, introducing himself and asking for a meeting. At the end of it, he told me I had the gig. They would put me on a retainer and I would write the big New York–based crime stories and sometimes edit smaller ones filed by staff writers. If there was a major crime story on the West Coast, I could choose to go to L.A. myself or oversee the coverage using some of the West Coast staff. I would have a desk in the office and should plan on being on-site two or three days a week. After I made certain I would be dealing mostly with Nash, I said yes.

I won't deny that I took some satisfaction in phoning Cat and announcing my news to her.

"*Celebrity* crime?" she asked, feigning true curiosity. "You mean, like when they steal clothes from a photo shoot or have too much collagen injected into their lips?"

Sarcasm was something she rarely directed my way, but I didn't let it irk me. I knew she had conflicting feelings about my departure.

I showed up at *Buzz* the next Wednesday. It was an interesting setup. The offices were all glass fronted, and about half of them faced an open area of workstations—a cube farm that looked like the bullpen at a newspaper. The rest of the offices ran along several corridors in the back half of the floor. A big part of the open bullpen area belonged to the art and production departments; a smaller section closer to reception, which included about twelve workstations, was filled with mostly reporters and writers. For some reason it had been nicknamed "the pod."

Mona's office was at the very end of the open area, near the art department and a section nicknamed Intern Village, where dazed-looking college students transcribed tapes and kept track of unfolding gossip on the Internet, on sites such as Gawker.com.

As a freelancer I didn't merit an office. The workstation I was shown to was in a four-desk section of the pod, shared by a hodgepodge of people. Directly next to me, separated by just a head-high gray partition, was a friendly-seeming writer named Jessie Pendergrass—about thirty, I guessed. Just behind us were another writer, Ryan Forster, and a photo editor named Leo something, who apparently spent his days screening paparazzi shots. As Jessie led me down one of the back corridors to show me where the kitchenette was, she explained that she'd recently switched out of "Juice Bar" to cover the music scene and general celebrity stuff and wouldn't get an office until she was promoted to editor. Leo, she said, should be in the art area but there wasn't enough room, and Ryan, like her, hadn't worked his way up to an office yet.

"Are they easy to sit near?" I asked, realizing that I'd have very little privacy.

"Leo's a good egg," she confided. "He used to be more hyper, but he started this nude gay yoga class and he seems much more mellow. Ryan's a loner. If you develop any insight into him, let me know."

The office decor was pretty bland—white walls, gray rugs, and gray partitions—though people had made an attempt to personalize their offices and workstations by sticking up pictures and tacky memorabilia. About sixty percent of the staff was female, and nearly ten percent of those seemed to have Johnny Depp photos staring soulfully at them from their cubicle partitions. What I couldn't believe was the amount of magazines lying around. Tossed on desks and chairs and strewn over the floor were endless copies not only of *Buzz,* but also of our main competition—*People, In Touch,* and *US Weekly,* as well as *Star* and the *National Enquirer.* People were constantly flipping through them for information.

The most amazing part, though, was the noise level. It was so much louder than at *Gloss*—in fact, you would have thought we were covering a war or a presidential election.

I spent the first half hour of the day having Nash's assistant, Lee, show me the computer system. I was basically familiar with it—just needed a brief refresher course. Nash told me he'd meet with me after the eleven a.m. daily staff meeting, so I spent a little while poring over a stack of back issues of *Buzz,* trying to soak up the style. I wasn't going to have to use words like glam, bling, or Splitsville in *my* copy, but neither did I want to be too heavy-handed. I also perused the daily "gossip pack," photocopies of everything from gossip columns to People.com to pages from the British tabs. By the time I finished, I knew far more than I'd cared to about Camilla Parker Bowles.

Every so often I'd glance up to see if Mona was in yet, but her office remained dark. Finally, I overheard someone say that she was making a television appearance and would be in around noon.

The daily meeting was over and done within fifteen minutes. It was run by a stern-sounding managing editor ("We call him the Kaiser," Jessie whispered) and focused on what stage every story was at. On the way back to the pod, Jessie informed me that Mona tried to hold idea meetings every week with a small group of writers and editors, but time didn't always allow for it. Cover story meetings happened only with the top-ranking people, and for secrecy reasons, very few people on staff knew what the cover story was until late in the game.

Mona finally arrived for the day moments later, stomping down the aisle along the pod with a frazzled expression, the kind you have on your face when you realize that your car has just been towed. Ten minutes later, she emerged from her office. She had several sheets of copy in her hands, and at first I thought she was headed in my direction. But she veered off into an office right near me.

"Why would you write a fucking lead like this?" she yelled from the doorway at the girl inside. I nearly rocketed out of my seat in surprise.

"I mean, it's fucking stupid," Mona continued. "Nobody cares about Maddox and his latest haircut. They want to know who Angelina is shacking up with."

Ouch. Robby had said she was tough. He hadn't used the term *she-devil*.

Even though I had my head lowered discreetly, I could see that after spinning around, Mona was barreling right toward me now. I wondered if I ought to hurl myself under my desk.

"Why did they put you here?" she asked as she reached my desk.

"I believe it's the only spot available, but it's fine," I told her. I noticed that all around me people's eyes went to their computer screens, as if she were a wolf or a police dog and they were afraid that making eye contact might trigger an attack.

"Suit yourself," she said, shrugging and walking off.

Midday a deputy editor e-mailed me to say that a reality TV star named Dotson Holfield had been arraigned that morning in Miami for indecent exposure. She asked that I work with Robby on the story. I had a few contacts in Miami that I offered him, and as I nibbled on a sandwich in his office, he reached one of them.

"What a loser," he said as he hung up the phone. "Holfield apparently wagged his penis at an undercover cop and told him to call it Brutus. I've got the perfect title for the story."

"Shoot."

" 'Dotson Holfield Proves He Really *Is* a Dick Head.' "

"See?" I told him. "You *can* write cute."

"How you doin', by the way?" he asked.

"Good," I said, forcing a smile. "I realize I'm not in Kansas anymore, but hopefully I'll get used to it."

I had no more *direct* encounters with Mona that day, though I was almost always conscious of her whereabouts. Each time she left her office, it was like a hurricane making landfall. She'd charge over to the art department to demand changes in a layout, complain in Nash's doorway about some annoying celebrity handler, and stride right over to people's desks and toss their copy back to them. Around two, I caught sight of her gesturing in annoyance at one of her two assistants behind the glass wall that blocked off their desks from the art department. Jessie rolled her chair over to me.

"Can you guess what that's about?" she whispered.

"Somebody wrote an unfunny caption?"

"No, I suspect it's about the chicken salad. Mona has it for lunch every day at two. If the celery content is over thirty-five percent, someone's ass is on the line."

I was too speechless to reply. What have I gotten myself into? I wondered. But in truth I hadn't seen anything yet. At around six-thirty, Mona came trouncing out of her office packed like an Italian sausage into an orange Dolce & Gabbana evening gown and asked an editorial assistant two desks away from me to put concealer on the eczema patches on her back. I had to fight the urge to gag.

"God," I muttered to myself, "this is going to be murder."

Six weeks later, to my absolute horror, I turned out to be right.

CHAPTER 2

As a crime writer, I've often had people remark to me that celebrities are treated differently by the legal system from the rest of us. Cops, for instance, supposedly handle them with kid gloves, and juries show them more leniency. I'm not sure if that's true—I've never seen any hard evidence on it. But there's one thing I know for a fact. When you commit a crime in New York City and are arraigned in court, you go through a series of humiliations that doesn't vary no matter how famous you are.

It starts with processing in the police station. That's where the paperwork is done. Afterward you are transferred to the courthouse at 100 Centre Street in lower Manhattan and are placed in one of the holding cells in the basement—more commonly known as "the pens." I've never been down there, but I hear they stink to high heaven, especially in summer. The courthouse opens at nine-thirty, and you are eventually brought upstairs to face the judge in one of the two arraignment courtrooms on the ground floor. They call this "producing the body."

I was considering what a great equalizer arraignment is as I sat in AR-1—arraignment courtroom number one—on a squelching hot Tuesday in July six weeks after my arrival at *Buzz*. The air conditioner seemed to be on the fritz, and four or five large standing fans were making such a loud whirring noise that you couldn't hear a damn word the lawyers or judge were saying.

The "body" I was waiting to behold was that of singer Kimberly Chance—or, as she'd been dubbed by "Juice Bar," *Fat* Chance—a twenty-seven-year-old white-trashy singer who had become famous a year ago after winning a reality TV contest called *Star Maker,* a rip-off of *American Idol*. Last night she'd become involved in an altercation with her boyfriend outside a downtown club. When a police officer attempted to break it up, she slapped him across the face—the cop, not the boyfriend. I learned of this development at six a.m. and had arrived in court at nine-thirty. It was now eleven, and though there was still no sign of Kimberly, I knew she'd come through the back door eventually. According to the law in New York, the body has to be produced within twenty-four hours.

Celebrities like Kimberly had been committing crimes at a steady pace this summer, enough to guarantee me two or three days of work a week at *Buzz*. To my surprise, I liked certain aspects of my job more than I'd thought I would. Granted, I was working at a magazine that published articles primarily about the binges, breakups, and botched plastic surgeries of the stars. Actually, "article" is probably the wrong word. Many pages were made up mostly of photos with deep captions or chartlike articles that someone on staff had dubbed "charticles." But my pieces were generally given more room and ran about the length of a crime piece in *People*. I even sort of liked covering celebrities. Their crimes as a whole just seemed more titillating than those of mere mortals.

And just as Robby had predicted, Mona appeared to be slightly in awe of me. She often sent me e-mails with tips she'd received, or she offered her own take on a story, but she delegated to Nash the job of editing my copy. The former editor of a now defunct men's magazine that the company had owned, he seemed too old and brainy to be at *Buzz,* but according to rumor he was biding his time until another number one gig opened up. He was a little mercurial—sometimes gruff, sometimes friendly, sometimes even flirty—but he was never a meany. He asked good questions and shortened some of my sentences, making my copy snappier.

I also enjoyed being out in the pod, the epicenter of action. Ryan pretty much ignored me, but I really dug Jessie—and Leo was unintentionally amusing. By week two he'd educated me on the difference between "stalkerazzi" and "cooperazzi" photos. Stalkerazzi were the ones taken against the celebrity's wishes. Cooperazzi shots looked like those of stalkerazzi, but, according to Leo, the celebrities actually *wanted* you to see them in those situations.

Unfortunately, that's where the good stuff ended. The atmosphere at *Buzz* was often vile thanks to Mona. Her verbal bullwhipping was never directed at me personally, but seeing others subjected to it was about as much fun as watching someone have his stomach pumped. I'd learned since I started work that there was even a Web site called "I Survived Mona-Hodges.com."

And it wasn't simply that she was a tyrant. What really incensed the staff was that she was always upending things, like a toddler in a high chair who's suddenly unhappy or bored with the SpaghettiOs and flips the bowl upside down. She would tear up pages of the magazine just before we went to press so that they'd have to be done all over again.

Even when she wasn't being difficult, she was just plain weird. She had this bizarre obsession with food, which led to all sorts of chaos. For instance, she swore that the French fries at the McDonald's on Ninth Avenue were the best in the city, and she frequently dispatched one of her two assistants all the way over there to purchase them.

Surprisingly, I rarely saw much of Robby other than at daily meetings, where he tended to keep his head low. His office was around the corner from the pod, near the entrance from reception, and he was generally there when I hightailed it out of the place at night. One day when I was using the copier near his office, I overheard Mona drop one of his stories on his desk and bark, "This sucks, do you know that?"

At first I told myself to give it time, that eventually I'd be able to ignore Mona and just focus on what I liked about the job. But I was near the end of my rope and had adopted a different strategy: to hang in through the publication of my book in the fall. Having the connection to *Buzz* would be an enormous advantage and would surely help me line up some press interviews. I would just have to do my best to not let Mona get under my skin.

It was actually Mona who called with the news about Kimberly. She had phoned me once or twice at home before, but never this early in the morning. As soon as I heard her say my name, I felt this large, prickly pit begin to form in my tummy, as if a porcupine had managed to wedge its way in there.

"Did you hear the news?" she asked bluntly. "Kimberly Chance was arrested last night."

Had I *heard* the news? Did the woman think I kept a police scanner in my bedroom?

"No, I didn't hear," I said. The truth was always best with Mona, because, as I'd suspected on the first day I'd met her, she could smell a lie the way some people could smell a dead mouse in the walls. "What for?"

"Hitting a policeman," she said. "They say she's going to be arraigned today. What does that mean, exactly?"

"It means she'll be going before the judge to plead—guilty or not guilty. I'll go down for the arraignment."

"Can you go *now*?"

"The courts don't start till nine-thirty," I explained. "Should I give Robby a call? He'd probably want to be there since it's his turf, too."

There was a long pause.

"No, I need him at the office today."

Before she hung up, she gave me a cell phone number for Kimberly that she had managed to get God knows where.

I hadn't planned on working on *Buzz* stuff today, so this was going to create havoc with my schedule. Not only would I have to spend a good chunk of my morning in court, but I needed to gather some background material on Kimberly so I could put her situation in perspective. Still in my underwear, I did a quick Web search. It was mostly stuff about her appearance on the *Star Maker* show. Though it would involve traveling in the wrong direction, I decided to stop by the office and comb through some back issues of the magazine. I knew that Kimberly had garnered lots of ink in *Buzz* since she'd won the contest, especially in "Juice Bar," but I'd never bothered to read any of it.

Other than Nash's assistant, there wasn't a soul in sight when I arrived. My guess was that plenty of people had probably been there closing the issue until the wee hours of the morning, and it was unlikely that anybody would surface before eleven. The eleven o'clock daily staff meeting was held at two on the day after closing.

After helping myself to the coffee in the kitchenette, I made my way to the room where they stored the back issues and grabbed an armful. To my total surprise, Jessie was sitting at her desk when I returned to my workstation.

"What the heck are you doing here at eight-fifteen?" I asked, smiling. Over the past few weeks, I had grown pretty fond of Jessie—and her flip sense of humor—and I hoped our burgeoning friendship would survive my tenure at *Buzz*.

"I have to get this damn Yoko Ono interview out of the way, even though it'll be buried in the back of the magazine.

Want to know something funny? She was wearing Stella McCartney sunglasses when I met her and didn't have a clue. What about you? I thought you weren't even coming in today."

I explained the wrench that Kimberly Chance had hurled into my plans.

"Oh yeah, I heard about it on the radio this morning," she said. "Are we sure the contest she won wasn't *Slut Search*?"

"How was the close last night?"

"More bearable than some. The high point was when Mona sent that new assistant of hers, Amy, out for this kind of Jamba Juice called Endless Lime. The girl went to every Jamba Juice in Manhattan and arrived back three hours later—empty-handed! It turns out they only sell that kind in California."

"When did people clear out of here?"

"Most people got out of here by twelve. The cover story was on freaky beauty rituals of the stars, so needless to say there was no breaking news that had to be incorporated."

"What freaky rituals *do* they like?"

"Well, apparently Chris Judd gets butt facials."

"Eew, please—I'm still drinking my coffee."

I let Jessie return to work while I combed the issues looking for items on Kimberly. In the very beginning there had been a brief lovefest between her and the magazine, like a fling between conventioneers. She'd appeared on the cover after winning her honor, and there were a few glowing tidbits in the weeks immediately following, especially as her single went platinum. But before long she was making regular appearances on the "Fashion Follies" page, dressed in outfits that you might expect to see on waitresses at an international smorgasbord: There was the Swiss miss getup—a ruffled skirt and laced bodice that she wore with her hair in fat pigtails—as well as a disastrous turn in a muumuu that may have caused Paul Gauguin to turn in his grave. In a whole other vein was the dress she wore to the Grammys. It was huge and puffy, as if she were stockpiling something underneath. The caption read: "News Flash! We've Located the Weapons of Mass Destruction."

Kimberly's sartorial indiscretions weren't the only things that *Buzz* had chosen to spotlight. Over the past months there were several photos of her coming out of hotels early in the a.m., generally with what appeared to be a bad case of beard burn. And last, but hardly least, was the diet. Not long after winning her title, Kimberly had begun packing on the pounds. At one point she announced that she was going on Atkins. "Juice Bar" immediately began running a regular box called "Kimberly Countdown." It started with her at 160 pounds, and in the following weeks the arrow always indicated an uptick rather than a decline in her weight. That was when the famous "Fat Chance" nickname was introduced to *Buzz* readers.

"Can I interrupt?" I asked Jessie. "Why have we picked on Kimberly so much? She seems pretty harmless to me."

"You've just stumbled upon what I call the 'white underbelly phenomenon.'"

"Say that again?"

"Mona despises weakness. The stronger you are and the more confident you seem, the more she leaves you alone. Just look at the way she treats you and me. But if she senses any vulnerability, any white underbelly, she can't resist the urge to sink her teeth in it. At first she liked Kimberly. Apparently Mona was kind of an underdog herself growing up—you don't get to be homecoming queen when one of your eyes is almost in the side of your head—and so she was fascinated by Kimberly's rags-to-riches story. When Kimberly started to chub up, when she proved she couldn't limit herself to four Krispy Kremes a day, Mona went in for the kill. I hear she even came up with the name Fat Chance herself."

"Jeez, I haven't been to the gym once yet this week," I said. "Do you think she's going to come up with a name for *me*?"

"Yeah, yours is going to be Golden Girl," she said. "Enjoy it while it lasts."

I was pretty sure she meant it as a compliment, but I didn't know her well enough to be one hundred percent sure.

With little time left, I stuffed the back issues under my desk and headed downtown on the subway to Centre Street. There were already at least a dozen reporters packed in benches in AR-1, and as I sat there staring at the scuffed brown linoleum, even more showed up, along with a fair share of rubberneckers. At twenty after twelve, Kimberly finally emerged from the door to the right of the judge's bench.

She looked like hell. Granted, no one would be much of a fashion plate after a few hours in the pens alongside druggies and hookers, especially in a heat wave, but she seemed to have weathered it especially poorly. Her hair, which had recently been dyed a shade of red you'd find only in a lipstick, had formed into a ratty mass on top of her head, looking exactly like hump hair, and she had a mean set of raccoon eyes. She was wearing a silvery blue baby-doll dress, which I suspected had actually been sold as a top.

Her lawyer, on the other hand, looked pretty spiffy, a high-powered babe in a crisp white suit. Because of the fans, I could make out only every few words, but I got the gist of what was going on. Her lawyer asked for a conditional discharge, stating that Kimberly was a law-abiding citizen with no prior charges, who something or other, and had struck the officer unintentionally during a fight with her boyfriend and greatly regretted what had happened. The judge listened with just a little less boredom than she'd displayed during the previous cases. It was determined that Kimberly would plead guilty to harassment in the second degree, which was a violation and not a crime, and as part of her conditional discharge would partake in both community service and ten weeks of anger-management classes rather than jail time. She was free to go.

All of us from the media bolted out of the courtroom in order to secure positions just outside the entrance of the building. That's where Kimberly and her lawyer would exit, and if we were lucky, they'd not only say a few words but answer questions.

Photographers were already waiting, a few with folding stepladders hung on their shoulders. They were for the most part freelance paparazzi, and *Buzz* would buy photos from one of them. Five minutes later Kimberly emerged, flanked by her lawyer in white and a man who I assumed, by the way he nodded to a couple of the reporters, was her publicist. Somebody must have passed Kimberly a tissue in the hall because she'd managed to remove a lot of the smeared mascara from beneath her eyes.

"Kimberly, Kimberly, over here," one of the photographers called in order to get a shot of her looking directly at the camera. She smiled wanly in his direction.

"Ms. Stanton," a reporter yelled to the lawyer, "what do you think of the verdict?"

"There was no verdict," she corrected with a tight smile. "The case was quickly and favorably resolved and Kimberly has not been convicted of any crime."

A few of us called out to Kimberly, asking her how she felt, and she smiled cautiously, clearly under instructions to remain subdued.

"I am very grateful about the decision," she said.

"Where's Tommy?" yelled some guy from *Access Hollywood*. "Are you guys still dating?"

She took a deep breath and shook her head. "That's not something I want to discuss," she said.

"How do you think your arrest will affect your career?" I asked.

"Since Kimberly hasn't been convicted of anything, it shouldn't affect her career at all," the lawyer said, taking over again. She went on to explain the meaning of a conditional discharge. While she spoke, Kimberly's eyes roamed over the faces of the reporters. She made brief eye contact with me, and

I saw her find the press tag around my neck and read my name and affiliation.

Abruptly the lawyer ended the makeshift press conference and led Kimberly away down Centre Street. Somewhere a car must have been waiting, but it was nowhere in sight. A few photographers trailed after them.

Back at my place, I wrote up the arraignment while it was fresh in my mind. I tried the cell phone number Mona had given me, hoping for an exclusive statement from Kimberly, but I heard a message saying that the cell phone customer I was trying to reach was out of range. For the rest of the afternoon, I worked on a story for another magazine and also fit in an hour at the gym. I was due to have dinner with a friend that night, so early in the evening I lay down for a catnap. I woke like a jolt when the phone rang. It was Robby.

"Got a minute?" he asked before I could even squeeze out a hello. It sounded as if he were choking back tears.

"Sure, what's the matter?" I asked, squinting at the clock on my nightstand. It was just after seven.

"I got canned today."

"What?"

"Yeah, and she did it herself. She often makes Nash do these things, but she handled my execution personally. Said I just didn't cut it. I think she actually derived some pleasure out of it."

"Oh, Robby, that's awful. When did it happen?"

"At around three. When she called me down to her office, I thought she was going to ream me out for a piece I did, but . . . She didn't even close the door. And then she told me that I had to leave *that* minute. I took my Rolodex and a few files, and they're sending everything else over tomorrow. I'd like to strangle that woman."

"Robby, listen to me. You will totally bounce back from this. There's plenty of freelance work out there. Besides, it's probably better for your sanity to be out of there."

"I know, I know, but it's the baby," he said, choking back another sob. "If I don't have a steady job, it means that our application may go to the back of the line and we'll have to start the process all over again."

"Oh God." I couldn't really think of anything else to say.

"That's part of the reason I'm calling," he said. "I realized after I got home that copies of two of my reference letters for the adoption are still in my desk drawer. I forgot to take them with me. There's no way I can get back in the building because they took my ID away. Would you be willing to sneak into my office and get them for me? I just don't want anyone to see them when they're packing up my stuff tomorrow."

"Of course. I'll go in early tomorrow before anyone gets there."

"I hate to do this to you, Bailey, but is there any chance you could go in there *tonight*? I can't bear the idea of anyone knowing my business. Troy, that guy who's in the office next to mine, told me he was coming in early. I'm afraid he'd see you. But there'll be no one there tonight. It's Tuesday."

"Umm, sure. The only problem is that I have a friend coming downtown to have dinner with me tonight and I just want to be sure she hasn't left her apartment yet. We're not supposed to meet for over an hour, but she'd said something about heading down this way to shop first. I'll try her right now and see if I can catch her."

"What if you can't?"

"Robby, don't worry. I'll get off the phone right now and call her and then call you back. Try to relax, okay?"

"I feel so wrung out and exhausted. Brock is away, and I haven't even been able to reach him. I just took an Excedrin PM and I'm going to try to crash soon."

I signed off and tried my friend. The line was busy. She was one of those people who rarely used a cell phone and didn't believe in call waiting. At least she hadn't left for the Village yet. After getting the busy signal constantly over the next ten minutes, I decided to take my shower but make it quick. As I was toweling off I rang her again, and this time I got an answer. I explained that I had an emergency and asked if she'd be willing to meet later than planned. She told me she was PMS-ing and was happy to just reschedule.

I called Robby back, but to my surprise I got only his answering machine. I waited ten minutes and tried again. Still the machine. Maybe the Excedrin PM had knocked him out cold. I left a message for him to call me when he woke up. Then I threw on a jean skirt, a white tank top, and a pair of sandals and hurried out into the hot Manhattan night. The subway arrived practically the moment I stepped onto the platform, and I was in midtown fifteen minutes later.

Times Square was teeming with summer tourists, fanning themselves with whatever they had in their hands. As I approached the building that housed Thomas Dicker's ever expanding media empire, I noticed limos and town cars double-parked outside, as well as a dozen or so paparazzi lined up behind blue police barricades. It was only then that I remembered something about *Track* hosting a party tonight for Eva Anderson, the singer/actress/style icon. Half Mexican, half Danish, she had a face that was both exotic and girl next door. She had become a megastar over the past two years, and her name appeared in *Buzz* as frequently as the phrase *on the rocks*.

Problem: There was a good chance that some *Buzz* staffers would be at the party, or, despite the fact that it was the night after closing, there might be people still lingering in their offices before they headed over to the other side of the floor. It wouldn't seem odd to anyone that I was stopping by; I'd just have to be careful not to be spotted going through Robby's desk. What fun for me—I'd get to play James Bond without the tux.

I flashed my ID at the security guard in the lobby, where a separate table had been set up to check people into the party, and then I rode the elevator alone up to the sixteenth floor. Two other security guards were standing in front of the doorway that led into the *Track* side of the floor. Emanating from behind them were the throbbing sounds of the party. I'd barely stepped off the elevator when a guy strode out of the party with a woman behind him. It took me a second to realize that he was Brandon Cott, Eva Anderson's husband. I had no idea who the woman was. She was blond and extremely tanned, at least ten years older than him. She put her hand on his arm, as if she were trying to restrain him. Curious, I paused, lowered my head, and pretended to rifle through my bag for something.

"Where've you been all night, anyway?" the woman demanded in just above a whisper.

"You're one to talk," he told her. "Every time I looked for you, you were missing in action."

"I was doing my job."

"Well, why don't you go back and keep doing it. I'm going to split."

"Brandon, please, no." Her voice was all sugary now. "If you leave now, everyone will say you bolted and it will be bad for her." She was obviously some kind of handler for Eva.

"What about what's good for me?"

"Please, stay. I'll owe you one."

With my head lowered, I stole another glance at the two of them. He was hunky in a brooding Johnny Depp kind of way, though he was shorter than I would have guessed, and his large head seemed disproportionate to the rest of his body— kind of like Mr. Potato Head. Maybe that worked well for TV. He'd been the star of a successful series that had eventually succumbed to ratings malaise. After two years of career doldrums, he had landed a series on TNT or USA about the FBI, and it had become a surprise hit. Which was lucky for him because Eva apparently didn't love losers.

"I can't stand it one more fucking second," Brandon said.

"Tell people I have jet lag. Or better yet, tell them I have that West Nile virus. Don't they have that in New York?"

Before they focused on my presence, I slid my ID into the slot and pushed open the main door to *Buzz*.

"You're making a mistake," the woman said as the *Buzz* door began to close behind me. Out of the corner of my eye, I saw Brandon stride toward the elevator.

Though I'd expected there might still be a few people hanging around, the *Buzz* office appeared empty. Most of the lights had been turned off, which meant that the cleaning personnel had already been through.

Robby's office was right off the reception area. I stepped in quietly and switched on his desk lamp. After checking once over my shoulder, I pulled open his desk drawer. There was a scattering of take-out menus, a tube of hand cream, and some *Buzz* envelopes all jammed in the front of the drawer. But no reference letters. Below the drawer was a file drawer, and I pulled it open, casting a brief look at the Pendaflex file tabs. There was nothing there that appeared to hold the letters. Clearly his desk hadn't been emptied yet, so Robby was mistaken about having left the letters behind. I yanked my cell phone from my purse and hit his number. His answering machine picked up once again. I sighed, mildly annoyed.

I wasn't planning on coming into the office tomorrow, so as long as I was on the premises, I decided to pick up anything that had accumulated in my in-box during the day.

As I turned the corner to head down the aisle toward the pod, I caught my breath. The lights were still on in Mona's office, the blinds drawn. That would have been rich, I thought— Mona working late and discovering me rifling through Robby's desk. But I reminded myself that Mona never worked late on Tuesday. Maybe the cleaning lady was still doing her thing down there. Sure enough, as I walked toward my desk, I noticed a cleaning cart parked outside the glassed-in vestibule in front of Mona's office, where her assistants had their desks.

I reached my desk, and without even turning on the desk light, I grabbed all the material from my in-box. As I stuffed the papers into my bag, I heard a sound—a moan. I froze in place, my eyes searching. I was pretty sure the noise had come from the direction of Mona's office, but I couldn't imagine what it might be. Had some guests from the party snuck over to have a quick shag? I checked my watch: 8:28.

I listened a few seconds longer but didn't hear anything else. I decided the smartest thing was to just get the hell out of there. As I stepped away, I heard the moaning again. But it was clear this time that it wasn't someone in the delirious throes of a desktop quickie—it was someone in distress. My heart began to pick up speed. I needed to find out what was going on.

Cautiously I inched my way down the aisle, along the outside of the pod and then the art department. The desks of Mona's assistants inside the vestibule blocked the lower half of the glass wall, but I could see the upper half and no one was in sight. The moaning must have come from Mona's office. The door was open only a few feet.

I took a deep breath and kept walking. I reached the cleaning cart, which was really just a huge rubber trash can on wheels, with bottles of cleaning solution and black trash bags dangling from the front and one of those big feather dusters stuck on the side. The cleaning person was nowhere in sight.

"Anyone here?" I called out haltingly. I was greeted by the honk of a horn sixteen floors below—and then another moan.

Quickly I stepped around the cart and into the vestibule. A blond-haired cleaning lady dressed in blue pants, a blue smock, and big rubber yellow gloves was on her knees next to Mona's office door, facing in my direction and rocking back and forth with her hands on her forehead.

"What's the matter?" I asked, rushing toward her.

She lowered her hands and stared at me. She looked dizzy, unfocused.

"Did you fall?" I asked. She said nothing, but her right hand instinctively went to the back of her head and dabbed at her skull by her hair bun. I squatted down and scrutinized the spot. Through the yellow rubber fingers of her gloves, I could see that there was blood oozing from the area. I straightened up, eager to find a cloth or paper towel for the blood. As I did, I heard an odd thumping sound through Mona's partially open door. I edged closer to the office and peered inside. One of the chairs to her small conference table had been overturned.

I glanced nervously behind me through the glass of the vestibule, out toward the darkened bullpen. There was no one else in sight.

I pushed the door to Mona's office fully open. She was lying on the floor just in front of her desk, face-up, dressed in black pants and top, her arms and legs twitching violently as if she had touched a high-voltage wire. Gurgling noises were coming from her mouth. And both brown eyes, even the one that never looked straight, were rolled back in her head.

CHAPTER 3

For a few seconds I just stood there. I felt paralyzed with both fear and uncertainty. Seizures . . . seizures? I thought, searching that section of my brain that may have committed itself during a first-aid course back in high school. I knew that doctors used to think that a person having a seizure was in danger of swallowing his tongue and that you were supposed to try to hold the tongue down—without getting your hand chomped off. But I was pretty sure that the only recommendation nowadays was that you protect the person from hurting himself and get medical attention fast.

Mona's head lay about an inch or two from the heavy wooden leg of her desk, and her body was being jounced in that direction by the spasms. I took three quick strides toward her, knelt down, and slipped my right hand under her head. I noticed immediately that the hair around her face was soaked with blood. Peering through the dark, wet strands, I spotted a huge, ugly gash on her left temple.

My heart wasn't just racing now; it was leaping all over the place. I'd covered seriously injured people as a newspaper reporter and I'd come across dead bodies in cases I'd investigated, yet I'd never grown used to being up close and personal with violence. Clearly, someone had attacked both Mona and the cleaning lady. Still squatting, I tugged Mona's body gently so her head wasn't so close to the desk leg. Then I swung around on my heels and stared anxiously out into the vestibule. The cleaning lady was the only one there.

"Mona? Mona, can you hear me?" I said, turning back to her. Her eyes continued to bounce around at the top of the sockets, and her left arm involuntarily pummeled my thigh. She was clearly not conscious of anything going on around her.

I stood up, hurried behind her desk, and dialed 911. I explained to the operator that two women had been attacked and were injured, at least one seriously. She told me to stay on the line, but I explained that the best I could do was set down the phone because I needed to check on one of the people who'd been attacked.

I rushed back out to the vestibule, where the cleaning lady was now struggling to her feet. She was younger than I'd realized—probably only in her mid-thirties.

"What happened?" I asked, putting my arm around her. There was a bloody smear on her face now, as if she'd dabbed at her wound with her glove and then touched her face. "Who did this to you?"

"My head," she muttered. "It hurts." She had a Russian or Eastern European accent.

"I know—you have a head injury. But I've called for an ambulance and they should be here soon. Why don't you sit down over here."

I guided her over to the desk of one of Mona's two assistants and eased her into the chair.

"What's your name?" I asked.

She hesitated for a moment, and I wondered if she might be suffering from memory loss.

"Katya," she said haltingly. "Katya Vitaliev."

"Katya, I want to find some ice for your head, but first I'm going to call for more help, okay?"

A sheet of phone extensions was pinned above the assistant's desk, and my eyes ran to the bottom of the sheet, where I found the number for the lobby.

"Who am I speaking to?" I asked as soon as someone picked up.

"This is Bob."

"This is Bailey Weggins on sixteen in the *Buzz* office. Someone has attacked two women up here. I've already called 911. The person who did it has probably already left the building, but you should try to prevent anyone from leaving until the police get here."

"All right, all right. I'm going to send somebody right up there."

I set down the phone and considered how I could obtain ice for Katya's head. The kitchenette was on the far side of the floor, and I was nervous not only about leaving her and Mona, but also about encountering the assailant. What if some kind of lunatic was wandering the floor? I realized that Mona must have a refrigerator. I glanced around the space and noticed a minifridge over by the other assistant's desk. I flung open the door. The freezer compartment was tiny, but it held a small tray of ice covered with about six months' worth of freezer burn. I popped the cubes into some paper towels and hurried back toward Katya.

"Here, can you manage to hold this against your head?" I asked. "It'll help control the bleeding."

"Yes, I will hold it." She accepted the makeshift ice pack with her bloodied yellow glove and touched it carefully to the back of her head. From the location of her wound, it appeared she'd been struck from behind. I wondered if she had even seen her attacker.

I glanced back into Mona's office. She was still twitching with seizures. I didn't dare do anything to *her* wound.

"What happened, Katya?" I asked again. "Did you see who did this to you?"

"I—I did not see him," she said, shaking her head. "I did not see anything."

"Were you attacked out here?" I asked.

"No," she said, shaking her head. "I start to go into the office. I saw her—the editor, Mrs. Hodges—on the floor. I start to go to her, to see if I can help. Then someone hit me. They—they were behind the door, I think."

"And then you came out here?"

"Yes. I was okay at first, but then . . . then I start to feel—dizzy." She pronounced it *deezy*.

"Do you have any idea how long you were kneeling out here?"

"I don't know. A little while, I think."

That meant the attack had probably occurred just prior to the time I'd been rifling through Robby's desk drawers—or perhaps even during that time. If that was the case, the assailant hadn't left by the main entrance because I would have seen him. He must have snuck down one of the stairwells—*or* had exited through the door on this floor that led to the *Track* offices.

"Okay, sit tight for a second," I told her. I rushed back into Mona's office. Mona's body was still twitching, but less than it had before. Her head was now drooping to the left. I wished there were something I could *do*.

From behind me I heard a commotion, and I stepped outside the office again. Lights suddenly flooded the bullpen, and I saw one of the building security guards running in our direction. A look of panic had formed on Katya's face.

"It's just the building guard," I told her. I stepped outside the vestibule into the aisle.

The guy was no more than twenty-five, a skinny Pakistani who looked terrified, as if up until this point the worst thing he'd encountered in his job was people sneaking out of the building with boxes of file folders.

"Where are they?" he yelled at me. "What happened?"

Before I could even answer, we heard more noise. Charging down the hall behind him were four EMS workers and two New York City uniformed cops and behind them one of the big burly security guys who'd been on duty outside the *Track* party. It looked as if he had hitched a ride to see what the excitement was. This was the first indication of just how much of a circus this was going to become.

The group reached the vestibule and came to an abrupt stop, staring at me expectantly. One of the patrol cops was a woman, thirty or so, African American, and the other was a white guy who seemed pretty green.

I pointed over toward Katya, explaining that she had been attacked and that there was a more seriously injured victim inside the office, the editor of the magazine. The security guard was told by the female cop to return to the reception area and make certain no one entered or left the *Buzz* offices. She also dispatched the young cop to make a sweep of the floor. Three of the EMS crew hustled into Mona's office, followed by the female cop, and the other went over to Katya. He examined the scalp wound and immediately took her blood pressure. A minute later the cop emerged from the office, speaking into her walkie-talkie. She signed off, pulled a chair up to Katya, and began asking her questions, taking the answers down on a pad inside a thick black leather holder. Katya told her the same thing she'd told me, though by now she seemed slightly more coherent.

When it was clear she'd extracted all she could out of Katya—which wasn't much—the cop turned her attention to me.

"You found the victims?" she asked after she'd jotted down my name and address and determined that I worked at *Buzz*.

"Yes. Just before eight-thirty I heard some moaning and

then I saw Katya kneeling down with her hands on her head. As I was trying to help her, I noticed the overturned chair in the editor's office and looked inside. That's when I saw Mona—"

"You were working *this* late tonight?"

"Sort of. I was on business outside of the office all day and I came by to pick up some work in my in-box."

I didn't like being less than truthful with a cop, but I'd made a decision a few minutes ago to leave Robby out of any explanation I offered about my presence here tonight. I was worried that I'd get him into trouble if I mentioned the secret mission he'd assigned me. Besides, I really *had* picked up work from my in-box.

"Did you see anyone else here?"

"No, not a soul," I said, shaking my head. "Though there are plenty of people over at the party."

She pointed to the art department, the area directly beyond Mona's vestibule, and told me to take a seat there. Detectives, she said, would want to speak to me after they arrived.

I picked up my purse from the floor, walked over to the associate art director's station, and plunked down in his chair. Attached to his bulletin board was a huge tabloid headline that read, NAKED SAMURAI SLASHER, and the desk was scattered with magazines, books, packs of gum, and a set of chattering teeth. I'd barely expelled my breath when four guys—two more patrol cops and what I assumed were two detectives—came charging down the aisle. They glanced over at me but made a beeline toward the patrol cop and the crime scene. Seconds later two of the EMS workers headed out with Mona on a stretcher, an oxygen mask over her face. They were moving fast, one guy holding an IV line. Mona no longer appeared to be twitching uncontrollably.

Moments later another stretcher was wheeled by, this one with Katya on it. She was twisting her head back and forth, and I saw one of the EMS crew lean closer and say something in her ear, perhaps to comfort her.

For the next five or ten minutes I waited, keeping my eye on the police activity and trying in my mind to make sense of what had happened tonight. Who could have possibly done this to Mona, and *why*? There was a chance, I supposed, that some sort of maniac or druggie had slipped into the offices and come prowling around looking for money. He may have popped into her office not expecting to find anyone and been startled when he discovered her. Perhaps she screamed or threatened to call security and he struck her on the head to silence her. As he was about to flee, he heard the cleaning lady come down the hall with her cart. He hid behind the door. As she pushed it open, he struck her, too.

But there was extra security in the building tonight, and the roving druggie theory didn't make nearly as much sense as another explanation: that someone Mona knew had done this to her. Someone who had learned that she was going to be in her office late on Tuesday—a rare occurrence—and had come by looking for her. Perhaps he'd had no intention of hurting her, but they'd had a confrontation and things had escalated. And there was an excellent chance that the person was someone who worked at *Buzz*.

I glanced across the area to the row of windows. There were already paparazzi down below, and before long there would be even more press. This was a big fat juicy story, and everyone would be covering it.

Suddenly, I heard the sound of activity at the far end of the floor. A man I recognized as Mona's husband, Carl, came barreling down the aisle along the pod, a wigged-out expression on his face and the tail of his jacket flapping like a flag. On his heels was a patrol cop I hadn't seen before. Before Carl reached Mona's office, one of the detectives stepped around from the vestibule and stood in his path. The detective spoke to him, and I heard him say the words St. Luke's—the name of a hospital in midtown where they must have taken Mona. A second later, Mona's husband turned on his heels and left with the cop in tow. He was obviously now heading to the hospi-tal. I assumed the officer had been told to take him there.

Only a few minutes later the two detectives strode over to-ward me, along with the female patrol cop. She told them my name and then retreated as they pulled out desk chairs and sat down.

The alpha male appeared to be the taller and bigger of the two, a six-foot-two guy, probably mid-forties, with receding pale brown hair, thick cheeks, and those glasses they make now without any frames so that sometimes you can't even tell they're there. His partner was short and chubby, maybe a little older, with a silver streak like a racing stripe along the side of his black brown hair.

"Miss Weggins?" the alpha male said, half question, half statement, as he glanced at a page of his notebook.

"Yes."

"We appreciate your sticking around. I'm Detective Randy Tate, and this is Detective McCarthy."

I nodded. I felt nervous, the way I always did when con-versing with cops. "Of course," I said.

"I know you told the officer what happened, but take us through it again, will you?"

I retold my story, starting with the part about hearing moans and skipping over how I happened to be at *Buzz* in the first place. I didn't want to lie again if I didn't have to.

"One thing I should tell you," I added. "I moved Mona's body a couple of inches—away from the desk. I know you're supposed to be careful about touching things in situations like this, but she was having a seizure and I was afraid she might knock her head against the leg of the desk. Do you know how she is, by the way?"

"We don't have any word yet," he said, sounding as if he wouldn't tell me even if they did. "Did the victim say anything to you?"

"Nothing. She was shaking badly, in some kind of convulsions. I did speak to the other victim—the cleaning lady. She told me that the person must have been behind the door when she entered the office. She said she never saw who hit her."

"Did you see anyone else on the floor tonight—at *any* point when you came up here?"

"No, it was empty—though when I was in the reception area I could hear a ton of people at the party over at *Track*. The attack must have happened just before I came in."

"Did Ms. Hodges often work late?"

"Most nights, yes—but rarely on Tuesdays as far as I know. Monday is the night we close each issue, and that's always a really late night. On Tuesday people try to clear out by six or so."

"But not you?"

Oh God, here we go *again*.

"Well, first of all, I'm, uh, sort of a part-timer and I don't work on the same schedule as everyone else. I was out on business all day—you know, covering a story—and like I told the officer, I needed to pick up work from my in-box."

As I gave the last detail I glanced down, directing his attention to the papers sticking out of my bag. I felt even more uncomfortable lying to Tate. He eyed me curiously. I couldn't tell if he suspected some prevarication on my part or was just trying to make sense of everything in his mind.

More voices and footsteps burst into the open space. The three of us looked up in unison to see four people come trooping down the aisle along the bullpen—the crime scene unit with equipment and two other guys in sports jackets, probably other detectives. Tate caught the eye of one and cocked his head in the direction of Mona's office. I assumed that the look he gave suggested he'd be with them as soon as he'd finished with his witness.

"Tell me, to your knowledge is there anyone here at the magazine who might be upset with Ms. Hodges?" Tate asked me, pulling my attention back to him. "Did anyone have a bone to pick with her?"

My brain seemed to freeze. God, what should I say? Robby, of course, had a big fat bone to pick with Mona, but he certainly hadn't killed her, and I didn't want to put him on the police radar unnecessarily. Nor did I want to do that to other people I'd heard Mona chew out. In a split second, I decided to err on the side of discretion and be vague with my answer. The police would be interviewing tons of people, including many who were far more entrenched at the magazine than I was, and they would hear soon enough about the staff's problems with Mona, including Robby's dismissal.

"I've only worked here six weeks and so I'm not really up to speed on everything that's going on," I said. "You should probably talk to Nash Nolan, the executive editor."

"All right, that will be all the questions for tonight," he said. "Our crime scene unit is here now, and I'd appreciate it if you'd show them exactly where you found the victim and explain how much you moved her."

"Of course," I said.

I followed Tate back to the area outside Mona's office. A portion of it, including the section where the cleaning lady had collapsed, was now cordoned off and there were about ten police types milling around—some inside the yellow tape, some outside of it. Detective Tate left me outside the office while he conferred with one of the crime scene personnel inside, and then he motioned that I should enter. The surreally bright crime scene lights made it seem as if Mona's office were being readied for a fashion shoot.

A young woman in an oversize navy blue jacket turned and looked at me. "You wanna indicate where you found the victim?" she asked.

"Her head was about an inch or two from the desk leg—in that direction," I said, pointing. "I moved her about six inches away so that she wouldn't bang her head."

Speaking of Mona's head, there was a big smear of blood on the beige carpet, and it glistened in the lights. I felt sick looking at it.

Tate led me out of the room. At first I thought he was walking me back to my seat, but we kept going and it became obvious that he was escorting me to the door. I was finally being sent on my way.

"Here's my card," Tate said, tugging it out of his wallet. "I want you to call me if anything occurs to you or if you notice anything odd at work this week."

I nodded with all the enthusiasm I could muster, considering that I felt like shit.

"And one other thing. I don't want you to speak to anyone about the specifics of what you saw in there tonight—is that clear? There may be certain details that we decide to hold back."

"Yes, I understand."

"Fine," he said, and then nodded at one of the patrol cops hovering nearby. "The officer will escort you out of the building so you don't get hassled."

He strode back toward the action, and the patrol cop stepped forward to play usher for me. As he pushed open the door to the reception area, I was startled by the scene that awaited us. More cops were congregated in the reception area and also by the door to *Track*. There was no longer any music, just the steady drone of a disgruntled crowd. Obviously, people were being held at *Track* until the police could interview each and every one of them.

But even more shocking was the scene that greeted me when I stepped out of the elevator into the lobby of the building. Through the glass windows to the street I could see throngs of people, including tons of press with cameras, standing behind blue police barricades. Mona, who had dispatched hordes of reporters and photographers around the world, had become the center of the kind of sizzling story that she always demanded they return with.

Though the noise of the crowd managed to permeate the lobby, it was muted and it wasn't until the police officer opened the door that the full force of the din hit me. It was like that moment when you leave the relatively hushed customs area at an international airport and step into the cacophony of arrivals.

"How were you planning to get home?" the cop yelled over the noise.

"I guess I'll just take a cab."

"I better help you get one."

He took my arm and ushered me through the gauntlet. Cameras snapped and reporters ambushed me with questions. "What's going on up there?" "Did you see anything?" "Have the police arrested anyone?" "Who are *you*?"

This, I realized, was as close as I was ever going to get to being Nicole Kidman.

The cop hailed a cab and helped me inside. As soon as it was in motion, I fell back against the sticky leather seat, completely wiped. Five hours ago, my plans for the evening had entailed going out for dinner at an Italian restaurant in the Village, where I'd hoped to have the roasted game hen and a glass of super Tuscan. Instead I ended up finding my boss beaten and bloodied. I was also now smack in the middle of a criminal investigation. Yet even if I hadn't stumbled onto that horrible scene tonight, the events would have caught up with me quickly. Tomorrow, *Buzz* would be a nuthouse as people reacted to the assault and worried about how Mona's fate would impact their own. She might have very serious injuries to her brain; in fact, she might never recover.

As the cab shot down Broadway, I dug my cell phone and BlackBerry out of my purse and found the number for Nash. I reached only his voice mail and left a message explaining what had happened in case he hadn't already heard and leaving my

cell phone number. Then I phoned Paul Petrocelli, an ER doctor I knew who let me badger him with basic medical questions when I was writing stories. Half the time when I called
him he was busy trying to stop a heart attack or remove a fish-
hook from someone's hand, but tonight I lucked out and
caught him between disasters. I described Mona's head wound
and seizure and asked him what he thought the prognosis
might be.

"It sounds like the blow to the head was pretty hard," he
said, stifling a yawn. "With this kind of injury, you might not
have a ton of *internal* bleeding, but the brain swells from the
impact, just like any tissue, and swelling is never a good thing
up there. The skull's a tight container, and there's just no room
to expand. The brain tissue gets compressed and you end up
with herniation down through the lower part of the brain. And
that compresses the respiratory center in the brain stem."

"There actually did seem to be a fair amount of external
bleeding," I told him. "Does that alter your diagnosis?"

"Okay, then, well, another possible scenario is that the
blow ruptured a blood vessel in the lining of the brain. If that
was the case, she would have had a large amount of bleeding
in the skull—not just swelling. Though you're looking at the
same end point."

"Could she die?"

"Sure. Head injuries are no picnic. Look, I'm getting a page.
Call me back later if you need more info."

Next I made a call to Lyle Parker, a former FBI profiler I
sometimes interview. I wanted her take on the crime, but her
voice mail picked up. I left a message saying that I needed to
pick her brain.

I had the cabdriver dump me on the corner of 9th and
Broadway and felt a rush of relief as I entered my place. It's a
fairly basic one-bedroom with an itty-bitty kitchen, but it sports
a few spectacular features that always provide me solace: a
walk-in closet that I've turned into a tiny home office, a big ter-

race, and an enchanting view to the west—a skyline of old
brick apartment buildings and nineteen wooden water towers.
My apartment was the one good thing to come out of my marriage, unless you want to include knowledge of how a football
pool works.

I poured myself a glass of wine, kicked off my sandals, and
plopped onto the couch with the force of something dropped
from a second-story window. I hadn't eaten a thing all night,
but my stomach was churning and I had no appetite. As I lay
against the throw pillows, I let thoughts of Mona consume me.
I kept wondering who had done this to her. The cleaning lady
hadn't seen the assailant, but Mona must have—she'd been hit
in the front of the head. Maybe the doctors at the hospital had
managed to stabilize her and she was even now whispering the
name of her attacker into the ear of a detective.

I realized suddenly that I needed to call Robby. Not only
was I eager to tell him the news, but I also wanted to report to
him about my little white lie to the police and make certain that
he didn't reveal the true purpose of my visit to *Buzz*. Last, I
needed to tell him that I had never found the letters he'd been
so concerned about.

I reached for the phone on the end table and tried his
number. This time he answered on the third ring.

"*There* you are," I said, my voice full of relief. "Look, I've
got some terrible news."

"Mona?"

"Yes, how did you hear?"

"Someone I know at *Track* called me. They're saying she's
in a coma at St. Luke's."

"Did you hear that I discovered the body?"

"*What?*"

"I'm not supposed to share any of the specifics, but, yeah,
I'm the one who found her."

"*You* found her?" he exclaimed. "You were *there?*"

"Of course I was there, Robby," I said, trying not to sound

irritated. "I went to get the letters, just like you asked me to—which, by the way, weren't anywhere in your desk. And which, by the way, I didn't mention to the police. I didn't want to drag you into it, so I just said I was picking up some work for myself."

"But you never called me back when you said you would," he said almost mournfully. "You said you were going to check with your friend and call me right back."

"It took me a while to reach her," I told him. "When I finally called your place, there was no answer. I figured you'd crashed, so I just left a message and headed up to the office. Why does any of that matter, anyway? You sound upset about it."

"It's just . . ." The tone of his voice was the vocal equivalent of someone wringing his hands.

"It's just *what*, Robby?" I felt myself growing aggravated.

"*I* picked up the letters. I went there tonight after I didn't hear from you."

CHAPTER 4

I took a few seconds to ponder the bombshell Robby had just dropped at my feet.

Robby had paid a visit to the *Buzz* offices tonight. He had been there around the time that Mona had been in her office. He'd been incredibly shaken about his dismissal. And now Mona lay in the hospital, a gaping hole in her head.

"Are you still there?" he asked.

"Yes, I'm here," I said quietly. "Did you see Mona tonight?"

"No, I never went down to that end of the floor. I just grabbed the two letters and left. Do you know what her condition is? Is she going to live?"

"I don't know, Robby. Tell me—how did you get into the office? Didn't you say they took away your ID when you left today?"

He expelled a nervous sigh. "Yes, they did. And I knew I wouldn't be able to get into the office without it. But I realized that I was still on the list for the *Track* party tonight. And I knew that all I would have to do was show up in the lobby, give my name, and present a photo ID—I used my driver's license. So that's what I did. They even had a separate security guard checking off names of people going to the party—some guy I'd never even seen before. Once I was on the floor, this guy who works freelance in the art department just happened to be leaving. I don't think he had a clue I'd been canned, so he held the door open for me."

"What time was this?"

"It was just a couple of minutes before eight. I checked my watch because I wanted to make sure it was late enough and that nobody would be around."

"*Was* there anyone around?"

"No, the place was empty. The guy from art must have been the last person to leave. Like I said, I just grabbed the letters and got the hell out of there."

"Did you leave the front way?"

"No, I went down the stairs—all the way to the lobby. I didn't want to take any chances. Why are you grilling me on this, Bailey? You don't think *I* had anything to do with this thing, do you?"

"I didn't say that. I'm just wondering how close you came to bumping into the person who did it. Did you notice the lights on in Mona's office?"

"No. I mean, they might have been on, but I never went around the corner."

My mind was reeling. I must have missed Robby by fifteen to twenty minutes. Was he telling me the truth? Or was he the one who had smashed Mona's skull? I couldn't imagine him being capable of such an act, yet he'd been despondent about being fired.

"Do you think the police are going to suspect me?" he asked, his voice suddenly filled with desperation.

"Hopefully Mona will be okay and she'll be able to tell the police what happened. But until she regains consciousness, you're probably going to seem like a very viable suspect. You have to talk to a lawyer as soon as possible."

"Oh God, this is horrible," he wailed.

"I don't know a ton about these things, but a lawyer may even suggest that you get hold of the police yourself. They'll be contacting you anyway. Someone saw you go into the office late, plus the cops are going to find out you were fired. It will probably look better if you take the initiative. But you need to get legal counsel and let them figure out the best course of action. Do you know a lawyer?"

"Well, we've talked to a lawyer about the adoption."

"That's not the right kind," I said, trying not to sound impatient. "You need a criminal attorney."

"Brock would probably know someone. He's in San Francisco this week trying to drum up some business. I haven't been able to reach him yet."

"If you can't find anyone, call me back and I'll do a little research. Are you going to be okay there by yourself?"

"I guess so. Oh God, this is so awful. Was she—was she in a coma when you found her?"

"Like I said, I'm not supposed to discuss any specifics, but she was in pretty bad shape. Call me back tomorrow and let me know what's happening, okay?"

"Okay," he said, choking back a sob.

I put down the phone and began pacing my living room. This was bad, really bad. But most disturbing wasn't that Robby might soon become the primo suspect. It was the fact that he might have actually *done* it. I just had to keep telling myself that the Robby I knew wasn't capable of such a despicable act.

I stripped off my jean skirt, kicked it into the corner of the living room, and wandered into the kitchen. I felt I needed something in my stomach, but toast was the only thing that held any appeal. As I was popping a piece of bread into the toaster, my cell phone went off in the other room. I raced for my purse and rummaged through it for my phone. Nash was on the other end.

"I just heard your message," he said. "Are you still there?"

"Where?"

"At *Buzz*."

"No, I'm home now. What about you? Had you heard before you got my message?"

"Yeah, I was at the *Track* party. I just escaped. They interviewed all of us, one by bloody one. I got moved up the food chain when I finally convinced somebody that I was worth talking to. What the hell happened?"

"Someone attacked both Mona and the cleaning lady. I have no idea why, though."

"What kind of shape is Mona in? Do you think she'll be okay?"

"She was unconscious when I found her and apparently, according to the news, she's in a coma—at St. Luke's. That's all I've heard."

"You said on the phone that she'd been hit on the head. With what, do you know?"

"No," I said honestly, but also mindful of the fact that I wasn't supposed to be talking about details. "It was a crime scene, and they don't appreciate amateurs doing any kind of inspection."

"What about the cleaning lady?"

"She seemed okay."

"Did she see anything?"

"I don't think so. Though she was pretty dazed. Maybe when her head clears, she'll remember some details."

"Wait, say it again," he said. "I'm in a cab in the park and you're starting to break up."

I repeated what I'd just told him.

"Christ," he muttered. "I'm probably gonna lose you again, so I better get off. You've got my home number, so call me tonight if you hear anything, all right? And I want you in there tomorrow. Stop by my office as soon as you get in."

"Sure," I said, wondering what he had in mind but deciding that this was not the time to ask.

"Hey, weren't you supposed to be in court today?" he said as an afterthought.

"I was," I said, trying not to sound defensive. "But I—I needed a few things from work."

It was silent at the other end, and I realized that I had lost him for good.

I finished making my toast and turned on the TV to CNN, but some talk show was playing and the crawl didn't offer any news about Mona. I figured that I probably wouldn't learn anything official until the eleven o'clock local news. For the next few minutes I paced my apartment, nursing my wine but barely tasting it. I didn't particularly like Mona, but seeing her injured like that was immensely disturbing.

For the first time in a long time, I also felt a desperate craving for the company of Jack Herlihy, the guy who'd been my boyfriend until January. Jack was a psychologist I'd met while researching an article about a troubled young girl who'd made everyone think there was a poltergeist in the house. Though I'd fought my initial attraction to him, we'd ended up in a steady, monogamous relationship last fall. A professor at Georgetown, he lived in Washington, D.C., during the week but flew to New York every weekend, and in the fall he would begin teaching at NYU. We'd spent our time together prowling around the Village, seeing movies, listening to music at little clubs, skiing, and having lots of very nice sex.

Then in January he'd knocked me off guard by telling me he wanted us to move in together—with the expectation that we would probably marry in the future. I was crazy about Jack, but as soon as the words spilled from his mouth I knew that I wasn't ready for that kind of commitment. I'd been divorced for just over two years, and I needed more time to figure out how I'd blown things so profoundly and how I could make sure I was never guilty of such bad judgment again. Jack broke things off with me, saying that it had to be all or nothing for him. It stung like a bitch at first, though I knew I'd made the right call. As the weeks went by, the ache subsided—perhaps more quickly than I'd anticipated.

But tonight all I could think about was how great it would be to have Jack to talk to. He had that shrink way of asking lots of the right questions, and when I answered them I generally felt an enormous sense of release, like floodwater gushing over sandbags. But there was no Jack anymore, and I was going to have to be a big girl and suck it up.

I headed for the refrigerator, this time in search of something sweet. In the freezer I found a tub of frozen vanilla yogurt, date and origin unknown. As I popped off the lid, I saw that it looked as old as the south polar ice cap. I scraped off the ice crystals on top and stabbed at it with a spoon. It tasted even worse than it looked.

As I was tossing the tub in the trash, my home phone rang.

"Tell me this isn't happening, will you?" someone said after I'd answered. There was a frantic edge to the voice.

"Who is this?" I asked.

"Me, Jessie," she said after letting out a big sigh. "I'm sorry. I'm just going out of my mind, and since I knew I was near your place, I dialed your number. This whole thing is just so— I don't know . . ."

"I know, I know. I'm going out of my mind here as well."

"Is it true—that you were there?"

"Yeah, I was there—I went by to pick up some work. How did you hear that?"

"I've talked to a million people from *Buzz* already tonight. I guess someone who was at the *Track* party heard you found Mona."

"Where are you, anyway?" I could hear cars rushing by in the background.

"I'm right around the corner—on University and Eighth.

Look, do you feel like getting together? We could just grab a cup of coffee or something."

"Why don't you come up?" I asked. "We could sit and talk on my terrace."

"You don't mind? I feel like a big buttinsky."

I told her I didn't mind and made sure she had the exact address.

I retrieved my jean skirt from the corner and wiggled into it again. I liked Jessie, but I didn't think she was ready to see me in a pair of hot pink boy briefs.

She arrived five minutes later, breathless, her long glossy brown hair shoved behind her ears.

"Hey, come on in," I said, opening the door to her. "I'm glad you called."

She was wearing low khaki green pants, a pale green T-shirt, and a necklace made of amber-colored stones. At around five seven or so, Jessie had a great figure—nice boobs, buff all over—but she admitted that her slightly wide hips bugged her. Her fashion strategy, she'd told me, was darks on the bottom and plenty of jewelry on top to deflect attention.

"I'm so glad you were *here*. I just needed to be with some-one—someone from work who could understand." We gave each other an awkward hug. We were on our *way* to being friends but not totally there yet, so it was kind of weird for us to be standing in my apartment late at night with our arms around each other.

"I can't believe you found her," Jessie continued, dropping her arms. "What—what had happened to her? I heard someone smashed in her skull."

"Yes, she'd been attacked. I'd love to talk about it, but I can't. The police practically threatened me with incarceration if I opened my mouth."

"Oh, I get it," she said. "It's one of those 'only the person who did it would know certain details' kind of things. But isn't it freaking you out—I mean, to have found her?"

"It wasn't pleasant. How about something to drink?" I pointed to the bottle of red wine on the dining table. "I've got wine. Beer. Sparkling water. And a bottle of port that someone brought as a hostess gift four years ago."

She smiled and thought for a moment. "Uh, just sparkling water if it's opened. But otherwise tap is fine."

She followed me to my tiny kitchen, looking around as we went. "This is a great place," she said, her eyes scanning the room.

"Thanks. Here you go. One sparkling water. Why don't we sit out on the terrace?"

I pointed toward the door and then followed her out into the night. There's something about the view from my terrace after dark that reminds me of the backdrop of a Broadway show—the inky blue black of the sky and the apartment buildings dabbed randomly with lights. It almost seems fake. I motioned for Jessie to take a seat at my patio table, and I lit a citron candle. Through the darkness, I heard her sigh.

"It's so beautiful out here," she said. "Do you mind my asking—do you *own* this?"

"Yeah, I was married once. This was the consolation prize."

"Gotcha. So what do you think is going to happen? You're a whiz at all this crime stuff. Will they be able to catch the person who did this to Mona?"

"You know, those *CSI*-type shows are really misleading. Yes, forensic medicine is amazing today, but often there's no real evidence to analyze or what they find is totally ambiguous. Hopefully Mona will recover and be able to tell the police exactly who did this to her."

"Recover?" In the pale light of the candle, I saw a look of astonishment form on Jessie's face, as if I'd just announced that Peter Pan was about to land on the wrought-iron railing in front of us.

"Yes, people *do* come out of comas."

"But she's dead—haven't you *heard*?"

I gasped. "Dead? How do you know that?"

"I have a contact at St. Luke's. I talked to him about a half hour ago and he told me that she had died from her injuries. I assumed the news was out there by now."

"Jesus," I said, leaning forward in my chair. "The last I knew, she was still alive." My mind was lurching all over the place. I wondered if Mona had ever regained consciousness and identified her attacker to the police.

"Is there any chance it was a robber?" Jessie asked, interrupting my thoughts. "I heard that one of the cleaning people was attacked, too."

"Its possible, I suppose. But security seemed especially tight tonight."

"I know. I thought they were going to scan my pupils."

"You went to the party?"

"Yeah—for just a while, though. I had another event to cover, so I left around eight. I was gone before they rounded everyone up."

"Who else was there from *Buzz*?" I was wondering who was still on the floor when Mona was attacked.

"Nash. Hilary, that blond chick who works for 'Juice Bar.' Ryan. I spotted him just before I left. And of course Mona and her husband."

"*Mona* was at the party?"

"Yeah, she always tried—*tried*—to go to stuff like that on nights when we weren't closing. Though obviously she went back over to the office at some point."

Why? I wondered. To meet someone?

"What do you think's gonna happen?" Jessie asked. "Will the place be crawling with cops?"

"Oh, you can count on that for at least the next few days," I said. "I suppose Nash will run things, don't you?"

"Yeah. Let's pray they give him the job. That way all of our jobs are safe."

"Oh gosh, we're missing the news," I said, peering at my watch in the candlelight. "Let's check it out, okay?"

But we were too late. By the time I turned on the TV in my bedroom, there were sports guys barking on every channel. Jessie and I went back into my living room and spent a few minutes speculating about what would happen over the next few days—what Dicker might do, how intrusive the press was likely to be in our lives, how people on staff would behave.

"Do you think someone we work with did this?" she asked.

"I'm afraid it's a possibility," I admitted. "Though everyone who was at the party is a potential suspect."

"I'm glad I left early. Well, I'd better get moving. Thanks again for letting me come up and hang for a while."

"Oh please, it was just what I needed," I said. "Before you go, one more question. Did Mona ever work late on Tuesday?"

"Not that I know of."

"So what was she doing in her office, do you think?"

"Maybe she went back to get some work she'd left behind—just like you did."

She might be right. I wondered whether the killer had been at the party and had seen Mona sneak away and followed her. Or was it someone who was at the office late and had gone down to Mona's office when he saw her pop in unexpectedly?

"Do you think someone at the *party* did this?" Jessie asked as if she'd been reading my thoughts.

"I don't know," I said. "Perhaps tomorrow we'll learn more."

"Yeah," she said distractedly.

"You going to be okay?" I asked.

"Oh sure. I mean, I feel overwhelmed by this weird floating anxiety, but do I think someone is going to sneak into my apartment tonight and smash *me* over the head with a paperweight? No."

"What makes you say paperweight?"

"Isn't it always a paperweight?" she asked, forcing a smile. "Good night. See you tomorrow."

I opened the door and watched as she headed toward the elevator.

"Oh, by the way," she said, turning midway down the hall. "You heard about Robby getting fired, right?"

"Uh-huh," I said, keeping my face as neutral as I could manage. "Were you there today when it happened?"

"Yes, and it was ugly. I don't think he threatened her or anything—he just crawled out of her office as if he were doing a scene from *The Passion of the Christ*. But once he was back in his office, he started slamming things around, kicking his wastebasket. They ended up sending security to escort him out. It's a good thing they yank away your ID when you leave. Otherwise the cops would be all over him."

I didn't say anything, just nodded as if I intended to give her comments some thought after she left. But as I shut the door, I sighed in worry. If the police didn't find evidence pointing to the contrary, Robby certainly was going to have the cops all over him. Could he actually have done it? And what kind of position did that put *me* in? I'd been less than truthful to the police tonight.

I undressed for bed, and after turning on the radio in my bedroom, I adjusted the dial to WINS, the New York City all-news station. Next I filled the bathtub and added some green-tea bath gel I had left over from a *Gloss* beauty giveaway. It was close to ninety out and taking a bath seemed borderline insane, but as soon as I sank into the water, my body almost moaned in relief. Unfortunately, the water did nothing to relax my brain. I kept thinking about Mona. If Robby hadn't attacked her, who had? From my bedroom I heard the droning of radio news—snippets about a rapist on the loose in Queens and a taxi that had jumped the curb in midtown. Then, suddenly the announcer was talking about Mona. The controversial, widely known editor of *Buzz* had been murdered in her office tonight, he reported. Another woman on the premises had been injured, but not seriously. No arrest had been made.

Before I fell into bed, I tried Robby again to see if he'd managed to track down a lawyer, but his answering machine picked up. I left a message for him to call me if he needed a name.

I slept fitfully, a million odd dreams appearing and then dissolving in my head before I could even grasp the story lines. In the morning, I wolfed down half a bagel and chugged coffee while scanning *The New York Times*. The Mona story was referenced in a small box on page one and then received full coverage in the "Metro" section. I was even mentioned indirectly, as in "her nearly lifeless body was discovered by an employee." There was an official obit in the back, detailing Mona's history of turbocharging magazine sales. They said she was known for being tough. What they didn't say was that she'd been an überbitch to work for.

I picked up both the *Daily News* and *New York Post* on the way to the subway, and they had Mona's picture plastered on the front page along with as many of the lurid details as they'd been able to gather. They reported that she'd been hit in the head but that the police weren't saying with what. There were also shots of party guests, including Eva Anderson, leaving the building. Eva's dress was a white Grecian design. A clasp midway down the deep V prevented her boobs from leaving the state.

The situation outside the office building was even zanier than it had been last night—there were photographers, reporters, TV crews, and lots of ordinary but curious citizens. The latter were probably tourists who'd been on their way to blow some money at the Disney store and ended up with Mona's murder as a bonus. Police barricades had been set up to keep the crowd at bay, and I had to flash my ID at a security guard before I even entered the building.

It was almost as crazy on the *Buzz* floor. Not only were two security guards in the reception area, but a patrol cop was cooling his heels there, too. The receptionist had this stunned expression on her face, as if she'd just heard that Godzilla had crawled out of New York harbor this morning and was now making his way up Sixth Avenue.

Inside the offices, the mood was an odd mix of somber and electrified. People were gathered in small clusters, talking, obviously pumping one another for details and speculating wildly. Some appeared sober, shaken by the news, but there were others who seemed to be containing their excitement, the way they'd looked the day Nash's wife had stormed into his glass-walled office, called him "a lying fuck-face," and hurled her purse at his head. As I walked by one of the clusters, a deputy editor volunteered that the daily meeting had been canceled.

The vestibule outside Mona's office was still cordoned off with yellow crime scene tape, and through the partially closed door I could see at least two people puttering around inside her office—police doing follow-up work. And lo and behold, Detectives Tate and McCarthy were in Nash's office, talking to him and Thomas Dicker, who was pacing the room like the proverbial caged tiger.

Neither Jessie nor Ryan was at their desks, but Leo was there on the phone, his computer screen displaying a grid of photos all featuring Jennifer Lopez dressed in a coral bikini. Apparently, life at *Buzz* hadn't ground to a complete halt because of Mona's death.

I threw my purse under my desk and checked my voice mail. To my dismay, I discovered that along with a couple of personal messages there were about ten calls from reporters and television producers hoping to talk to me. Word was obviously seeping out that I'd been at the murder scene. It was going to be tough to stay beneath the radar over the next few weeks. Among the personal messages was one from Cat anxious for details (natch!) and another from my next-door neighbor Landon, saying he'd heard about Mona and was desperate to chat. I left a message on his answering machine saying I'd catch up with him later.

Next I headed for the kitchenette. Several staffers I recognized but barely knew were congregated there, talking in low voices. They stopped speaking as I entered and eyed me curiously. After pouring myself a large cup of coffee, I slipped down one of the back corridors to do something I'd been unable to accomplish last night: check out the passage between *Track* and *Buzz*. I'd noticed the door before when I was back in the magazine storage room and someone had come through from *Track*, but I'd never been through it myself.

It was a big heavy metal door, closed at the moment. I glanced around, made sure no one was skulking about, and pushed down the handle. Though there was a lock on the door, it wasn't locked now. On the other side, I saw a deserted back corridor area similar to the one I was standing in but obviously belonging to *Track*. Along one wall was a row of framed posters of albums from the sixties, including *The Free-wheelin' Bob Dylan*. Anyone would be able to pass from one magazine to the next.

How ironic, I thought. You practically needed to be strip-searched to gain entrance to *Buzz* or *Track* from both the street and the reception area, but once you were at one magazine, you could easily sneak into the other if you desired. There was every chance that the murderer had slipped through the door last night—perhaps leaving the party for a confrontation with Mona or then returning there after killing her so he wouldn't be seen coming out of the main door from *Buzz*. On the other hand, the killer might have been a *Buzz* staffer who had never gone to the party but had lingered late at the office. He could have gotten away by slipping into the party or simply by heading down the stairwell. Or, of course, the killer could be Robby.

As I returned to my workstation moments later, Nash was walking in my direction and he indicated with a fast cock of his head that I should follow him back to his office. The detectives were not in sight at the moment, and neither was Dicker.

"Take a seat," he said in that no-nonsense way of his.

I obliged, dropping into one of two leather-and-chrome chairs in front of his desk. He was a husky, fairly attractive guy, somewhere in his forties, with silver-tinged black hair that he wore slicked back at the sides and a pair of black reading glasses perched perennially halfway down his nose. He looked a little fatigued today but nonetheless totally in command. He was wearing a tie for a change, a black one against his black shirt and jacket.

"You hear about Robby?" he said, peering with his deep blue eyes over his reading glasses.

"What about him?" I asked warily.

"He apparently snuck into the building last night. Says he was looking for some letters in his desk. You didn't see him when you were here, did you?"

So the word was out. That meant Robby was in deep doo-doo. I only hoped he'd tracked down a good lawyer.

"No, the place was empty when I arrived," I said. "Do you think the cops believe Robby did it?"

"All I know for sure is that they had him at the precinct for questioning early this morning. And one of the detectives here today asked me all the details about his firing. How pissed he seemed, whether he made any threats."

My stomach sank. "Do you know if he had a lawyer with him?" I asked.

"I wouldn't know. He's your buddy, isn't he? Do *you* think he did it?"

"Robby's a wonderful guy. I just don't think he's capable of something like this."

"Well, the cops clearly have him in their sights. Speaking of which, the reason I called you in is that we have to cover this crime and I want you to be in charge of the reporting."

"For *Buzz*?"

"Yeah, for *Buzz*. Mona wasn't an Oscar winner, but she *was* a celeb of sorts and even people in Oshkosh know her name. Besides, she edited *this* magazine. We can't ignore the story."

"Of course. . . ." I paused for a moment.

"What's the matter? You're not too upset about this to write it up, are you?"

"Of course not. But the very fact that I'm personally involved presents a problem. I can't exactly be objective."

"Look, Bailey, in case you haven't noticed, we're not *The New York Times*. Just cover the story the way you'd cover any other celebrity crime for us—and plan to do as many follow-ups as necessary."

"Okay, but there's something else. The killer could very well be someone who works here. Are you going to feel comfortable with us airing that amount of dirty laundry?"

"We don't really have a choice. We have an obligation to report on this. Besides . . ." He stopped himself. "Let me worry about any fallout."

I couldn't help but imagine what he'd been *tempted* to say. It was probably something like "Besides, newsstand sales will go through the fucking roof."

"Fine," I said. "Thanks for the opportunity. You know people at *Track*, right? Can you get me a list of everyone who attended the party last night?"

"I'm already working on that. You should know that we're going to do a big sidebar on the party—on all the VIPs who were toasting Eva right next door to where Mona was attacked. Are you thinking some party guest did it?"

"It's certainly a possibility. All those people had access to our offices. I'll have to talk to some of them, too."

"Not a problem. Just keep me posted each step of the way with your story," he said, gazing at me over his glasses. "As you say, this could involve someone here. I need to know everything major that *you* know—with a lag time of no more than four seconds. Hear me?"

"Of course. Where are Betty and Amy, by the way?" I asked, referring to Mona's two assistants. I was hoping one of them could shed light on why Mona had gone back to her office last night.

"Betty left for vacation yesterday. Amy is going to help Carl for a while, but she'll be back later. A couple of detectives ambushed her this morning in Great Neck where she lives with her mother and she's scared to death. She's terrified she's a suspect because of an incident involving the quest for some Jamba Juice concoction."

"*Could* she be a suspect?"

"I doubt it. She's too inept to murder anyone—and she apparently was on the Long Island Rail Road when Mona was killed."

"Have the police told you *anything*?" I asked.

"Not a thing. Dicker was pressuring them for info, but they're being totally closemouthed."

"What kinds of *questions* have they been asking? Obviously they wanted to know about any problems Mona had with people on staff."

"Yeah, that's how Robby's name came up last night. But there is one thing you should know about. They asked me to take a look at her office and see if anything was missing. It didn't look like anything had been stolen. But then it became pretty obvious that they were thinking about something that could have been used as a weapon. And I realized that this paperweight she kept on her table—the one she was given when she was named editor of the year—seemed to be missing."

"Really?" So Jessie was right about the paperweight. "Sounds like the killer might have taken it with him—or her."

"Looks that way. Something else you should know about. I've asked Ryan to do a separate piece on Mona. A profile of her, kind of a tribute. He's dying to get in on this story."

"Isn't there a chance our stories will overlap?"

"They might a little. But I'll take care of that in the editing."

"Speaking of editing, what's going to happen *here*?" I asked. "Who's going to be running things?"

"Nothing's official yet. Look, I've got to get busy. The police have already eaten a big chunk of my morning. If you need anything at all on this, just ask. And I want to be kept abreast of *everything,* okay?"

"Fine, but when you have a chance to catch your breath, I'll need to talk to you again."

He frowned. "What do you mean?"

"I need you to help me flesh out details for the piece. Background info about the party."

"Okay, but later in the day."

"Just one last thing. Any word on Katya?"

"Who?"

"Katya Vitaliev—the cleaning lady."

"From what I hear, they kept her overnight for observation but she's out now."

"Can you get me her phone number from the cleaning service?"

"Yeah," he said distractedly, starting to thumb through some phone messages on his desk. "I'll see what I can do."

As I headed back toward my desk, I spotted two men hovering there. Moving closer to them, I realized it was Tate and McCarthy. *Great.*

"We'd like to have a word with you, Miss Weggins," Tate said as I approached. He didn't look at all happy to see me, and my stomach began to knot as I followed them down one of the hallways toward the back of the floor—with every eye in the place glued to my ass. We reached one of the small conference rooms, and Tate gestured for me to enter. He shut the door as soon as we stepped inside and told me to take a seat. Four or five empty soda cans and a wadded-up baked-chip potato bag littered the table. I realized that poor Katya had never gotten around to cleaning the room last night before she was injured.

McCarthy remained standing, his arms crossed, but Tate took a seat across from me. He stared hard at me for at least half a minute before speaking. With all my might, I fought the urge to squirm in my seat like a four-year-old.

"So tell me, Miss Weggins," he said finally, his voice hard as a car hood, "why did you mislead us last night?"

CHAPTER 5

"Mislead you?" I said. "What do you mean?" As I spoke, I could feel a nervous flush begin its way up my chest, relentless as General Sherman's march to the sea. I prayed it ran out of firepower before it reached the top of my tank top.

"You don't know what I'm talking about?"

"No, I'm sorry, I don't. I described everything about the crime scene as accurately as I could."

"That's not what I'm referring to," Tate said, and allowed his remark to hang in the air. Gosh, he did the pregnant pause thing almost as well as Cat Jones did. I fought off a momentary urge to confess to burning down several warehouses or killing Jimmy Hoffa and sat there with what I hoped was a look of innocent bafflement—or baffled innocence—on my face.

"I'm talking about the real reason you were here last night," Tate said finally, his voice laced with frustration. "It wasn't to collect your work, was it?"

So did this mean Robby had given me up? I couldn't believe it. Why would he have done that? I knew that I had to come clean quickly rather than end up any deeper in a hole.

"It sounds like Robby Hart mentioned to you that I was supposed to find some letters for him last night," I said. "But it was only *one* of the reasons I came by here. I also picked up my work. I'd been out all day on a story, and since I was hoping to avoid having to come into the office today, I wanted to grab my stuff. I figured I'd kill two birds with one stone."

As soon as the words were out of my mouth, I realized how idiotic they sounded in light of everything that had happened.

"You couldn't have arranged for someone to send you your work today?" Tate asked.

I shrugged in a helpless gesture. "I'm basically a freelancer, and I don't have an assistant," I said.

"Why not tell us about it last night?"

I gathered my words carefully. "Robby feels very private about the adoption, so I didn't want to mention it when there seemed to be no reason to. If I'd thought it had any bearing on things, I would have. The way I saw it, I was here, I heard moaning, and then I discovered that two women had been assaulted. The *reason* I was on the floor didn't really seem to matter."

He smiled with half of his mouth, a sarcastic smile that suggested I'd just said something totally naive or ridiculous, like a predilection toward violent behavior was partially due to consuming too many raisins during one's childhood.

"No *bearing*?" he said. "We're talking about a request from a man who had been fired that day and was extremely angry with Ms. Hodges and you didn't think it had any bearing?"

"But his—" I was about to elaborate but caught myself. I would have loved to point out that if Robby had begged me to *off* Mona, I might have thought it had some bearing, but since he'd asked me only to run what amounted to an errand, it wasn't worth mentioning in my view. It was time to shut up, however. I'd covered enough crime stories to know that the biggest mistake someone can make with cops is to *overexplain*. Plus, since I was now reporting the story, I was going to have to rely on these guys for information in the future. It wasn't a good idea to get off to a cantankerous start with them.

"I'm very sorry if it seemed I misled you," I said instead. "I really didn't mean to."

"Tell us about the phone call Mr. Hart made to you yesterday evening," Tate demanded. "What exactly did he say?"

I tried to take a deep breath without them noticing it. I was afraid they'd think I was attempting to fortify myself for a round of truth obfuscation.

"He told me that he'd gotten fired and, as you might expect, he was feeling upset," I said. "Then he mentioned that he'd forgotten the letters and asked if I'd pick them up for him—they'd taken away his ID, so he couldn't get into the building."

"Did he say anything threatening—about Ms. Hodges?"

"No. No, he didn't." I had a vague recollection of Robby suggesting that he'd love to throttle Mona, but it had been pure hyperbole and I wasn't going to reveal it.

"No?" McCarthy asked skeptically. It was the first time he'd opened his mouth.

"No. Robby's a terrific guy and a very *gentle* guy. I can't imagine him feeling vindictive toward anyone."

"So if he asked you to retrieve the letters," Tate said, "why do you think he came up here and did it himself?"

I described the follow-up conversation I'd had with Robby after I'd returned home last night, in which I discovered that he'd gone to the office after failing to hear from me. Tate and McCarthy exchanged a look that I couldn't decipher, and then Tate told me that was all—for now.

I needed to make one more effort, though, to smooth things over.

"I apologize again for being less than straight with you last night," I said. "But I really had no idea Robby had come down here. He told me he'd taken an Excedrin PM as he was going to bed. Plus, he had no ID card to get into the office."

Tate offered a small smile, begrudgingly, it seemed, while McCarthy regarded me skeptically.

"You may go now," Tate said.

"Just one more thing. I do most of the crime coverage for the magazine, and I'm the person on staff who will be reporting this story. I'll have to be in touch with you over the next week."

Tate's expression soured. "I hope you remember what we discussed. I don't want to read anything about Mona's injuries or the position of the body."

"You have my word."

I slunk down the corridor, trying not to look as rattled as I felt. I'd ended up trapped in a lie and paid the price with my discomfort, yet I still didn't regret my decision to protect Robby last night. What I didn't understand was why he had put me in such a vulnerable position today—he'd obviously told the cops about the secret mission he'd sent me on. I wondered just how much trouble he was in and how good of a lawyer he'd managed to rustle up.

Jessie was at her desk now. We smiled wanly at each other, and as soon as I sat down, she rolled her chair closer to me.

"What was that all about? I saw those two cops walk off with you just as I was coming in."

"Oh, just some follow-up questions about last night. You haven't seen Ryan, have you?" I not only wanted to ask him about the party, I also wanted to discuss our assignments and make certain we didn't end up stepping on each other's toes over the next few days.

"No, but I heard someone say he's due in around noon."

"I'm going to need some help from you if it's okay. Nash wants me to cover Mona's death for the magazine."

"Of course. What do you need?"

"Nash is going to get me the party list, and I'd like to go over it with you. You know lots of those people, I don't. I'd also love to have a conversation with that contact of yours at the hospital, the one who told you Mona had died. Do you think she'd talk to me?"

"*He.* Yeah. But he'd probably only do it on the phone, and he'd never let me tell you his name. You'll just have to trust me that he's a doc there."

"Great."

Over the next five minutes, I drew up a quick plan for myself. I was going to have to interview a ton of people for this story: party guests, Mona's husband, Mona's assistant Amy, Katya, Jessie's doctor friend, my cop contacts, and of course as many *Buzz* staffers as possible. I was going to be a very busy girl.

One of my biggest challenges was how to set up my story about Mona's murder. The crime had fallen in an awkward part of the weekly cycle for *Buzz*. We'd just closed an issue, and the next issue—with my article in it—wouldn't be shipped until next Monday. By the time we hit newsstands on Thursday, people would have learned tons of details about the murder from TV and newspapers. I was going to have to find a fresh take.

One possibility would be to play up the insider angle. That's something I had that no one else could duplicate. I even wondered if I should write the story in the first person. Granted, I couldn't divulge the details that I'd promised Tate I'd keep confidential, but I could certainly describe the overall situation and how chilling it had been. The decision on this one would have to be Nash's.

Though interviewing *Buzz* staffers was going to be a critical part of the process for me, it would have to wait until at least the afternoon. Tate and several other detectives were now making the rounds, questioning people. Tate wouldn't be at all pleased if I spoke to someone before he had the chance.

What I could do, though, was make sure that my priority list—the people besides Jessie who had attended the party—saved time for me. I called Nash's assistant, Lee, and asked her to set up an appointment for me to talk to him again later in the day. I'd grab Ryan as soon as he showed up. That left Hilary, the "Juice Bar" reporter who Jessie said had been in attendance. When I called her, she announced in a slight southern drawl that she had urgent business to take care of this morning and couldn't make time to talk to me until three. I wondered what business was more important than Mona's death.

Next I left messages for my contact in the medical examiner's office and some of the cops I knew, who I hoped would give me a heads-up on anything in the case. I also secured official statements on Mona's death from the police department, from St. Luke's, and even from Dicker's corporate PR department. I wasn't necessarily going to use the stuff, but it was always good to have, especially before you started interviewing people. Once, when I was working for the *Albany Times Union,* I learned through an official statement that a victim was forty-one, not thirty-six as she had led the whole world to believe. That piece of info had given me an invaluable edge when I talked to people. As I was hanging up from one of my calls, Jessie was setting down her phone, too, and gave me a thumbs-up.

"That was him—the doctor," she said to me. "He can talk to you right now." As she scrawled his number on a page from a *Buzz* pad, I glanced down toward Mona's office. There was still police activity in there, but I had the sense that it was slowing down.

I took my cell phone and went down the hall in search of a quiet spot. The police were still using the small conference room that Tate had grilled me in, so I slipped into the other one around the corner. Since I worked at home a good part of the time, I hadn't minded the lack of privacy for me at *Buzz,* but it was going to turn out to be a problem while I was doing *this* story. I needed to be on-site, but I also needed to be away from curious eyes and ears. And no one in the world was more curious than the staff of *Buzz*.

I hit the number Jessie had given me, and a guy answered, with a voice that suggested he was around thirty or so. My guess was that he was an intern or resident. I identified myself, and as I was about to ask my first question, he cut me off.

"Just so you know, I've got time for three questions, tops," he said brusquely.

"Okay. What injuries did Mona Hodges have? I saw one wound on the left temple. Was there anything else?"

"No, just the head wound. It looked like she'd been hit very hard twice, maybe three times. The blows triggered a massive brain hemorrhage."

"Could it have been done with a paperweight?"

"Possibly. Whatever it was, it was heavy. And it was probably roundish."

"Was the same weapon used on the cleaning lady?"

It was so quiet for a second that I thought he was gone.

"Yeah, seems like it," he said finally. "She had a concussion, but there wasn't any internal bleeding. She went home today."

"Did Mona ever regain—"

"You're over your limit."

"Just one more, *please*."

He didn't reply, so I kept going.

"From what you know, did she say anything before she died?"

"Negative."

He disconnected the phone without a good-bye.

Now that I knew exactly what Mona's injuries entailed, I was in a better position to speak to Lyle Parker, the former FBI profiler I knew. Before I headed back to my desk, I tried her again. This time she picked up.

"Hey, sorry not to call back last night," she said, sounding as if her nose were stuffed up. "I've been consulting on this case in Chicago and I've been racing from one plane to the next. What's up?"

"Does the name Mona Hodges ring a bell?" I asked.

"You mean that editor who was just bludgeoned to death in her office?"

"That's the one. I haven't had a chance to tell you that I started working at *Buzz* a few weeks ago. *I* found the body."

"Again?" she exclaimed. "Boy, you get around. I've actually been following the case a little on airport CNN. Have they arrested anyone yet?"

"No, that's why I was hoping to grab five minutes with that fabulous mind of yours."

"I was just about to say I'd have to call you back, but they're flashing a notice that my flight is delayed. Remind me never to come to Illinois again in the summer. There's a thunderstorm every time you turn around."

"So can I describe the situation and have you give me your thoughts on it?"

She sighed. "You know I hate to do this without seeing a report—so it's gonna be nothing more than a guess."

"Okay, here goes, then. Mona Hodges returned to her office from a party and someone hit her twice, possibly three times on the head with a round, heavy object. Seems like a paperweight is missing, so that may be the weapon. She was in convulsions when I found her and she died a few hours later. While the assailant was still in the room, he apparently heard the cleaning lady coming, hid behind the door, and bopped her on the back of the head when she entered the room. That blow didn't cause any major damage. Are you with me so far?"

"Yup."

"So what does it look like to you?"

"Were Mona's clothes disturbed?"

"No. From what I could see, there was no sign of it being a sexual assault."

"Anything taken?"

"No sign of robbery, either. The only thing that's missing apparently is the weapon."

"What part of the skull was Mona hit on?"

"Upper left side, close to the front."

"A frontal attack like that suggests a prior relationship and a sudden burst of anger," said Lyle. "The fact that the paperweight from her office was used to kill her means that the attack probably wasn't premeditated. Like I told you, all you're getting is a guess from me, but I'd say that someone stopped by and had a confrontation with her—a confrontation that got overheated and then out of hand."

"Though *could* it have been premeditated?" I asked. "Let's say someone was nursing a real grudge against Mona. He found out that she'd be coming back and then waited in her office for her, paperweight at the ready."

"I'd bet not. Two blows just don't suggest a longtime grudge or festering rage. Remember that case you asked me about a year or so ago, the one where the sixteen-year-old boy stabbed the girl next door? There were like sixty or seventy stab wounds to the body. That case involved a lot of rage. He'd loved her for years, and when he finally confessed to her, she rebuffed him. He brooded on it for days. When you stab someone sixty times, you're more or less saying, 'I hate you, I hate you, I hate you.' But two blows to the head is different. It's more spontaneous. It's as if you're saying, 'How *dare* you?' "

That's exactly what must have been running through Robby's mind yesterday, I thought. But I couldn't let myself draw any conclusions—yet.

When I returned to my desk, I saw that Nash's assistant had dropped off the guest list while I was away, and I asked Jessie if she had time to review it with me.

"You bet," she said.

"I'm not taking you from anything?" I asked.

"Nothing that can't wait."

"One of the conference rooms is available. Why don't we do it back there?

I folded the guest list and stuffed it in my purse so people wouldn't wonder what secret document I was carrying. Nonetheless, curious pairs of eyes followed us as we walked one behind the other out of the pod. People were hyped up, desperate for info, and blowing your nose was enough to pique someone's curiosity today.

We slipped into the small conference room and sat side by side at the table.

"Here, let me take a look," Jessie said, reaching for the list before I had it halfway out of my bag. I liked Jessie, but there were two things I needed to keep in mind about her: One, I didn't know yet if I could totally trust her; and two, she was a reporter for *Buzz,* as eager for dirt as anyone else on the staff. I needed to be cautious about how much I shared.

Something must have flickered on my face because she yanked her hand away without taking the folded sheaf of paper.

"Sorry to be so grabby," she said. "I'm just worked up about this whole thing."

"Understood," I said. "I just have to be sure I keep all of this hush-hush. I don't want anyone getting even a hint of the information I have."

"Point taken."

"First tell me more about the party last night. Give me the lay of the land."

"Well, it was pretty mobbed by the time I left at around eight or so. The point was to celebrate Eva's August cover of *Track*—and the release of her new CD. Their space is a little different from ours over there, and they've got this big open area they use for parties. People schmoozed, mingled, nothing too exciting. The *Track* people tend to look down at us, but they're required to invite us since we're in the same company."

I unfolded the paper and flattened it with my hand. There was an orange Post-it note that read, "Nash, here's a list of everyone who checked in at the table in the reception area. This is the list we put together for the NYPD." It was signed "Max." He was the editor of *Track*.

I peeled off the Post-it and gazed down at the long line of names. There were over a hundred.

"I suppose you recognize plenty of these names, right?" I said to Jessie, passing the list to her.

"Yeah, it's a lot of the usual suspects," she said, letting her eyes fall down the page. "*Track* staff, record label people, music trade press. Eva, of course, and her husband. Her publicist, Kiki Bodden. Her hair and makeup people."

I took the list back from her and glanced down at it. "You, Hilary, Mona, Nash, and Ryan. Are these the only people from *Buzz* you saw?" I was wondering if someone from *Buzz* who wasn't invited had slipped in the back door, perhaps after a fateful confrontation with Mona.

"Uh-huh. That's it—at least while I was there."

"Question," I said. "I can see why Hilary would go to the party—to pick up gossip. But why would Ryan go? And Nash? And Robby mentioned to me the other day that he'd been invited. Why would that be?"

I hoped I'd said it casually enough so she wouldn't suspect I knew anything about Robby's whereabouts last night.

"Well, Nash likes to schmooze and scope out the chicks, so that would explain his presence. Ryan's always looking for leads, so he would have gone to check out the celebrities, mingle. Robby must have had his reasons. He probably got wind of some reality TV star who'd RSVP'd or maybe he just felt like he wanted some free drinks and finagled an invitation."

She turned back to the list and ran her long tan finger down the ladder of names.

"Oh, okay, this might explain Robby's invitation," she said. "Kimberly Chance was there. I didn't see her."

"*Kimberly Chance!*" I exclaimed. "The same day she got arrested?"

"Well, you know how those stars are. After they fuck up in some major way, they like to get their image rebuilding started immediately. She's on the same record label as Eva, so she probably ended up on the guest list that way. My guess is that Robby knew that she was going to be there, and since he covers reality TV, he asked for an invite. Mona was always hungry for stuff on Kimberly."

"Your white underbelly theory."

"Yeah. Actually, Kimberly would make an awfully nice suspect," Jessie said.

I'd just been thinking the exact same thing.

"Because of all the nasty items?" I asked.

"Yes, but there's more to it than that. One thing I didn't mention to you yesterday morning—I mean, it didn't seem relevant to the story you were doing on her arrest—is that the Fat Chance nickname ended up costing Kimberly a beauty contract."

"Now *that's* a reason to be pissed."

"Don't get me wrong. Kimberly was never going to be the face of Giorgio Armani or anything like that. It was for some small company, apparently, but it did mean more money and more time in the public eye. Once every DJ and comic and gossip columnist started using the Fat Chance name, too, the company withdrew the offer. At this point she'd be lucky to sign with Jenny Craig."

"And you heard she blamed Mona for the loss?"

"Yup. A few weeks ago, Kimberly approached Mona at an event and called her the devil. I'm sure this is on the police radar by now. Enough people were aware of it."

"You should say something to them, though, regardless."

She cocked her head. "If you think I should, okay," she said. "Speaking of suspects, what about *Robby*? I just heard that he came up here last night."

"Who told you that?" I asked.

"It's all over. Hey, you know what? I bet he used his party invite to get onto the floor."

I shrugged, again trying to seem nonchalant, ignorant of any info or opinions in this area.

"Do you think Robby did it?" she asked.

"I can't imagine that," I said, shaking my head. But Jessie was smart enough to realize that I'd already considered the possibility.

"Tell me about Hilary," I said, changing the subject. "I'm going to interview her at three and I'd like to get your take on her."

Jessie rested her head on her hand, squinting with her caramel-colored eyes as she thought.

"I'll be perfectly blunt. Hilary is a little bitch who'd run over her grandmother in a Hummer if she thought she'd learn some salacious tidbit about a star."

"So why don't you tell me how you *really* feel about her," I said, smiling.

"Look, I have to give her credit. She's gutsy as hell. Remember when Paris Hilton shot the homemade porn film? Well, Dennis—the guy who runs the L.A. office—told her to just *get* the story. So she flew to Hong Kong, where Paris was hiding out, but she couldn't get within a mile of her hotel room. Then she heard that Paris was coming back, so Hilary called the office and said she absolutely had to have a first-class ticket back to New York so she'd have a shot at Paris. It cost eight fucking thousand dollars, but they gave it to her anyway and she managed to trick Paris into talking to her on the plane."

"Wow," I said.

"Oh, and get this. When Julia Roberts was on bed rest in the hospital—right before she had her twins—Hilary flew to L.A. and apparently tried to pass herself off as a candy striper."

"So what makes her a bitch?"

"It's the way she does it. It's one thing to scoop the competition, but she'll try to undermine people on *our* staff. The worst thing is she talked Mona into letting 'Juice Bar' start running anonymous items. You know, 'Which TV actress is really a cocaine-snorting dominatrix?' sort of thing. That means we all had to start playing that game, and it lands you in some pretty disgusting territory. That's part of the reason I wanted out of that section."

"Can I at least count on her to cooperate with me?"

"Since Nash has given you the assignment, she'll probably behave. Unless she has some personal agenda we're not aware of. Her number one priority is always Hilary."

She snickered, then continued, "She's this real southern debutante type and she may act snooty toward you—but I'll tell you something that will keep you from letting it get to you."

"What's that?"

"I know a guy who hooked up with her, and he said she was this totally bossy bitch in the sack. She kept making comments to him like 'Buddy, it's going to take a little more effort than that.' The poor guy told me it was like going to bed with the navigational system in a car. And then about a month later he ran into someone who went to college with her and found out that her nickname there was the Cock Nazi."

"Gee, what a lovely image to carry around in one's mind," I said. "One last question. Mona's husband. What's the deal there, do you know?"

"I guess they got along. He's a playwright, but the kind no one's ever heard of. His plays are all spoofs of Shakespearean plays, apparently, and they're produced in those little forty-seat black box theaters around New York. He was totally dependent on Mona."

Worth investigating, of course. He could have easily slipped back to Mona's office.

"Thanks for all your help. I think I'm going to stroll over to *Track*. I'll catch up with you later."

I'd been introduced to the editor of *Track* by Nash one day in the lobby as our paths had intersected. He was a short, slightly geeky guy with glasses who was only thirty-two and looked eleven. I assumed he was the kind of guy who'd never had a date in high school but had owned four thousand CDs.

I made my way back to the door I'd discovered earlier, and after opening it, I slipped along the maze of corridors. It *was* a different setup over there—with the open area where the party must have been, but no bullpen section of desks. Finally, I had to ask someone where Max's office was. As I approached it, I spotted him standing outside at his assistant's desk, looking as if he were proofreading or checking out something over her shoulder. He was wearing jeans and a black T-shirt.

"Excuse me, Max, I'm Bailey Weggins," I said, interrupting. "Nash introduced us a couple of weeks ago."

"Uh . . . right," he said, slightly flustered by the ambush. "What's up?"

I explained that I was covering the story of Mona's death for *Buzz* and I wanted to review the party with him. He ushered me into his office.

"The police just left," he said. "It's been crazy here."

"At our place, too. Can you tell me about the party? I hear Mona wasn't here for very long."

"That's right. She shot in here halfway through—I'd say around seven-fifteen, maybe a little later—and probably didn't stay longer than a half hour." His voice was on the high side, and you could tell he made a conscious effort to speak in a lower range.

"Did you see anyone with her when she left?" I asked.

"I didn't see her leave. Like I explained to the cops, I was busy doing diva duty with Eva. But Travis, one of our columnists, says he saw her head toward the back door close to seven forty-five. She was alone at the time."

"Anything happen at the party that seemed significant?"

"Well, there was one incident, and I'm sure the cops are already checking this out. Eva's publicist, this woman named

Kiki Bodden, walked over to Mona when she was standing all by her lonesome and tore into her."

"Really?" I exclaimed. This was big, something Jessie apparently hadn't witnessed. I wondered if Kiki was the woman I'd seen trying to coax Brandon into staying last night. "Is Kiki fortyish with long curly blond hair?"

"Yup—and a real ball buster," he said. "Mona apparently went a little green around the gills, and then Kiki headed off for the bar. That was the thing about Mona. I've always heard that she could dish it out but she wasn't very good at taking it."

"So what was the spat about?"

"I don't have a clue. From what I've been able to determine, nobody was close enough to overhear the spat. But aren't you barking up the wrong tree? I was told someone on your staff got fired yesterday and threatened Mona. He sounds like a pretty logical suspect."

"Well, I have to look at every possibility. Kimberly Chance was at the party. Did you see much of her?"

"I spotted her once, early on, but that's it. I don't have much interest in someone who does covers of old Barry Manilow songs, so no, I never said more than hello to her. Didn't she get arrested yesterday?"

"Yeah, for slugging a cop."

He glanced at his watch without trying to disguise the fact.

"Just one more question," I said. "Is there anyone on your staff who might have been angry with Mona?"

"*My* staff?" he said, coiling back.

"I'm just wondering if someone who worked here once worked for *Buzz* and might be nursing a grudge."

"Not that I know of. Like I said, I think you need to look closer to home. Like that dude who was canned."

I thanked him for his help and made my way back along the maze of corridors and through the door to *Buzz*. The tussle between Kiki and Mona might be very significant, and I needed to find out what the subject matter was. As I passed the small conference room, I saw that Jessie was still there, flipping her cell phone closed.

"My sister called just as you were leaving," she said as explanation. "Do you have any siblings who drive you insane?"

Before I could reply, we heard voices in the hallway and looked in unison toward the door. A stream of five or six people were making their way down the corridor.

"What's up?" Jessie called out to one of the senior editors.

"They just sent an e-mail telling everyone to come out to the front," he said. "They're going to make an announcement."

"Omigod," Jessie said to me in a hushed voice. "Maybe they've made an arrest."

CHAPTER 6

Jessie and I followed the sullen-looking *Buzz* staffers out to the open area of offices up front. Nash was waiting at the very end of the pod, by the table where the daily meetings were held. It was as far away as possible, it seemed, from the spot where Mona had lain last night, her body writhing like a hose that someone had accidentally dropped to the ground as the water spurted out. Next to Nash stood Tom Dicker, dressed in a slim-fitting navy suit and yellow tie. His face, which seemed to be forever pinched in irritation, was a splotchy bronze color, as if he'd applied self-tanner with a blindfold on. From where I stood, his small eyes looked no bigger than dimes. He was rocking nervously, suggesting that he'd soon be making an announcement.

This ought to be good, I thought. Dicker was known in the industry as "the prince of malaprops."

The space wasn't ideal for such a big gathering. While some people moved up near the table, others hung back, snaked around the workstations in the pod.

"Come on up this way," Dicker demanded, gesturing impatiently to those who were hanging back on the periphery, unsure what to do. "I have a few things I need to say."

The people he was gesturing to shifted in position but barely moved, refusing to be herded. Dicker made no attempt to hide his displeasure. Someone once wrote in a profile of the man that he related to people on the creative side about as well as a puma would relate to a parakeet. Nash whispered something in his ear, and Dicker took two steps forward.

"Let me start by saying that I'm sorry I didn't have the chance to talk to you earlier," he announced, his voice strident. "I've been dealing with the police and all the media—though I know Nash has had the chance to speak to some of you folks.

"First things first. I am terribly sorry about Mona, as we all are. She was a terrific editor, and she made this magazine a great, great success, and I'd like for us to all join in a minute of silence for her."

People lowered their heads, but there were no tears, at least not any that I could see, and many pairs of eyes darted around the room, checking out everyone else's reactions. For all the remorse people were showing, you would have thought Dicker had asked us to bow our heads in memory of Betamax recorders or the Backstreet Boys.

"Okay," he said brusquely before a minute was even up, "the next piece of news is that the police are hard at work on the situation, but at this point in time there's nothing to announce. Of course, if any of you know anything that the police ought to know, you oughta tell them. I've also tightened up security, so there's no reason for anybody to feel nervous."

One of the fashion editors raised a hand, and Dicker glared. "This is *not* a damn press conference," he seemed to say with his eyes. He nodded begrudgingly in her direction.

"Will there be any kind of, like, memorial service for Mona?" she asked.

"It's gonna be private," Dicker said. "Down the road we'll

probably do something ourselves, but we have to coordinate that with the family.

"Okay, next on the list," he continued. "Nash will be taking over here for the time being. I know that telling you to return to normal is easier said than done, but we have a magazine to put out and we can't misunderestimate how important it is to stay focused on that right now. And I don't want to hear about anyone talking to the press. That's against the rules here—and anyone who does it will be suspect to termination."

Oh God. He was making George W. Bush seem like William Jennings Bryan. As he'd been speaking, I'd discreetly scanned the crowd. A few people were smirking. Most, however, looked anxious. I figured it had as much to do with the professional precariousness they now found themselves in as it did with the murder itself.

"Oh, and one more thing," Dicker said bluntly. "I know some of you were wondering about the barbecue at my place in East Hampton on Saturday. That's still on. I think it's important for us to follow normalcy as much as possible. The buses will be in front of this building at eight o'clock. Be on time."

A few other hands shot up around the room, but Dicker, ignoring them, turned to Nash and spoke something under his breath. Then he blasted toward the door to reception like a speedboat taking off from a dock.

"I know you all have a lot of questions," Nash said with uncharacteristic softness to his voice, "but unfortunately there's not much I can add. The police aren't releasing a great deal of information. Right now, let's put all our energy into turning out a great magazine. If I hear of anything significant that I can share, you'll all be the first to know."

Something told me that wouldn't be the case, but Nash nonetheless managed to radiate both credibility and concern. I glanced around the room. Whereas some people had practically scoffed as Dicker spoke, everyone seemed to be lapping up Nash's words.

"And speaking of sharing," he continued. "Some of you have asked if we'll be covering the crime in *Buzz*. The answer is absolutely yes. Mona was a celebrity in her own right, and we're in the business of covering celebrity news. Bailey Weggins will be overseeing our coverage of the crime, and Ryan is preparing a profile of Mona. Please cooperate fully with them. We'll be following this story for as long as necessary."

People disbanded slowly, reluctantly, as if they believed that by lingering they might pick up a few more scraps of information. I scanned the crowd one last time. Several staffers were gazing in my direction, perhaps intrigued by the news that I would be writing up Mona's murder. One of those eyeing me was Ryan, who had finally surfaced today. I was anxious to talk to him, but I saw him drift off down one of the corridors, and I decided to wait until he was free and we could do the interview with some degree of privacy.

Back at my desk, I stuck the guest list in an unmarked file folder and checked my voice mail. Nash's assistant had called earlier to say that he could meet with me around six but that he'd prefer to do it outside the office. She offered the name of a nearby bar. Then I dug out the number Mona had given me Tuesday morning for Kimberly. This time I reached voice mail at least: "I'm not here—leave a message." The twang was familiar, and I was pretty sure it must be Kimberly. I left my name and my affiliation and said that I wanted to speak to her about the party for Eva Anderson.

I was tempted to track down a number for Kiki and call her, too, but first I wanted to learn if Hilary knew anything about the altercation. The more information I had in my possession, the better my advantage in any conversation with Kiki.

Since the police were now gone from the premises—for the time being, at least—it was safe for me to begin interviewing people on staff. I placed an order over the phone for lunch, then grabbed my notebook and began to make my way around to people's desks and offices—in no particular order. I nabbed people when I found them and when they weren't on the phone, though I kept an organized master list of names so I'd be sure to miss no one.

Over the next few hours, I talked to about twenty-five people on staff—mostly from fashion, art, and production. During the first few interviews, I realized that people seemed defensive—perhaps they were feeling guilty for having harbored animosity toward Mona. Because of that, I proceeded gingerly with my questions, trying not to appear as if I were creating a suspect list in my mind. First I asked what time each person had cleared out last night and whether he or she had seen Mona at any point. From what I could tell, there had been almost a mass exodus around six. However, a designer in the art department nicknamed Spanky admitted that he hadn't split until seven-thirty, and when he had there was still one person left in the art department, a freelance designer named Harrison. That was most likely the guy Robby had said held the door open for him. Harrison wasn't scheduled to come back to *Buzz* until Friday. I jotted down his number from the art director.

After I'd learned each person's schedule, I probed deeper. Do you have any idea who could have done this? I asked conspiratorially. I tried to make it seem as if the name of the person I was interviewing had never crossed my mind. But, of course, everyone was a possible suspect, and I watched people's reactions carefully.

At three, I cut short one interview and headed toward Hilary's office. She was on the phone when I stepped into the doorway, a sly smile on her face that made it seem as if the person on the other end might be describing a booty binge with George Clooney. She signaled with a long manicured finger that she'd be just a sec.

I hadn't had any trouble relating to what Jessie had told me about Hilary. In the month and a half I'd known her professionally, I'd never seen Hilary with anything other than an expression of smug self-possession on her face. Women like her seemed incapable of being rattled by *anything,* whether it was a roomful of strangers or an insanely cute boy or even one of life's endless curveballs. I just wished *I* could be more like that. It seemed that no matter how much experience I gained in life, I walked around occasionally looking like someone who just realized that she'd locked the keys in her car.

Hilary's appearance was like that of no one else who worked at *Buzz.* She wore pastels rather than black, and her look was pure Junior League, the south of the Mason-Dixon line branch—big blue eyes, shoulder-length golden brown hair tousled just a bit, and lips so thick with gloss that they could snare a small dog. She was slightly plump by Manhattan standards, but if you plopped her on a country club lawn in Georgia, she'd be considered the toast of the town.

Today she was wearing a minty green skirt and a long-sleeved white shirt, unbuttoned low enough to reveal the lacy edge of her bra.

"So you're the one who found Mona," she declared as soon as she set down the phone. She motioned for me to take a seat in a black chrome chair in front of her desk.

"That's right," I replied, trying by my flat tone to display *nada* interest in revisiting it. "As Nash was saying, I'm going to be—"

"And she was still alive when you found her?"

"Unfortunately, I can't really discuss the details."

"Saving it all up for your story?" she asked coquettishly.

"Actually, the police have asked me to withhold the details."

She stared at me, her gleaming lips pursed as if she were mulling over whether or not to believe what I'd just said. "That's got to be tough, then," she announced finally.

"What?"

"Keeping details from *yourself.* I mean, if you're writing the story and you're the one who found her, you have to be a real good girl to hold back."

"True," I said, wondering if she'd ever had one good-girl instinct in her entire life. Despite the Junior League attire, she came across, just as Jessie had said, like the kind of chick who was always conniving, plotting, trying to make sure she scored exactly what she wanted. "It's a delicate balance. But anyway, the reason I'm here is that I'd like as much background on the party as possible. I need to retrace Mona's last steps for the story. You saw her there, right?"

"Um-hm. Though she wasn't there for very long."

"What about other people from here? Who did you see at the party?"

She arched her back in a stretch, her breasts straining against her shirt, and sighed as she recollected. I tried not to stare at her boobs, but it was tough because they were about three inches from my face.

"Ryan and Jessie were there. And Nash—though he came in latish. Mona's husband, Carl, was there, too, if that counts—I guess no one was staging a production of *King Lear Jet* last night or another one of his riveting plays. And from what I hear, your friend Robby was *supposed* to be there—to cover Kimberly—but I never saw him. *Apparently* he used the party as a way to get back in the building. He seems to be suspect *numero uno*. Would that upset you—to find out he did it?"

"It would upset me to find out that *anyone* I knew did it," I said. "I hear Mona had a fairly unpleasant confrontation with Eva Anderson's publicist. Did you happen to see it?"

"See it, yes. But I didn't hear it. I skedaddled over there to find out what was going on, but by the time I worked my way through the crowd, it was over. I tried to find Mona later—to see if she wanted me to write it up as an item—but she'd disappeared."

"But can—"

"I told the police, by the way. I thought they ought to know, even though Robby seems to be their personal favorite for the murder."

"But can you take a wild guess about what Kiki and Mona went toe-to-toe over? Do you think it had to do with something you guys had written about Eva?"

She shrugged her crisp white shoulders. "I really haven't a clue," she said. Her tone was cagey, and for all I knew she was lying—or *pretending* to lie in order to look as though she had a big bag of secrets.

"Of course, it could have been about another client alto-gether, right?" I asked.

"Kiki doesn't have any other clients that matter to *Buzz.*"

"Is she with one of those big celebrity PR companies—like PMK?"

"No, she runs her own small firm. Her specialty is hot new talent—and she guards them ruthlessly. Unfortunately when her clients become superstars, they tend to move on to the big-ger agencies. Eva is one of the few who've stayed."

"Tell me about Kimberly Chance, will you?" I said, switch-ing gears. "I hear she wasn't too fond of Mona."

Hilary chuckled wickedly. "Try *despised,*" she said. "She blames us for all her woes, including losing a beauty contract. She has a passable voice, I suppose, but about as much charisma as a carrot stick. Of course, if she included a few of those in her diet, it might make all the difference. Have you seen how much she's porked up? I can't believe someone even *considered* giving her a beauty contract."

"Is it true that Mona made up the nickname Fat Chance?"

"Now, Bailey, you know what our motto is, don't you? What happens in the 'Juice Bar' department *stays* in 'Juice Bar.' I mean, I could tell you, but then I'd have to kill you."

"Come on, Hilary. You heard what Nash said. I have to file a story."

"Yes, it *was* Mona," she admitted. "Who told you that, any-way—Jessie? I notice that you two have gotten pretty friendly lately."

God, what was *with* this chick? I wondered. I felt tempted to ask for permission to treat her as a hostile witness.

"Did Mona have something against Kimberly?" I said, ignoring her question.

"She liked her initially, but then she hated how she let herself go. But mostly it was just because Mona enjoyed making up nicknames. She's the one who came up with Lara Thin Boyle and Monica Lewdinsky."

"What was Kimberly up to last night at the party?"

"She was boozing it up at the bar for a while. I went over to her to try to get a quote about her arrest, and she told me that we were monsters and to stop hounding her. After that I lost sight of her."

"Do you think she might have wanted to have a few words with Mona last night?"

"My, my. I see where you're headed with this, Bailey. It's possible, I suppose."

"You said Mona disappeared after the confrontation with Kiki. Do you think that's when she came back to the office?"

"Maybe—because I never saw her after that. Mona's policy with parties was to come late and leave early. She likes—or should I say she *liked*—to go to those sorts of things because she wanted the press, but she was hopeless at party chat. That's the funny thing about her that most people never knew. She hated interacting with strangers. I was driving in a limo with her once and the air-conditioning was too high. You know what she did? She called the limo company on her cell phone and had the *dispatcher* ask the driver to turn it down."

"But you never saw Mona leave?"

"I believe I just said as much, didn't I?"

I thanked her for her help and asked if she could provide a number for Kiki.

She shifted toward her computer and tapped a few keys. Then the printer whirred. She held out a limp hand in anticipation, her cantaloupe-colored nails glistening almost as much as her lips. When a piece of paper was half through the printer, she snapped it out the rest of the way.

As I accepted the sheet from her, I mentioned that I might circle back and talk to her at some point during the next couple of days.

"Sure," she said perkily, as if I'd just requested her recipe for crab dip. "Anything I can do to help." If I were really lucky, I'd never have another reason to speak to the girl again in my lifetime.

On my way back to the pod, I went in search of Mona's assistant Amy. She was back from helping Carl and had been set up in the office of someone out on assignment. I found her staring listlessly at a piece of paper. She was so short that her shoulders were barely visible above the borrowed desk. Whereas Mona's main assistant, Betty, was a forty-something executive secretary, Amy was in her early twenties, the classic editorial assistant who'd graduated from someplace like Georgetown or Barnard and was hoping to rise through the ranks. From what I'd heard, Mona had required the person in this spot do everything from be backup secretary to write her speeches to go on quests to fulfill her quirky food cravings, and the job turned over every four to five months. Amy had arrived at *Buzz* shortly before I had. On more than a few occasions, I'd seen her looking ready to bawl.

I rapped on the door frame and her head shot up.

"Hi, Amy," I said. "I don't think you were at the meeting this morning, but I'm going to be covering Mona's death for *Buzz*. I'd like to ask you a few questions."

"Okay," she said morosely. "I guess I really don't have a choice, do I?"

"I don't want to make you feel uncomfortable," I said, stepping into the office. "I just need some basic information for my piece."

"I'm sorry," she said. "It's been such a zoo. I've had a million reporters calling wanting to get sordid details about Mona.

Do you know that one guy from the *New York Post* even asked me if it was true that Mona used to borrow clothes from designers and then say she couldn't give them back because she'd gotten her period. Isn't that disgusting?"

"It's not true?"

"Between the two of us, it *is* true, but that someone would actually ask me such a gross question on the phone just blows me away. Plus I've had to help Mona's husband with the funeral arrangements and all that."

"Carl must be awfully upset," I said, slipping into a seat by the desk.

"Yeah. And not only is he hearing from everybody who knew Mona, but he's got all the press calling him, too. After I finished talking to the police this morning, I spent three hours at Mona's apartment just answering the phone and helping him with arrangements. If Betty were here, she'd be doing it, but she's still on vacation in Spain."

She had a habit of repeatedly tucking her chin-length brown hair behind her ears as she spoke. Each time she did it, her hair would immediately fall forward again.

"Will Betty fly back for the funeral?"

"No. I mean, she got a special deal on the airfare and she'd have to pay way more to get an earlier flight."

It was enough to make you feel sorry for Mona.

"What I'd like to do," I told her, "is to retrace Mona's steps last night. Did you leave the office first or did Mona?"

"Well, I was *supposed* to leave by six because Tuesday's the early night, and I knew Mona'd be going to the *Track* party. But then she didn't leave till after seven for the party, and I was stuck here."

"Did her husband pick her up?" I asked, beginning to jot down notes as she spoke.

"No, he called from the reception area and she told him she'd meet him out there." Amy rolled her eyes and let her mouth sag open. "And then she kept him waiting out there for at least fifteen minutes."

"What was keeping her so busy?"

"She was waiting to hear from Mary Kay Mason. You know, that old consultant for us out in L.A.? They'd talked earlier in the day, and I think Mary Kay had some important tip or something for her. She was supposed to call back before the end of the day, but we hadn't heard from her. Even though I left messages on the woman's cell, her home office number, and her home number, Mona kept having me try them over and over. Mona was one of those people who think that if they press the elevator button a hundred times, it's gonna come faster. Mary Kay finally called at seven."

"How long did Mona speak to her?"

"That's the thing," she said, tucking her hair behind her ears again. "Mona was in her bathroom when Mary Kay called. It turned out Mary Kay was about to go on a live radio show, so she couldn't hold. She said that Mona should be at her desk at seven forty-five."

"And she'd call her then?"

She twisted her mouth, thinking. "That's what she meant, I'm sure. But what she said was just, 'Tell her to please be at her desk at seven forty-five.' Maybe she was a little annoyed that Mona kept trying to call her and then was in the bathroom when she finally called back."

This explained why Mona had returned to her office last night. But it was an odd way for Mary Kay to have phrased her instructions. I wondered if she could possibly have been arranging a meeting for Mona with someone. I'd have to speak with her to find out.

"So what happened after that?"

"I got up to leave right after that, and Mona walked out with me—I figured she was going to come back from the party to take the phone call. Or maybe she was going to blow off Mary Kay. That's the kind of thing Mona would do. She once had me spend the entire afternoon trying to track down this Gucci bag. They didn't have it at the Fifth Avenue store, so I had to go to the one on Madison and then she made me drive out to a mall in New Jersey, where I found it. And then in the end she didn't want it."

"But you saw Mona go into the party?"

"First, she *had* to see Mr. Dicker. As I was leaving, she went up the stairwell to his office—it's two floors above us."

It couldn't have been a very long visit. Max had seen Mona at the party at around seven-fifteen.

"Do you know what the meeting was about?"

"No. It must have been some impromptu thing, though, because it wasn't on her calendar. And she wasn't looking forward to it, I'll tell you that. She said, 'Wish me luck,' when she walked off. She hated the fact that he kept his nose in what she was doing. She thought he was a total asshole."

Boy, was that ever a case of the pot calling the kettle black.

"What about Carl?" I asked, suddenly remembering the husband cooling his heels in reception.

"Oh, Mona told me that when I went through reception I should tell Carl to go into the party without her and that she'd meet him in there later."

"He take it in stride?"

"I guess. He didn't look that happy, but he went into the party anyway."

"They have a pretty good marriage?" I asked casually, hoping not to look too obvious.

"Yeah, I guess. He called her twenty times a day. Sometimes she'd put him on hold forever."

"Just a couple more questions. Who was still at *Buzz* when you left?"

"Practically nobody. There were two people in the art department. One, that guy they call Spanky. He told me he wasn't staying much longer. There was another guy there—some freelancer. I don't know how long he stayed."

"Harrison?" I asked.

"I don't know."

"Look, you've been very helpful," I told her. "This is the last thing. I need a number for Mary Kay—and then I'll be out of your hair."

I knew Mary Kay Mason only by reputation. She was a former B actress who morphed into a gossip columnist and, most recently, into Mona's L.A. consultant. The theory I'd heard was that because Mary Kay was a free agent and reported directly to Mona, her presence helped prevent *Buzz*'s West Coast bureau chief from becoming too big for his britches. Sixty and single, Mary Kay was apparently a piece of work.

"Sure," Amy said, spinning through a giant Rolodex that clearly had belonged to Mona. "But you'll have to wait till later to reach her. She's on a flight to New York even as we speak. Mary Kay wouldn't miss this for the world."

"Thanks," I said, accepting the notepaper she handed me. "Let me know, too, will you, if there's anything I can help *you* with. This must be a very tough time for you."

"Yeah, well, what am I gonna do?" she said ruefully, shrugging. "I just thank God I wasn't still in the office when that crazy person showed up there last night."

"Do you have any idea who could have killed Mona?" I asked.

She sighed and allowed her body to droop. "Everybody's saying that Robby might have done it," she said. "I guess that makes sense. I mean, Mona was wretched to everybody, but yesterday she was soooo awful to him in particular."

"You overheard?"

"Of course. I sit right outside her office. She didn't just fire him. She told him *why* she was firing him. She must have used the word *clueless* about ten times."

"Did Robby threaten Mona in any way?"

"No, he just slunk out of her office like a kicked dog. But I heard he got all feisty in his office later. That was the way it always was. People would love to rant about Mona behind her back, but when they were face-to-face with her, they were meek as sheep."

Before I left, I mentioned to Amy that I'd been trying to get in touch with Carl and asked if she'd help arrange an interview for me. As I walked back to the pod, her phrase kept echoing through my mind—the one about how no one had the nerve to confront Mona to her face. Well, last night someone finally had.

I placed a call to Dicker's office once I was back at my desk. The idea of talking to him made me anxious, but it was going to be a necessity so I could confirm Amy's version of events and be sure of my timeline. With icy politeness, his assistant informed me that she would have to get back to me. Based on her voice, I was pretty sure she could have played the receptionist in one of those movies about a futuristic company that is secretly turning people into robots or harvesting their organs for experiments with aliens.

I tried the number the art director had given me for Harrison but reached only voice mail. I had better luck with Travis, the *Track* columnist. He was not in the office, but I was given a cell number for him and he confirmed that he'd seen Mona slip through the back door at seven forty-five or just before. He'd been in his office, rather than at the party, and had glanced up just as she'd strode by.

Next I called Kimberly's cell phone again—still voice mail—and then Kiki's office. Some guy answered the phone with the name of the agency and told me, truthfully or not, that Kiki was out of the office. I left a message saying I was from *Buzz* and that I wanted to interview her for my article. Something told me not to hold out a lot of hope of hearing from her.

If she didn't return my call, though, it was going to be tough to figure out what the tiff had been about. No one had apparently been close enough to overhear it. I wondered suddenly if the answer might lie in the pages of *Buzz*.

I tucked my notebook into my drawer and walked down to

the room where the back issues were stored. I gathered up the last nine months' worth and lugged them back to my desk.

There turned out to be an absolute ton of stuff on Eva. In fact, it was fair to say that not a single issue of *Buzz* appeared on the newsstand without at least two items on her. It didn't rival the page count of *The Lord of the Rings* trilogy, but it felt close. There were the endless red-carpet shots—Eva, with her long, glossy brown hair, in Versace or Dolce or Cavalli or in the occasional "vintage" dress, all with deep V necklines that showcased her broad shoulders and big, perfectly shaped boobs. There were also endless tips from her stylists and makeup people. She apparently couldn't go a day without wiping her face with a glycolic acid pad, and part of the reason for the incredible glow of her skin was that she used *two,* not one, shades of bronzer. Oh, so *that's* the secret, I thought.

And then there were the gossip items. Her looks fueled lots of speculation: Had she had her nose slimmed? Her forehead Botoxed? Most perplexing of all, had those awesome, mediagenic boobs been a gift from God or a plastic surgeon? But the most ink had been used for rumination on her love life. In the last six months alone, *Buzz* had run five cover stories about her marriage (number three) to not-nearly-as-successful-as-her actor Brandon Cott. A February cover described the star's yearning for a baby (EVA: "GOD, PLEASE GIVE ME A BABY"), with an insider claiming that the couple was exploring adoption. In May there were hints of marital discord (IS IT OVER?—EVA'S SECRET HEARTACHE), along with rumors of flings on both their parts.

I thought back to the discussion I'd witnessed between Brandon and Kiki. Clearly there was trouble brewing in Eva's marriage, because Brandon hadn't seemed to give a damn about the embarrassment his early departure would cause that night. I suddenly recalled something significant that Brandon had said to Kiki—he had wondered where she'd been during the evening. Had Kiki snuck back to Mona's office to follow up on their heated discussion at the party?

I returned to my reading. Unlike stars who swear that they loathe media attention, Eva apparently thrived on it. She never seemed to dodge the paparazzi and was always eager to provide a quote. I'd been at *Buzz* long enough to learn about the dreadful dangers of celeb exposure, but Eva demonstrated no concern that her public might one day experience Eva fatigue. I mean, the woman showed up at the premiere of animated Disney flicks when she wasn't even one of the voices.

I looked through the last four issues particularly carefully, focusing on "Juice Bar." There was absolutely nothing nasty on Eva, at least by "Juice Bar" standards. So what had made Kiki so ticked? Something that *Buzz* had *yet* to run?

"Jessie, have you got a minute?" I said, interrupting her train of thought. "Can you think of any reason Eva Anderson would be pissed at *Buzz*?"

She straightened her back, something Jessie did when she was curious or surprised, the way other people widened their eyes.

"Not off the top of my head," she said. "For the most part I think we've been pretty decent to her, considering that she's far more talented at launching fragrances than she is at either singing or acting."

"Why did Mona treat her with such kid gloves?"

She let out a deep breath. "Mona always loved Eva. I think part of what made Mona so good at her job is that she's—she *was*—star crazy. She filled the magazine with all the stuff she was dying to know—whether Brad cheated on Jennifer in their marriage, how much Kirstie Alley eats a day. She was especially obsessed with Eva, don't ask me why. Eva is half Mexican, half Danish, and Mona was some crazy mix, too, I think. Maybe that's what she related to. But I don't think she was such a big fan of Brandon's, at least lately."

"What do you mean?"

"She dissed him at one of the daily meetings recently. She seemed irritated with him, though I have no idea why."

"Is there any way for me to find out what triggered that?"

"Mary Kay might know. You know her, right—our consultant on the West Coast? Hilary might know, too, of course, but Mary Kay would be more likely to tell you."

"Got it," I said.

"Where are you going with all this? My curiosity is piqued."

"Just trying to get a sense of the dynamics at the party last night."

"You're not thinking Eva could have killed Mona, are you? She was surrounded by bodyguards the whole night."

"I'm not really trying to figure out who did it. I'm just trying to describe Tuesday night as well as I can."

"Come on, Bailey. Your reputation precedes you."

"They've got half of NYPD on this. They don't need me."

I returned the back issues to the storage room and glanced at my watch. The day was slipping away from me. I had hoped to reach Katya before the end of the afternoon, but I still hadn't received a number from Nash. I decided to stop by his assistant's desk to see if I could move the request along faster.

Like Mona's main assistant, Nash's assistant, Lee, was more the classic secretary type—a middle-aged woman who could reportedly type a hundred words a minute and wore her jet black hair in a cut just an inch longer than most men's. She was also apparently brilliant at securing Nash a table at any restaurant in New York. She was setting down the phone as I arrived, and she looked weary for the first time since I'd known her.

"Nash is at a meeting, Bailey. He'll meet you at your location."

"I know, I'm going to be heading out shortly. I was actually stopping by to see if he'd been able to locate the number for Katya, the cleaning lady who was injured last night."

"He didn't say anything to me about it."

"It's awfully important. I really need to interview her for my piece."

"Hmm. Let me call someone I know in building maintenance. He may be able to track it down for me through the cleaning company."

I returned to my desk so I could pack up before my meeting with Nash. Jessie was gone, and from the look of things on her desk, she may have split for the day. But Ryan was finally at his desk.

"Hey, Ryan," I called out to him. "Got a minute?"

"Just," he said, sounding as though he really didn't.

I started to ask him if he'd be willing to head down to the conference room with me so we'd have some privacy, but there was a fair amount of noise in the office that would provide cover; besides, he didn't seem in the mood for doing me any favors. I crossed the few feet to his workstation with my notebook in hand and perched on the countertop above his file cabinets. I'd never been so close to him, and for the first time I noticed that his pale blue eyes were rimmed with a darker blue. That effect, along with his sharp, beaked nose, gave his looks a hard, unfriendly edge. He shifted his lean body in discomfort, and I sensed he was feeling that I'd invaded his space. I eased into a standing position.

"You were at the party last night, I hear," I said. "Did you see anything worth noting?"

"Worth *noting*?" he asked with a trace of disdain. "You mean, did people get smashed? Or were Eva's nipples showing through her dress again? Or did anyone slip Kimberly Chance a hundred dollars thinking she was a hooker?"

"Worth noting in terms of Mona's murder," I said, keeping my voice neutral despite how obnoxious he was being. "Did you see the confrontation between Mona and Kiki Bodden?"

"Nope. I missed it."

"You saw Kimberly around, though?"

"At one point. She was pounding drinks back at the bar in a pair of low riders. You can recognize that butt crack from a mile away."

"Did you ever see her and Mona speak to each other?"

"Nope."

"Did you see Mona leave the party? She apparently came through the back door."

"Must have missed that, too."

What a jerk, I thought. It was as if he were trying *not* to help me. I was pretty certain my next question wouldn't elicit much of a response, either.

"Okay, on another note," I said, "I was wondering if you wanted to talk about our pieces—so that we could avoid overlap."

"Why would there be any overlap?" he asked suspiciously. "My story is about Mona's life and career. There's nothing in it about the murder."

"Well, we're just . . . Okay, never mind. I guess if there's any problem, Nash will take care of it in editing."

"Yeah," was all he said, and turned back to his desk dismissively. He'd never been particularly nice to me, but this was a new level of curtness.

I stepped back to my desk and started to pack up all my stuff to take home. I wasn't anywhere near ready to start a first draft of my article, but hopefully I'd make enough progress tomorrow to begin before the end of the day. I scooted my notebook and composition book into my tote bag and then reached for the folder with the invitation list. It wasn't there. I sifted through the scattered magazines, junk mail, and pieces of paper on my desk, but the folder was nowhere in sight.

Someone had taken it.

CHAPTER 7

Whant I really wanted to do at that moment was give myself a swift kick in the head. It had been, in the words of the late Mona Hodges, "f—king stupid" of me to leave the folder with the guest list on my desk. I should have known better, not only because I was a reporter, but also because I worked at *Buzz,* which employed people so snoopy they knew when you were ovulating. The worst part of the whole thing: I was going to have to ask Nash for another copy.

But what concerned me just as much was *why* someone would take it. Was it out of pure curiosity? Or competitiveness? Only Ryan and I were covering the story—if you excluded the party sidebar—so it wasn't as if I'd had something in my possession that other reporters on the staff coveted. And speaking of Ryan, he'd been so curt moments ago. Had he taken the list to see what I was up to?

Trying not to give away my discomfort, I glanced discreetly back in Ryan's direction. He was staring at his computer screen with a scowl on his face, as if he were a day trader who didn't like the way things were going down. After a second, I sensed him watching me out of the corner of his eye.

I resumed my preparations to clear out for the day, and as I did I stole a glance toward Nash's office. Lee was talking on the phone. If I was lucky, she had a copy of the party list and I could talk her out of it without Nash being the wiser. I walked over to her desk, my purse and tote bag slung over my shoulder.

"Oh, Bailey," she said, hanging up the phone. "I'm so glad you didn't leave yet. That was Nash. He's been delayed in Mr. Dicker's office and he's going to have to postpone your meeting."

"Did he say when he wants to reschedule?"

"He just said he'd try to do it tomorrow. He's got so much on his plate right now. He's supposed to not only run the magazine but deal with Mr. Dicker *and* the police."

I told her I understood completely, hoping that my agreeableness would make her more likely to take pity on me in my current jam. I explained the situation of the missing guest list with one teensy-weensy alteration: I said that I needed another copy because mine was sopping wet with spilled coffee.

She didn't bat an eye at my request. All she did was step into Nash's office and return with what I assumed was a copy she'd made earlier. As I waited for her to return from the copier, I glanced over toward the pod. Ryan was staring directly at me.

I didn't totally mind being blown off by Nash. I was both mentally and physically fried from the events of the past twenty-four hours. I thanked Lee for her help and headed out. Though the floor had been bustling only moments earlier, it was quieting down quickly. My guess was that people felt creepy being on the premises—perhaps they even feared for their own lives.

When I arrived home, my apartment felt like a car that had been baking all day in the parking lot of a shopping mall, and

I quickly flipped on the air conditioner to high. As I was drawing my blinds against the setting sun, I heard a knock on my door. I knew it had to be my seventy-year-old gay next-door neighbor, Landon; he must have heard me come in. A second later, I was staring at his face through the peephole.

"You poor dear," he said as I flung open the door. "I'm dying to hear everything. Are you in need of sustenance?"

"God, yes," I said. "And I feel too wrung out to even wash a lettuce leaf."

"Well, I'm about to throw a steak on the grill. Are you up for something thick and juicy?"

"Absolutely. Though it's been so long since I've seen anything fitting that description, I may not know how to handle it."

I requested that he give me thirty minutes so I could take a quick shower and change my clothes. As soon as I closed the door, a little part of me regretted having said yes to the invitation. My aching body craved the couch, plus I wanted to review all the notes I'd taken that day. But I also knew that it would be helpful to spend time with Landon, and not just because he was a fantastic cook with a fantastic wine cellar. Conversing with him for an hour or two would help clear my head and enable me to return to my work with a fresh eye.

I had struck up an acquaintance with Landon soon after my divorce. I had some great girlfriends who offered their shoulders for me to cry on back then, but I was embarrassed to hang with them after my husband blew town. They'd listened to me foolishly rave about the guy, given up their Labor Day weekends to come to my wedding on Cape Cod, and bought me Tiffany place settings—and then my marriage had ended up lasting about as long as a car fire. Of course, at the time I had no idea my husband was a compulsive gambler, the kind of guy who would bet on anything short of a cockfight. But I looked so stupid *not* knowing. I kept imagining my friends' comments to their other pals and significant others: "Couldn't Bailey *tell*?" "Weren't there any signs?" "Isn't she a *reporter* for god's sake?" Besides, so many of my friends were starting to have babies by that point, and the last thing I needed in my postmarital melancholy was to hear someone describe how many centimeters dilated she was by the time she arrived at the hospital or how raw her nipples were from breast-feeding. Landon asked me for a drink one night, and for a while it just became easier to have *him* as a buddy.

I peeled off my clothes, showered, and slipped on a pair of shorts and a cotton T-shirt. Before I left, I took out my notes from my interviews and left them on the pine dining table at the end of my living room. When I returned from dinner, they'd be ready and waiting for me.

"So tell me everything," Landon said as I sat on his terrace, the steak sizzling and popping behind us on his Weber grill. He was wearing shorts, too, a madras pair teamed with a navy polo shirt. He was the preppiest gay man I knew, and tonight, with his walnut-colored skin and close-cropped silver hair, he actually *looked* like Ralph Lauren. "I know that your boss was a bitch, but did she really deserve to die?"

"It looks as if it were done in the heat of the moment. Mona was probably having a contentious discussion with someone and things escalated. The person got angry or upset and smashed her in the head."

"Any ideas about who might have done it? Other than the entire population of Manhattan?"

"Oh, I'd venture to say she cut an even wider swath than that."

I told him then about Robby and how right now, at least, all signs were pointing in his direction.

"Do you think he did it?" Landon called over to me as he flipped the steak with a long pair of silver tongs.

"God, I hope not. I'm not what you'd call a super close friend of Robby's, but we're pals and he's always struck me as such a sweet guy. But that's so often the case with crimes like this. They're committed by people you'd never imagine capable of such things. With career criminals and psychopaths it's only a matter of time before they kill someone. They set the family cat on fire at age nine and then progress inexorably from there. But someone who commits this kind of crime might never have done a violent thing in his life. It just takes the right set of circumstances. You know, when I found out that my ex-husband had hocked my jewelry, I fantasized about shoving him off the terrace. Who knows—if we'd been standing on it at the time I learned the truth, I might have done just that."

"Of course, I would have come forward and said I saw him leap," Landon said. "Let me just get a platter for the meat."

Taking my glass of Cabernet with me, I stood up from the table and walked toward the railing of the terrace. The sunset just moments ago had been positively Turneresque—filmy yellows and oranges that had bled across the entire sky—and now that same sky was a swirl of dark blues and black. I let my eyes roam over the skyline and all the wooden-shingled water towers, and then glanced down to the courtyard fourteen stories below.

"Calculating how big of a splat your ex would have made if you'd pushed him?" Landon asked, emerging through the door with a white ceramic platter.

"Not at this particular moment. Did I ever tell you the story about my brother Cameron and the girls on the seesaw?"

"No, but it sounds perfectly poetic."

"After my father died, Cameron and I went to stay with my aunt in Boston for a week or so. I think my mother thought we could do with a change of scenery, but we felt totally abandoned there, considering that my little brother was back home with her. Well, my aunt lived in a fancy apartment building, about twenty stories high. Every day Cameron would look down below at this little playground in the park. I finally asked him what he was staring at, and he told me he was looking at two girls in red coats on the seesaw. He wondered why they never went inside. I looked down and I realized that there were no girls—what he was seeing was a red circle painted on each side of the seesaw."

"That's what my sister used to call an optical *confusion.*"

I smiled, considering the phrase. "I didn't have the heart to tell him that there were no girls in red coats," I continued. "I hope he didn't obsess about them for very long."

We ate our steak along with an arugula-and-Parmesan salad and touched on other topics of conversation: Landon's upcoming trip to Nantucket, a lobby he was designing for a small hotel in Florida, and our super's newest toupee, which made his head look as if it had been laid with strips of sod.

"Speaking of men, how's your love life?" Landon asked.

"Not so great. I'm having a hard time finding what I'm looking for."

"And that would be . . . ?"

"I was hoping to have a great summer fling. Back in May I kept picturing myself meeting some guy who was visiting Manhattan just for the summer—you know, some paleontologist who was, let's say, a guest lecturer at the Museum of Natural History. And we'd have this passionate romp for three months and then he'd go back to the University of London or wherever paleontologists go."

"So just a sexual thing?"

"Not exactly. I was hoping for some good conversation, too. I'm a girl. I've got that stupid chat gland, so sooner or later I'm always overwhelmed with the urge to converse."

"But what if you fell in love?"

"I wouldn't let myself. I told Jack that I didn't want to commit to anyone right now, and I meant it."

"And you don't think you might discover that you really *are* ready to commit—it was just that Jack was the wrong guy for you?"

"Ooh, don't say that. It hurts my heart to think that. Besides, it's all a moot point anyway. I haven't met anyone. There seems to be a paucity of decent guys around this summer."

"Maybe they're all at *foreign* universities as guest professors. What about at work?"

"No way. There are a few straight guys there, but I just can't picture myself with a man whose job involves keeping tabs on Jude Law's love life or what shoes Cameron Diaz was wearing at the Oscars. Do you think it could possibly be an age thing? You know, I was walking across Washington Square Park the other day and this guy wearing a *fanny pack* tried to pick me up. Please tell me that it was just a fluke and has nothing to do with the fact that I'm over thirty and this is what's in store for me."

Landon laughed. "Is a fanny pack that terrible?" he asked. "Maybe he was just the outdoorsy type, the kind of guy who likes to ride a bike up a mountain. Now if it were a *money belt,* then I would have worried."

He forced himself up to fetch coffee, and when he returned our conversation swung back to Mona's murder.

"If Robby didn't do it, then who did?" he asked.

"Well, it certainly doesn't seem as if anyone could have walked in off the street and committed the crime. There was too much security last night. So it was either somebody from *Buzz* who hung around or someone who snuck over from the party."

"Are you going to play Nancy Drew and try to figure it out?"

"Of course I want to know who did it," I admitted. "But my main priority right now is to report the story and follow whatever developments unfold over the next days."

He offered me another glass of wine, and because I was feeling so relaxed suddenly—and enjoying a wedge of key lime pie left over from his recent dinner party—I was momentarily tempted to accept. But I declined, knowing that I had work to do. I hugged Landon good night and let myself back into my apartment.

My notes lay spread on the table, beckoning me. I popped two Advil and before sitting down grabbed some pencils and an empty black-and-white composition book. Whenever I'm working on a piece, I always use a composition book to jot down questions to myself, along with pertinent quotes from people and incongruities that surface. There's something about the combination of a composition book and a newly sharpened number two pencil that always jump-starts my brain—and allows me to scrutinize the situation from fresh angles.

Before touching pencil to paper, I read through all the notes I'd taken during my interviews that day. I circled interesting details here and there, like Lyle Parker's comment about the murderer thinking, How *dare* you? and the revelations about Kimberly and Kiki. When I was all done, I cracked open the composition book and wrote out a timeline for Mona on the last night of her life.

7:00: Mona goes into her private bathroom. Misses phone call from Mary Kay.

7:05 (or so): Mona leaves office. Walks with Amy to stairwell. Says she's going to Dicker's office. Amy tells Carl to go into the party without Mona.

7:05: Robby calls me.

7:15 (or so): Mona arrives at party; is ambushed by Kiki.

7:30: Spanky leaves *Buzz.*

7:34 (or so): Mona leaves *Track* party for her office—Travis sees her go.

7:50: I leave for *Buzz.*

7:55: Robby arrives at *Buzz,* Harrison lets him in.

8:02: Robby says he leaves *Buzz.*

8:20: I arrive at *Buzz.*

8:28: I hear moaning, discover Katya and Mona.

My game plan tomorrow would be to flesh out the timeline by talking to as many more people as possible—including

Mary Kay and Tom Dicker, though I'd have to handle Dicker delicately. As of right now, it appeared that Mona had spent only a few moments in Dicker's office ("Was he not there?" I scribbled), come back downstairs, attended the party just long enough to be bitched out by Eva's publicist, and then returned to her office just in time to take the call. Had the call come through? Or had she already been attacked by the time the phone rang? The police would know this by now from examining the phone records. I wouldn't know until I spoke to Mary Kay. Once I had that piece of information, I'd have a better idea of the time of death.

One thing that still piqued my curiosity—the phrasing Mary Kay had used with Amy: "Tell her to please be at her desk at seven forty-five." It almost sounded as if Mary Kay had been arranging a call or meeting with *another* individual.

I also hoped that by tomorrow I'd have a number for Katya. Not that I expected to learn much more from her than I had already, but there was a slim chance that she had remembered something now that her head wasn't throbbing and her dizziness had abated.

I dropped my pencil and leaned back in the chair. For a few minutes, I let my mind play with the idea of Robby as the killer. By his own admission, he had arrived at *Buzz* when Mona was back in her office. Perhaps he saw the light and wandered down there to tell her off, knowing that now he had nothing to lose. And then she had hurled a few more insults at him. Indignant, he'd smashed her over the head with the paperweight.

But though that was the easiest scenario to imagine, there were certainly other possibilities that *didn't* involve Robby. After all, he wasn't the only one at *Buzz* who had hated Mona. Someone else could have been hanging around last night, someone Amy hadn't noticed—someone, for instance, with an office toward the back of the floor. And then there were the people at the party to consider. From what I'd learned so far,

Kimberly Chance despised Mona, and Eva Anderson's publicist had been pissed at her. Perhaps one of them had seen Mona leave the party and had slipped away quietly after her.

I wanted to talk to Robby, to find out how he was doing, but he had placed me in an awkward situation today and I thought that it might be best to keep my distance for the time being. I didn't want to get in any more hot water with the police.

Before long, I could feel fatigue overtaking me, and I used my reserves of energy to make a few more notations in my notebooks. When I finally did go to bed, I slept restlessly, rising periodically during the night to turn off my air conditioner because the noise drove me insane and then back on because it was hot as hell. I would have loved to leave my window open, but for security reasons I had never felt comfortable doing that. My bedroom, like the living room, faces out onto the terrace, which adjoins the roof on the south side—and there was access to the roof from a back stairwell.

Fortunately, I fell back to sleep each time within twenty minutes. I had suffered badly from insomnia during the two years after my divorce, and only recently had it gone into remission.

I didn't show up at *Buzz* until nearly eleven the next morning. When I'd dragged myself out of bed, I'd discovered a message on my cell phone from one of the cops I'd called and he agreed to meet me for coffee on the Upper East Side. The trip uptown and back ate up over two hours of my morning, and I came away with only one new piece of information: The cops liked Robby for the crime, but so far they had no real evidence linking him to it. His fingerprints had been found on the door frame of Mona's office, but of course he'd been in there earlier in the day when she'd fired him.

Buzz was bursting with activity when I arrived, and it seemed on the surface, at least, as if life were almost back to normal. I didn't think people had put Mona's death behind them, but they had next week's issue to produce, and they needed to accelerate to full speed. After all, America was waiting with bated breath for its celebrity news—the bitch-fests, the breakups, the butt-ugly clothes, and, of course, the mind-blowing body language revelations.

As I plopped down at my desk, I noticed a note from Lee with Katya's number. Great, I thought. She'd left it right out there, in a perfect spot for anyone to see, including my little desk snoop, whoever that might be.

I didn't waste time being annoyed. After quickly checking my voice mail, I called the number, which based on the area code was in either Brooklyn or Queens. A man answered, maybe in his thirties or forties, with an accent similar to Katya's. I gave my name and said I was calling from *Buzz*.

"Why is it that you need to speak to Katya?" he asked warily.

"I need to find out some details about Tuesday night—on behalf of the magazine and also the corporation."

Okay, granted, I was making it sound like this big official thing, but I was afraid if I didn't, he'd try to dodge me.

There was a long pause, and then he announced that he was Katya's brother, André.

"Katya is still not feeling good," he added.

"I'm so sorry to hear that," I said. "But it's very important that I speak to her. It won't take long, I promise. We just want to make sure she's okay. And we hope she can provide some information about the attack against Ms. Hodges."

God, I sounded like a cross between a bureaucrat and a funeral director, but he bit. He told me that she could see me that night at seven. The address he gave was on Brightwater Court, one block east, he said, of Brighton Beach Avenue.

"In Brighton Beach," he said. "You know, Little Odessa."

"Sure," I said, though the only portion of the borough I was really familiar with was Brooklyn Heights.

As soon as I hung up the phone, I turned around to ask

Leo for help. He lived in Brooklyn, and I figured he might be able to tell me the best way to reach Little Odessa.

"When did you need to be there by?" he asked.

"Seven."

"The traffic on the BQE at rush hour is a nightmare, so believe it or not the subway's probably your best bet for getting out there and back."

"Is it safe to roam around out there?"

"Well, it's not *Chelsea,* but you'll be okay—as long as you haven't done anything to offend the Russian Mob."

I had roughly six hours before I left for Brooklyn, and I was going to use the time to gather as much info as possible so that by the end of the day I could begin a rough draft of my piece. Before beginning my interviews with *Buzz* staffers, I left messages for Detective Tate ("Is there any news to report on the case?"), Mary Kay, Kiki, Harrison, and Kimberly. I called Dicker's office again and said that I would like five minutes of his time, though I was conscious of not wanting to hound him. And I also put in requisitions for photos with the photo department. I figured Nash would want the article to feature shots of people leaving the building after the party, the more famous partygoers—especially Eva—and shots of Mona's office.

Then I started on my colleagues. Perhaps because I had learned so little yesterday, I had this vague sense that the laws of probability would work in my favor today and I would stumble on a great nugget of info. But it didn't happen. I came away with absolutely nothing new. Everyone I talked to claimed that they left in the vicinity of six on Tuesday night, just as the others had. Therefore, no one had seen anything. And though it was clear people had mixed feelings about Mona, no one was willing to serve anyone up as a suspect.

In between interviews I checked my voice mail, but that proved just as fruitless. I didn't even score a meeting with Nash. In midafternoon, Lee apprised me that he was "crazy busy" and would have no time to meet; tomorrow looked more promising. As long as I had her on the phone, I asked her for the name of the hotel Mary Kay was ensconced in. My previous messages had been on her cell, but this time I left a message on her room phone.

When I returned to my desk, I saw that Ryan had materialized. He was glaring intently at his screen and pretended not to notice me. His pale skin seemed sallow today, as if he'd been so busy working on his profile of Mona that he hadn't bothered with any of the four food groups. Though it was hot as blazes today, he was wearing a T-shirt with a gray hoodie over it, the kind of getup you'd see on a fall day in the East Village. Clearly, if he was due to interview any luminaries in Mona's life, he wasn't dressing for it.

By the time I was supposed to leave for Brooklyn, I felt wiped. I'd spent the day interviewing over thirty people and had so little to show for it. And I still hadn't reached several key sources. I prayed that my interview with Katya would yield something of value.

I'd checked online for directions, and after leaving the building I hoofed over to Rockefeller Center, where I picked up the B train for Brighton Beach.

Though the subway trip may have been shorter than going by car, it still seemed interminable, and just when I thought I couldn't take one more second, the train rocketed out of the tunnel and up onto an elevated track. I should have realized part of the trip would be aboveground, but I hadn't been expecting it. We rattled along the track, past endless grim, grimy red-brick buildings. A few seconds later, we pulled into the stop I was looking for: Brighton Beach Avenue.

I climbed down a long, litter-strewn stairway that led to the street and checked out my surroundings. The scene in front of me was so foreign looking that I might as well have stepped out in Abu Dhabi or Bhutan. Nowhere else in America could you find a scene like the one I was gazing at: Brighton Beach Avenue, a four-lane road below the elevated train, was lined with endless storefronts—delis, hair salons, bookstores, dentists, funeral homes, palm readers—all with signs in Russian. People rushed past me, half of them barking words I couldn't understand into cell phones. The air was filled with the smell of cheese, cooked meat, and cigarettes, and from a deli directly in front of me came the refrains of a woman singing hauntingly in Russian.

I walked for a half block to try to get my bearings. I passed half a dozen street vendors, their tables crowded with everything from pastries to DVDs to ugly argyle sweaters, improbably for sale on a hot summer evening. A little old lady, shopping with a metal cart, ran her thumb over a shabby piece of fabric.

"Are you buying it or not, woman?" the female vendor scolded her in English.

I realized after a minute that people were checking me out, probably because I was so clearly a fish out of water. That wasn't a good thing. You never wanted to appear out of your element in New York. It made you vulnerable. I wondered, though, if I had much to worry about here. From what I'd read, the way you ended up in trouble in this part of town was when you tried to muscle in on someone's caviar business.

According to André, Katya's apartment building was on a street that ran parallel to Brighton Beach Avenue. I walked up to the first intersection and glanced to the right. At the very end of the street I could see only sky behind the buildings, and I realized that the Atlantic Ocean was on the other side and that Brightwater Court must be in that direction.

I took the right, onto a street of short red-brick apartment buildings that were the shade of old bloodstains. Parked cars lined both sides of the road, but there were very few people around, just a couple of men gesticulating wildly to each other as they stepped into a building and another old lady struggling along with a metal shopping cart. When I reached the end of the street, I saw from the sign that it was indeed Brightwater

Court. Not knowing which way to go from there, I took a left, only to discover a block down that it was the wrong way. I retraced my steps and headed back in the other direction. The sun was setting now, and the street was eerily quiet after the bustle of Brighton Beach Avenue. There was only the muted sound of traffic in the distance and what I thought must be the gentle pounding of the ocean. Though I couldn't see it, I knew the Atlantic was behind the buildings on the other side of the street. Everything seemed so alien that it was hard to believe I was only a few miles from Manhattan.

I found the address André had given me, directly across the street from the back entrance of a restaurant. Oceanfront dining, I guessed. The apartment building was seven stories high, brick like the others around it, with a dingy yellow stucco vestibule and lobby. When I swung open the glass door from the street to the vestibule, I was nearly knocked off my feet by the smell of something hot and cabbagey. I found the name Vitaliev on the buzzer and pressed. I waited and pressed again. Nothing. Oh God, please don't tell me I've come all this way for nothing. As I started to rummage through my bag for the phone number, a male voice shot through the intercom, asking who it was.

"It's Bailey Weggins," I said.

"Come to the fourth floor," he told me.

The door to the lobby released and I glanced once over my shoulder before letting it slam behind me. Across the street, near the back entrance to the restaurant, two men leaned against the wall by a sign for valet parking.

The elevator was one of those ancient numbers that groaned every few seconds and moved with the speed of a hippo on land. André answered the door of the apartment, beckoning me into a tiny foyer. He appeared to be in his thirties, about five ten, with shiny, short-cropped dark hair. He was wearing black flat-front pants and a black T-shirt that showed off muscular arms the yellowy white color of an old refrigerator. Around his neck was a chain with a thick gold cross.

"Good evening," he said. "Katya is this way. Please follow me." In person, his accent didn't seem as strong as hers.

He led me into a living room whose small size was exaggerated because it was crammed with oversize pieces of dark furniture, as if a small herd of water buffalo had wandered in to graze. There was a huge chocolate brown sofa, two matching armchairs, and a tall mahogany piece that I believe in my grandmother's day had been known as a highboy. The room reeked of stale cigarette smoke, and the cabbagey odor was conspicuous here, too—though I couldn't tell if that was because the vegetable in question had been boiled in their own kitchen or if the smell had simply bullied its way in from the hall when André opened the door for me.

Katya was on the sofa, huddled at the end of it with a moss green blanket over the lower half of her body. She looked so different from how I remembered her, partly, I supposed, because she was out of her blue uniform, and her blond hair was hanging lankly around her face rather than pinned up. She still looked pale and shaken, and I wondered if she was suffering side effects from the concussion.

"Thank you for seeing me, Katya," I said, stepping closer to her.

"Of course," she replied with a wan smile. I could barely hear her words over the drone of a window air conditioner. "Thank you for helping me."

"I just wish I could have done more."

"I did not realize when you called that you were the person who assisted my sister," André said behind me. "Then I am very, very grateful to you. Please, take a seat. May I provide you with a drink?"

"No, that's not necessary," I said, perching on the edge of one of the armchairs. "I just have a few questions."

"So you are investigating this crime for the owner of the

magazine?" André said. He'd taken a seat in the other armchair so that we both faced the couch.

"Well, sort of. I'm going to be writing this up for the magazine. We have to cover it, you know." I turned my body so that I was facing Katya directly, not wanting André to monopolize the conversation.

"How are you feeling, Katya?" I asked. "Did you need stitches?"

"No stitches," she said, her hand instinctively touching the injured spot of her head. "But I have pain still. And I am very dizzy all the time."

"I know we talked a little bit on Tuesday night. But could you go through what happened again, starting from the beginning?"

She sighed, the sound an odd combination of melancholy and vexation. She had obviously told the story one too many times by now.

"I want to remember, but it is very hard."

"You had gone to clean Ms. Hodges's office, right? Your cart was outside."

"I start in the outer office, where the two women sit. Then I hear a noise in the big office."

"The light was on, right?"

"Sorry?"

"Ms. Hodges's light was on."

"Yes, but I did not think she was in there. She never turned the light off—never." She sounded annoyed. Clearly she wasn't going to let Mona off the hook, even after death, for such an infraction.

"So what happened then? After you heard the noise?"

"I look in her office and I see her lying—on floor. I go inside and then I feel pain in back of my head. Someone was behind the door. I lean over, grabbing my head, and this person runs out the door."

"Did you see the person—even a glimpse?"

"No, I did not see him. And when I stand up, he was gone."

"You said 'him.' Do you think it was a man?"

"No, I cannot be sure."

She paused, her mouth slackening as if she were about to say something. I cocked my head expectantly.

"Are you remembering something?" I asked.

"There was one thing," she said softly. "A little thing." She pronounced little as "leetle."

"Yes?"

"I think I feel the sleeve of what the person was wearing. It was long sleeve."

"A long-sleeved shirt?"

"Yes."

"How tall are you?"

"I am five feet four. Why do you need to know?"

"Because of the angle at which you were hit. The person must have been taller than you."

"I don't know," she said, shaking her head in despair. "I don't know how tall this person is."

"My sister is still not feeling well," André interrupted. "We really should not trouble her longer."

"Just one more question. After you stood up, what happened then?"

"I want to get help for me—and Mrs. Hodges. I go out the door. But then I get so dizzy."

"Did you see anyone at that time?"

"No, no one," she said, shaking her head. She stopped and then stared at me. "Except you, of course."

"Well, like I said," I told her, oddly defensive, "I'm glad I was able to help you."

Her brother rose, a sign that the interview was over. I crossed the short distance to the couch and offered Katya my hand. She seemed momentarily startled but then accepted it limply.

Her brother walked me to the door, lighting a Marlboro on

the way. I suspected he'd been fighting the urge during my visit and had pegged me for one of those snooty New Yorkers who'd threaten to sue him if he smoked.

"Thank you for your time," I said. "Will Katya be going back to work soon?"

"Why?" he asked after shooting a stream of smoke from the side of his mouth. "You need to talk to her more?"

"I don't think so. I was just curious."

"Yes, she needs to have the work. Jobs aren't so easy to find here. But she is worried."

"About having to be on the floor where the attack occurred?"

"Yes. And maybe the person who did this being there. Thinking that she may know more than she does. She . . . Well, that is our problem, not yours."

"Tell me. Maybe it's something I can help you with."

He smiled in exaggerated politeness. "No, it is nothing," he said.

Though the interview had lasted only ten minutes tops, the sun had already set when I stepped outside. The streetlights cast only a dim light, and it seemed so much darker than it had when I'd entered the building.

Across the street, by the restaurant's valet parking sign, I could see the outline of someone—perhaps one of the same guys who'd been there earlier—and the red pinpoint of a cigarette near his hip. As I stood there, he flicked the butt into the street and slunk inside the restaurant.

I started for the corner. I didn't like how deserted it was, and I tried to walk confidently, like a woman who knew what she was doing. Just ahead of me, two people emerged from a car and crossed the street to the restaurant. As I reached the corner I heard a sound behind me, the scrape of a shoe on pavement. I spun around. The street looked empty. But I could sense there was someone behind me, somewhere.

CHAPTER 8

I picked up my speed, checking behind me again as I turned the corner. There was no one there. Maybe my imagination was running wild.

I was now on the same street I'd come down originally, and far up ahead I could see Brighton Beach Avenue. Cars streamed by in both directions, but it couldn't have been more desolate down where I was. Far off, on another street, I thought I heard a voice call out, but it was the only sound around. I cursed myself for not arranging a car service at least for the way back. I bet Cat Jones, the patron saint of town cars, never found herself, heart in mouth, hauling ass down a deserted New York street.

I was halfway up the block when I heard a sound behind me again. I whirled around just in time to see a dark slim figure, in what looked like a baseball cap, slip stealthily into the vestibule of an apartment building. Shit. He was following me.

Without giving myself time to think, I broke into a run. My heart was pounding in my ears, but above it I could hear footsteps behind me—running, too. I didn't dare turn around because I was afraid I'd lose momentum or maybe stumble. I also didn't dare try to dash into one of the apartment buildings. The doors would be locked, and even if I could convince anyone to buzz me in, the guy would catch up with me.

I tried to cry for help, but I was breathing so hard from running that it emerged from my mouth like the yelp of a Chihuahua. I had to think of something to do. When I reached a spot where two parked cars weren't touching each other's bumper, I shot out through them and began to run down the middle of the street. The footsteps were closer now, in the road, too. In seconds he would catch up with me. I felt crazy with panic.

Then I did something that shocked me, without it even forming first in my mind. I dropped to the ground and rolled under one of the parked cars in the street.

It was something I'd heard once from a personal-safety expert I'd interviewed for an article. It must have been leaning against some door frame in my brain for years, biding its time until I had a moment to use it. As soon as I was beneath the car, I wiggled closer to the curb. It was pitch black and I couldn't see anything, though I could sense the chassis of the car one inch from my nose. My panic began to swell even more. Was this the dumbest thing in the world to have done? The expert had told me that this strategy was built on the fact that dragging a woman out from under a car would take too much time and attract way too much attention. But what if the guy had a gun? He could shoot at me.

Clumsily, I shoved my hand into my purse and groped around in desperation for my cell phone. I touched my notebook, my BlackBerry, my blush, my keys, but not the damn phone. I froze for a second and just listened. I wasn't sure, but I thought I heard quiet footsteps making their way toward the car.

My hand began another frantic search, and this time it found the phone, hiding in a fold of the lining. Once it was in my palm, I slid my hand carefully up the length of my body. I flipped open the phone and tried to read the numbers. But I couldn't get it far enough away from my face. I shifted my body so that I was partially on my side and I could hold the phone at enough of a distance to see. As I was about to hit 911, the toes of two athletic sneakers appeared at the edge of the car, their whiteness illuminating them in the darkness. I felt so scared, I thought I might puke.

"Get away!" I shouted. My voice echoed oddly against the steel of the car. "I have a cell phone. I called the police."

The shoes shifted slightly, as if they were thinking. Then they disappeared completely. I felt an iota of relief trickle through me, and I exhaled for the first time in what seemed to be ages. I was deliberating what to do next when the shoes appeared again, this time even closer. The white leather toes were under the car, almost in my face.

I punched 911 into the phone. I only had to wait two rings before an operator picked up.

"Someone is chasing me," I said. "I'm under a car, between Brighton Beach Road and Brightwater Court," I said.

On what street? she wanted to know. Christ, I couldn't remember. Despite the fact that it was pitch black under the car, I closed my eyes and tried to make the name appear. Nothing. When I opened my eyes, I saw a hand reaching toward me in the darkness.

"Get away!" I screamed as I pressed my butt against the curb. "The police are coming."

The hand paused, then pulled away. And two seconds later the shoes were gone, too. I heard the *tsk tsk* sound of rubber soles breaking into a run.

"Miss, miss, are you still there?" asked the operator.

I told her I was, but I wasn't sure of the name of the street. I then said that it was just a block up from the train stop. She told me to stay on the line while she dispatched a patrol car. While I waited, listening to the hum of noise behind her, I heard footsteps again. Oh God, please, no. My eyes had adjusted to the darkness and I stared terrified out toward the edge of the car. But this time two sets of feet appeared—one in black leather, one in high heels.

"Are you all right?" someone called out. It was a man's voice, no accent.

"Who are you?" I asked.

"We were walking down the street," a woman's voice said. "We saw what happened."

I scooched my body over the pavement so that I was closer to the outer edge of the car. Then I strained my neck so that I was looking out and up. Two heads peered down at me. From the glow of the streetlight I could tell it was an ordinary-looking, young couple, probably headed off for dinner someplace. I shimmied the rest of the way out from under the car and stood up, helped by the man's extended hand. My body felt cramped, as if I'd been under the car for days.

"Thank you," I said, looking quickly up and down the street. There was no one in either direction, so I turned back to the couple. She wore a black dressy dress, and he, implausibly for July, was in a black leather jacket. "You said you saw what happened?"

"We came out of my mother's apartment building," the guy said, "and we heard you calling out from under the car, and he was reaching under there. Were you having a fight?"

"God, no," I exclaimed. "That was some stranger following me."

They exchanged worried glances.

"We thought it was a lovers' quarrel," the woman said. "That you were hiding from him under the car."

"No, I slid under there so he wouldn't catch me," I explained. "Did you see what he looked like?"

"Not really," the guy said, shaking his head slowly. "He had a baseball cap on and some sort of dark shirt or jacket. He was about my height, I'd say. Five ten or so."

"And he took off when you came out of the building?" I asked.

"He didn't see us at first," the guy said. "He was stooping, reaching his hand under the car. As soon as he spotted us, he took off like a bullet."

"Shouldn't we call the police?" the woman asked.

As soon as she said it, I glanced down at my hand. I was still squeezing my cell phone, though I could tell when I looked at it that I'd lost the connection. I hit 911 again and explained to the operator who I was and that someone had come to my aid. I said that I would walk over to the train stop and wait for the police there.

The couple told me that their car was parked on the street and offered me a ride. I thanked them but asked instead that they walk me to the corner. As far as I knew, my stalker might still be lurking around. I wondered suddenly if it was the guy I'd seen by the valet parking sign, the one who had slipped inside after I'd stepped out of Katya's apartment building. Had he come right back out again, having donned a baseball cap?

Brighton Beach Avenue was even busier than it had been earlier, and it seemed so absurd that I could have been in danger just a short distance away. When we reached the stairs to the subway, I thanked the couple again profusely and said I would be fine from here. They hurried off back to the side street, the girl almost on tiptoes trying to keep up with her boyfriend's long strides.

It was only a few minutes before a New York City police car pulled up, and I walked over to fill in the two cops who emerged from the car. They were both female and they seemed genuinely concerned, though at this point there was little they could do.

"Where'd you hear that tip about rolling under the car?" asked one, a few strands of blond hair peeking out from beneath her cap.

"A safety expert. Do you think it was a bad idea?"

"Well, seems a little chancy. But it worked. I mean, it bought you some time. So I guess that's all that matters."

"Mind telling us what you were doing in the neighborhood?" the other one asked.

"I'm a writer. I was interviewing someone for an article."

"Not on the Russian Mob, I hope," said the blonde. "That's the sort of thing that would get you chased."

"Nothing like that," I told her. "It's about a murder in midtown. The woman I was interviewing was injured during the assault."

Her eyebrows shot up. "Whoa," she said. "Sounds like it could be connected."

"I don't see how," I said. "I didn't tell anyone where I was going."

"Well, just watch your back," she said. "You never know."

The train ride back seemed even more interminable than the journey out. I checked out the passengers who boarded with me, but no one was tall and thin or even suspicious looking. I kept thinking about the cop's suspicion that the attack was linked to the murder. If the killer was someone from *Buzz,* it *was* possible, I supposed, that he could have figured out where I was going. Katya's number had been lying on my desk. I'd asked Leo for directions to Brooklyn. I'd strode out of the office purposefully, a woman on a mission, while the place was still packed. I'd gotten only a glimpse of the person in the baseball cap, but his shape didn't seem familiar.

I was famished by the time I let myself into my apartment. Landon had sent me home last night with a piece of leftover steak, and as soon as I'd changed out of my pants and T-shirt, which were streaked on the back with dirt, I sliced the steak and tossed it with a bunch of limp lettuce leaves and oil and vinegar.

It wasn't until after I'd wolfed down my dinner that I checked my voice mail. There were five or six calls, some from friends just checking in, one from a reporter who'd managed to score my home number, one from my mother saying she'd heard the news and wondered if I was okay ("*Buzz* is the magazine you work for these days, right?" she asked), and the last, thankfully, from Mary Kay. She said she would meet me at breakfast tomorrow. Eight o'clock sharp at the Mark Hotel. She sounded as imperious as a duchess asking for her bath to be drawn, but I was grateful I was finally going to connect with her.

There were also two hang-ups. I hated hang-ups, both on general principle and because of my experience with them in the past. When I had investigated the death of Cat's nanny over a year ago, the killer had called me, monitoring my whereabouts. I checked my caller ID. They were both from a cell phone, and offhand I didn't recognize the number.

I took a shower, not only to scour away the grime, but also to try to take the edge off. I felt wired both from the attack and from the hang-ups. As I soaped the backs of my legs, I noticed scrape marks that had been made by the pavement through my pants.

Though they didn't amount to much, I took my notes to bed with me, the ones I'd taken during my conversation with Katya. I had traveled all the way out there and been pursued by a stranger down a dark street—and had learned only that the assailant had worn long sleeves. I pictured Robby in his plaid button-down shirts, the ones he wore even in the dog days of summer. *Had* he done it? No, I just couldn't buy it.

Actually, there was one *other* detail I'd come away with from my visit with Katya and her brother: that Katya seemed not just upset about the incident in Mona's office, but worried, even fearful. As if she were expecting the other shoe to drop. This had been reinforced by André's expressed concern that the killer might believe Katya had seen more than she had. André had started to reveal something and stopped. Had Katya made a guess about who the killer was?

Then a thought nearly knocked me over. What if the man

who had followed me from the apartment *had* been the one outside the restaurant, and he'd been watching Katya's building? Was it the killer, fearful that Katya might be able to identify him? Had he realized that I'd gone to see her and then followed me when I'd emerged? Was that the secret Katya and André were hiding—that they sensed they were being watched? There was no way I could be certain that the man who'd followed me was the one in front of the restaurant or connected to the murder, rather than your run-of-the-mill New York mugger-rapist, but it was essential I tread carefully from now on, just in case.

Finally, barely able to keep my eyes open, I turned off the lamp on my nightstand. I felt relieved and safe now that I was back in my apartment, yet as I stretched out along one side of my queen-size bed and gazed at the empty half next to me, I was suddenly overwhelmed by loneliness—from seeing that large vacant patch of pale yellow sheet. Of course, I could have just *moved over,* but that was one of the odd things about life after a man. For weeks, even months, after his departure, you couldn't bring yourself to take title to the whole bed again and instead slept just on your side. I'm not sure why. Maybe it was just habit, this vague sense that if you sprawled out across the mattress, it would turn out he'd just gotten up to take a leak and when he came back he'd flop into bed on top of you, breaking your nose with his ass. Or maybe there was some psychological barrier—or sadness—to claiming what was once his, despite your perfect right to it.

I thought of Jack. I doubted he was suffering from Sad Bed Syndrome in his new Village apartment. He was hunky, successful, charming, and highly desirable. I bet it would be only a matter of months before I'd be strolling down Bleecker or Sullivan Street one Saturday afternoon and bump into him with some gorgeous, adoring thing by his side.

"Bailey," he'd say, "I'd like you to meet my fiancée, Lake."

God, the sheer thought of it made me want to sob, though I was the one who had kicked the man to the curb.

I was trying to push thoughts of Jack, his fiancée, and their sterling silver pattern out of my head when the phone rang. The sound of it, so loud in the silent room, slammed my heart against my chest like a baseball.

"Hello," I said, trying not to sound as if I were already in bed.

There was only silence. Oh Christ, I thought, not this again.

But then someone spoke my name. It was Robby.

"Hi," I said, using my free elbow to push up into a sitting position. "I've been thinking about you."

"Have you? I tried to call you a couple of times tonight."

"Those were your hang-ups?"

"Yeah, sorry," he said. "I didn't want to go into some long, involved message. I sort of thought *you* would have called *me* by now—I mean, to check on how things were going." The last sentence was delivered forlornly.

"Well, like I said, I've been thinking of you. But I was a little concerned by the fact that you left me out to dry with the police. They weren't too happy when they found out that I'd been looking for your letters on Tuesday night but hadn't informed them of that earlier."

"I'm sorry," he said regretfully. "I know you said that you'd been mum about that. But my lawyer told me to admit that I'd sent you to collect the letters. He thought it added legitimacy to my claim that I'd gone there that night for the letters and not to kill Mona."

"So you found a good lawyer?"

"Yeah, he seems decent enough. Of course, I'm going to go broke paying for him. And if they charge me . . . God, Bailey. I don't know what to do."

"Robby, you know there's a chance your phone may be tapped."

"I don't have anything to hide. Bailey, I swear I didn't do

it. You know me, I couldn't hurt a fly. I never even saw Mona that night. I just went in, took the letters, and left."

"The guy from the art department, the one who let you in—was his name Harrison?"

"I'm not sure. He has long blondish hair. He's only freelance."

"No one else was there?"

"No, I told you that the other night. You don't believe I'm innocent, do you," he added plaintively. "You think I killed Mona."

"I didn't say that. You just threw me a curveball, that's all, by not letting me know you were going to share that information about the letters with the police. Tell me, what does your lawyer say? What's his assessment of your situation?"

He let out a long, despondent sigh. "He says that right now, they don't seem to have any evidence. How could they? There *is* no evidence. But who knows what will happen if they don't figure out who the murderer is? They may charge me on circumstantial evidence, based on the fact that I had a motive and I was *there*. Because they don't have anyone else to blame."

He was sounding noticeably more agitated as he spoke.

"Robby, try to stay calm," I urged.

"You've got to help me, Bailey," he said. "I'm so worried I'm going to be railroaded. Is there anything you can do?"

I gathered my words carefully. There was a lot brewing, and some of it might be of value to his lawyer, but I had to be circumspect with Robby—with *anyone*—until I knew what I really had.

"I don't know if you heard this, but I'm writing up the story of Mona's death for *Buzz*," I told him. "I'm doing a lot of investigating on the case. If I find anything that might help clear you, I will turn it over to the police immediately and let you know, okay?"

"What have you learned so far? Do you have any ideas who could have done it?"

"No, I don't have anything yet. But like I said, I will definitely let you know if I learn anything significant. In the meantime, I want you to do two things. Listen to your gut about your lawyer. You said he seems decent enough, but if you have even the vaguest thought that he's not as smart as he should be or not giving you his full attention, you need to find someone else. People who get screwed by their lawyers often admit later that they had a bad feeling but didn't put it into words or felt reluctant to act on it. Also, you have to be straight with your lawyer. One of the biggest mistakes innocent defendants make—at least from what I've seen—is not being forthcoming enough. Don't leave anything out. Don't convince yourself he doesn't need to know certain things. Okay?"

"Yeah, thanks. That's good advice. I just feel so miserable. I think of that drink we had in that wine bar and how I wish I could have my old life back again."

"You will," I said with as much reassurance as I could muster, which wasn't much at all.

We said good night, and I was aching inside as I hung up the phone. It would be horrible to be in his shoes right now.

The next morning I was up by six-thirty. I still felt unsettled about the incident last night and the chance that it might be connected to Mona's death. A shower and a cup of coffee, enjoyed on my terrace in the balmy quiet of the morning, did a pretty good job of chasing away some of my anxiety. Plus, I kept reminding myself that no one knew exactly where I was going last night, so chances were it wasn't connected to Mona's murder.

By ten of eight, I was seated at the restaurant in the Mark Hotel on Madison and 77th Street. I wanted to get the lay of the land before the duchess arrived so that I'd remain in control of the meeting. From what I'd been able to surmise by both her tone and office chitchat, she was the wily type who could strip you butt naked—metaphorically—before you had a clue what was going on. The dining room of the hotel was dark and hushed, filled mostly with banker types in expensive, well-draped suits and middle-aged female tourists.

At exactly eight Mary Kay appeared in the doorway, dressed from head to toe in pink Chanel, probably a size twelve. I'd never met her but I'd seen photos. Her champagne-colored hair was in a large, tight French twist, which except for the color looked identical to a hornet's nest. "That's Mary Higgins Clark," a woman at the next table announced sotto voce to her three fellow diners. "I'm sure of it." The maître d' led Mary Kay to my table, where she waited regally for him to pull out the chair for her.

"So you're the famous Bailey Weggins," she said as she shifted in her seat for a comfy position. She was wearing more bling than I'd ever seen on a woman before noon.

"Famous?" I asked with a polite smile. "I don't know who would call me *that*."

"Excuse me if I sounded facetious," she said. "What I meant to say is that I've heard a great deal about you. Mona—God bless her soul—believed you were making a wonderful contribution to the magazine. And Nash clearly thinks you're the bee's knees."

"I didn't know you dealt much with Nash."

"Well, I do *now*, of course," she said. "He'll be named editor, don't you think?" Her eyes were a faded blue, as if the color had been leached out over the years, but they managed to hold mine tightly as she spoke.

"I'm probably the worst person to ask about that," I said. "I'm still too new to be privy to much inside information. And Dicker didn't give away anything about his intentions when he spoke to the staff."

She had slid pink reading glasses onto her powdered nose in order to study the menu, and she peered curiously over them in my direction. "I suppose he's all worked up—Dicker, I mean. He always seems so overheated, doesn't he? Maybe it's all because of that unfortunate name of his."

"I've never had much contact with him, actually," I said. "Mona did, of course, but not the rest of the staff."

"And how *is* the staff? Does anyone seem truly saddened by Mona's death? Or are they all crying crocodile tears?"

"Well, like I said, I'm new and no one is going to confide in me. But I sense that people are very upset and disturbed by what's happened. Whether anyone is actually grieving for her personally, I don't know."

She considered my comment without remarking on it and then turned her attention to the menu, which she perused briefly and tossed on the table. As she flicked her wrist, her thick gold and diamond bracelets clicked together.

"Do you know what you'd like?" she asked.

"Just some scrambled eggs."

"Wonderful," she said, signaling for the waiter. She motioned for me to give my order first and then offered her own: two poached eggs, moist but not runny; whole-wheat bread toasted twice and already buttered; a selection of jams, but only berry and no marmalades; cantaloupe, sliced thin; and coffee, very, very strong. My guess, just from looking at the waiter's expression, was that she had about a sixty percent chance of receiving everything she'd requested.

"Now tell me, what can I do for you?" Mary Kay asked as the waiter walked away still scribbling. "You seemed very anxious to talk."

"I don't know if you've heard yet or not, but I'm writing the story about Mona's death for *Buzz*. I need to interview people on staff, and Nash has asked everyone to cooperate with me."

"I hope you understand, dear, that I was on an airplane for a good part of yesterday. I returned your call as soon as I could."

"Um, of course . . . I know that," I said, sputtering. "I was just explaining the reason for my wanting to see you. I need to ask you some questions for the story."

"I thought someone else was doing the profile of Mona, a young man."

"You mean Ryan. Yes, he's doing the profile. I'm reporting on the actual crime—on Mona's murder."

"What could I possibly contribute? As you know, I was in Los Angeles at the time of her death."

The waiter arrived with a white ceramic pot and poured coffee for both of us. Mary Kay took a long sip of hers, leaving a pink lipstick mark that might require a blowtorch to be removed.

"I know," I said. "But you called Mona's office at around seven. And you asked that she be at her desk at seven forty-five. I need to know if you talked to her again that night."

Mary Kay just stared at me. Through the pale blue eyes, I could almost see her mind working.

"I assume Mona's assistant told you that," she said finally, her tone huffy. "Yes, I *did* call Mona's office at seven, but I did *not* call at seven forty-five."

"Then why did she need to be at her desk?"

"I had arranged for someone else to call her—a photographer."

That explained the confusing phrasing Amy had relayed to me.

"And do you know if he made contact with her?"

"I don't know, actually," she said vaguely. "I was just the middleman, as they say."

From Mary Kay's caginess it was clear that something was up, but I didn't have a clue what. Surely Mona talked to photographers all the time.

"Who was this guy?" I asked. "Is there any chance he came to see Mona in person that night?"

"Good heavens, no," she said. "The police would be all over him in that case. The photographer's in Los Angeles, and besides, I don't think he's ever even met Mona. He's just a paparazzo who had some exclusive information that he thought

Mona might be interested in. He wanted me to talk to her first so that she'd take his call."

"*Information?* I thought paparazzi sold *photos.*"

"Of course. But sometimes, in the course of their work, they turn up extremely valuable information."

She made them sound like guys doing stem cell research.

"And what information did this photographer have?" I inquired.

"I don't see how that could possibly be relevant to you," she said after fortifying herself with a sip of coffee. "Besides, I don't *know* what it was. Like I said before, I was just the middleman in the situation."

I fought the urge to yell, "Liar, liar, pants on fire." It wasn't that Mary Kay couldn't tell a fib convincingly, but it was hard to believe that a busybody like her had been out of the loop.

Our food arrived and conversation ground to a halt as the waiter set it before us, then lifted off the silver warming covers. Mary Kay rested her palms, slightly cocked, on the edge of the table and surveyed her plate as if she were inspecting a blue velvet-lined tray of raw diamonds.

"Well, I'd like his name and number," I said as soon as the food show was over. "I need to talk to him, to find out if he spoke to Mona or not. It will help establish exactly when she died."

Mary Kay winced and set down her knife and fork as if she had briefly lost her appetite. "Dear me, how gruesome," she said. "And what an unpleasant assignment for you."

"Oh please," I was tempted to say. This was a woman who'd had small parts in some of the worst movies ever made.

I used the rest of the breakfast to inquire about her career—how she got started, the highlights. Generally, pumping people about their life's story is a sure way to soften them up, but Mary Kay never came round. She seemed to dislike me, as if she considered me beneath her. Maybe it had something to do with my being a crime writer, that she'd finally found another professional that she, a gossip consultant, could look down on. Sensing that she was anxious to leave, I ordered the check the moment the waiter cleared our plates. As I was paying the bill, I reminded her of my need for the photographer's name and number. From her handbag she withdrew a black address book as thick as a club sandwich, flipped quickly to the correct page, and then jotted down the name and number for me.

"I'm not thrilled to be doing this," she said, sliding it across the table to me, "but since Nash has asked that people cooperate, I will. And please be sure to tell him that I gave you all the help I could."

I glanced down at the piece of paper. The name on it was Jed Crandall and then a phone number that I assumed was for a cell phone.

"Oh, just one last question," I said. "Why did Mona take a sudden dislike to Brandon Cott?"

"That nasty little man? Sooner or later the whole world will take a dislike to him."

"But did he do something to her?"

"It was at a premiere party that *Buzz* sponsored in L.A. It wasn't particularly rude by Hollywood rudeness standards, but Mona found it humiliating. There was a photo op with several people, including Mona and Brandon. He kept ramming her with his hip, forcing her out of the picture."

"Was he angry with her for some reason?"

"No, that's just how men with little—little *minds* amuse themselves."

As soon as I'd said good-bye to Mary Kay in the lobby and she'd headed for the elevator, I tried the number for Crandall. It was voice mail. I left a message saying simply that I was from *Buzz* and I wanted to talk to him.

In the taxi to the office, I had a chance to cogitate on why Mary Kay had seemed so evasive. Perhaps she *did* know what information Jed Crandall had in his possession but was afraid that if she passed it to me, I'd go blabbing it somewhere and there'd be no more exclusive. Or maybe she really didn't know. After forty years as a gossipmonger, she might just exude caginess.

I also used the taxi time to check my voice mail. More calls from reporters, one call from a contact in NYPD saying he was on vacation and had nothing to share. No word on my meeting with Nash, no message yet from Mona's husband, and no message either from Tom Dicker. I needed to talk to him to help establish my timeline.

As I strolled through the black marble lobby of the building, an idea occurred to me—that I might have better luck with Dicker's assistant if I approached her face-to-face. Rather than take the elevator to sixteen, I pushed the button for eighteen, where the corporate offices were located and where Mona had gone before the party. Actually, I realized, maybe Dicker hadn't even been there Tuesday night, which would explain why Mona's visit to the floor had been so brief. Regardless, I needed to find out the details.

I'd never been on the corporate floor, and it took me by surprise. I hadn't expected it to look like the *Buzz/Track* floor, but I'd thought it would feel like a media empire. It didn't at all. Opening the glass doors to the reception area, I saw that everything was colored beige—from the walls, to the couches, to the wall-to-wall carpet under my feet—and it was so quiet that you could almost *hear* the hush. I might as well have been in the corporate headquarters for some company that made aluminum cans.

There was a tall blonde at the reception desk, someone so good-looking that it made you suspect she had passed a screen test for the job. I headed toward her. As I did, I noticed that there was a guy in the reception area, his back to me. He was talking on his cell phone while attempting to rifle through a briefcase that was balanced on his bended knee.

"Sure," he said. "Just say the word." He flipped the phone

closed, stuck it in his jacket pocket, and hoisted the briefcase closer to his chest. Hearing my footsteps, he glanced behind him and our eyes met. Out of nowhere I felt a wallop, as if someone had just shoved me hard, and the weirdest thought flashed through my brain.

One day I'm going to marry that guy.

CHAPTER 9

"Can I help you? . . . Miss, can I *help* you?"

The chick at the desk was speaking to me—and in this especially annoying tone, the kind salespeople in stores use when you're pawing merchandise that they're certain you can't afford. I forced myself to turn around and face her.

"My name is Bailey Weggins," I said. "I'd like to speak to Mr. Dicker's assistant. I work at *Buzz* and it's a matter of great importance."

That seemed to grab her attention. Everyone on this floor was surely chattering about the murder at *Buzz* and eager for any crumbs of info they could find.

"Let me try her. What was the last name again?"

"Weggins," I said. Would it seem odd, I wondered, if I added my phone number? Cell, work, and home. So that the guy behind me, the one who'd rendered me instantly and insanely lovestruck, could sear them on his brain if he so chose. I turned my head ever so slightly back in his direction to see what he was up to. He was still looking at me. He was in his thirties, I guessed, maybe just a little older than me—or maybe not. It was so hard to tell these days. He had dark, dark eyes, brown hair on the longish side, at least just long enough to tuck behind his ears, and he was tanned. Not been-caught-in-a-rust-storm tanned like Dicker, but the kind you ended up with when you'd spent the first half of your summer windsurfing every weekend or maybe just lying in the warm sand in a faded pair of board shorts.

Christ, I'd seen him for ten seconds and I already had him half-naked. I started to turn back toward the receptionist so I wouldn't appear like a total goofball, and as I did the mystery guy offered me a cocky smile, the kind where only one side of the mouth pulls up. I tried to smile back, but nothing happened. My face seemed permanently frozen into the gawking expression someone might wear after witnessing an exploding manhole cover.

"She's checking," the receptionist announced. My attention had been so diverted by the guy behind me that I hadn't even heard her make the call.

"Thank you," I said. Fearful of looking even more like an imbecile if I just stood there agog in the middle of the reception area, I walked over to the couch on the other side and perched on the edge of it. I stole a glance across the room. The guy was now shifting through his briefcase again, a nice-looking soft leather one with a shoulder strap. I wondered who he was waiting to see. He certainly wasn't the corporate type; he was wearing jeans below his black sports jacket.

Any minute now someone was going to come out and fetch him, and then that would be it. I racked my mind for some sort of strategy that would enable me to make a connection with him. The old standby "Aren't you so-and-so?" would be pathetically obvious. So would "May I borrow your cell phone?" And though it wasn't beneath me to saunter over to a guy like him and boldly ask for his digits, I certainly wasn't going to do it in front of the snooty blond receptionist.

As I was trying desperately to formulate a plan, I heard a

snap and glanced up to see that he had just secured the flap of his briefcase. Then, to my horror, he strode across the floor and opened one of the glass doors to the elevator bank. He offered me another sly smile and passed through the doorway.

Whatever appointment he'd had here today was *over,* not about to begin. God, I might never set eyes on him again. Should I run after him? Throw myself on the floor and snare the leg of his jeans with my teeth? Too late. I heard the muted *ding* announcing the arrival of the elevator and glanced up just in time to see the back of his jacket as he boarded. I felt as if I were being sucked into quicksand.

No need to panic, I told myself. I took four strides toward the reception desk.

"Can I ask you a question?" I said to her, throwing my pride to the wind. "I swear that guy who was just here roomed with my brother at college. Does his last name start with a D?"

She glanced down at a paper on her desk. "No, R," she said, too dense to be suspicious. "Regan."

"And the first name is . . . ?"

"He didn't say."

"I think that's him, though. I think the name was Regan. Who was he here to see?"

"Why? That's not really information I should be giving out."

I was tempted to tell her that there was no damn law against it, that it wasn't as if she were a psychiatrist and I was demanding to see her patient records.

"Oh, I was just wondering," I said sweetly. "My brother's been having a tough time lately, and I'd know he'd love to hear from him again. They kind of lost touch."

"Well, if you must know," she said, almost in a whisper, "he was here to see Mr. Dicker."

As if the sound of his name were a cue, the phone rang right then and I could tell by the way the receptionist shot a glance at me while she was talking that it was Dicker's office on the other end.

She set down the phone and pursed her lips. "That was Mr. Dicker's assistant. She said she's sorry, but Mr. Dicker is extremely busy and he doesn't have any time available at the moment. She'll see what she can do about squeezing you in later."

"Thank you," I said, annoyed by the brush-off. But I didn't want to take it out on her. After all, she had at least told me the last name of the man who had left me in such a delicious tizzy.

I returned to the couch, picked up my purse and tote bag where I'd left them, and prepared to head down to sixteen. But lo and behold, just as I was about to swing open the glass door to the elevator bank, Tom Dicker charged out of the open door to the right of the reception desk. He was headed toward the elevator bank and moving at the speed of a cardiologist answering a code blue.

This was my opportunity to make a move. I opened the door and held it out, allowing Dicker to grab it. He offered a curt nod as it closed behind us.

"Mr. Dicker, I'm Bailey Weggins, a reporter at *Buzz*," I said once we were standing by the bank of elevators.

"How ya doin'?" he said, face pinched as he stabbed at the Down button with his finger. He was like a massive ball of energy tightly packed in a suit, almost like a bag of freeze-dried coffee. You couldn't help but have the feeling that if you tore a hole in his jacket sleeve, all that energy would burst out from the inside.

"Pretty good," I said. "Actually, I've been trying to get in touch with you. I cover celebrity crime for the magazine, and Nash put me in charge of writing about Mona's death. I was hoping to be able to speak to you."

"I already spent an hour with that other guy—Ryan," he said with another jab at the elevator button. "Isn't that enough? I'm very busy, as you might imagine. I'm trying to keep a lot of balls on the field right now."

"Right. Well, Ryan's, doing the profile," I told him, "but we also have to report on the murder. That's what I'm doing. I'm trying to establish a timeline for Mona's last hour. I hear she came up to see you shortly before she was attacked."

He froze, all the jitteriness vaporized in a split second. It was disconcerting to see him totally still, staring at me with those too small blue eyes.

"I saw her that night, sure," he stated. "What's the big deal, anyway?"

"It's not—I mean, it's not a big deal," I said falteringly. "Like I said, I'm just attempting to create a timeline, a sense of where she was and for how long. It seems like she was in your office for only a few minutes." I could tell by his expression that I was irritating him, and that was not a good thing. I smiled weakly, a feeble stab at keeping things light.

"That's right," he said. "She just wanted to tell me what cover she'd gone with. I like to know these things up front, in case the subject calls my office threatening to sue me for a hundred million bucks. But I'd been out of town the day before when it shipped."

"'Freaky Beauty Rituals of the Stars.'"

"Huh?"

"The cover story this week. 'Freaky Beauty Rituals of the Stars.'"

"Yeah, that's right. Don't ask me why, but people go nuts for that kind of shit. And it's a winner, too. I got the retail scan numbers on it."

"Just one most question, then. According to her assistant, Mona came up here just after seven. How long did she stay?"

"Just long enough to tell me what the cover was. Five or ten minutes, tops."

The elevator announced its arrival with a *ding,* and Dicker was so anxious to board that he had to force himself to allow me to go first. I figured it wouldn't be too smart to ask him the full name of the hottie who'd been in to see him. Instead I simply thanked him for his assistance.

"What did you say your name was?" he asked as the elevator door opened on sixteen, his face now looking even more consternated than usual.

"Bailey Weggins," I answered. I felt as if I were giving it to a teacher who had just caught me writing graffiti on the walls of the school.

The reception area on sixteen was quiet today—just the receptionist on duty, no cops hanging about—but inside, things were really jumping. Before going to my desk, I headed straight for the art department. This was the day Harrison was due in, and I could see a mop of long blond hair sitting at the desk he supposedly occupied. As I approached, I saw that he was working on a layout for what appeared to be a page of "Fashion Follies."

I introduced myself, explaining that I was writing the article on Mona. I asked if I could talk to him privately.

"Yeah, I guess so," he said, lifting his shoulders awkwardly. I led him down to the small conference room I'd been in before.

"Thanks," I said as he looked at me expectantly. "I've been trying to reach you."

"Oh yeah? Well, I'm keeping my head down. This whole thing has been a real bummer, if you know what I mean."

"I can understand. I hear you worked late the night of the murder, and I was hoping to ask you a few questions."

He sighed, lifting his shoulders nervously again. They nearly reached his ears this time.

"Man, I hate havin' to talk about this stuff," he said. "I already spent an hour with the police."

"I promise not to take too long. Nash has requested that people share as much information as possible with me." I hoped that invoking the name of the boss would help.

"My head is just messed up about this thing. I let that dude in here that night. And now it looks like he might have killed her."

"You mean Robby Hart?"

"Yeah. But I had no idea he'd been fired. I'm just freelance, so I'm the last to hear anything."

"I can relate to that since I'm freelance, too," I said with a smile, trying to find some common ground. "What time did you leave—do you remember?"

"Like I told the police, it was just before eight. I had to meet somebody downtown at eight-thirty. You know how when it takes you thirty minutes to get someplace and you leave two minutes after you're supposed to, you're gonna be ten minutes late, but if you leave just two minutes *before,* then you're on time?"

"Uh, yeah, I know what you mean," I said, trying not to look skeptical. "So as you were leaving, Robby was coming in?"

"Yeah, I was just going out the door. He yelled for me to hold it and so I did. I mean, the guy's a senior editor, so I didn't think twice."

"How did he seem to you?"

"Sweaty."

"Sweaty?"

"He just looked sweaty, like he'd been hurrying around or on the subway. His head was kind of shiny."

"Did he seem upset?"

He shook his head slowly. "Not upset, but tense. I thought he'd probably forgotten something."

"So who was around when you left?"

"Nobody. By six-thirty there were only a few people here anyway, and then gradually they all split. To be honest, I was working on some personal stuff 'cause my computer at home crashed. When I left, there was nobody here—except Mona, of course."

"You saw Mona?"

"Yup. She'd been here earlier but then left for a while. I guess she went over to that party and then came back. She came right down the corridor." He pointed to the one that led to the back offices and eventually to the door to *Track*.

"Was anyone with her, or did anyone come in after her?"

"Nope, she was all by her lonesome."

"Was there anything at all that struck you as odd?"

"Well, she had that new haircut, the one that made her look like she was wearing a wig."

"I don't mean *that* way. I'm just wondering if you noticed anything out of the ordinary."

"Nope. I didn't even make eye contact with her," he confided. "A guy who worked here before told me never to do that 'cause then she would notice you. But she talked to that guy Ryan, the one who sits over by you."

"*Ryan?*" I said, stunned. "But you said only Mona was here when you left."

"Yeah, that's right. Ryan left *earlier,* about ten minutes before me."

I flashed back on my conversation with him. No, he hadn't once mentioned he was here when Mona returned.

"Do you know what they talked about?"

"No, I couldn't hear. She only spoke to him for a second and then he took off."

"And you never saw anyone go into Mona's office?"

"No, but she was on the phone when I left, that much I know."

"You could hear her?"

"No, I could see her through the glass as I was standing up to go. She was sitting at her desk, talking on the phone."

I thanked him for his help, and he beat it. Based on what he'd told me, it seemed likely that Mona had managed to have her conversation with the paparazzo before she died, though I would have to confirm that when I finally reached the guy. Once I knew how long the call had lasted, I would be able to almost pinpoint the time she'd been attacked. Harrison's revelation about Ryan was odd. Amy hadn't told me. Neither had

Spanky, but then I'd been pressing him about the identity of the last person in art that night. Why hadn't *Ryan* mentioned to me that he had seen Mona before he left for the party? Perhaps because Ryan wasn't willing to help me with any aspect of my story. Or was something else going on? According to Harrison, Ryan was one of the last people to have spoken to Mona before she was attacked. Had he been angry at Mona for some reason?

As I walked along the aisle toward my desk, I craned my neck to see if I could spot Nash in his office. I wanted to forewarn him about my encounter with Dicker in case the man said something to him. But he was on the phone, his back to the glass wall. As I passed by, Lee signaled for me to come over.

"Nash would like to reschedule your meeting—for tonight," she said. "Same place, at six-thirty. He'll be coming from the outside."

"Perfect," I said. I needed the meeting not only to learn what Nash knew about the party, but also to discuss my piece. But I felt uneasy now. What if Nash was on the phone with Dicker right this minute and was being told, "Bring me the head of Bailey Weggins on a silver platter"?

Jessie was pounding away at her computer as I reached the pod, and she spun around in her chair to face me. She looked really cute today, dressed in black pants and a pale pink kerchief top.

"So there you are," she said. "I thought we were going to have to send out the highway patrol. What have you been up to?"

"Just scurrying around trying to do this story."

"Any developments?"

"I've managed to fill in a few holes. But it's slow going."

It would have been nice to share more with Jessie, to confide in someone close to the action, but I had to remain circumspect, keep my own counsel.

I checked my e-mail and voice mail. I was still receiving

calls from various reporters and TV producers. To my relief, there was also a message from Mona's husband, Carl. In somber tones, he announced that he could see me on Sunday at three and gave me the address for his and Mona's apartment. That was one person off my list, but I still had to reach Kiki and Kimberly.

"Sorry to interrupt," Jessie said as she caught me staring into space, wondering how I was going to connect with people who didn't want to connect with me. "You're going tomorrow, right?" she asked.

"God, is that tomorrow?" I said. I knew she was referring to the barbecue at Dicker's. Ordinarily, it wouldn't be something I was dying to do—in fact, as far as I knew I might be banned from it after my encounter with Dicker today—but at this point it would be an important opportunity for me. I would be able to check out my colleagues with their defenses down, perhaps even pick up information.

"I've got a car," I told her. "Why don't you meet me in my lobby at eight tomorrow?"

"I thought you'd never ask. I can't bear the thought of being on the same bus with the Cock Nazi."

"Let me ask *you* for a favor now. I'm having a hard time getting either Kimberly Chance or Kiki Bodden to return my calls. I've got Kimberly's cell phone number, and I figure if I call it enough, she's likely to pick up. But with Kiki, I just end up being put off by her receptionist. Can you think of a way for me to finagle a meeting with her?"

"Kiki Bodden?" she said, straightening her back in that way of hers. "Why would you need to see her?"

"She bit Mona's head off at the party, and I'm trying to weave that into the story."

"*Really?* Well, that's going to be tough since Kiki refuses to have much to do with anyone working for *Buzz*. I have an idea, though. Publicists often get their clients through celebrity managers, and therefore they're usually pretty eager to please them. There's one manager who owes me a big favor. I could try asking him to pull a few strings."

"Great, I'd really appreciate it. What's Kiki like, anyway?"

"She's sort of sad, if you ask me. She's about forty-five, but she runs around in minis and tries to act all hip. And she's a total swag whore."

"A what?"

"Swag whore. Swag is all the free stuff that stars receive— you know, the goody bags at award ceremonies and stuff like that. Kiki loads her trunk with whatever she can get her mitts on."

"Hilary told me she protects her clients like a harpy eagle."

"I can't believe I'm agreeing with something Hilary said, but yes, that's totally true."

"What if someone was going to print information that her client might not like? What would she do?"

"What so many of them do—scream and yell and threaten to blackball you and your magazine. It's like no one has ever told them that they might be able to accomplish more by trying to negotiate. Sometimes I think it's just so they can call the client and say that they screamed and yelled."

Kiki had indeed yelled at Mona, at the party. Was Eva the client she'd been in such a boil over? And had she taken the matter further? I considered how it might have happened. Perhaps Mona had dismissed Kiki and refused to address her concerns. Kiki saw Mona leave the party and then slipped away after her. After all, Brandon had even muttered something about Kiki being missing in action during the evening. Kiki then tried to return to the contentious topic, hoping for closure, but Mona refused to hear her out. Furious, Kiki struck her—and then again. But if that was what happened, how did I explain the man in Little Odessa? Was he just a predator after all? Or perhaps someone working with Kiki? Just thinking of the incident again—of those moments of terror under the car—made my stomach knot.

Chasing the memory out of my mind, I settled down to work. I took out my reporter's notebook and jotted down what both Dicker and Harris had told me. Then I pulled my composition book out of my bag and thumbed through to the timeline I'd created, making a note that Mona's visit with Dicker had supposedly lasted five or ten minutes "tops." Something about Dicker's story bugged me. I picked up my notebook and thumbed back through until I found the notes from my interview with Amy. According to her, Mona had said, "Wish me luck," before she'd headed up to Dicker's office. That was a phrase you used when you thought you might be in hot water or when you were about to say something that might put you there. Yet according to Dicker, Mona had stopped by only to tell him about a fairly benign cover story. Why hadn't Dicker seemed familiar with the subject matter? And why hadn't Mona taken a print of the cover with her to show him?

I slipped out of my desk and walked back to the office Mona's assistant Amy was holed up in. She was staring glumly at a piece of a paper, almost as if she hadn't moved since the last time I'd seen her.

"Are you going to move back to your old desk?" I asked, stepping into the room.

"Maybe when Betty gets back next week. It's too creepy to be down there all by myself. Besides, I don't even know if I'll have a job."

"I'm sure things will work out for you. Look, Amy, I need to ask you one more question about the other night. When Mona went up to see Mr. Dicker, do you think it could have been to tell him what the cover story was that week?"

"She didn't have the cover with her."

"But maybe she was simply going to tell him what the subject matter was."

"Then she would have just called him. Trust me, she found any excuse possible not to have to be face-to-face with that guy."

So did this mean that Dicker had out-and-out lied to me?

"Do you have *any* idea why she went up there?" I asked. "What might she have needed luck for?"

"Huh?"

"You told me the other day that she'd said, 'Wish me luck.' "

"Oh right. She probably had to tell him something he wasn't going to be happy about. Like we were over budget again. That always made him blow a gasket."

"Okay, thanks," I said. It sounded as if I really might have caught Dicker in a lie. Why would he want to misrepresent the reason for his meeting with Mona? I wondered if he had lied to the police as well. I turned to go and then stopped in my tracks.

"Just one more thing. The other day when we spoke, you mentioned that Spanky and Harrison were still here when you left. Was Ryan here?"

She lifted her eyes upward and to the left. "I didn't tell you that?" she asked.

"No, you didn't. Was he here?"

"Yes, he was here, too, when I was leaving. I'm sorry I didn't mention it. I guess because Harrison and Spanky sit closer to me, I was just more conscious of them."

I thanked her and returned to my desk. I still had some holes to plug—I needed quotes from Kiki and Kimberly, and it was essential that I speak to the paparazzo—but I finally had to start writing the story. Hopefully I would be able to obtain all the info I needed before Monday night.

Over the next hours, I crafted a rough first draft of my piece. I tried both a straight-on reporting approach and a first-person account (leaving out certain details about the body and scene, as promised), and though it was distressing to relive the night of the murder, I felt the first-person tack worked better. When I was done, I routed it electronically to Nash. I hoped he'd be able to take a look at it before our meeting.

I thumbed back through my notebook to the page where

I'd jotted down Dicker's comments. If Mona's meeting with him hadn't been about the cover, what *was* its purpose? And why had it lasted only five or ten minutes?

A thought wiggled its way into my brain. Cat Jones had her ear close to the ground on everything related to the magazine business. She might very well know if there had been more than the usual degree of tension between Mona and Dicker. Hopefully, she was still feeling guilty enough about giving me the boot that she would find time to see me before the weekend was over.

I called her number, and naturally her assistant picked up. I explained that I was hoping to grab a few minutes with Cat today or possibly on Sunday, since I had the Dicker barbecue tomorrow. I explained that it could easily be done over the phone if that was best for Cat.

"Cat's in a meeting right now. But hold on for a second. I think she'd probably want me to interrupt."

Good. Feeling even guiltier than I'd imagined.

I was on hold for about two minutes. As I waited, I pictured life at *Gloss*—the familiar faces of staffers that I'd taken for granted and now missed; the sullen models who crowded the reception area on go-see days; the nutty fashion department, dressing the mannequin they'd dubbed Fat Ass in their big office across the hall from mine. I had been gone only six weeks, yet in some ways it seemed like an eternity.

"You still there?"

"Yeah."

"How about meeting for drinks tonight? At Cat's place. Around eight?"

"Sure," I said, surprised. Now that's what I'd call industrial-strength guilt. Timing-wise, I'd be cutting things close because of my meeting with Nash, but I didn't want to miss the opportunity to pick Cat's brain about Dicker.

Thinking of Dicker led me back to the mystery man in his reception area. Over eight hours had passed since then, and I could still remember the charge I'd felt at the sight of him. Next, I did something so silly that I actually felt embarrassed for myself. Using my cell because my landline number would show up on caller ID, I dialed Dicker's extension.

"Hi, I'm calling on behalf of Seymour Regan," I said to his assistant when she picked up. I was a hundred percent certain that his name was not Seymour, but I wanted a name that would jump out as *wrong.* "He had an appointment with Mr. Dicker earlier today, and he may have left his cell phone there."

"You mean *Beau* Regan?" she asked, confused.

"Oh God, I'm sorry. I'm new here."

"Let me check," she said without much enthusiasm.

She took so long, I started to worry that she was checking out the story with Beau Regan on another line. But she finally returned and reported coolly that no cell phone had been found but she would keep an eye out for it.

Beau Regan. I had his full name, at least.

I leaned back into my chair. One of the junior editors who occupied the far end of the pod walked by my workstation at that moment and nodded at me. She'd seemed a little in awe of me since I'd started, and she probably thought I'd just hung up from a call with the director of the FBI. Wouldn't she be impressed if she knew what I'd really been up to?

I glanced at my watch. I had about thirty minutes before I had to split for my confab with Nash. Just as I was considering the best way to use my remaining time in the office, I heard a commotion up by the big conference table. A woman was standing there—someone who from a distance, at least, wasn't recognizable to me—talking to one of the editorial assistants. The assistant pointed her finger toward our end of the floor and the woman swiveled her head, surveying the length of the room. She then started to move in this direction.

I would have returned to my work, but I couldn't take my eyes off the woman's outfit. She was dressed in pants the color of a Granny Smith apple, and they hung dangerously low on her extra-wide thighs. She'd paired them with a sleeveless hot-pink top with a cowl collar, the kind that dipped in the middle, exposing a yard of cleavage. On her head was a newsboy cap in the same shade of green as the pants. She'd tucked all her hair under the cap, so it wasn't until she was within ten feet of me that I realized to my utter shock that it was Kimberly Chance.

My first thought was that she was coming to see Nash. And then, about the time I heard Leo mutter, "Uh-oh," I realized that she was actually barreling right toward me.

"Are you Bailey Weggins?" she asked harshly as she lurched to a stop next to my desk. The only thing I'd managed to do in the time since I'd realized she was gunning for me was sit up straighter in my chair.

"Yes. Hi, Kimberly," I said, discombobulated. "I've been trying to reach you."

I saw a look of recognition flash in her eyes.

"You were outside the courtroom the other day, weren't you?" she demanded. There was the hint of a twang in her voice, but it was almost edged out by her anger. "Who the fuck gave you my cell phone number?"

Except for the ringing of phones, the office had gone utterly still, and people seemed frozen in place.

"Look, why don't we go somewhere and talk," I said, rising from my chair. "There's a place down the hall where we'd have more privacy." With her stilettos, she had about four inches on me—to say nothing of the seventy pounds.

She cocked her head in a mocking way. "I don't think so. Now tell me: Who gave you my fucking cell phone number?"

"Mona did," I said. "After you were arrested." I wasn't turning all stool pigeon. I wanted to see how she responded to Mona's name.

"Why doesn't that surprise me?" she blurted out. "You worked for Satan, do you know that? And you oughta be ashamed of yourself. Do you have any idea how much you fuck up people's lives? We're just normal folks. Maybe we're a little more talented than everybody else, but we just want to lead normal lives and be left alone. And then you go and mess that up."

I couldn't help but wonder what my co-workers were all thinking, but I kept my eyes trained on Kimberly.

"Did you have a confrontation with Mona on Tuesday night?" I said. Might as well take the bull by the horns.

"Oh, I see what you're thinkin'," she said, forcing a big fake smile. "You're thinkin' I killed that bitch. But I was with a guy all night at the party. Just ask the police."

"I appreciate the information," I said, hoping that by appearing calm, I could prevent things from escalating any more.

"I've got another tip for you," she said, her blue eyes hard and cold. "You know what happens to people who work for Satan? They end up burning in hell."

On that note, she turned on her three-inch-heeled pink sandals and stormed off.

No sooner was she out the door than people started to cackle, and someone yelled, "Way to go, Bailey." I wish I could have found it as amusing as everyone else did.

Jessie rose from her desk, leaned against the partition, and smiled at me sympathetically.

"So what did you think of that?" I asked ruefully.

"My guess is that she's making a pitch to be the next Mister Greenjeans, but I don't think she's going to get the job."

"Did the entire office hear it?"

"Well, everyone on this side of the floor. The other half is just making their way down here now."

As if on cue, one of the deputy editors sidled up to my desk and asked if I was okay. After I assured her I was fine, she asked that I write up everything that Kimberly said so that they could run it in "Juice Bar." Oh, that was going to make Kimberly *real* happy.

I wanted to extricate myself from the spotlight, so I headed to the kitchenette. As I waited for the machine to release coffee in my cup, I finally exhaled. Kimberly claimed to have an alibi for the night of the murder, but I had no reason to believe her. Based on the tear I'd just seen her on—and the fact that she'd thought nothing of slapping a cop—she was a girl who had a real problem with anger management. I could easily picture her smashing in Mona's skull. I considered her comment about me ending up in hell. Had she meant it literally or figuratively? Until I had confirmation of her alibi, I had a new reason to watch my back. I wondered how she'd managed to talk her way past the receptionist. People weren't supposed to be allowed through without checking with the party they were visiting.

I opened the refrigerator and pulled out a carton of milk. As I splashed some into my coffee, I heard someone come up quietly behind me. Still on edge, I started to turn around.

"What the hell do you think you're doing?" a male voice barked at me.

CHAPTER 10

I spun completely around. Ryan was looming behind me in the entrance of the kitchenette. Because I was fresh from my encounter with Kimberly, I just assumed his anger had something to do with that, but I couldn't imagine why it would leave him all hot and bothered.

"What are you talking about?" I demanded.

"You know exactly what I'm talking about." He was still in the doorway, and his eyes darted to the right, as if he were worried someone coming down the hall might overhear him.

"No, Ryan, I really don't. You aren't taking Kimberly's side, are you?"

"*Kimberly?*" he said, clearly baffled. "Kimberly who?"

"Kimberly Chance. She just showed up in the pod and tried to have me for dinner."

"I don't know anything about that. I've been back here," he said dismissively. "I'm talking about the way you're stepping all over my territory. I'm the one who's supposed to be doing the profile of Mona, but you're calling all my sources. You talked to Dicker. You've been hounding Carl. And now I hear you took Mary Kay out for tea and crumpets."

"Ryan, I tried to have a conversation with you the other day to discuss this very matter," I said. "I was worried that there might be a small degree of overlap in our reporting, but you couldn't be bothered. Of *course* we're going to be talking to some of the same people. We don't have a choice. Those three people you mentioned fit with your story, but they fit with mine, too. They all spoke to Mona the night she died."

"But it sounds exactly like you're trying to profile Mona."

"No, I'm *not* doing that. I've been asked to write up her murder. I have absolutely no interest in delving into the life and times of Mona Hodges."

The rage bled from his face and I could sense that my explanation had mollified him. He started to turn to leave.

"Before you go, I have a question for *you*," I said.

"What?" he asked contemptuously.

"When I asked you about the party, you never told me you'd left here so late."

"You never asked."

"You were here when Mona returned. You and she spoke."

"And your point is . . . ?"

"My point is that I've been trying to create a timeline of Mona's last hour, and you never volunteered that you saw her only a short time before she died. Nash wouldn't be very pleased if he knew you were withholding information from me."

He snickered. "I assure you I have nothing worthwhile to contribute to your story. And for your information, I've already told the police. It's really *their* job to be asking these kinds of questions."

"What did you and Mona talk about when she returned?" I asked.

"She simply asked me if I was going to the party. I explained that I was heading over there shortly, and then she told me to keep an eye on Eva and her husband. Who said I talked to her—that nerd in the art department?"

"Yes," I conceded. "Was he the only one around out here?"

"As far as I could see."

"Did you get into the party through the back way or through reception?"

"The back. Why does it matter, anyway?"

"I'm wondering if you saw someone in the back part of the floor."

"You mean some enemy of the queen skulking around the corridors, waiting to bash in her skull?"

"That's right. You and Harrison supposedly were the last people here that night. But I'm wondering if there was someone still in the back part of the office. Or perhaps someone from the party snuck over here and was hanging around back there."

"Not that I saw. I passed the cleaning lady as I was leaving. She was pushing that ridiculous trash can cart of hers down toward the front of the office. And then I—"

He caught himself and looked off to the right, thinking. Clearly, a lightbulb had gone off in his head.

"What?"

"Nothing."

"You were about to say something. 'And then I . . .' "

"And then I went through that back door."

"You didn't just remember seeing something?"

"Nope. I was just trying to get the sequence down in my mind."

I was almost a hundred percent certain he'd experienced an epiphany.

"Well, I hope if you recall something, you'll let me know. We should be helping each other out on our stories."

"It sounds like you're doing more than writing a story. You're being a little detective, aren't you. But I don't think the police are going to like that."

Ignoring his comment, I tired to edge past him out of the kitchenette.

He didn't budge, which forced me to brush against his bony bare arm as I passed through the doorway.

Alarm bells were going off in my head as I hurried down the corridor. Ryan seemed more than competitive. There was a menacing quality to his attitude. I wondered *why* he was being so snide and elusive and whether I should accept his explanation of the exchange with Mona. Most important, I wondered what he'd recalled right before my eyes but had refused to divulge.

I glanced at my watch and saw that it was nearly time for my meeting with Nash. In fact, I'd hoped to be out of here even earlier, and now I was going to have to fly. While I grabbed my purse and tote bag from my drawer, Jessie told me that she'd heard that Kimberly had managed to gain entrée by telling the receptionist she wanted to surprise me and convincing an editorial assistant that we had an appointment. People were still gawking at me as I dashed through the bullpen toward reception.

It was steamy outside, as hot as it gets in July, and the tourists were dragging their heels. I spotted a small passage through the throngs and took it at a clip, because I was now two minutes late for my meeting with Nash.

The place he'd chosen turned out to be a spot I'd walked by dozens of times but had never been in—a sleek, overly air-conditioned bar-restaurant decorated in shades of gray. Muted jazz seemed to seep through the walls like a vapor. There were about a dozen businessman types at tables, a few with young chicks in skimpy outfits who might have been hookers or just girls who worked in the area and had dressed so they wouldn't sweat. No tourists, though. I guess they gravitated only to the spots that served the silo-size drinks with little umbrellas in them.

Nash wasn't there yet. I deliberated between the bar and a

table and opted in the end for the bar since it would be faster. Nash had been antsy this week, and he was probably planning to go back to the office after our meeting.

He strolled in fifteen minutes late, with me halfway through a not-cold-enough beer. A couple of the women followed him with their eyes. He *was* a good-looking guy, and once I'd even allowed myself to imagine what he was like in the sack—though he wasn't at all my type.

"Sorry," he said, hoisting himself onto a stool. "As you can imagine, it's been a real zoo." For once he didn't have his reading glasses perched on his nose, though I spotted them peeking out of the pocket of his jacket. He cocked his chin upward for the bartender and ordered a very dry martini.

"Speaking of zoos," I said, "I better fill you in on something that just happened back at the office." I described my dressing down by Kimberly.

"Jesus," he said when I'd finished. Though he was shaking his head in concern, I saw a hint of a smile, as though he was also mildly amused. "You've got to add that to your story. Do you believe her?"

"That we should leave celebrities alone?"

"No, that she was with someone the whole night."

"As far as I know, she could simply be trying to get me off her back. I'll make a few calls and see if I can find out whether this mystery man exists or not. Did you see her around that night?"

"I didn't set eyes on her until after the police showed up and shut down the party. If she had some guy with her at that point, I didn't notice. I just remember thinking she looked pretty wasted."

"Speaking of the party, that's what I wanted to talk to you about."

"Yeah, but first there's an issue we've got to discuss."

He sounded stern suddenly, and I felt my stomach do a backflip. I bet he was about to bring up Dicker.

"I know you meant well," Nash continued, "but you just can't go charging up to see Dicker like that. You threw him into a total tizzy."

"Sorry," I said, more meekly than I would have liked. "I was just trying to set up an appointment with him, which I would have told you about as soon as I had it arranged. But then he came out into the reception area and I grabbed him while I could."

"But why do you need him for your story? It's Ryan's job to talk to Dicker for his profile of Mona."

The bartender set down the martini on the bar, and after sucking the olives off the little stabber doodad, Nash took a long sip.

"Part of what I've been doing is trying to retrace Mona's steps the night of the murder. And she went up to see Dicker less than an hour before she died."

"*Really?*" he said, frowning. "I thought you were going to keep me abreast of everything you found out."

"It didn't seem like such a big deal. He *was* her boss, after all. But I'm a little confused about the reason for that particular meeting. He *says* she went up to tell him who was going to be on the cover this week."

I let the comment hang in the air. I felt uncomfortable asking Nash point-blank if Dicker could be lying, but I figured that simply revealing this little piece of info might elicit the same response.

"*You're kidding?*" he said, clearly surprised. "I would have thought she'd told him by then. He likes to know what's on the cover as early as possible. *After* it's gone to press is a little late in the game." His comment gave credence to the fact that Dicker had misrepresented the situation.

"Dicker didn't ask for my head, did he?" I asked.

"No, you've been granted a reprieve—as long as you don't go ambushing him again. So what else have you turned up? Don't leave anything out this time."

"There is one thing that I keep noodling about. As you saw in my article, I spoke to Katya, the cleaning lady. I didn't include one point—because there's no way to prove it—but I sensed there was something she wasn't telling me."

"Like what?" His face registered alarm.

"Something about the assailant. But I'm not sure what it could be, or why she'd hold back on it. Maybe the police will figure it out. By the way, what do you think of the first-person approach with my story?"

"I think it works," he said, following another sip. "It's different for us, but then the situation is so fucking different, none of the old rules necessarily apply."

We talked for a few minutes about the piece and he offered a few comments, suggesting little fixes I should make here and there. And he didn't even have the article in front of him. Mona might have known how to make things tart and clever, but Nash was a brilliant line editor, probably the best I'd ever worked with.

"I'll polish things up over the weekend, add the stuff about Kimberly, and then fill in the holes on Monday," I told him. "Those were great comments, thanks."

"Well, you're a great writer, Bailey. I know this is just a pit stop in your career, but it's been terrific to have you here. I hope you're going to stick it out."

I tried not to look as giddy as I felt from his compliment. "I've loved working with you, too," I admitted, "but I guess it depends on who the new editor is. It might even end up being someone who doesn't want all this new crime coverage in the magazine."

"Look, I think I can trust you, so I'm going to share something with you. But I want you to keep it under your hat. I'm being tapped for the job. That's why I've been out of the office so much. I've been with Dicker, working out some of the details."

"That's great, Nash," I said, feeling my face light up with a smile. "I'm so happy for you."

I meant it. And on a purely selfish basis, I was happy for me, too.

He took another long sip of his martini, nearly polishing it off. As he set down the glass, he suddenly glanced at his watch, as if he were afraid it was about to burst into flames.

"Jeez, I've got to split," he announced.

"Just one more minute. I need to ask you about the party."

"Shoot."

"Mona and Kiki Bodden had a contretemps that night. Do you know what it was about?"

"No, I was on the other side of the room. By the time I worked my way over there, it was done—and Mona had disappeared, so I couldn't ask her for details."

"Any guesses?"

"Not really. Mona had mentioned to me lately that in hindsight she thought our cover stories on Eva had been too soft and that she wanted to play it a little bitchier in the future. But there was nothing planned on Eva at the moment."

"I—"

"You don't think *Kiki* did it, do you? She gets paid to be protective of her clients, but I don't think that includes killing for them."

"But what if the information someone was going to run about a client was bad enough?"

"Like I said, we didn't have anything planned on Eva."

"Well, regardless, I need to mention the fight in my article, and I'm having a tough time trying to reach Kiki for a specific comment."

"That woman won't give anyone at *Buzz* the time of day. I have absolutely no clout with her. You might try Mary Kay. She's the queen of pulling in favors."

"Speaking of Mary Kay, I have one more question. I haven't added it to the piece yet, but I found out that Mona was re-

turning to her office to take a call from a photographer—a paparazzo—who apparently had some information to share. Mary
Kay arranged the call but claims she doesn't know what it was
about. Do you have any idea?"

"A paparazzo? That's odd. Usually if they have something
for us they call the L.A. office and negotiate through them. Do
you know who the guy is?"

"Yeah, I've left a few messages for him."

"Well, stay on it and let me know what you find out. Look,
I really need to split, okay? If you've got any more questions, we
can catch up at the barbecue tomorrow. You're going, right?"

"Yes, I'm driving out with Jessie."

I hadn't told him about Ryan, because I was afraid that
would incite the situation even more. Nor had I told him about
the attack in Little Odessa. I was reluctant to bog him down
with that if it wasn't related to the murder.

"Got plans for tonight?" Nash asked, tugging a twenty out
of his wallet as he slid off the stool.

"Just seeing an old friend."

"Well, have fun. And I'll see you tomorrow."

He leaned over and to my surprise gave me a kiss on the
cheek. It wasn't such a big deal, really. People did it all the
time in New York, including co-workers. In this case, it could
easily have been a nonverbal way of saying, "We work together and we like each other and we've been through one
hell of a week." But here was the problem. He laid his left
hand on my back when he did it, and there was something a
little too intense about the press of his fingers and a little too
long about the amount of time they were there. I knew that
kind of touch—what woman didn't? It wasn't at all about working together and being through a tough week. It was the kind
of touch that said, "I'd like to have my way with you."

But there was nothing lascivious in the look on Nash's face
and I felt perplexed. We said good night, and after seeing me
outside, Nash merged into the human traffic flow. For a few

moments I lingered on the sidewalk, watching him weave through the crowd and replaying our conversation in my mind. I had told him I liked working with him and that I liked his editing. Nothing misleading on my part, I was sure of it. Maybe it was just Nash being his Mr. Flirty self.

Still standing in front of the bar, I took a few seconds to figure out which subway line to take. A FedEx truck that had stopped directly in front of me suddenly gunned ahead, and as soon as my view cleared, I spotted Hilary standing across the street in front of a deli. She was staring right at me. It was obvious that she recognized me, but she gave no indication of that and then hurried off. I wondered if she'd seen me leave the bar with Nash. She'd be just the type, I realized, to start some ugly rumor. Gosh, what a fun day so far.

I ended up taking the R from 49th and Seventh Avenue, getting off at Prince Street and walking the rest of the way. For years Cat had lived in a town house on the Upper East Side, but her nanny had been murdered there last spring, and after discovering that no amount of scouring or redecorating could purge the negative vibe, Cat had sold the town house and moved in February to a loft downtown. I had visited there only once, just before I left *Gloss*.

Her place was on Lispenard, just to the west of Chinatown. Cat answered the door herself when I arrived, dressed in tight tan capris and a black top with what I believed would be described in the pages of *Gloss* as little cap sleeves. Her long blond hair was pulled back into a low ponytail, and she'd forgone her usual pink or red lipstick for a nude-colored one tonight. She'd topped it with a thin layer of clear gloss or Vaseline—not just on her lips, but on the very outside edges, too, making her mouth appear even fuller. I'd seen this glistening trick on a few other women, but when I'd attempted it myself I had looked as though I'd just eaten a hunk of whale blubber with my hands.

"Bailey, it's so good to see you," Cat announced. This was

the first time I had laid eyes on her since I'd left *Gloss*. She hugged me in the awkward, arms-held-stick-straight way that Cat was famous for, but nonetheless I could feel warmth in her touch. She really did seem pleased.

"It's quiet here," I commented. "Are you on your own tonight?"

"It's just me and Tyler," she said. "Want to say hi?"

"Sure."

She led me toward his bedroom at the far end of the loft. The place looked smashing, in a much more finished state than when I'd been there previously. It ran east to west, the entire floor of a small building, so there were wonderful views of both uptown and downtown. The walls had been painted white, and Cat's off white couches and chairs from her town house fit in well, accented by her collection of black-and-white photographs. One wall showcased a huge abstract painting of red splashes that must have been newly acquired.

Tyler was in animal-decorated jammies, looking precious and watching a *Dora the Explorer* video. He gave me a little handshake when I said hello, but he seemed about as interested in talking to me as he would be in hearing a lecture on cybernetics, so Cat and I drifted back to the living space. She motioned for me to take a seat on the couch and poured us each a glass of Bordeaux. On the black coffee table in front of us was a board of cheeses, as creamy colored as her couch and chairs, and little cloth cocktail napkins bordered in gold. Man, I felt like a passenger on the *QE II*.

"So how *are* you?" she asked, settling into one of the big armchairs across from me.

"Still kind of rattled, I guess. And as you've probably heard, the police have their eye on Robby Hart. You remember him from *Get,* don't you?"

She nodded, though I wasn't sure if she really did. Cat often fell short of knowing the names of the low-rung people on her staff. "Start from the beginning," she said. "I want to hear it all."

Ahh, perhaps that's what I owed the gold-trimmed napkins to—Cat's desire to learn everything she could about Mona's murder. I complied by offering her a ten-minute overview. She peppered me with questions, some of which I felt comfortable answering, some of which I had to play dumb to.

"I've got a couple of questions for *you,* actually," I said. I tried to make it sound casual, so that she wouldn't suspect it was the only reason I'd hiked down to TriBeCa. "I'm writing the story up for *Buzz,* and I could use some background information."

"*Buzz* is actually *covering* the murder?" she asked. I could tell by her expression that she was both surprised and mildly annoyed with herself for not having realized it.

I nodded quickly, and then, not giving her a chance to lob any more questions at me, said, "Tell me what you know about Mona's situation there. What was her relationship with Dicker like?"

"From what I hear, she couldn't *stand* the man," Cat said. "Mona was hardly to the manner born, but she apparently thought Dicker was the crudest thing she'd ever come across."

"He certainly liked to keep his nose in what she was doing—looking at covers, stuff like that."

"Oh yeah, and that galled her, I hear. It's one thing to be stuck with an editorial director, but at least they occasionally have something worthwhile to say. Dicker's just a business type who started off selling women's shoes, and suddenly he's trying to make suggestions to her about putting out a magazine. I heard he even had the nerve to suggest cover lines from time to time."

"She supposedly got paid over a million a year. Doesn't that make all the hassle and interference worth it?"

"Not to someone like Mona. In fact, not to most editors. Who wants some former shoe buyer in a Hugo Boss suit telling them what to put in their magazines? I heard lately that Mona's contract was coming to an end, and though Dicker offered her a fat new one, she'd been sitting on it for weeks. And he's not a patient man."

As soon as she said it, a memory shot through my mind: Dicker dashing out of Mona's office the day I was there for my job interview. I sipped my wine, trying to conjure up the words he'd uttered that afternoon. They were something like "Take time to review it, but we need to get moving on it." He may very well have been referring to the contract. Had Mona gone up to his office Tuesday night to tell him she wouldn't be signing it? Had she asked Amy for luck knowing how pissed he'd be when he heard the news? This was getting interesting.

"Do you think she was going to take another job?" I asked.

"Possibly. There were always rumors—including one that she might try TV. But I hadn't heard anything specific."

"So what would Dicker have done if she didn't sign up again?"

"Been extremely pissed. Not only is she good at what she does, but Dicker's put up with a lot from her and he probably felt she owed him."

"Couldn't he have just given the job to Nash?" I asked, feigning ignorance.

"The rumor around town is that Nash *is* actually going to get it. But I think he lucked out because of all the turmoil right now. I don't think he would have gotten the job if Mona had simply not renewed her contract. Dicker would have taken his time and done the search of the century for a hot new editor. . . . Do *you* think Nash has a chance?"

"I haven't been there long enough to have any intuition about the politics of the place," I said, pleased with the way I'd avoided answering. "I'd *like* to see Nash get the job. He seems like a good guy—and he's a terrific editor."

"Yeah, that's what they say about him. That he's a terrific editor." She'd left something unspoken.

"But . . . ?"

"Well, he's a great word editor and a great boss, but he's no visionary. His staff loved him when he was editing that men's magazine, but he bombed at the newsstand."

"What's the deal with his marriage? Do you—"

"Oh please. He's a total tomcat. But his wife doesn't deserve any sympathy. Apparently, all he has to do is beg for two minutes and she takes him back."

"What about *Mona's* marriage? Do you know anything about that?"

"I met the guy once. He seemed like a loser. He writes these ridiculous plays. He's got a kid from a previous marriage, and I can only imagine what kind of stepmother Mona must have been. But enough about all of them. Tell me about you. What's happening?"

I explained that there was nothing much to report: My book was still slated for the fall and my love life was in a holding pattern.

"What about you?" I asked. "How's the new, improved *Gloss*?" It slayed me to have to inquire, but it would seem lame not to.

"Good, I suppose," she said. "It'll take a few months to see how readers are responding to it. I'm trying not to let the material bore me to tears."

"You mean all those articles on living your best life ever and sniffing vanilla to reduce anxiety?"

"Yeah, those. I hope you're not still mad at me, Bailey. I miss having your articles, but I had to change *Gloss* or it was going to catch up with me. I'm in a lifestyle with a huge overhead, and I can't take any chances. You know, I envy you. You've created a life for yourself in which you're pretty much a free agent. You don't have to do things you don't like."

Oh sure, I wanted to say. I was a real free agent. That's why I was working at a magazine that used endless amounts of ink to speculate about the authenticity of women's tits.

"Well, look, I'd better get moving," I said. "You need to put Tyler to bed and I've got an early morning tomorrow."

"I'm so glad we reconnected," she said warmly as she un-bolted the door for me. "Let's plan on seeing each other again soon."

"Absolutely," I told her. It had been nice to break the ice tonight. Yet I felt a gap between us, a distance that had never existed in all the years she'd been my boss—and certainly not when I'd investigated the death of her nanny and Cat had saved my life.

I opted for a cab home, stopping at the deli at my corner for a few supplies. My place was like an oven all over again. There was a note under my door from Landon, announcing that he'd gone to Bucks County for the weekend and that I should feel free to drive out if I wanted to. After firing up the air conditioner, I stripped off my clothes and made an omelet with the eggs and mushrooms I'd bought at the deli. I drank a glass of wine, too, hoping I'd feel more relaxed; but as I stuck my plate in the dishwasher in my tiny kitchen, I realized that I was even more tense than I'd felt earlier. Everything that had happened over the past twenty-four hours seemed to have hardened in my gut, like one of those giant rubber-band balls that some people keep on their desks and snap when they're bored.

For starters, there was the lingering fear from the episode in Little Odessa. I couldn't get those terrifying white shoe tips out of my mind. If the guy was connected to the murder, he might even be spying on me here in Manhattan.

Then there was all the crap that had gone down today: Kimberly's visit and her threat about me burning in hell; Ryan's outburst and his snide remark about how I shouldn't play de-tective. Why was he being so nasty—and what was he hiding from me? I could still feel his bony arm as I'd brushed past him. A terrifying thought suddenly occurred to me: Ryan was tall and skinny, just like the person in the baseball cap and white sneakers.

And let's not forget Nash, I thought. Had I imagined the

suggestiveness in his touch, or was it for real? Was he just constantly putting out feelers and seeing what woman bit, or did he have a particular interest in bagging me? The last thing I needed in the middle of this mess was my boss propositioning me.

Last, but hardly least, was Cat's revelation about Mona and Dicker. If she was right, Mona's visit to Dicker on Tuesday night might have related to a decision on her part not to sign a contract. That would explain the brevity of the meeting (Mona might have told him simply that she wasn't signing up again or that she still hadn't made up her mind and that there was nothing more to say until she had) and confirm Amy's suspicion that Mona had needed courage for her encounter.

No wonder Dicker had offered that seemingly bullshit story about Mona visiting him to discuss the cover. He'd probably offered that version of events to the cops, too, because he wouldn't want it known that his meeting with Mona had been contentious. Was Dicker the killer? Had he become enraged when he'd learned that Mona was leaving and later shown up in her office to continue his fuming?

I had too many suspects. And too few pieces of real information.

I opened the door to the terrace and slipped outside with my wine. Through the wood stockade fence on the right, I could see the amber light on Landon's terrace. To my left, beyond a low wrought-iron fence, was the open roof area, filled with shadows. I'd never been nervous sitting out on my terrace before, but tonight I felt creeped-out. I went back inside.

In my bedroom, I turned on the ten o'clock news and laid out an outfit to wear to Dicker's—little jean skirt, pink flip-flops, white top, and pink beaded belt. I also packed a carryall bag with provisions, including sunscreen, a towel, and a bathing suit, though I had *nada* intention of prancing around in a bikini in front of my co-workers.

I was about to crawl into bed when an idea occurred to me.

I padded down to my office and turned on my computer. Then I went to Google.

Slowly, I typed in Beau Regan's name in the search space. I felt positively sophomoric. Doing a Google search on the guy reminded me of being fifteen and swooning over a boy I'd had a five-minute conversation with on the sidewalks of Provincetown. He'd been from Erie, Pennsylvania, and I'd spent the next month researching everything I could about Erie. I'd even investigated what colleges were there in case I wanted to go to one. In the end I researched the place so thoroughly, I knew how many pike they pulled from Lake Erie each year.

Beau Regan was an unusual name, so I figured I wouldn't get many hits. There were a bunch of listings in which both the name Beau and Regan turned up, including the open bitch category of the Yankee Golden Retriever Club. Both a Beau Geste and a Regan had walked away with a ribbon. There also turned out to be a Beau Regan on the board of supervisors in Fort Lauderdale who had attended a meeting at the Holiday Inn.

Then I found someone I was sure had to be him. Producer and director of documentary films. He even had a Web site, though when I hit the link, it said it was under construction.

Before crawling into bed, I made one more attempt to contact Jed Crandall. I left a message saying that I was calling on behalf of the magazine and urgently needed to speak to him before the weekend was over.

Jessie was right on time the next day. She looked really cute dressed in burnt orange shorts and a white T, the halter strap of her orange-and-pink bathing suit peeking out. She was carrying both a big straw tote bag and a shopping bag filled with food.

"We weren't supposed to bring a hostess gift or anything, were we?" I asked as we walked the half block to my garage.

"No, this is for you and me."

As soon as I'd maneuvered onto the FDR Drive at 23rd

Street, she pulled out two large cappuccinos in paper cups and a bag of muffins and bagels.

"I've got bran in case you do low-carb."

"Let me maneuver out of this traffic and then I'll help myself to something," I said. "So what do you think the mood is going to be out there?"

"I'd say it's going to be pretty weird," she predicted. "I don't think anyone is bawling their eyes out over Mona, but still it's freaky—and eating barbecued spareribs isn't going to make that feeling go away."

"I see you're wearing your bathing suit," I observed. "Are you actually going to let people you work with see you in it?"

"It depends on the weather," she said, licking some foam from her cappuccino. "It's supposed to get crappy later, but if it doesn't rain, I'll probably succumb. Why—does it wig you out?"

"Sort of. You live day in and day out with people, but there are certain lines you just don't want to cross. When I worked for this newspaper in Albany, we had an outing on Lake George one day, and one of the guys on staff, somebody you'd never suspect would do it, wore a banana hammock to swim in. You could totally see the outline of his dick—the only thing that was left to the imagination was genital skin tone. God, I couldn't look him in the eye after that."

"Of course, the danger works both ways. I'm not what you'd call thrilled about allowing Nash a closer inspection of my body."

"Oh yeah?" I'd been hoping to find a way to raise this very subject with her without having to reveal what had happened last night. "Have you had problems with him?"

"If I look away when I'm talking to him and then look back, his eyes are *always* glued to my boobs. I feel like I've got magnets in my nipples."

"That time his wife came in and slugged him with her purse. That was about another woman, right?"

"Yeah, but I haven't a clue who. Apparently, she yelled something about him keeping it in his pants at work, so it might even have been someone at *Buzz*. Do you think he keeps those glasses on when he's doing the deed?"

"Yup—and I bet he likes it with the lights on, too. Are he and his wife still together?"

"As far as I know, but I hear she's trying to keep him on a very short leash. She apparently calls about five times a day. Please, don't tell me you've got a thing for him?"

"God, no. Can I pick your brain on something?"

"Of course."

"Mary Kay told me that paparazzi traffic in information as well as photos. Is that true?"

"Yeah, definitely. We've got a million stringers out there and their job is to provide tips, but we also receive them from stalkerazzi."

"Stuff they hear when they're waiting around?"

"Absolutely. Those guys stalk stars and go to events primarily to take pictures, but they pick up stuff, too—things stars say, tips from the valet parking guys, you name it. What I hate is that part of the time they *make* things happen."

"What do you mean?"

"They're agents provocateurs. They're always trying to get a rise out of celebrities so they end up with the best picture possible. I mean, these dudes lie on surfboards in the ocean just to zero in on a chick's cellulite when she's on the beach, so they're capable of *anything*. They'll shove a camera in someone's face, for instance. Or they make a provocative remark. I have a friend who was at a movie premiere a few years ago. Ben Affleck was there. A few days before, he'd been at an awards ceremony with his mother, and one of the stalkerazzi yells out, 'Hey, Ben, your mother looked like a whore the other night.' Just to make him pissed. That's what I mean."

"But what about the info they overhear? They sell it?"

"Sometimes. Or they may barter with it. Use it to help them get assignments. Why the sudden interest in them?"

"I've just always wondered how it works."

Jessie and I let go of the conversation while I maneuvered my way onto the Triboro Bridge and then picked it up again once I'd merged onto the Long Island Expressway. That was the rhythm we established for the rest of the trip. We'd talk for a while—about Mona and work and even a little about our personal lives—then fall into a comfortable silence as we listened to CDs. I drank the offered cappuccino and devoured a blueberry muffin. Being with Jessie felt a little like road-tripping with a pal in college, and I sensed some of my anxiety dissipate. When we finally drove into East Hampton, it was hard to believe we'd been on the road for over two hours.

We knew Dicker's digs would be impressive, but we both went bug-eyed as I drove down the lane leading to his beachfront house. We spotted a tennis court through the hedges, as well as several outbuildings, and finally pulled up to a circular gravel area, where four or five cars were parked. The house was a big shingled rectangular box up on top of the dune.

"God, I've gotta pee so bad," Jessie said as we pulled our bags out of the car. "I think I'll go up to the house and find the bathroom."

"Okay, why don't I meet you down here?" I said, pointing to a large wooden gate in the hedge. Behind it was the sound of water gushing, like a waterfall. "I don't think the bus has arrived yet because it sounds too quiet."

As Jessie hurried up the wooden stairs to the house, I lifted the black latch on the gate.

It felt as if I had just stepped inside a secret garden. There was a swimming pool that looked more like a pond, dark bottomed rather than turquoise and with a waterfall cascading over large boulders. There were flowers everywhere—in purple, pinks, reds, and yellows. A cluster of fir trees stood off to the far side of the perfectly manicured lawn. They seemed improbable here, right by the ocean, yet they made the place all the more enchanting. No one was about, though there was a huge rectangular black grill and a table lined with bottles of booze and soda. I took a step in that direction.

To my left I heard footsteps. I turned toward them.

Beau Regan was walking in my direction.

CHAPTER 11

"Hello again," he said, though I could tell it had taken him a few seconds to realize that it was me, the girl who had mentally stripped his pants off in Dicker's reception area. "Still searching for Mr. Dicker?"

"Actually, no," I said, flustered. "I'm looking for some people I work with."

He was wearing stone-colored pants today and a black linen jacket. On the left side, his brown hair was tucked behind his ear, but on the other side it fell forward, over his eye. Now that I was closer to him, I could see that his eyes were not as dark as they'd seemed from a short distance yesterday but more of a chocolate brown. My heart was thumping ridiculously hard, as if this guy were my long-lost love whom I hadn't seen since he'd left for an RAF bombing mission over northern Germany one night.

"The tour bus hasn't arrived yet, apparently," he said. "But there are a few people who came by car. I believe they're up at the house having mimosas."

"Well, I'm not a big fan of those, so maybe I'll just check out the scenery—if that's allowed."

"Of which ones?"

"Excuse me?" I said, puzzled.

"Which ones aren't you a fan of—mimosas or the people who came by car?"

"Possibly both," I replied, smiling in spite of myself. "I'm Bailey Weggins, by the way."

"Beau Regan," he said, reaching out to shake my hand. Though the day was warm, his hand was dry and slightly rough to the touch.

"I thought this event was just for people from *Buzz*," I said.

"I believe you're right, overall. I may be collaborating with Mr. Dicker on a project, and when I mentioned I'd be out this way this weekend, he suggested I stop by for the barbecue and check out his digs."

"It looks amazing here," I said. "I can't believe he's got a waterfall in his pool."

"You can have one, too, you know," Beau said. "It'll cost you a hundred grand, though—at least that's what he told me. I'm surprised he doesn't have the soundtrack of *Last of the Mohicans* piped in. Here, would you like a seat? I was just about to sit down and enjoy the scenery."

He gestured toward one of the patio tables near the pool, a green wrought-iron one with a mosaic top. Without waiting for my reply, he took several steps toward it and pulled out a chair for me. As I sat down, I stole a glance back toward the gate, thinking of Jessie. She might not be able to contain her laughter when she discovered that in the two minutes she'd left me alone, I'd managed to pick up a guy.

"So you like sitting and gazing at waterfalls?" I said. "That's kind of a Zen-like activity, isn't it?"

He laughed over the sound of the splashing water. "Yes, I suppose so. I spent three years in Asia, and I developed an appreciation for that sort of thing."

"What took you to Asia for so long?" I asked.

"I made a couple of movies over there—I do documentary films. I studied Japanese in college and I thought I'd tried to marry both interests. I didn't plan to stay nearly so long, but I couldn't seem to drag myself away.

"And what about you?" he added. "Are you one of those journalists who delves into the secret sex lives of the stars?"

Just hearing him say the word *sex* made my tongue feel numb.

"No, I'm a crime writer and I was brought in to handle celebrity crime stories."

"And does that include covering your boss's murder?" He raised one eyebrow as he asked the question, a trick I'd never been able to master.

"Yes, that's certainly the crime of the week."

He bent slightly at the waist and pulled off his jacket. Underneath he was wearing a black polo shirt, and the muscles on his arms were tanned and well-defined. For a second I imagined peeling off all my clothes and diving into the pool, then beckoning Beau Regan to follow me.

"So what project are you doing with Dicker? A *Crouching Tiger, Hidden Dragon* featuring media warriors instead?"

He laughed. "We haven't nailed anything down yet. It was supposed to be a longer meeting the other day, but because of the murder it was cut short."

"It's been a pretty crazy time for everyone."

"Actually, an odd thing happened to *me* there," he said. "Or rather, it occurred not long after I left."

"Really?" I asked, my curiosity piqued. "What do you mean?"

"I got a call from Dicker's assistant several hours after my appointment saying that she hadn't been able to locate my cell phone. A young woman had called earlier in the day saying I may have left if behind. But I didn't lose my cell phone. And my assistant is a twenty-two-year-old guy."

Thank God my cheeks already were flushed from the heat because I could feel a surge of blood heading in their direction, like a crowd crashing the stage at a rock concert. I had to do everything in my power to fake a look of genuine surprise on my face.

"How absolutely bizarre," I said. "You should report it to the police. Maybe it's connected to the murder."

"I'll have to do that," Beau said, his mouth turned up on one side in a half smile. "Thanks for the tip."

Over the sound of the waterfall, we suddenly heard the crunch of gravel and the chugging of a big engine.

"That," said Beau, "must be your merry band of co-workers."

I rose from the table and turned in the direction of the gate. Above the fence, I could see the very top of a dark green coach bus as it lumbered up the gravel drive. It ground to a halt outside the gate, and seconds later there was a *whoosh* from the pneumatic release of the door. Any second now a couple dozen people would come through the gate, and that would put an end to my interlude with Beau Regan. Would he be here all afternoon? How could I make sure I talked to him again? He'd clearly brought up the cell phone hoax because he knew that I was the culprit and my stunt had amused or intrigued him.

"Bailey," a voice called behind me, and both Beau and I glanced back over our shoulders. Jessie, two glasses in hand, was descending a tree-lined set of flagstone steps that obviously led from the house to the pool area.

Before I had a chance to respond, I heard someone come up behind Beau and me from the direction of the tennis court and outbuildings. I turned to see a tall blonde in dangerously high-heeled sandals wobbling across the lawn.

"*There* you are," she called out, making no attempt to disguise her annoyance.

She seemed to be looking straight at me. I stared back, perplexed. Then, to my complete chagrin, I realized it was Beau she was addressing. Great—he had a date.

"Well," I said to Beau, "it sounds as if you're being summoned." It was bitchy to say, but I was ticked at the unfairness of it all. He'd been busy making my pulse pound when all along he'd been in the company of this bleached blond fashionista.

Before he could respond to me, I strode across the lawn to the steps where Jessie stood.

"How about checking out the beach," she asked as she handed me a sparkling water.

"The bus just pulled up, but I'm game for a short walk," I told her. My main mission today was going to be snooping and observing, but at this moment I was happy to remove myself from the presence of Beau and his date. I could sense the chick's eyes on my back as Jessie and I bounded up the steps.

After reaching the top of the stairs, we walked along the side of the house toward the patio, and then descended another set of steps—weathered gray wood ones—that led down a large sand dune. The sun, though not overhead yet, was hot and the sky nearly cloudless. Rain was supposedly in the offing today, but there wasn't even a hint of it now.

"God, that sun feels good," Jessie said, peeling off her shirt and stuffing it into her big straw bag. "I suppose there are worse ways to spend a Saturday."

"Oh yeah, what are they?" I asked.

"You'll warm up to it when you see the spread Dicker's putting out for lunch. I know you love to eat."

"Really? I'd heard he's such a famous tightwad, I thought he might serve us hot dogs and beans."

"No way. I peeked in the kitchen and saw all this great food, including a huge platter of bruschetta, my absolute favorite. There's a whole team of waiters getting ready to serve it."

"Was Nash there yet?"

"Uh-huh. Mary Kay had him in a corner of the living room, and there was no sign she was ever going to let him go."

"So *Mary Kay* is here?"

"You bet. She's not going to miss something like this. Wait till you check out her getup. She's dressed head to toe in pink and yellow, and she's got this silk paisley scarf tied around her head like a pirate."

"What about Ryan? Do you think he'll come today?"

"Ryan? Why would you care about him?"

"I've been curious about him lately. He's been acting very aloof towards me, almost sullen—and last night he nearly bit my head off. Is he usually so difficult?"

"He always struck me as someone with more than his share of demons. But, yeah, lately I guess I'd say he seems even *more* bothered than usual."

"What do you know about him personally?"

"Not much. From what I hear, there are some dead spots on his résumé. He worked for *People* a few years ago and supposedly was on the fast track there. Then he left to write a book, but the book has never come out as far as I know. He was apparently freelancing before he came here. Mona always seemed to like his writing—though I noticed some copy on his desk last week with a lot of ugly Mona scratch marks on it. I guess no one was totally immune to that."

"Does he have a girlfriend?"

"Don't think so. He gets personal calls, occasionally, but they seem to be mostly friends, not dates. He's really a loner."

"So maybe he wouldn't want to be packed on a bus with the rest of the staff today."

"Yeah, maybe not. Though some people besides us were planning to drive. Maybe that's what he'll do. Oh, you know who drove out? Hilary. I saw *her* up at the house. Maybe she wants to get her claws into Dicker."

"Dicker and the Cock Nazi. Now that's a match made in hell."

"Speaking of matches, who was that hottie biscotti you were talking to by the pool?"

"His name is Beau Regan. He says he's working on some project for Dicker. Unfortunately, it looks like he brought a date with him."

"You mean that stick chick that was staggering across the lawn as if she'd never been in grass before? Well, he appeared totally gaga when he was talking to you, so I wouldn't let her get in your way. You're not seeing anyone these days, are you?"

"No. I broke up with someone a few months ago and I'm sort of taking a sabbatical from any kind of serious relationship."

"I bet this Beau guy could change your mind."

"Not if he's going steady with that blonde in the fuck-me sandals," I said.

"Didn't you hear that naggy voice she used with him? He's not going to put up with that for very long."

"What about you?" I asked. "Are you seeing anyone?"

"I'm in between guys myself right now. Though I'd love to find someone who wants nothing more than to worship me."

The beach had started to fill up with sunbathers and their paraphernalia. A few people had decided to brave the water, though the waves were high and rough today. Watching them peak and then spew their foam into the sand was mesmerizing. High above us, a formation of tiny silver planes began to write a message with their contrails. Jessie and I walked for a few more minutes and then, almost in unison, stopped in our tracks and turned around. Dicker's brown-shingled house had disappeared into the haze.

"Do you mind heading back?" I asked. I was anxious to observe the dynamics today and see if any revelations unfolded.

"No, that's fine," she said. "Just promise that you'll eat lunch with me. Otherwise this day has the potential of being a real cluster fuck."

We walked back in that easy silence we'd established in the car. Every few minutes my thoughts fought their way back to Beau Regan. His date might have been egregiously naggy, but it had sounded like the brand of nagginess that comes only with familiarity—and full possession. Despite what Jessie had said, the odds might definitely be against me. Yet I also knew we had clicked in those brief moments we'd spoken.

The house came into view. From below we could see that there were now around two dozen people mingling on the patio that ran along the front. We mounted the weathered steps and came face-to-face with Dicker and Nash.

"Well, look what the waves washed in," said Nash, smiling. "Been enjoying the sand and surf?"

"Yes, it's gorgeous down there," Jessie told him.

"Tom, I believe you've met Bailey Weggins," Nash said. "This is Jessie Pendergrass, one of our writer/editors. Tom Dicker."

"So nice to meet you," Jessie said, extending her hand to Dicker. He was dressed in khaki-colored stay-pressed pants and a navy Ralph Lauren polo shirt. In the harsh sunlight his fake tan looked even orangier today, as though he'd been dipped in a glass of Tang.

"Hello, Mr. Dicker," I said. "I'd like to apologize about ambushing you the other day."

"Not a problem. Why don't you ladies get yourselves a drink," he added, as if he'd already spoken far longer than he'd like.

"What were you talking about?" Jessie asked after Dicker had moved off.

"I better tell you later," I said.

We drifted over to the bar. The entire front wall of the house was nothing but windows and doors, though because of the glare, all you could see was the reflection of the people on the patio. In addition to the booze and wine being offered at the bar, there were large frosty pitchers of iced tea and lemonade.

We both asked for lemonade. It was absolutely delicious, just the right combination of tangy and sweet. As I sipped it, I surveyed the patio. Though there were a bunch of *Buzz* staffers mingling up here, at least eight to ten people appeared to be corporate types from the eighteenth floor—reinforcements for Dicker probably. The vast majority of my co-workers were probably on the beach or by the pool.

As my eyes reached the end of the patio, I spotted Beau and his date chatting with two guys in sports jackets. Beau saw me as well and, squinting from the sun, smiled at me across the patio. I smiled back pleasantly. That was all he was going to get while he had a date.

Two writers from the staff, pals of Jessie, ambled onto the patio from the side of the house and asked us to come explore with them.

"Go ahead," I told Jessie. "I'll be down in a few minutes."

This, I decided, would be my chance to check out Dicker's house. I certainly didn't expect to find a sampler pillow that announced, "I bludgeoned Mona Hodges to death," but I was hoping to gain more of a feel for the man. A minute after Jessie took off, I slipped inside.

It wasn't a huge house, and it wasn't particularly special architecturally—just a very big rectangle, really—but it was stunningly decorated. The ocean side of the house consisted mostly of a double-heightened glass-fronted living room. What walls existed were white, and the floor was made of old stone tiles that looked as though they might have been looted from Bethlehem or Baghdad. There were two huge, ornate armoires, Indonesian in flavor, and lots of Balinese fabrics—in orange, blue, and yellow. A painting of a tiger hung above the massive stone fireplace, not one of those tigers on black velvet but a gorgeous, slightly abstract oil. Clearly, everything had been done by a decorator, so it was hard to arrive at any real sense of Dicker himself.

At each end of the living room was a smaller room: On the

north side was a glassed-in dining room that looked as if it might have once been a porch and on the other side a small but charming study with bamboo shades drawn against the sun. Making sure no one saw me, I ducked into the study. The walls were lined with photographs of Dicker with celebrities and dignitaries as well as a few shots of him on board a sailboat the size of Nova Scotia. He clearly had made a fortune with his empire. I wondered how much it would have damaged his worth if Mona had bolted on him. Though the study seemed more personalized, it didn't offer up any worthwhile info. Fearful of being caught, I glanced around quickly and left.

At the back of the house, away from the ocean, I found the kitchen—a sleek modern one currently bustling with cooks and waiters. A tall, slim guy with a shaved head, dressed in white shirt, black pants, and bow tie, stood near the entrance loading glasses onto a tray.

"Excuse me, what time is lunch?" I asked. He glanced at me quizzically and then looked down again, ignoring me. He either couldn't be bothered or didn't speak English.

I headed back into the living room. The room was still empty, but I heard a voice and realized it came from a mezzanine above the living room. Curious, I mounted the enclosed steps. The mezzanine had been turned into a small seating area with a television. Mary Kay was lolling on one of the two sofas, talking into her cell phone. She gave me a fake smile and one of those little flapping waves, as if she were working a sock puppet. As Jessie had reported, she *did* look like a pirate— Captain Jack Pucci.

Since it was clear she didn't want me eavesdropping on her conversation, I descended back to the living room. Standing at the bottom of the stairs was none other than Beau Regan. I caught my breath when I saw him. It was pretty obvious he'd seen me go up the stairs and had been waiting for me to descend.

"Having a tour?" he asked.

"More or less," I said, wondering why his date had let him off the leash. "It really is quite amazing. There's no Mrs. Dicker at the moment, right?"

"I believe Mr. Dicker is what my mother would call an unattached gentleman."

"Are you from the South?"

"What makes you ask that?"

"The words your mother used. And Beau. It's a southern name."

"My mother's from Georgia, but we never lived there. She met my father when they were both working in Washington, and a few years later they moved to Manhattan. What about you?"

"Look, I'd love to talk," I said, "but won't your date come looking for you again? I'd hate to see you subjected to a tongue lashing in front of all these people."

He flashed the irresistible grin. "How nice of you to look out for me. Why don't you give me your number, then? Maybe you'd let me take you out for a drink this week."

"Wouldn't your girlfriend mind?"

"That's actually *not* my girlfriend. Just a date for the weekend. And what about you?"

"What *about* me?" I asked.

"Is there a boyfriend in the picture?"

"At the moment, no. This summer I'm enjoying being free as a bird."

God, how lame, I thought. In my attempt to be intriguing, I'd ended up sounding like a member of Greenpeace. Hoping he wouldn't hold it against me, I reached in my carryall, dug out a scrap of paper and a pen, and scrawled down my numbers.

"I put my cell on there, too, since I'm out so much," I said, handing him the paper. "I'm going to be pretty busy this week, but I could probably get away for a drink." I sounded casual, but my heart was thudding.

"Great," he said. "I'll be in touch."

I turned on my heels and headed toward the back of the house again. In the corridor off the kitchen, I came face-to-face with Hilary—in a lime green Izod shirt, short white skirt, and Jackie O-style sunglasses pushed up on her head.

"Having a nice time?" she drawled. She didn't sound as if she gave a damn one way of the other.

"Yes," I said. "How about you?"

"Just fine, thanks. I bet this is kind of tough for you—a company picnic when you're new. Do you have anyone to hang with?"

"Actually, I'm doing okay. But I appreciate your concern."

"Oh, that's right. You've got Jessie to pal around with. You two are really buddy-bud."

God, having a normal conversation with her was like trying to fit a cobra into a shoebox.

"Well, if you'll excuse me," I told her, "I think I'm going to head down to the pool."

"Who was that guy I saw you talking to in the living room?" she asked before I could get away. "Is he one of the lawyers on the eighteenth floor?"

There wasn't a chance in hell I was going to encourage the Cock Nazi to make a run at Beau.

"Actually, he said he was Mr. Dicker's valet," I told her. "See you."

I found the back door and headed down the stairs. The sounds of the Gipsy Kings blasted across the lawn, and the air was filled with the smell of grilled meats.

I scanned the crowd. Forty or fifty people from *Buzz* had gathered on the lawn by the pool—standing in clusters, stretched out on the grass, or inching along in the queue that snaked toward the buffet table. Most people were in very casual summer wear, and a few even in bathing suits, but everyone from the art department was dressed the same as they would be for work: cropped pants, weird T-shirts, sneakers or black sandals. Though the mood was somewhat subdued for a barbecue, people were at least smiling and gabbing. In such a good setting and with so much booze and food, it was hard not to enjoy yourself.

I didn't see Jessie, but I spotted Ryan off by the fir trees. This, I thought, was my chance to chat casually with him and try to smooth matters over. But as I sauntered in his direction, he made eye contact with me, then purposely turned and walked through the trees. I couldn't have asked for a more obvious snub.

I pulled up a lawn chair and waited for Jessie to appear on the scene. After about ten minutes of watching people pile plates with food, I decided to join the line for lunch. There was barbecued chicken and ribs, Caesar salad, potato salad, the previously ballyhooed bruschetta, and corn on the cob, and I requested a little of everything from the waiters sweating through their white shirts. As I was surveying the lawn for a patch of grass to sit on, Jessie came bounding over.

"Hey, where've you been?" I asked.

"Just checking out the property. Why don't you sit over there by the trees? I'll just grab a plate and join you."

"So what's it like?" I asked when she plopped down beside me a few minutes later.

"Surprisingly tasteful for Dicker. And it's bigger than it looks. The roof you see over there is a guesthouse with two bedrooms. Some people are eating lunch there because it's air-conditioned. Behind that there's a tennis court. And way back there's this kind of super clubhouse with a bar and billiards table and a Ping-Pong table. There's a sauna in there, too, and even a room with a massage table."

"That's one of life's little pleasures that's high on my wish list—a sauna."

"Well, it's on right now, so clearly Dicker expects people to use it if they want. Speak of the devil, he's decided to join the masses."

I followed her gaze to where Dicker had pulled up a chair at one of the tables, along with Nash, two of the corporate dudes, and—make me gag—Beau Regan and his date. Their backs were turned to us, and at one point she draped her arm possessively across the back of his chair.

Jessie wrinkled her nose. "Want me to shove her in the pool? Her shoes must weigh ten pounds each, so she's not likely to surface."

"Let me think about it," I said.

The two writer pals of Jessie soon joined us on the grass. As we talked desultorily about rest-of-the-summer plans, I kept an eye on the crowd, observing. Ryan had returned and was sitting sullenly on the grass next to a few designers from art but not really interacting with them. Gradually, the mood of the party picked up, probably from all the booze being sucked down. A couple of people jumped in the pool, splashing around like lunatics under the waterfall. Someone here could very well be a murderer, I thought. It might even be Dicker. But from the outside, nothing seemed amiss.

Just as Jessie announced that she was going in search of brownies, Nash sauntered over in our direction.

"Okay, Bailey," he announced, "a little bird told me that you play a mean game of volleyball. Is that true?"

"You've got me confused with another Bailey Weggins," I said, lying.

"Don't bullshit me. We're getting two teams together and you're on mine."

"Oh, Nash, no," I protested. "I haven't played in years."

"It'll come back to you. Anybody else?"

Jessie fibbed and said she had a heel injury, but one of the writers jumped up eagerly and the two of us followed Nash to a big expanse of lawn back near the tennis court where a volleyball net had been staked in the ground. About a dozen people were already milling around. Nash and one of the deputy editors began sorting out the teams.

Nash was right. I'd played volleyball in both high school and college, and though I wasn't a brilliant athlete, I did seem to have a knack for it. I could serve hard, set nicely, and deliver a dangerous spike. Of course, that didn't mean I was eager to play in front of my co-workers.

The teams were finally worked out, and we took our positions. Hilary had been picked for the opposite team, and she eyed me gleefully. I wondered if she'd been volleyball champ in some country club in Texas. By this time, a big chunk of the staff had drifted over, some in bathing suits with beach towels slung around their shoulders. Mary Kay had dragged over a lawn chair and was sitting in it with a big bowl of strawberries, as if she were about to take in a match at Wimbledon. To my dismay, Beau was there, too, sitting on the grass with his date practically curled up in his frickin' lap.

It was clear from the get-go that ours was the stronger team—and Nash was a fabulous captain. Despite how rusty I was, I managed to play well—getting in all of my serves, setting and bumping nicely, and spiking the ball wickedly on two occasions. Before long our entire team was high-fiving one another obnoxiously after every point. Out of the corner of my eye I saw Beau watching me intently.

Contrary to my initial suspicion, Hilary turned out to be a disaster. She rarely managed to return the ball, and once, when I spiked it in her direction, she covered her face with her hands. Our team won all three games, and when the last was over, she had a look on her face that suggested she planned to boil my firstborn child in a vat of oil.

"Great playing, Bailey," Nash said afterward as his assistant, Lee, along with Jessie and a few others, came up to congratulate us. He leaned over and kissed me on the cheek, and I had that sense, as I had last night, that he lingered a hair too long.

"Right back at you," I replied perkily. As I pulled back, I caught Beau checking me out. Good, let *him* feel a little jealous, I thought.

The sky was finally clouding up and the air was cooling. The sauna suddenly sprang to mind. I suggested Jessie join me, but she said she'd like to take one more walk on the beach while the weather was still decent.

I started off in the direction of the clubhouse, which was off by another cluster of fir trees. The crowd drifted off in the opposite direction, back to the pool and the booze.

The clubhouse was amazing, just as Jessie had described, but it had that vaguely musty smell of rooms that were rarely used. I found the sauna along a little corridor that shot off the main space. The heat was still on, and thankfully I had the place all to myself.

I dropped my carryall on the floor outside and, after glancing over my shoulder, stripped off my clothes. I pulled a towel from my bag and wrapped it around me. There was a timer on the wall, and I adjusted it to fifteen minutes on the off chance I dozed off.

The moment I sat on the hot dry boards, I could feel my tense muscles start to release. Fifteen minutes of this was going to work wonders, I predicted. Yet after a few minutes, I felt restless, almost claustrophobic. I had wanted to relax, yet my mind kept wrestling with the same old disturbing questions: Who had tried to grab me Thursday night? Had Dicker lied about his meeting with Mona? What was bugging Ryan so much? Was Nash trying to make a play for me?

I checked my watch. I'd been in the sauna only five minutes, but I was too antsy to stay. As I stood to go, I heard a sound in the corridor, or at least I thought I did—a bump, sort of. I twisted the towel tighter across my chest; the last thing I wanted to do today was accidentally flash my boobs at a co-worker.

As I stepped down from the upper shelf, I peered through the narrow window in the door. No one was there. I reached toward the wooden handle and pushed.

The door wouldn't open.

CHAPTER 12

I tried the door again. It refused to budge. I wondered if it might be swollen and thus sticking. Next I used my hip to ram it—once, twice, three times, delivering solid blows—but still there was no give. Sauna doors never locked, for obvious reasons, but clearly something was preventing this one from opening. I felt a tiny swell of panic.

Glancing around the room, I looked for a device that I could use as a ramrod, but there was absolutely nothing. I stood up and shoved at the door again, hoping that its reluctance to open earlier had been due to my approaching it from some odd angle. But nothing happened. With the last blow, though, I became aware for the first time that the door seemed to give just the tiniest bit and then catch against something. It felt as if there was an object on the other side blocking the door.

I froze as a sickening feeling overtook me. I'd heard that bumping noise moments before I'd tried to leave. Had someone pushed an object against the door so I couldn't get out?

I sat back down on the lowest shelf and gathered my

thoughts. Nothing bad was going to happen. Not only had I put the timer on, but Jessie knew where I was and would certainly come looking for me at some point. I glanced at my watch again, not even recalling what time it had been when I'd looked moments before. It was four. The buses were due to leave at around five, which meant that if she became preoccupied, she might not seek me out for at least a half hour, maybe longer. The thought of staying in that dry, hot space with the overwhelming cedar smell filled me with dread.

I peered out the window again, trying to see, but there was nothing visible below the window. Stepping back, I hollered for help as loud as I could. I also yelled Jessie's name four or five times, hoping she might be in the vicinity.

The only reply was the clanging of the sauna heater.

I was sweating up a storm by now, and I sat back down again to rest. It seemed my only choice was to stay calm and wait. The heat would shut off in just a few more minutes, and eventually Jessie would find me.

Who could have done this? I wondered. And why? The chance of it being an accident—someone putting something against the door without realizing I was there—seemed next to nil. It could very well be an ugly practical joke. Both Hilary and Ryan struck me as capable of giving me a little scare to teach me a lesson.

But then the incident in Brighton Beach suddenly flashed into view. I had allowed for the possibility that the incident that night might have been a random mugging attempt, but two threatening occurrences within forty-eight hours seemed more than coincidental. I felt my panic balloon as I realized that this could be the murderer at work.

The heat had started to make me light-headed. My skin felt scorched and prickly, as if I'd been adrift on a raft on the ocean in full sun, and my nostrils stuck together from the dryness, making it hard to breathe. I glanced at my watch again. I had been in here over ten minutes and it still felt hot as blazes. The timer guaranteed that the heater would shut down before too long. But if someone had blocked the door, whoever it was might have also changed the timer. If no one found me, I could die from heat prostration. I stood up and screamed for help again. I hated myself for feeling so scared, but something about the heat and the closed space had caught up with me. When I finally stopped, my voice was nearly hoarse.

The sweat was now pouring from my face, and I felt truly faint. From far off in the distance I heard what I thought was the sound of thunder. The threatened storm was finally coming. What if everyone retreated to the main house, and Jessie, thinking I was safe and dry down here, didn't bother looking for me for close to an hour?

In an act of desperation, I threw my entire weight against the door again. It flew open, spilling me onto the stone pavement of the corridor.

For a few minutes I just sat there stunned, the towel half off me. I glanced up and down the corridor. There was no sign of anything that could have blocked the door. I listened. It had begun to pour, and rain pelted a small window in the corridor. The clubhouse was silent.

Carefully, I eased myself onto my feet. I'd come down hard on my left elbow, and it throbbed. Securing the towel back up around my boobs, I walked up and down the length of the corridor, glancing into the massage room and a linen closet stacked with white sheets, towels, and robes. There was no object or piece of furniture that could have been dragged over to block the door. Had the door simply stuck and needed the right push from the right angle?

I quickly dressed and shoved my feet into my sandals. After stuffing my towel into my carryall, I walked cautiously out to the big room.

It was dark in there now because of the storm, and I fumbled at the switch of a table lamp before I turned it on. I searched the room with my eyes. After a moment, my gaze fell on a pile of wood in a low basket by the stone fireplace. The logs were all neatly stacked—except for one that lay haphazardly in front of the basket.

I crossed the room and picked up the piece of wood. It was about three feet long. Leaving my bag on the floor, I carried the wood back into the corridor and stood it by the sauna door. The log was the perfect height to prop under the handle. Kneeling, I examined the area under the handle. There were scratch marks there. It seemed possible that the log or a similar object had been positioned under the door. I propped the log under there, at around a fifteen-degree angle, and then tried to open the door. It wouldn't budge.

Then I heard a noise, something muffled from another part of the clubhouse. My stomach did a flip-flop as I hurried out into the main room. It was empty, just as I'd left it. I heard the noise again and realized it emanated from a small room off the other side of the entranceway. It was the sound of someone moving quietly around.

"Who's there?" I called out.

To my surprise, Jessie emerged from the other room into the entranceway.

"God, there you are," she said. "I thought I'd better come round you up. The bus left early because of the rain—there was a mad, hilarious scramble. We can split now, too."

"What were you doing in there?" I asked.

She turned back and glanced at the doorway she'd just emerged from. "Oh, it's just some small sitting room," she said. "I hadn't noticed it before, so I was checking it out."

"You didn't see anyone leaving here, did you—or in the general vicinity?"

"No, why? Are you okay?"

"I think someone tried to lock me in the goddamn sauna," I told her.

"*What?*"

I described what had happened to me, and after grabbing

a bottle of spring water from the refrigerator, I took her back to the corridor, where I showed her the piece of wood that I'd wedged under the door pull.

"Are you sure the door wasn't just stuck?"

"I considered that for half a second, but just look at how easily it opens and closes. And look at these scratch marks."

"This is insane," she said. "Why would someone do that to you?"

"I'm not sure. Either I'm their least favorite co-worker or . . ."

"Or what? Do you think it could have been the murderer?"

"Maybe."

"So you think it's someone on staff, then?"

"Look, let's talk in the car. I'd like to get the hell out of here."

"But shouldn't we tell someone?"

"I need to think this over. There's a chance it was just a nasty practical joke." What I didn't want to tell her was that Dicker was on my suspect list, too, and I didn't want to raise any alarms just yet. Plus, what proof did I have?

"It's your call," she said, shrugging.

The rain had stopped as quickly as it had started, as if someone had simply upended a huge bucket. It was a mess outside. The grass was soggy, and many of the boldly colored garden flowers had been completely flattened. By the time we'd made our way across the lawn, my sandals were squishy. As we approached the gate, we could see four waiters balling up wet tablecloths and breaking down tables. Their shirts were plastered to their backs.

We pushed open the tall wooden gate and saw that the bus was indeed gone, but half a dozen cars were still parked there. We tossed our bags into the backseat of my Jeep and then climbed into the front.

"Were there people still up at the house when you left?" I asked Jessie as I maneuvered out of East Hampton.

"Just Dicker, Nash, and some of those creepy corporate dudes. A couple of other people from the staff apparently drove out, but they left when the bus did. How are you feeling, by the way?"

"A little better," I said. "At least I don't feel like my skin's on fire anymore. But I'm still pretty rattled about the whole business."

"I've got a question for you. Why do you think the person blocked the door and *then* took the wood away?"

"Well, like I said earlier, it might have all been a nasty prank. Even if it *was* the murderer who did it, the goal may simply have been to scare me silly. Maybe he—or *she*—senses that I'm getting close to the truth, but he doesn't want another body on his hands. So he gives me a warning to back off."

"*Do* you know something?"

"Not anything that points directly to who the murderer is. Unless it's something that I know but don't *know* that I know." I hesitated. Jessie had been incredibly helpful to me. Maybe it wasn't smart to completely trust her as a confidante, but I knew I could use a sounding board at the moment. "This is actually the second time since the murder something has happened to me."

"You're kidding!" she exclaimed.

"I went to interview the cleaning woman, Katya—you know, the one who was injured with Mona?—at her apartment in Brooklyn Thursday night, and afterwards some guy chased me down a street and tried to grab me. I rolled under a car just in time."

"Wow, does Nash know about this?" she asked.

"No, not yet."

"Don't you think you should tell him, or the police, maybe?"

"What exactly would I say? That I got scared by a man who might have been the murderer or in league with the murderer or might have been just a plain old garden-variety mugger?

And then someone supposedly shut me up in Dicker's sauna, which may or may not be connected to Mona's murder? Nash couldn't do anything about it, and the police would just tell me to stay away from the case. Until I can be sure about what happened, there's no point in sounding the alarm. And you've got to promise to keep all this in confidence, Jessie, okay? First, I don't want to put *you* in any danger. And I don't want anyone to know that I'm digging into this so deeply. That might really stir up more trouble."

She went quiet for a moment. "Okay, I guess I understand. I won't talk to anyone about what happened with the sauna. But you're a ballsier woman than I am, Bailey, that's for sure."

"I think you may mean 'foolhardy,' not ballsy," I told her, smiling ruefully.

Later, as we rolled into Manhattan, I asked Jessie if she'd like to grab a late dinner, but she begged off saying she was going to crash at her place. I hoped I hadn't freaked her out too much; I was frightened enough for both of us. Once home, I ordered take-out barbecue chicken and slaw, which was okay but not nearly on par with the spread at Dicker's. I left a message for my mother, trying to sound chipper. Then I dug out my DVD of the original *Thomas Crown Affair* and for the next two hours attempted to divert my attention.

Lying in bed later, though, I couldn't get those moments in the sauna out of my mind—the panic I'd felt when I knew the door wouldn't open, the horrible discomfort of not being able to breathe in the heat. If it had been Mona's killer who trapped me in there, why remove the wood and let me out? Was it because, as I'd suggested to Jessie, he was just trying to scare me off? Was it because it would have been too risky to kill out at Dicker's house? Or maybe the person who murdered Mona wasn't a killer by nature, just someone who'd given in to momentary passion that night.

Dicker popped into my mind. He'd been watching the volleyball game and could have observed me heading toward the clubhouse afterward. Then there was Ryan, who'd scurried away like a spider when I'd tried to talk to him. Perhaps *he* was the guilty party, warning me off from my investigations either because he was worried I'd expose him as Mona's murderer or simply because he wanted my story to appear lame in comparison with his. I also couldn't rule out the nasty practical joke angle. Hilary had looked ready to skewer me after the volleyball game. And there was also Beau's platinum blond date. If she had spotted how he'd looked at me during the game, she may have decided to give me a hint of what it was like to be dry-roasted alive.

Which led me to thoughts of Beau. I wished that he would call *right this minute.* I wanted him to tell me that he was home, in bed, watching the Yankees game he'd TiVoed and thinking of me. But I knew that more than likely he was in bed with his date, banging the hell out of her. He'd said she wasn't his girlfriend, but that didn't mean he wasn't in lust. What was I thinking, anyway, developing an industrial-strength crush on a guy named Beau? With a name like that, a guy just seemed to announce: "Hey, I'm good-looking—so what are you going to do about it?"

I holed at home for a good part of Sunday. I reread my article, tweaking little parts here and there, and also Googled Mona's husband in preparation for my interview with him. In addition to *King Lear Jet,* he was responsible for several other absurdly titled plays, including *The Taming of the Shrewd.* I was anxious to talk to Carl, eager to try to discover how damn sad he was over Mona's death, but at the same time wasn't looking forward to it. My least favorite part of being a crime writer has always been interviewing the friends and relatives of the deceased. It's so hard to find an entry point when you're face-to-face with raw grief, so tough to summon anything to say other than trite and tired phrases of condolence. I used to think that talking about the situation at least led the grief-stricken to experience a brief catharsis, but I don't believe that anymore. All the talking just seems to flog their wounds.

Even more discombobulating is when you encounter a person who craves the attention. Once, after the publication of an article I wrote about a murdered college student, I received a call from a woman I'd interviewed but had ended up not quoting.

"Is this what you like to do?" she demanded. "Bother the friends of dead people by interviewing them for hours and then never quote them?" I realized at that moment that she'd been looking forward to seeing her name in print.

The address Amy had provided for Carl was on 23rd Street off Broadway, not very far from me, so a little before three I set out on foot. As I emerged from my apartment building, I checked up and down the street, just to be sure no one was lurking around. With two frightening incidents possibly related to the murder, I knew I had to be on orange alert.

Mona's apartment turned out to be in a modern condominium building, probably expensive to live in but hardly the height of chic. A concierge announced me, and the person he spoke to apparently had to check whether or not I had clearance because there was nearly a two-minute wait before the man nodded that I could go up. The apartment was on the fifteenth floor, and the door was opened by a pale-faced, vaguely pretty young woman with choppy brown hair. For one moment I wondered if she was Carl's daughter, but after quickly doing the math, I realized that it wasn't possible. Plus, when she spoke she had a British accent.

"Why don't you have a seat," she said. "Carl is just finishing up a phone call."

She led me to the living room and then trotted off to parts unknown. The place looked fairly spacious—a three-bedroom, at least, I guessed. It was that sort of loft-style apartment you sometimes found in newer downtown buildings, an attempt to offer the best of both worlds—the elegance of an uptown space and the less predictable layout of a SoHo loft—that didn't achieve either, really. The living room had huge windows offering a view of the Empire State Building, and there was a raised dining area at the far end, just big enough to hold a table for eight. The furniture was ultramodern, not especially expensive looking, and the walls were nearly bare of art. Though Mona surely had been making a great salary and good bonuses at *Buzz,* her job history was checkered. She'd never met a magazine she couldn't jump-start, but in some instances she'd soon run afoul of management and been booted out despite her hefty newsstand numbers. That lack of continuity may have prevented her from ever building up the kind of equity someone like Cat had accrued.

There was no sound or sign of movement in the apartment for the next ten minutes, so I just sat there studying the view.

"Sorry to keep you waiting," Carl said when he finally padded in, wearing jeans, a beige sweatshirt, and a pair of moccasins. "I wish I could just turn the damn phone off, but there are too many things to attend to right now."

His longish brown hair was limp, possibly dirty, and it had none of that studied unkempt quality that he'd sported on the couple of occasions he'd dropped by Mona's office. As he moved closer to me to take a seat on the couch, I noticed that the rims of his eyes were red, as if he'd finished a crying jag only moments ago.

"I'm very sorry for your loss," I said. "I can't imagine what you're going through."

"Thank you. Your name is Weggins, you said?"

"Bailey Weggins. Mona hired me just a couple of months ago, to write crime stories."

"Oh right. How ironic," he said mournfully. "Well, look, I'm not sure what I can do for you. I already spent time with this other guy from *Buzz.* I gave him photos and a huge list of names of people to talk to."

I explained how my story was going to be different from Ryan's and promised to take only a short amount of his time.

"I'd really appreciate it if you could tell me a little about the night of the party," I said. "You went in ahead of Mona, is that correct?"

"Yes, that's right. She got tied up on some business, and one of her assistants, Amy, came out to the reception area and told me that Mona would meet me in there shortly."

"What time did Mona finally arrive?"

"Not much later. I'd say it was somewhere around seven-fifteen, maybe a little later."

"I hear she had words with Eva Anderson's publicist. Did you witness that?"

"I saw it, but I didn't hear what was said. I'd gone to get a drink for Mona, and while I'm waiting by the bar I see this woman walk over to her. I could tell by her expression that she was livid. Her teeth were clenched and there was fury in her eyes. Before I could get over there, the woman walked off."

"Did Mona tell you what the woman was so upset about?"

"No. Just that it was Eva's publicist and that she would tell me later. I mentioned it to the police, of course. As I'm sure plenty of other people did, too."

"Who else did Mona speak to at the party?"

"No one, really. She didn't actually seem to know many people there. Someone from *Track*—I'm not sure of his name—introduced her to one of the heads of the record company, but she didn't say more than a couple of words to him. In fact, she wasn't really at the party all that long. She"—his voice choked—"she went back to her office to take a phone call."

"Do you have any idea what the phone call was about?"

"No, Mona really didn't talk too much about her work to me. I think she thought I found it frivolous. But I never viewed it that way. I would never have been able to do my own work if it wasn't for her."

"You're a playwright?" I asked.

"Yes, despite the fact that the press likes to say I'm unemployed."

"How did you and Mona meet?"

"We met in high school."

"Really? But you have a daughter, don't—"

"Mona and I broke up our last year in college, and I married someone else. But eventually we found our way back to each other. It was a very magical experience to rediscover what had been lost." He choked back a sob during the last few words.

Wow, here was someone who, on the surface, at least, actually seemed to care for Mona. Could he be faking it?

We had drifted from talk of the party, but I needed to get back there. And I needed to learn what his alibi was, without being too disgustingly obvious.

"Go back to the party for a minute, will you?" I said. "When did Mona leave for this phone call?"

"At about twenty to eight. I'm sure of that because I looked at my watch when she left."

"It must have been hard for you to hang at the party without really knowing anyone."

He put a hand to his forehead and dragged it across, letting his fingers knead his temple. "Generally that's the case at these shindigs," he said. "But as soon as Mona left I bumped into a guy I knew from years ago. He works at an ad agency that does business with *Track*. I was still talking to him when one of the security guards came looking for me and told me there was an emergency. It was fortunate for me. Otherwise I'm sure I would have been an attractive suspect—the dilettante househusband of the world's hottest editor."

So Carl supposedly had an alibi. That would have to be confirmed. And there was still one piece of information I needed from him.

"Just one last question," I said. "Mona went up to see Tom Dicker right before the party. Do you know why?"

His gray eyes shot off to the right quickly and then back, and I could see his brain was working way too hard.

"I'm not certain," he said. "They were *always* meeting. Dicker was her boss."

"Could it have been about her contract?"

"Who told you that?" he asked, his brow wrinkled.

"Several people have mentioned that Mona's contract was up for renewal, and that she was reluctant to sign it."

"Well, perhaps initially there was some reluctance on her part," he said haltingly. "Mona turned the magazine around, and she wanted to be adequately compensated."

"Mr. Dicker didn't want to give her what she deserved?"

"He played hardball with her at first, but that's to be expected in these types of negotiations. They were getting close, however. I've been out of town a lot lately—a small college in Rhode Island is producing one of my plays—so I'm out of the loop somewhat. But I do know that she and Tom were . . . how shall we say? . . . closing the gap in their discussions."

"But I heard she was considering taking another job," I said.

He looked startled. "Mona did talk to some people, but it was exploratory," he said. "Like I said, she and Tom were getting very close on the contract."

This was the exact opposite of what Cat had sussed out. Which wasn't surprising considering how news became distorted in the magazine business, like a game of "Telephone." Unless, of course, Carl was so out of the loop that he was clueless about Mona's true intentions. Or was he lying for some reason?

"I know Tom has a reputation for being a pit bull," Carl added as I was digesting his revelation, "but he's really a good man on many levels."

"Carl, you have a call. It's your sister." The British girl had quietly reentered the room.

"I need to take that," he said to me. "Sophie will show you out."

I took my time getting up, giving Carl a chance to disappear into the recesses of the apartment.

"I'm Bailey, by the way," I said to Sophie. "I was one of Mona's reporters. Do you work for the family?"

"Just a few days a week when Molly's here. I'm kind of a combination nanny and tutor."

"How old is Molly, anyway?"

"Eleven."

"Isn't that a little old to have a nanny?" I asked.

She glanced back over her shoulder. "Yes, but it's still too young to be left alone at night," she said, turning back to me. "So when Carl and Mona went out, I watched Molly. I was here with Molly the night Mona died."

"But if Molly was here only a few nights a week, why go out those nights?"

She allowed a hint of a smirk to form on her face. "That's what Molly always asked, too. But Mona said she couldn't control the kinds of obligations she had for her job. Carl's a dreamy guy, but Mona called the shots."

"Do you have any idea who might have killed Mona? Did she ever mention a problem with someone?"

"Mona had a problem with just about *everybody,*" Sophie declared. "Except Carl. I think she felt so lucky to have him that she was usually pretty sweet to him. And so he spent half his time making excuses for her or smoothing over her messes."

"Am I right to assume Mona wasn't an angel to you?"

Again she glanced over her shoulder. "I really shouldn't be talking out of school like this."

"I promise to keep it between the two of us. It would only be background for my story."

She shrugged. "Most of the time she managed to ignore me, but if I accidentally got in her way, she could be a real tyrant," she said. "One day I'd let Molly wear one of Mona's cashmere sweaters and she went absolutely ballistic. She raised her hand and I thought she was going to slap me. But she caught herself at the last moment. If it wasn't for Carl and Molly, I would have left that second."

"Do—"

"Look, if you don't mind," she said, "I really have to get back to Molly."

Before making my way to the street, I found a small café on 20th Street, where I ordered a cappuccino and made notes in my composition book. I'd come away with more information than I'd anticipated: Carl supposedly had an alibi. And if he was telling the truth about the contract negotiations, Dicker no longer had a lovely motive.

I'd also learned a fascinating tidbit from the English nanny. Mona could be provoked to raise her hand in anger. In the six weeks I'd worked for her, I'd discovered that she was demanding and obnoxious, but I would never have imagined her getting physical in her anger.

While waiting for the bill, I checked my voice mail. Jessie had called just to take my pulse and see how I was doing. I appreciated her concern. All day long, I'd felt a low hum of anxiety in my body about what had happened yesterday, and it was nice to know someone was thinking of me.

To my surprise, the paparazzo Jed Crandall had also finally attempted contact. And he'd done so only ten minutes earlier, when I'd been sitting in Mona's apartment. I called him back immediately, and a husky, sleepy-sounding voice answered.

"Sorry I've been hard to reach," he said after I'd identified myself. "I've been a very busy man lately."

"Well, I appreciate your calling me back," I said. "As I mentioned, I'm a reporter at *Buzz,* and I'm writing about Mona's death. I know she was expecting a call from you the night she was killed. Did you speak to her?"

He must have taken a sip of something, because there was a long pause during which I heard him swallow.

"My, my, you're quite the detective, aren't you?"

"Just doing my job. So did—"

"I really don't like to get into these things on cell phones, which I assume you're on because it sounds as if you're in a fucking wind tunnel. Why don't we meet and discuss it."

I hesitated for a second. "With everything that's going on, it wouldn't be possible for me to get to L.A. this week."

"L.A.? I'm in New York now. I flew in for some work."

"Okay," I said, surprised. "Then I can definitely meet you. Could you do it today?"

He said he was staying at the Hudson Hotel and suggested that I meet him there in an hour, in the outdoor bar. I signed off, mystified by the fact that he was suddenly making himself so available to me.

It seemed senseless to return to my apartment and then travel up to the hotel, which was at 58th between Eighth and Ninth, so I headed straight to the Hudson. It's an offbeat, surreally decorated hotel, favored by young businesspeople and minor rock bands. You enter a small foyer, with eerie backlit green panels that make you think you've just boarded a spaceship. You then ride an escalator to the lobby. It's a dark, mysterious space, with brick walls, wood floors, a huge crystal chandelier, and ivy cascading from the ceiling. It's like being in a dream—nothing quite makes sense.

Because I was early I lounged for fifteen minutes in the library bar, in a butterscotch leather chair near the billiards table, which was covered with purple felt and positioned under a huge dome light. Finally it was time to meet Jed, and I moved out to the bar he'd suggested. It was in an open-air courtyard surrounded by the walls of the hotel, and though there were a few tables, most of the seating was on wooden daybeds. In the middle of the courtyard was a gigantic silver watering can that could almost convince you that you were Alice in Wonderland.

The space was only half-filled tonight, probably because it was so muggy out and anyone with half a brain was indoors. I scanned the area, looking for a very tall, slightly bald man in his late thirties—Jed's description of himself. And finally I spotted him on one of the daybeds, his long legs sprawled in front of him. I imagined his height gave him a real advantage when he was leering over walls, hoping to snag shots of Jennifer Aniston sunbathing topless. He shook my hand with a large, sweaty paw and indicated I should take a seat.

"Do you travel back and forth between the coasts a lot?" I asked as he took a long slug from his beer.

"I'm mostly L.A. based," he said, "but I have a bit of business here occasionally. To tell you the truth, I'm in Europe half the time these days."

"Really?"

"Yeah," he said with a grin. "Beckham's kind of a specialty of mine. I had one of the first shots of him with that tarty little assistant of his."

"It must be fairly dangerous work," I said. "With the way stars take swings at you and stuff these days."

"Man, some of these dudes can get real nasty—they kick, they punch, they scratch your car with their keys. Especially when you use the flash. They just hate the fucking flash."

"So why do it?"

"Hell, it's exciting. One night, just after I got in the business, I was on a stakeout with an old Scottish photographer—a real legend in the business—and we were waiting for this hot-headed actor and his slutty date to come out of a restaurant. The Scottish bloke leans over to me with a shit-eating grin and says: 'D'ya feel yer heart pumpin'?' It *was* pumping—and I liked it. Besides, the money's ridiculous. You can get a hundred grand for the first shot of some new couple if they're big enough names."

"So Mary Kay set up the phone interview with you and Mona?" I asked, easing into what really mattered.

"Yup, I had something I thought Mona would really like, and it was a little too sensitive to take to her West Coast bureau guy. Mary Kay arranged for me to talk to her. You know, don't you, that I was probably the last person to talk to Mona—before the killer, that is?"

"Did you make the call at the time it was planned, at seven forty-five?"

"On the dot. We only talked for about five minutes. I told her what I had, and she said she'd get back to me."

I'd just filled in another part of my timeline. That meant Mona had been bludgeoned somewhere between seven-fifty and eight twenty-eight, when I'd discovered her.

"So what were you offering Mona—pictures of some celeb misbehaving?"

He shook his head, beer hoisted midway to his long, thin mouth. "Nope. It was information."

"Information? I thought you sold photographs." Mary Kay and Jessie had told me about the new currency paparazzi dealt in, but I wanted to play dumb in order to see how Jed responded.

"Guys in my line of work sometimes come across information that's pretty powerful," he said cockily, as if he were a spy. "You're going through a garbage can looking for invites and you find something else, something you weren't expecting, mixed in with all the coffee grounds and other crap. Or you overhear something outside of a party. It's all in a day's work."

I remained as still as possible, trying not to look too eager. "So you had some information worth sharing with Mona. Who was it about?"

"The lovely Eva Anderson," he said. "And it was pretty damn explosive."

CHAPTER 13

I offered a sly smile, hoping he'd see me as a fellow conspirator.

"Do tell," I said softly. "It sounds really juicy."

He tossed his head back and laughed. "Now, you're enough of a detective to know that I can't tell you what I've got. As far as I know, you'd scamper off in those cute little red pedal pushers and tell someone before I could market the information."

Obviously there was no point in explaining to a big know-it-all like Jed that they were *capris*.

"Come on. I'm a crime reporter. I just want it for background."

"No can do."

"Then why'd you have me come all the way up here?" I asked.

"On the phone you said you were interested in knowing if I'd spoken to Mona that night. I thought I'd be a nice guy and tell you.

"And besides," he added, smiling, "I thought you might actually be able to help *me* a little—in exchange for what I passed along to you."

I felt an urge to wipe the stupid grin off his face with my purse, but instead I smiled sweetly. There was still a slim chance that if I played nice, I might extract more from him.

"Sure. I'd be glad to help if I can," I said. "Tell me what I can do."

"Mona was hot for this info," he said, shifting his long, gangly body into a more comfortable position on the daybed. "She wanted proof, though, and I told her I'd show her when I got to New York this week. So now that she's dead, I do the right thing and go to this guy Nash or Dash or whatever the fuck his name is. But he doesn't seem to understand the real value of what I've got. I'm hoping you can put in a good word for me."

I tried to imagine what could be so good that Crandall would deem it explosive. Eva cheating? Brandon cheating? These days almost nothing really blew up in a star's face. If having a sex video of herself go public hadn't torn an irreparable gash in Paris Hilton's chance at stardom, I couldn't imagine what could pose a threat to Eva Anderson's career.

"When did you meet with Nash?" I asked. "He was at a party in the Hamptons all day yesterday."

"Last night. He and Mary Kay met me right here where we're sitting at about ten-thirty. Mary Kay was nice enough to set it up for me."

"So Mary Kay knows what your information is?"

"She does now. I hadn't let her in on it previously, but since I'm using her to try to broker a deal with this new guy, I figured I'd better share with her. And just so you know, I didn't blab to the cops about this. They know Mona and I talked that night, but I told them it was about some photos. The last thing I want is for my info to turn up on *Access Hollywood,* thanks to the NYPD."

"Haven't you considered that the information you shared with Mona could be a motive for murder?"

"How so? Mona was killed right after I talked to her, so nobody ever knew she had it. Look, are you gonna help me or not?"

I smiled, submerging my exasperation. "Sure, like I said, I'll try to help," I told him. "It would make it easier if I knew the broad outlines of the information. I could really make a case for it then."

He snorted. "Nice try, sweetheart. Hey, I'll tell you what. If you convince this Dash guy to buy the info, I'll let you in on it. I mean, we'd all be on the same team then anyway."

It was clear that short of using a sledgehammer, I wasn't going to extract anything more out of him. Unfortunately, he had just ordered his second beer, and since he might prove useful down the road, I didn't feel I should bolt on him. So I spent the next ten minutes listening to him justify the use of the telephoto lens. He told me that stars really *needed* the paparazzi because they helped to create their images. Plus the public liked knowing that stars were real.

"When you see a star pushing a grocery cart with no makeup on or picking underwear out of her butt crack, it makes people feel better about themselves," Jed told me. By the time I paid the check, I felt in need of a barf bag.

I was tempted to call Nash the minute I escaped the hotel and urge him to fill me in on his meeting with Jed. In fact, I felt annoyed that he hadn't brought me up-to-date already; after all, he certainly knew I was trying to retrace Mona's last steps, and her conversation with Jed was one of those steps. But in the end, I resisted the desire to phone him. I didn't want to put him on the defensive again. Instead, I would find a way to raise the topic gingerly tomorrow.

I've never loved Sunday evenings, and this one had the potential to be a real loser. In addition to the normal blues that came free of charge with the night, I felt frustrated about the case—and also still fearful. My biggest problem was that I didn't know what I should be watching my back *for*. Being attacked on a dark street was one thing—and I could take precautions about stuff like that in the future—but being locked in the sauna seemed so random. It meant that I wouldn't be able to guess when and where I was vulnerable.

During the cab ride down Ninth Avenue, I decided to buoy my spirits by cooking myself something yummy for dinner. Three words suddenly burst into my mind, words that promised solace: spaghetti alle vongole. I'd been a maniac for it ever since I'd eaten a bowl at a little restaurant in Venice. I had the taxi drop me at a market on Sixth Avenue, where I picked up baby clams, pasta, garlic, fresh Parmesan, parsley, and a baguette. I hoofed the rest of the way home. Wondering if Landon might be back from Bucks County and want to join me, I rapped on his door before going into my apartment, but there was no reply.

Based on how overcast and muggy it had been all afternoon, I was surprised when I opened the door to my terrace to discover that the sky was beginning to clear and the air seemed suddenly fresh, cooler. I stuck in a Maria Callas CD and filled two pots with water. My meal was going to involve a frightening degree of carb overload, but just the thought of it began to make me giddy. When I was married, my husband and I ate most of our meals out in restaurants (I didn't know it at the time, but being on the move created the illusion for him that he was a few steps ahead of his creditors). After the divorce, I finally taught myself how to cook. I'm not exactly a genius at it—in fact, during my learning phase I gave a dinner party in which I dried out the swordfish steaks so badly that the edges curled and you couldn't imagine they'd ever been within a thousand miles of water. But over time, I've managed to master a dozen dishes or so.

As the water heated, I strolled out onto my terrace. Lights were beginning to wink on in all the buildings to the west, and I envisioned the occupants puttering about their apartments, preparing dinner like me, and perhaps imagining both the good and the bad that lay ahead in the week. On a terrace far-ther down the block, I spotted a cluster of people holding cocktail glasses and speaking animatedly, and I felt a fleeting desire not to be alone. Partly it was because of the episodes in Brighton Beach and Dicker's sauna, but I knew it was also due to being a divorced chick alone on a Sunday night. One mo-ment you are giddy as hell as you consider your brilliant way with a clam sauce, and the next minute you feel as if someone is pinching your heart between their fingers.

Staring off at the setting sun, its light seeping through a rib-bon of clouds, I didn't realize at first that inside my apartment a buzzer was going off. I scurried inside, thinking it was Lan-don at the door. But it turned out to be the intercom, with my doorman at the other end.

"Hey, Bob," I said.

"You've got a visitor, Bailey."

Because of everything that had happened, a warning sounded in my head. "Really?"

"It's a Mr. Beau Regan."

My heart nearly stopped. God, what in the world was he doing here?

"Umm . . . Okay, send him up, I guess."

I glanced back at my apartment. It was *clean* because my twice-a-month cleaning lady had come late last week, but there was junk flung around on various surfaces—three days' worth of *The New York Times,* a CVS bag with tampons and tooth-paste, the hard copy of my story, the bra I'd torn off since my return from the Hudson Hotel. I hurried around the living room gathering it all up, then heaved it into my office as if I were unloading a dead body over the side of a ship. When the doorbell rang I was in the bathroom putting on lip gloss. It was called Flirty Pink, and I wondered if it would live up to its name.

"Hi," Beau said as I opened the door, his deep brown eyes smiling mischievously. "I said I'd call, but I was in the neighborhood—on Broadway and Mercer—and I thought I'd just stop by instead. I hope I'm not interrupting anything."

"Umm, actually you're not. I just got back from doing an interview and was fixing myself some dinner. Do you want to come in?"

"Thanks."

He wandered in, surveying my place. He was wearing black pants and a white linen shirt just wrinkled enough to confirm he'd been out somewhere for the afternoon. Maybe I should have been concerned about his tracking me down, but there was nothing creepy about the vibe he gave off.

"How did you know where I lived?" I asked.

"They've got this amazing new service these days—411 Info. They can tell you phone numbers, addresses, movie times . . ."

"Wow, I'll have to check it out," I said facetiously. "Can I get you a beer? Unfortunately, I just have girl beer—Amstel Light."

"That'll do," he said. "Not expecting any boys?"

"Well, not tonight, anyway."

Jeez, Bailey, I thought. Skip the attempt at being a mystery woman. It didn't work with the so-called pedal pushers.

"What's that amazing smell?" Beau called out as I fetched the beer from the fridge.

"Spaghetti alle vongole—you know, spaghetti with clam sauce. I felt a craving for it suddenly and—"

As I turned around, he was standing right there in the doorway of the kitchen, a foot away from me.

"So you cook?" he asked. Over the aroma of garlic, I noticed that he smelled of musk and something else exotic, and I also saw, for the first time, that he had a small jagged scar on the right side of his face, just above his soft full mouth.

"Uh, yeah, a little. I'm not going to give Marcella Hazan a run for her money, but I can manage to serve the pasta al dente. . . . Would you like to stay? For dinner, I mean?"

"God, I thought you'd never ask," he said, grinning.

"You're not a serial killer, are you?" I said. "I mean, the type of guy who meets a woman at a party, asks for her number, then comes to her apartment and strangles her with a pair of panty hose?"

"No. I'm just the type of guy who usually waits a few days to call for a date but didn't feel like it this time. Besides, you don't look like you own any panty hose."

I laughed. "Okay then, I'll give you a job," I said, opening a drawer. "Put these napkins and placemats on the table out on the terrace."

It felt sort of dumb to turn him into Mommy's little helper, but I needed a minute to *think.* Had I done the right thing inviting him for dinner? Shouldn't I be acting more coy? As I'd fantasized about Beau since Saturday, I'd imagine a phone call, a drink, plenty of time for me to proceed carefully and not do anything that would backfire. It all seemed to be moving too fast. Yet hadn't Beau just admitted that he'd decided not to be coy? So why should I be that way?

And then there was the dinner. All I'd planned to consume myself that night was the pasta and bread, but that didn't seem like enough for a man. I rooted through the drawer in my fridge, scoring a few mesclun leaves. They were slightly past their prime, but I thought I'd be able to defibrillate them with a tart vinaigrette. I also pulled out an amazing Bordeaux that I'd been saving, a gift from someone's stockbroker boyfriend when they'd come for dinner. As I scrambled around my kitchen, my stomach felt as if it were riding a pogo stick.

"So what were you doing in this neighborhood?" I said as I set down the salad plates a few minutes later. I'd given Beau the job of opening the wine, and then instructed him to relax on the terrace while I'd finished things in the kitchen. He pulled out a chair for me at the table. "For that matter, where do you live?"

"My apartment's over in Chelsea, and so is my studio. I love being able to walk to work in the morning, but unfortunately I've outgrown my studio and I can't find the right one near me. I was checking out a place on Broadway."

As he reached for the wine bottle and poured us each a glass, I stared at his right forearm. It was perfectly shaped, lightly covered with hair, and tanned from the sun. It was impossible not to wonder what it would be like to have those forearms around me. I felt my cheeks redden.

"What kinds of films do you do mostly?" I asked.

"It's really a mixed bag," he admitted. "I guess if there's any common denominator, I would say I like the dynamics between people. I did one film on bond traders. They're a greedy, obnoxious, unrepentant group, but they fascinated me. I shot another one about actors doing an off-off-Broadway play."

"So what have you learned about human dynamics that the rest of us don't know?"

"God, this wine is great. . . . I don't think I'm any kind of expert on human dynamics. I just like to observe and shoot it—people trying to connect with one another or trying to pull the wool over each other's eyes, or even betraying each other. Since you write about crime, you've got to be covering the same stuff, right?"

"Oh sure. It's mind-boggling what people do. Though a lot of the people I end up covering are sociopaths or borderline personality types. They have no conscience, no sense of remorse, so you're not really dealing with people who follow the normal rules of human interaction."

"What made a nice girl like you decide to write about murder and mayhem?" he asked. He did that thing he'd done the other day—lifting one eyebrow but not the other.

"A few people have surmised that it's because my father died when I was twelve and it endowed me with a fascination for the macabre, but I don't think that's it. Around that time someone started writing awful notes to me and leaving them in my locker at school. It scared me—not just because of the pure meanness of the notes, but because I hadn't a clue who it was. I would walk down the halls every day wondering, Is it her or him or her or him? It made me feel I had no power. So I played detective, and I trapped her. I think she was just jealous of me, probably for some ridiculous reason like I got my period ahead of her. But I loved that sense of control that came with being able to learn the truth. And I guess that's why I like writing about crime—trying to find the truth."

"Does it ever get to you?"

"Sometimes. I'll feel kind of down after working on a story if there's a lot of brutality to it. And I don't cover stories that involve violence toward kids. I just couldn't bear doing that." I glanced at my watch. "Oops, I better check the pasta."

I was afraid that I might have overcooked it—and after bragging about being the master of al dente, no less. But it was perfect. As I dumped the spaghetti into the drainer, the steam billowed back into my face. If I got any hotter, I was going to have to hose myself down.

As I mixed the sauce and clams with the pasta, I considered how things were going. I still felt slightly discombobulated by the surprise nature of his visit, but other than the fact that I'd raised the topic of menstruation during the salad course, I wasn't doing anything to humiliate myself. It was also clear that we were clicking as much as we had when we'd spoken briefly by the pool in East Hampton.

"I hope this isn't death by garlic," I said as I carried the pasta bowl to the table and spooned the contents into the smaller bowls at each place.

"I'll forgive you if that's the case," he said. "It smells amazing."

The sun had set when I'd been inside, not much of a sunset, just a smudge of pink along the horizon. Before sitting down again, I lit the hurricane candle on the table and several candles along the edge of the terrace.

"So what about you?" I asked, twirling spaghetti around my fork. "Does it ever get to you, tracking the bad things people do to each other?"

"I try not to let it. And anyway, I don't just cover the evil things people do. I also focus on the good connections between people. When I was shooting the film about the actors, one woman in the cast—she was about thirty—fell head over heels in love with this kind of tubby character actor who had a minor role in the show. It was amazing to see it. From the very first second she set eyes on him, you could tell she was a goner. It was like Paul on the road to Damascus."

He held my eyes as he said it, not letting them go. Was he suggesting that *he* was like Paul, too—struck by a thunderbolt?

"Unfortunately," he said, breaking into a smile, "she was married to a soap star and it turned into a big fat mess. Good for my film, though."

For the rest of the meal, we talked effortlessly. Beau asked lots of questions and listened intently—not exactly in that riveted (sometimes *too* riveted) therapist's way Jack had, but as if my answers intrigued him. He wanted to know where I was from, how I'd ended up at *Buzz,* how I'd learned to play such a mean game of volleyball. I learned more about him, too. He was thirty-four, had gone to a private high school in Washington and the Tisch School of the Arts at NYU, and he was hoping to make his first feature film before long. He'd never been married, though he said he thought it had to do with the fact that he had spent those three years in Asia and that his real life in New York hadn't actually begun until his thirties.

"So your parents live in New York?" I asked.

"That's right. Up in the Seventies."

"Are you close to them?"

"When I'm not driving them insane. Actually, I think we're pretty tight these days, but we had a few rocky years. They're both high-powered career types and they wanted that for my brother and sister and me. The filmmaker thing threw them for a loop. They couldn't quite understand my interest in the life of Buddhist monks.

"But thank God my brother makes two million a year now," he added, smiling. "That's taken a hell of a lot of pressure off."

There was something both fascinating and incongruous about the mix of his personality: He was outgoing and charming—that sexy grin—but also introspective, the observer. Was *that* what attracted me to him? That paradox? I had no idea. Maybe it was all purely physical attraction, my first real experience with the hypnotic power of deep brown eyes.

"What exactly are you talking to Tom Dicker about, if you don't mind my asking?" I said. We had finished our pasta but were sitting there with empty bowls, finishing the wine as the city twinkled around us.

"I don't think it's supposed to be a big secret, but it's probably best if you don't mention it to anyone. He wants me to shoot a behind-the-scenes documentary for him. About race car drivers. One of his smaller magazines is about race car driving, and he'd like a short film as a way to promote it. He'd seen my film on bond traders and thought I was right for the job."

"Are you going to do it?"

"I don't know. The money is good, but I have to find out more about it. Plus I don't know if I'd really enjoy having to answer to him."

"Well, you're not the only one. Apparently, Mona hated having to answer to him. . . . I don't have much in the way of dessert tonight. Just some blueberries. Is that okay?"

"I don't know what more I could ask for after that fabulous pasta, but sure, I'll take some blueberries."

"Coffee?"

"That'd be great, but let me help."

"No, that's not necessary."

"Didn't I do a good job with the placemats and napkins?"

"Absolutely, but you should just relax and enjoy the view."

I carried the bowls back into the kitchen, where I quickly put on water for coffee and spilled blueberries into two goblets. I covered each with a dollop of sour cream and some brown sugar, something Landon had taught me from his "gay gourmet" bag of tricks.

"So tell me . . ."

I spun around. Beau stood in the doorway again, leaning against the frame with easy confidence and staring at me, a small quizzical smile on his face.

"What?" I asked.

"Why did you call Dicker's office posing as my assistant?"

"You think *I* did that?" I exclaimed, smiling. "Why would I have done something so ridiculous?"

"You said it yourself. You like to play detective. Did you do it to find out what my name was?"

"Is that why you came here tonight? To try to solve that little mystery?"

"I think you know why I came here tonight."

I caught my breath when he said it.

"Oh really? I—"

Before I could speak another word, he reached out with one of his gorgeous forearms and pulled me close to him. And then he kissed me.

The kiss was long, but soft and gentle. I could taste the Bordeaux on his mouth. I let myself enjoy the kiss, but at the same time my mind was racing. What did he mean by "you know why I came here"? Had he shown up at my door because he couldn't resist me, because he'd been struck by that damn lightning bolt? Or was this just a booty call?

He released me and stepped back, looking into my eyes.

"Shall we have our blueberries now?" I asked, picking up a goblet in each hand. *Shall we have our blueberries now?* Jeez, I sounded like a freakin' kindergarten teacher. Next I'd be asking him if he wanted to watch a video of the *Care Bears*.

"We could," he said. "Or we could save them until later."

"Save them?" I asked. "And do what?"

"I was thinking how nice it would be to go to bed with you right now."

I could feel myself flush. I'd let myself toy with such an outcome as I sat through dinner, but now that he'd announced his intentions so boldly, I didn't know whether I should be flattered or offended.

"That's a little presumptuous, isn't it?" I smiled as I said it.

He laughed. "True. But you did mention this was your summer of being a free spirit. And if it's any consolation, I don't generally act so presumptuously."

I set down the goblets, momentarily conflicted about how to proceed. Here I was in my kitchen with a ravishingly attractive guy who wanted to go to bed with me—and my instincts about him were the same. Granted, we hadn't even had a date yet, but why not surrender to the moment? As I'd reiterated to Landon the other night: I wasn't looking to be a *girlfriend*.

"Well," I said finally, "you've sort of managed to slip by on a technicality. I don't like to sleep with someone on a first date, but we haven't *had* a date yet."

"Ahh, how lucky for me," he said. "Will it wreck it if I ask you for dinner tomorrow night?"

"No, it won't wreck it," I said.

He pulled me to him and kissed me again, this time firmer and longer. He slipped his tongue in my mouth, but deliciously slow. There was something so exotic and mysterious about the kiss—perhaps because of the way he smelled and tasted, or because he was so damn sure of himself. He was holding my waist, and his hand edged up higher until just the edge of his palm touched my breast.

A moment ago I'd felt unsure of exactly what I was going to do, but now I gave in to the kiss, kissed him back urgently this time. His hand moved onto my breast and massaged it. A second later he slid his hand under my shirt and took my breast into his cool, rough hand. Then both breasts in both hands. As I leaned in closer to him, I felt his erection between my legs.

"Look," I said, pulling back, "since I wasn't expecting a night of wild sex, why don't you give me a second to make sure my bedroom doesn't look like a war zone."

He smiled. "As long as there's a bed, I don't care."

As soon as I'd closed the bedroom door behind me, I exhaled enough to blow out my windows. Again I wondered if I was a fool to be going through with this. It seemed so delicious to just give in to my desire, yet I knew how guys could be unforgiving if you refused to play the third-date game. I remembered, suddenly, my first impulse when I'd seen Beau in Dicker's office—the thought that I'd marry him someday. It seemed silly and overly romantic now, but I hadn't felt that sort of industrial-strength reaction since I was with Jack. I couldn't ignore it. On the other hand, if I just gave in, like I wanted to, maybe my head would clear.

I checked the room. It looked decent. I fluffed up my comforter and opened the two windows to let the breeze blow in.

When I returned to the living room, Beau was standing in the doorway to the terrace, staring out at the darkening sky.

"So," he asked, turning to me. "Did you hide away all those photos of you with old boyfriends?"

"Actually, I was putting away my Scrabble game. I often play alone on Sunday nights."

"See, I knew I was interrupting something. Well, hopefully I can find a way to please you as much as a game of Scrabble."

When he said that about pleasing me, my legs turned rubbery. Before I could respond, he stepped closer and kissed me again. I let my own arms go around him and stroked his back. Through the fabric of his shirt, I could tell how taut his body was.

With both hands he took the bottom of my tank top and pulled it up, breaking the kiss for only a second as the fabric flew over my head. He caressed my breasts softly. He traced my nipples first with his fingers, then with his tongue. As he leaned in closer to kiss me on the mouth again, I could feel the hardness between his thighs.

"I'm offering a lovely evening breeze in the bedroom," I whispered.

"Lead the way," he said.

The sex was like him in certain ways: sometimes fast, intense, passionate (what you'd expect from someone who just showed up at your door after meeting you once) and other times unhurried, deliberate, and almost unbearably pleasurable (was that inspired by all his exposure to Zen?). I'd never experienced anything quite like it.

And he seemed reluctant to stop. I would drift off to sleep and wake to find his fingers inside of me or his mouth moving slowly up my thighs.

At around seven, as the early light was seeping through the windows, I opened my eyes to find him sitting on my side of the bed, fully dressed and cupping my face in his hand.

"Bailey," he whispered, "I should get moving. I have someone coming by my studio at seven-thirty."

"No breakfast?"

He grinned. "If you do breakfast as well as dinner, I hate to say no. But I'm already running late."

"Okay," I said, wondering whether or not my hair was in a faux Mohawk. "I'll let you out."

I pulled on a robe and walked him to the front door.

"Thanks for last night," he said, smiling. "For the pasta, the wine—everything."

"Thank you, too. It was a very nice surprise for a Sunday."

"Better than Scrabble?" he asked.

"Scrabble has yet to make my toes curl."

"I'll call you later, okay? About dinner." He leaned in and kissed me softly on the mouth.

"Great. But we're closing so it will have to be late."

I crawled back in bed for a while, with just the sheet pulled over me. There was no denying how I felt. I had a monster crush on Beau Regan. As I lay there feeling the breeze blow over my body, I swung back and forth between luxuriating in my infatuation and wondering where in hell it would take me.

Once I was finally in the shower, with hot water streaming over my body, I forced myself to refocus on the case and my story. I was anxious to speak to Nash and find out what secret Jed had placed up for sale. I also desperately needed to hook up with Kiki. And I was going to have to watch my back every step of the way. With Beau in my bed, my anxiety had temporarily subsided, but as I toweled off I felt it return with a vengeance.

I was at *Buzz* by nine-thirty (trying not to do the post-shagathon shuffle) and there were already more than a few people at their desks. Soon the place would be filled with the manic "We gotta close today" energy of a typical Monday at *Buzz*—as people frantically finished their stories, fiddled with layouts, and wrote cute captions about Brad, Jessica, Angelina, and Colin. I'd overheard that the cover story this week was going to be on "love rats," bad boys in the celeb world who cheated on their girlfriends or simply broke off the relationship without explanation. Like FREAKY BEAUTY RITUALS OF THE STARS, it was one of those timeless stories that was kept in the can in case there was no breaking celeb news.

Jessie was already tapping at her computer. She cocked her head quizzically at me. "How you doing?" she asked.

"Still rattled," I said. "I appreciate your call yesterday. I just wish I could figure out who did it."

"I'm going to snoop around and see what I come up with," she announced just above a whisper. "I'll keep you posted."

"Thanks. Is Nash in yet?"

"Hm-hmm. Hilary was in there earlier. She looked frazzled. Maybe Lindsay Lohan called her up and screamed at her for suggesting she was a slut."

I hurried down to Nash's office. Lee wasn't out front, but I could see Nash inside working at his computer. I poked my head in.

"Got a sec?" I asked when he looked up over his reading glasses.

"Sure. Any new developments?"

"Nothing significant," I said, stepping into his office. I'd toyed with sharing the sauna incident with Nash but didn't want to until I knew more. "I'm going to send you my latest draft in a minute. We may get caught with our pants down between tonight and when we come out on Thursday, but I hedged in the piece as best I could."

"We'll just have to take our chances like we do with everything else."

"There's just one loose end that I was hoping you could help me on."

He'd been playing with a yellow pencil as he spoke, tapping the eraser end and then flipping it over and tapping the point. He let the pencil drop and looked up at me. "Shoot."

"I talked to Jed Crandall last night. As I guess you know, he spoke with Mona on the phone right before she was murdered. He informed me he met with you Saturday night—and that he told you what the call was about."

Nash pursed his lips, and I could tell he was deliberating about how much to reveal to me. After a second, he lifted his chin and pointed in the direction of the door. "Shut it, will you?"

I moved slowly toward the door and closed it. Lee was back at her desk, and she smiled absentmindedly at me.

"Look, Bailey," Nash said when I turned around, "I wasn't going to drag you into any of this, but I should have realized you'd find your way there. I'm going to be candid with you, but you can't share this with anyone, okay? And there's no way it's going in the story?"

"Okay," I said. I stood perfectly still, waiting.

"This guy Jed is a real lowlife, and he had some information that he was trying to sell to Mona."

"It was about Eva Anderson, right?"

"Yes. And you're not going to believe it. According to him, Eva Anderson was born a hermaphrodite."

CHAPTER 14

"Wait," I said. "A *hermaphrodite*? You mean when . . ."

"Yes, when someone is born with the genitalia of both sexes," Nash said, pulling off his glasses and tossing them onto his desk. "A vagina *and* a penis."

"But what about her husband? He doesn't look like the type who would go for that kind of kinky. Handcuffs maybe, a threesome definitely, but a *penis*? No way."

Nash shook his head hard. "No, no," he said. "She's not a hermaphrodite *anymore*—technically. I looked up stuff on it after I met with Crandall, and apparently they would have removed the penis after she was born and possibly done some surgery. They may have also given her female hormones. She would have developed like a woman from that point on."

"But how did Jed find this out?"

"These guys come across all kinds of crap when they're working. You know what he told me? He's an expert in what he calls 'garbology'—going through people's trash. But that's not how he discovered this piece of info. He claims someone passed it along to him."

"Do you think what he has is legit?"

"I don't know. He isn't going to show me his so-called proof until I make a verbal agreement to buy it. I do know this, though. There's been a rumor around for a while about some female movie star being a hermaphrodite. I never would have guessed Eva."

"Was Mona really interested in buying the information?"

"Crandall says she was, but of course you're dealing with a major bullshit artist. I'd say there was a chance she was considering it. As you've probably noticed, she was making 'Juice Bar' nastier these days. The competition is getting fiercer every minute. Mona believed that if we added some real tabloid stuff, it would goose our sales. And by keeping it quarantined in 'Juice Bar,' it would prevent the overall magazine from seeming too bitchy."

"But would she have really run an item saying that Eva Anderson was once half man?"

"Probably not. My guess is that she would have done it blind, but not so blind that people couldn't put two and two together. I'm sure she believed that as long as she had proof, Eva couldn't sue."

"So what are you going to do?"

"Stall the guy for a while. I know the pressure Mona was under, and I'm under it now myself. But if it's at all possible, I want to avoid getting too down and dirty with the magazine. I don't want to run blind items—and I certainly don't want to *pay* for items. Believe it or not, I used to write the word *journalist* in the spot on a form where it asks for your occupation. And besides, Dicker hates the tabloid stuff. He thinks we finally have a shot at getting advertising in the magazine, but it's not going to happen if we turn into a rag."

"But you're going to tell the police about this, right? It's a motive for murder."

"Come on, Bailey. You're not suggesting Eva Anderson offed Mona, are you?" he said.

"No, Eva was apparently always surrounded by an entourage. But as you know, Kiki chewed out Mona that night. Maybe it had to do with this hermaphrodite information. Later, when she saw Mona leave the party, Kiki may have followed her and attempted to talk some sense into her."

Again, the hard shake of his head. "I really don't think so. Because Kiki didn't *know* what Mona knew. Mona never made it back to the party after the phone call."

"But why was Kiki so angry that night?"

"It might have been anything. That woman gets her panties in a twist if you run an item saying a client hadn't been asked to the prom back in high school."

I could tell by his expression that he was reading the skepticism in my face.

"Look, Bailey," he said, "if I thought this had anything to do with the murder, I would go to the police, trust me. But it can't possibly. Mona's skirmish with Kiki was *before* her phone conversation with Jed. And to be perfectly blunt, I don't want to tell the cops about this because if it comes out that we're in—or were once in—the business of buying and using that kind of information, it won't be good for us. Dicker would be seriously pissed."

I was tempted to argue, but I bit my tongue. Nash was a breeze to talk to, and I could be easily lured into thinking I could share my mind with him without worry. But he was my boss after all, one with more than his share of testosterone and known for sudden mood shifts. I had a sneaking suspicion that it would be smart not to challenge him. That said, I wasn't going to just let the matter drop. The information he'd shared with me might be of consequence, and I intended to snoop around and find out what I could.

"I hear you," I said, trying to sound as though I really meant it. "It seems like it's best to sit tight for the time being."

"Good girl," he proclaimed, smiling.

"Do you still want me to keep pursuing the story—for next week's issue?" I asked.

"Of course," he said. "People are going to be interested in how all this plays out. We should plan on follow-ups for as long as it takes the case to unfold."

As I left Nash's office, every pair of eyes around checked me out. People were speculating about why the door had been closed: What did I know that they didn't?

As promised, once I was back at my desk I forwarded the latest version of my story to Nash. Then I went online and dug up what I could about hermaphrodites.

Cases of true hermaphrodites were extremely rare, I learned, and it was more than likely that Eva Anderson had been born an intersexual, an umbrella term used to describe people with ambiguous sexuality. An intersexual might have the chromosomal makeup of one sex but the anatomy of another—or both, for that matter. Though in cases of both, neither sex was fully developed. The penis, for instance, might be nothing more than a stump. In the past doctors operated within days, refashioning the genitalia to fit one sex. More often than not, doctors chose to make the baby a girl, because it was easier to create a vagina than a penis. Hormone injections would often be part of the treatment, especially in cases where the chromosomal makeup didn't indicate clearly what sex the person was. Unfortunately, down the road the person might manifest all the personality attributes of the other sex because doctors had made the wrong choice. There was thinking these days that parents should wait until the child was older to take any action.

The one thing that doctors couldn't create was reproductive organs. If Crandall's revelation was true, it would explain why Eva was considering adoption.

I summoned an image of Eva in my mind: the long, lean body, flat stomach, broad shoulders, and of course, the huge boobs, rumored to be surgically enhanced. Despite how sexy Eva was, there *was* something slightly masculine about her.

If it was true that Eva was a hermaphrodite, what impact would disclosure have on her career? Today it seemed that an A-list celebrity's reputation could rebound from just about any-thing—addiction, bisexual flings, a shoplifting conviction, pub-lic feuding, a hit-and-run car crash, an amateur porn flick. But I wasn't so sure that a brilliant bounce-back could occur with *this* particular news. On the surface no one could possibly hold it against Eva, but it might harm her anyway, might tarnish that dazzling, multimillion-dollar girl-next-door image. Because it would mean that she wasn't really the girl next door. She was the girl/boy next door.

Which quickly brought me back to Kiki. If she had learned that this information was on the black market, she would have been desperate to stop it from seeing daylight. Even a blind item could possibly damage Eva. What if Mona had a hint of what information Jed was peddling *before* that phone call? Maybe she'd even talked to him once before. And maybe Mona had someone call Kiki for her reaction, just to test the waters. My idea was a bit of a stretch, but it would explain why Kiki was so fired up that night. And if Kiki *had* known about the information that was coming into Mona's possession, she would have had good reason to tear into her.

I didn't want to lose track of other people on my suspect list—Kimberly, for instance, Ryan, and even Carl, whose alibi I had yet to validate. I phoned my contact in NYPD, the one who'd met me for coffee last week, and asked for any verifi-cation on Carl's story that he'd spent most of the party with an old friend and Kimberly's tale about hooking up with a guy. He called back fifteen minutes later, stating that Carl did seem to be in the clear, but he could not confirm Kimberly's version of events.

So she was still on the list. Kiki, however, was looming even larger at the moment. She, after all, had skirmished with

Mona. Of course, if she *had* killed Mona, how did that relate to what had happened to me in Brighton Beach and in Dicker's sauna? Were those random events after all, unrelated to the murder? Or could Kiki have paid someone to try to scare me off?

I picked up the phone and called Donna Lapp, one of the company lawyers who vetted my articles and much of the other material that *Buzz* churned out. She was an expert on libel and slander and guided us so we wouldn't wind up getting sued.

"Got a sec?" I asked when she answered her phone.

"I'm all yours," she said in that no-nonsense way of hers. In the weeks I'd been at *Buzz,* I'd thought more than once how much I'd hate being cross-examined by her in a courtroom.

"How much danger is there in running blind items? You know, where—"

"I know exactly what you mean. I hate them. And I think they're *real* dangerous."

"How so?" I asked.

"In the first place, the sources always seem to be so shifty—a-friend-of-a-friend-saw-the-person-backstage kind of thing. And if the subject is recognizable and the information is untrue, the person could bring a cause of action for defamation, just as he could if we named him."

"But what if it *is* true?"

"You still could be looking at an invasion of privacy claim. As you well know, celebs forfeit some of their privacy protection because they're public figures, but if the information that's published isn't at all newsworthy or a matter of public concern, there could be grounds for a suit."

"But if the information was damaging enough, the celebrity might decide not to sue so they wouldn't have to drag it out in the open, right?"

"Possibly. But my view is why should we chance it? There's too much to lose."

"Can I assume then that you haven't been very happy about all the blind items we've been running lately?" I was fishing, hoping that if Mona had advance word on what Jed was trafficking in, she might have consulted with Donna.

"No, I'm *not* pleased. I warned Mona several times about them."

I felt the hairs on the back of my neck stir. "Oh really?" I said. "Did—did Mona speak to you about any item in particular?"

"No, it was actually I who called her," Donna admitted. "I told her I'd noticed the increase and that she needed to be careful. She didn't mention anything in particular to me. In fact, she seemed annoyed by my call. Look, I've got a conference call I need to take. Is there anything else?"

After I hung up, I leaned back in my chair and stared at the ceiling, trying to distract myself from a conversation Leo was having with an editor about butt flab. I hadn't a shred of evidence that the spat between Mona and Kiki related to Jed's "scoop," but the whole thing seemed so coincidental—Jed peddling the info this week and Kiki blowing a gasket. I hadn't learned anything from Donna, but I knew someone who *might* shed some light on the matter. I took a hike back to the office used by the West Coast staff. Earlier I'd caught a glimpse of Mary Kay in the hallway, and I was pretty sure she must be back there.

She *was* there, and her appearance nearly knocked my socks off. She was decked out in another Chanel suit, this one in lavender and yellow, but she had about a dozen silo-size red Velcro rollers in her hair and her entire face was covered with white makeup, as if she were about to perform in Kabuki theater.

"I was hoping I could speak to you for a second," I said after rapping on the door frame and making her jump.

"All right," she said begrudgingly. "But you'll have to excuse my appearance. I'm doing an *ET* segment in a little while."

She had set up one of those light-up magnifying mirrors on

the desk, along with a big pink bag of beauty goodies, and as I took a seat she dabbed a makeup sponge into a compact and began applying pressed foundation the color of mannequin legs onto her face. The white stuff, I guessed, must have been some kind of primer, a spackle for the face.

"Nash filled me in on the conversation the two of you had with Jed last night," I told her.

She halted her dabbing for a millisecond as she digested the news, and I could sense she was surprised at Nash's decision to spill the beans to me.

"I take it, then, you're capable of guarding a state secret, Bailey?"

"Yes, Mary Kay, I am."

"Good. Because Nash and I feel very strongly that this information must be kept under wraps for the time being."

"Well, you can count on me. Quite a revelation, though, huh? Have you ever heard one like that before?"

"Not like that, no. But many other things. You know, dear, at the end of the day, stars are just people. They don't escape life's travails or fate's fickleness. One of the great actresses of our time was born covered with body hair as thick as fur. I'm sure there are many heartbreaking things even I am not privy to."

"Were you aware of what information Jed had for sale?"

She snapped her head in my direction. "As I told you at breakfast, no. I simply arranged the contact."

"That wasn't the first time Mona had spoken to him, though, was it?"

She dropped the sponge into a little plastic bag and picked up a powder puff, slipping her hand snuggly through the silver ribbon on the back. She appeared to be preoccupied with her toilette, but I sensed that she was weighing what I'd just said and considering how to answer me.

"I'm not sure what you mean, Bailey."

"I know that Jed had talked to Mona once before, hadn't he?"

I felt slightly uncomfortable lying to her, but she was a cagey thing, and I didn't know any other way to flush out the truth.

She turned to me again, her brow furrowed. "Who told you *that*?"

"I don't recall. It's in my notes somewhere."

"Well, I wouldn't know. This was the first call *I'd* been involved with."

"Thanks for the help," I said. "I'll see you around."

I couldn't discern whether she'd been telling the truth or not. The furrowed brow had indicated that something was going on underneath those jumbo rollers on her head, but she might have simply been irked by the fact that there were details about the Jed situation that she wasn't *privy* to. It looked as if the best way to find out if Kiki knew anything was to speak to Kiki herself—and so far I'd had zero luck pulling that off.

Back at my desk I waited for Jessie to get off from a phone call, then rolled my chair in her direction.

"I hate to be a nudge, but have you made any progress on the Kiki front?"

"I was just going to tell you. I spoke to my manager pal about an hour ago and he said he'd think about it, but that was his secretary saying that he couldn't do it. He doesn't want to piss Kiki off. Sorry about that."

I touched my fingers to my forehead, thinking. "What's the address for her agency?" I asked.

She flipped through her Rolodex, found the address, and jotted it down for me. By the time she handed it to me, I had my purse slung over my shoulder.

"Omigod, you're making a cold call there, aren't you? Nervy girl."

My term for it was the cannonball approach. If you tried everything possible to finesse your way in and it didn't work, you ran to the edge of the pool, jumped and grabbed your knees in your hands, and hoping that you didn't drench anyone who really mattered. At this point, I didn't feel I had a choice. Beyond my suspicions about Kiki, I still needed a quote from her for my article.

The office was on the East Side, in the 40s, on the fourth floor of a fairly small building by Manhattan standards. The reception area was small and modestly decorated, like one of those fake starter apartments in a decorating magazine. There were two slim pale green armchairs, a striped sofa, and some old framed movie posters on the wall, including one with Sean Connery that I'd never even heard of. In addition to working for individual celebrities, publicists often promoted movie launches.

A young, very hunky African American guy sat at the reception desk, thumbing through the *New York Post*. He looked up and smiled politely as I crossed the room to him. Do not be fooled, I told myself. The trappings of the office might seem innocuous, even inviting, but I knew from my short time at *Buzz* that celebrity publicists ate their young.

"May I help you?" the receptionist asked softly. He wore a silver nose stud that sparkled in the light.

"My name is Bailey Weggins. I'm here to see Kiki Bodden."

"Do you have an appointment?"

"Actually, no," I said. "But it's important that I see her today. I need to speak to her about Mona Hodges."

His eyes grew wide, as if I'd just announced that Tom and Nicole had decided to get back together. "Unfortunately, Ms. Bodden doesn't see anyone without an appointment. I—"

"I think she'll want to talk to me. Just tell her that I'm writing an article about Mona's murder for *Buzz* magazine, and since I have to include Ms. Bodden in the article, I want to give her the chance to speak for herself."

He raised his shoulders and exhaled, obviously considering the smartest course of action. "Okay, just a moment," he said. "Why don't you take a seat."

While I retreated to the sofa, he picked up the phone and whispered into it. Just by the expression on his face, I assumed he was talking to Kiki's assistant rather than the head babe herself, and sure enough, he'd barely hung up before a twenty-something blonde in flat-front pants and a button-down shirt strode into the reception room flashing plenty of haughty 'tude.

"What's this all about?" she demanded. I repeated what I'd said to the receptionist.

"Are you telling me there's something about *Kiki* in the story?" she asked indignantly.

"Yes, and I think she'll probably want to comment on it."

"Wait here," she demanded, and strode off, her arms at full swing by her side. The receptionist eyed me with a mixture of trepidation and pity, as if I'd just been pulled over at customs and been told to unzip my bags.

Five minutes later the assistant returned, looking even less pleased than she had before. "Come with me," she declared.

I followed her through a warren of nondescript offices. If it weren't for the rows of movie posters staggered on the walls, I might have assumed I was in a real estate sales office.

Kiki was on the phone, or else pretending to be. She let me stand in the middle of the room for two minutes while she said, "Perfect," eighteen or twenty times to the person on the other end. She was wearing a tight-fitting brown T-shirt and I could see the top part of a leopard-print skirt or pants. On her ears and arms and around her neck were what appeared to be the world's largest supply of pavé diamonds. Being in closer proximity to her today than I had been last week, I could see that she was what Jessie called a "Photoshop blonde." That's a woman who from a distance looks twenty-five, but when you step nearer you see that she's been kind of digitally corrected—there's a ton of makeup over Botoxed and collagened skin. In fact, Kiki's forehead looked smooth enough to ice-skate on.

"Please, have a seat," she said after she'd finally hung up the phone. Her words were polite enough, but her voice was so cold that it almost hurt. "I wouldn't normally let someone just barge in here, but I like to show respect to the members of the press—though unfortunately I don't always get that in return."

"I appreciate it. I know how busy you must be this week with Eva's new CD."

"You're actually very lucky to have caught me. Eva's still here doing press, and I've been out of the office more than I've been in. What is it that you want from me?"

"*Buzz* is running a story on Mona Hodges's murder and I've been trying to reach you. I wanted to double-check some information with you."

"My goodness," she said. "Don't tell me that *Buzz* has added fact-checkers. This must be a new development since Mona's death."

"I'm actually the reporter on the story. You had a conversation at the party with Mona that was witnessed by several people, all of whom said it looked fairly heated. Do you mind telling me what it was about?"

She laughed, though it was really a harsh little bark, the sound a Yorkie might make before it was about to sink its tiny teeth into the mailman's pants leg.

"You want me to tell you about a private conversation I had that night? I can't imagine why you think I'd be willing to share that."

"I'm sure the police have asked you about it."

"Yes, and I have an obligation to be forthcoming with them. But I don't have the same obligation with you. And frankly, I don't see what relevance it has."

"You have a heated exchange with someone less than an hour before she's murdered. That could seem pretty relevant to some people. I have to include the conversation in my article, and I thought you'd like the opportunity to put it in perspective, explain why it really *isn't* relevant."

"First of all, it wasn't all that heated," she said. "If you'd like to see heated, I'll show you heated. And secondly, if I were going to kill Mona Hodges, I wouldn't smash her head in. I'd choose something like rat poison so she'd be guaranteed a slow, agonizing death."

She smiled when she said it, but the rest of her face remained frozen in place. She was keeping her cool with me, but that didn't mean she couldn't have flown off the handle in Mona's office.

"Were you upset with Mona about something the magazine was doing?" I asked.

"Look, if you must know for your story, I'll tell you. I'd heard through the grapevine that *Buzz* was going to give a bad review to Eva's CD. I'd never try to persuade someone to alter a review, but I wanted to register my opinion. I thought what they were doing was unfair, because frankly the album is brilliant."

That was her story, and as they say, she was sticking with it. I decided to try another tack.

"Does the name Jed Crandall ring a bell with you?"

Bingo. Her brows lifted involuntarily and the lower rims of her eyes reddened. A nerve had just been pricked.

"He's a stalkerazzo, isn't he?" she said. "Scum of the earth?"

"That's right. Do you know why he would have arranged to call Mona on the night of the party?"

I could tell just by the way she pulled a breath that she was about to lie to me.

"I haven't a clue," she said. "I make it a point to stay away from scum like that."

"Are you making a generalization about paparazzi, or do you happen to know something uniquely deplorable about Jed Crandall?"

"They're *all* pond scum, but yes, he's particularly despicable from what I hear. It's all about money for these guys. Stoop as low as you can go and then find the highest bidder. Now, if you don't mind, I have work to do." As she said it, the preppie-looking assistant reappeared in the office, as if she'd been hovering outside waiting for a cue.

There was one more question and I had to ask it, though I knew I might get hurled from the office.

"I happened to be on the floor the night of the party, and I heard Eva's husband ask you where you'd been. Do you mind telling me what you told the police when they inquired about your whereabouts that night?"

"There was never a single moment when I wasn't doing my job. Now get out."

The assistant stayed right on my heels as I left, as if I were being tossed from a club where they'd discovered I didn't have a membership. It was a relief to finally be on the street again. I found a café a block away and bought a cappuccino, and though it was almost as muggy inside as out, I parked myself at a table still sprinkled with sugar. Something Kiki had said was gnawing at my brain, yet I couldn't see the shape of it. I pulled my notebook out of my bag and jotted down my conversation with her to the best of my recollection. And then I had it. It was the part about guys like Jed Crandall always trying to find the highest bidder.

Let's say that Nash was absolutely right—that until Crandall made the call to Mona, she'd had no inkling about the information he had. Theoretically, then, she wouldn't have had time to relay to Kiki the ugly secret she now possessed and thus enrage Kiki with it. But what if Mona wasn't the first "bidder" Jed had approached? He may have called other media outlets, and Kiki could have gotten wind of it. Perhaps—oh, and I liked this theory—he'd phoned Kiki herself and given her a chance to make an offer on Eva's behalf. Kiki would have known that buying the information wouldn't have kept it under wraps for long, so she may have refused. Jed might have divulged that Mona was next on his list. When Kiki approached Mona at the party, it may have been to tell her that she knew Jed was going to be calling her and that if she was smart, she wouldn't hear him out. When Mona showed no interest in being cooperative,

Kiki may have followed her back to her office. I desperately needed to arrange another conversation with Jed.

Before I closed my notebook, I thumbed through the pages again, thinking. In light of Nash's revelation, there was one other name I needed to consider seriously as a suspect: Brandon's. Just as Kiki would have a vested interest in protecting Eva's reputation, so would he. I didn't know who his publicist was, but it hardly mattered because there'd be no way she would set up a meeting for me with him. My only hope of coming into contact with him was to make an appearance at a location where I knew he'd be. I'd seen one photo of him in the *Post* this week—out with friends sans Eva one night. He'd probably been left to his own devices while she was fulfilling her diva duties with the press. I rummaged through my purse for my cell phone and called Leo.

"I'm coming back in a few minutes, but I wondered if you'd do me a favor. I'm trying to figure out where Eva Anderson is staying in New York and where that charming husband of hers is hanging out. Do you think some of your paparazzi contacts would know?"

"When do you need the info by?"

"Right away."

"I'll try. But I'm scrambling on last minute stuff Nash wants for this issue."

After I hung up, I left a message for Jed. And I checked my voice mail at work. My heart was skipping like an idiot as I listened to a Swedish television producer ask for an exclusive with me, Landon inquire how I was doing, and some guy I'd met months ago say he had tickets for a Mets game and did I want to go. And then to my utter relief—and I felt so *dumb* being so relieved—there was Beau's voice.

"It's Beau Regan," he said. "Call me on my cell, will you? You know, the one you thought I lost." Then he gave the number.

The thought of seeing him again tonight, the thought of

having sex like that again, made me momentarily light-headed.
I hurriedly hit the digits.

"Hi there," I said. "How are you?"

"I'm barely able to walk. How about you?" he said with
laughter in his voice.

"Ditto."

"I look forward to being in your company again. But I need
to plead for mercy. I realized when I got in here today that I'd
set up dinner with a potential investor tonight, and I hate to
blow him off. Can we do it tomorrow night instead?"

"Uh, sure," I said, my heart sinking. "At least I think so. Let
me call you back after I check my schedule."

"Good. I'll be shooting later, but just leave a message and
I'll call you back."

I felt like hurling my cappuccino cup across the room. Was
he blowing me off? I felt vaguely mortified and pissed at myself. Why in the world had I slept with him? I was now in slut
limbo—just where I deserved to be. So much for Bailey's easy
breezy summer.

When I returned to the office, I was halfway into a funk. At
least Leo had good news for me.

"They're staying at the Four Seasons," he said. "They've
been out to dinner once, but mostly he's been on his own
while she's done press and stuff."

"Has he been going out?"

"Oh yeah," Leo said devilishly. "For two nights in a row he
showed up at Scores—you know, that stripper place?—with a
bunch of guys who looked like their combined IQ was just
over a hundred. Then he totally switched gears and started
going to Soho House each night—you know, that members-
only place? My bet is that Eva gave him a spanking when she
heard he was out enjoying lap dances."

"Thanks, that's great."

The only thing not great about it was that I had no way to
gain entrance to Soho House.

Jessie returned from an appointment moments later, anxious to know how my meeting with Kiki had gone.

"I'm sporting a few singe marks from the experience, but at least she gave me a statement," I said. "Listen, is there any way you can get me into Soho House tonight?"

"Soho House? Why, what's up?"

"Brandon Cott has been hanging there most nights this week, and I'd like to find a way to talk to him. I want to try to pry a quote from him, too, about the night of Mona's murder. It would add a little flavor to my piece."

If Jessie suspected I wasn't telling her the whole story, she didn't let on.

"I think I can pull it off," she declared. "But you've got to give me a little time."

For the next few hours, I stayed focused on my article: I added Kiki's lame explanation of her flare-up with Mona. Since I couldn't add the word *bullshit* in brackets afterward, readers would have to decide for themselves how legitimate it sounded. As I worked, I occasionally stole a glance at Ryan. Though he'd been away from his desk more often than not lately, he was now pounding away intently at his computer.

Late in the afternoon, I also met with the fact-checker to go over his questions on my piece and then clarify details he was confused on. A little before five I phoned Detective Tate, just to be sure the police weren't about to make a critical announcement. He answered my questions warily, as if he still didn't trust me as far as he could throw me. The investigation, he said, was progressing, but there was nothing to report at this moment.

"There are some people at the party who had reason to dislike Mona—Kimberly Chance, Eva Anderson's publicist, Kiki Bodden. And then there's Eva's husband. Do all of them have alibis? Or are any on your suspect list?"

"I'm not at liberty to discuss those details with you at this time."

"And Robby? Are you still considering him a suspect?"

"All I can say is that he hasn't been removed from the list."

"All right, thank you," I said. For nothing, I wanted to add.

"I hope I'm not going to read any surprises in your article when it comes out," Tate said. "I expect if you learn something of interest, you'll contact me."

"Absolutely," I said. Of course, at the moment I was with-holding information that might be incredibly valuable—the whole hermaphrodite angle—but I wasn't going to tell him until I'd verified things. And I would tell the police only after running it by Nash. I also hadn't informed Detective Tate about the attacks. Maybe I should have, but I still had no evidence they were related. Plus, if I told the police about them, they might try to do something to curtail how deeply I'd become involved.

Dinner that night was catered, as it always was on closing night. Jessie had nicknamed this weekly buffet the Starch Bar, because so much of it was loaded with carbs. Despite how bad it was, people always lined up the minute it arrived, as if they hadn't eaten a meal in days, and if you waited and sauntered down thirty minutes late, all that was ever left was the decorative lettuce with the pink tips. As I helped myself to a dish that could be described only as chicken in butter and fat, I couldn't help but think of Beau and the dinner date that wasn't going to be. I hadn't called him back yet to tell him my Tuesday night was free. I decided it was time to play a little tougher to get.

Just before seven I headed back to the coffee station, needy of caffeine. As I turned one of the corridors, my heart nearly stopped. A cleaning cart was parked outside one of the small conference rooms and Katya was standing next to it, emptying a wastebasket. It was like seeing a ghost. I must have startled her, because she spun in my direction. She looked haggard and tired. She also looked terrified.

CHAPTER 15

"Katya," I said, moving toward her, "are you okay?" I could see that the shadows under her eyes were now even deeper and darker than they'd been when I'd visited her.

"Yes. Thank you. I am okay."

"Is this your first day back?"

"Yes," she said without further explanation. She right-ended the wastebasket and stepped into the conference room with it, placing it in a corner. After hesitating for a second, I followed her into the room. She hardly seemed receptive to speaking with me, but I couldn't just ignore how shaken she appeared.

"Are you sure you're ready to come back to work?" I asked. "You don't look all that great."

She pulled the left side of her mouth into a sardonic smile. "I will try not to be offended by that."

"I'm sorry," I said. "What I meant is that you just look so tired and . . . Have you been back to the doctor?"

"Yes. And he said it was possible for me to return. Please, if you'll excuse me. I must get back to work."

"Well, what about changing locations? Working in another building or on another floor, at least?"

"Perhaps. For now, as my brother said, it is important to be strong." There was a trace of bitterness in her tone.

Oh great. André clearly had little empathy for the emotional pain she was experiencing.

"Well, I'll be here most days this week, so just let me know if there's any way I can help, okay?"

"Thank you," she said without making eye contact. She slipped by me, out into the corridor again. As she began to push the cart away, I hurried after her.

"Katya," I said in a whisper, "is there something important that you haven't told anyone? Why do you seem so frightened?"

"I am only frightened about not getting my work done," she said dismissively. "If they fire me, then I will really be in trouble, won't I?"

"The night I went to see you last week? Someone tried to attack me near your apartment building. It might have been a random mugging attempt, but I've wondered if someone was actually lurking near your building, keeping an eye on you. Have you sensed someone is watching you?"

Alarm registered in her eyes, but I couldn't tell if it was because what I'd told her was a revelation or that I was putting too much pressure on her, adding to her anxiety.

"New York City is very dangerous," she said, beginning to push her cart away. "We must all be careful."

She hurried down the corridor, leaving me to watch her back. Did she know something or was she just still distraught from what had happened to her?

As I walked back into the pod, Jessie flashed me the thumbs-up sign.

"Good news," she said. "We're on for Soho House. It'll have to be after nine, though. I won't be done before then."

"That's fine. I won't be, either."

"There's just one hitch. We've got to go with this sort of ditzy girl I know. She's the member."

"Beggars can't be choosers," I said.

Over the next couple of hours, I worked in bursts of activity. My article arrived in first form with about fifty lines of run-over copy, and I made the necessary cuts. I also wrote the pull quotes and the captions for the photos. The main photograph was of Mona out one night at some event, flashbulbs popping behind her, which I think was supposed to suggest that it had been taken at the *Track* party, but I knew it hadn't because of the clothes. There was also a photo of the crowd scene outside the building the night of the murder and one of Mona's office, though mercifully the bloodstain in her carpet had been removed, either with a nuclear-strength carpet cleaner or from the picture itself with the aid of Photoshop. There was also a small photo of me, a head shot that they'd apparently had on file. I could see the point of it, since the story was in first person, yet it made me feel self-conscious. I wondered if I should write a caption like "Too slutty for her own good?" At least there wasn't a shot of Robby. I'd had no choice but to mention briefly in the story that the police had questioned him, but running his picture would have been mortifying for him.

While I waited for my piece to return in the final fit, I picked at a platter of brownies and lemon bars in the conference room. The room had emptied out, and I was alone when Hilary strolled in. She was dressed in pink-and-yellow Lily Pulitzer–style pants and a white tank top, with a ribbed pink sweater knotted around her neck. She looked as if she'd just played eighteen holes of golf and was now making a beeline for a tray of gin and tonics. This was my first sighting of her today. The "Juice Bar" staff worked the phones like crazy on Mondays, their last chance to deliver truly salacious items.

"Well, if it isn't Bailey Weggins, true crime reporter," she said, her voice both sweet and sour.

What I should have replied was, "And if it isn't Hilary Wells, part vixen, part vampire," but I just nodded pleasantly. She clearly didn't like me, yet I wasn't going to try actively to piss her off.

"I guess I should add volleyball champion, too," she said. "That's such an . . . *unusual* talent to have."

"Should I take that as a compliment?"

"Of course. How's your story going, by the way? Am I going to find out who murdered Mona when I read your piece this week?"

"I'm afraid not. If the police have any ideas, they're not saying at the moment."

"But *you* must have some ideas, no? I hear you've been *very* busy looking into things."

"I'm just trying to stay on top of what's going on with the investigation. Can I ask you a question?" It had just occurred to me that if Mona had gotten wind of the hermaphrodite revelation *before* her phone call with Jed, Hilary might know about it.

"Let me guess. You want to know if Brad Pitt is as well hung as everyone says. Unfortunately, I don't think Brad would approve of my sharing that information."

"Blind items," I said, ignoring her. "I know you guys have been running them lately. Had Mona mentioned that she hoped to run one on Eva?"

Her eyes widened and the edges of her mouth curled up almost imperceptibly. I might have been wrong, but it didn't seem to be a look that said, "How do *you* know?" It was one that said, "What do you know that I don't?"

"Maybe if you'd be more specific, I could help you," she said. Man, she was cagey.

"Unfortunately, I don't have much more to go on." I was afraid if I led her any more, it might get back to Nash that I was stirring up interest in Eva when he'd asked me to keep my trap shut. Plus, I was pretty sure she didn't know what I was talking about.

"Well, if you get any more, do tell. Maybe I could be of more assistance."

"Sure, thanks," I said, beginning my retreat. "Talk to you later."

I headed to my desk with my brownie and nibbled at it as I leafed through almost a week's worth of newspapers that I'd saved. I wanted to be sure before my article closed that there was nothing of importance I'd overlooked.

At around eight-thirty I walked over to Nash's office, needing to make certain he didn't have any final questions. He was standing in the middle of the room with the art director, staring at about ten variations of this week's cover that were strewn across his small round table.

"Sorry to interrupt," I said, backing out of the doorway. "I just wanted to touch base with you before I took off for the night."

"Here, take a look," he said, beckoning me back into the room. I crossed to the table and stood with him and the art director, inspecting the batch of covers.

Five or so of the covers featured two hot young male stars in a split-screen effect, but there were others with three or four guys and then one with just a single photo and lots of little pictures ringed around it. The headline on all of them was HOLLY-WOOD LOVE RATS. Underneath, there was a deck that announced, "Former girlfriends and wives reveal how these guys cheated, lied, broke their hearts—and then begged to be taken back."

But obviously what Nash had wanted me to see was what's called the roof, the big bar that runs above the logo. One-half of it was devoted to Jessica Simpson and the other half to Mona. The headline read, BUZZ EDITOR MURDERED IN OFFICE, and underneath that was, "The Inside Story." The little head shot they'd included of Mona showed her more in profile, so that you really couldn't tell she'd been wall-eyed.

"It just seems surreal," I said. "Mona on the cover of her own magazine. But I like the way you set it up. It works."

"Wanna vote on your favorite love rat cover?" Nash asked with a grin.

"I like the split-screen one—with the two heads. How about you?"

"Yeah, that's what I'm leaning toward," he said, arching his back in a stretch. He seemed like the cock of the walk, totally thrilled to be calling the shots.

"I'll let you two get back to work," I said. "The final on my piece should be coming through any second, and then I'd like to head out if it's all right with you. There's a lead I want to pursue downtown for the follow-up on my story."

He lifted one eyebrow. "Do tell."

"It's nothing concrete, and it may not amount to anything. But I need to check it out. I'll have my cell phone on, so if you have any questions on my piece, just call me. I can come back if you want me to."

"I'll call if I need you," he said. "One of the first things I want to do is straighten out the hours here."

"Great. Oh, by the way," I said, trying to sound real casual. "How did the profile turn out? Ryan's piece?"

"It's good. It will be a nice companion piece to yours. He's working on a follow-up, too, for next week."

"A follow-up to his *profile*?"

"Yeah, he says he's got some good stuff he couldn't fit into his story this week. We'll have to wait and see what it amounts to."

I wondered, too, what could possibly make up a part two of a profile—"Mona Hodges: The Early Years"?

In the end the final didn't come through until nine-fifteen, and it was nine forty-five by the time Jessie and I were finally in a cab barreling downtown. It was hot again, and the driver had the AC cranked up so high, I was soon shivering.

"Look, I need to talk to you about something," Jessie said after giving the driver the address of her friend. "I don't think you're going to like it."

"Is it about the sauna?" I asked, thinking she may have discovered something.

"No, it's Ryan. I think he may be trying to horn in on your territory."

"How do you mean?" I asked, alarmed.

"When you were out of the office earlier, ambushing Kiki, he was on the phone to some pal of his, and he was trying to keep his voice real low and secretive. But I heard him say, 'Big, man. It's gonna be really big.' Like he's sitting on the scoop of the century."

"But that might relate to something totally different from the Mona story."

"That's what I thought at the time. But then tonight, when I was having dinner, I sat with that guy Harrison—you know, the art guy you were looking for last week. I know he's kind of a loser, but he's really into music and I was picking his brain. At one point we started talking about Mona's murder and he mentioned that you'd interviewed him about it. And then he mentioned that *Ryan* had interviewed him, too. I almost spat out my chicken."

"Shit," I said. "Did Harrison say what questions Ryan asked him?"

"All about the night of the murder. He wanted to know exactly when Harrison left and what was happening then. Of course, Harrison just thinks you two are doing some sort of team coverage."

As the city flew by us, I could feel my stomach start to prick with anxiety. In the last few days, Ryan had acted so weirdly that I'd wondered if he might be the killer, if he'd doubled back from the party and confronted Mona on some matter, knowing that she was at her desk. I thought he'd been trying to find out what I'd dug up on the case. But maybe the reason for his odd behavior toward me was that he had made a discovery about the murder and was going to trump me.

What could he have stumbled on? When I was quizzing

him on Friday, he'd seemed to remember a key detail—there'd been that telltale flicker in his eyes. But he'd refused to come clean. Had he recalled something Mona said to him before going into her office to take the call from Jed? Or something he saw or heard, which, after chatting with me, suddenly seemed significant, something that might identify the killer? I remembered what I had just asked him: Had he seen anyone on his way to the back door to *Track*?

"What are you going to do?" Jessie asked, pulling me from my thoughts.

"There's not much I *can* do. I'm not going to garner any sympathy from Nash if I go charging into his office and announce that Ryan's on my turf. Nash isn't going to care where the scoop came from as long as he has it. Is there anything else you can think of that might indicate what Ryan's up to? My copy of the invitation list for the party was lifted off my desk one day last week. I bet Ryan took it."

"It wouldn't surprise me. The only other thing I can think of is that he's seemed hyperinterested in anything you've been working on. Like today, when you were talking to Leo about Brandon, you had your back to him but I could tell that he was eavesdropping."

"*Great.*"

"I've got one other interesting tidbit, though it's totally unrelated. Remember how Hilary was out at Dicker's house early, ahead of the bus? Guess who she probably hitched a ride with?"

"Count Dracula?"

"Nash."

"*No.* How did you find this out?"

"Like I promised, I've been doing a little snooping about events on Saturday. In the process I found out that Hilary unexpectedly ended up taking the bus *back* with everyone. Which means that her ride fell apart. Then I heard that Nash was apparently asked to hang around for dinner in East Hampton with Dicker. My guess is that Nash gave her the ride, and then when he had to stay, she was forced to find other transportation. I bet she was pissed. She's not exactly the Peter Pan Coach Tours type."

"So do you think he's screwing her?"

"Oh please. They're probably doing it on his desk after everyone leaves. I can just hear her shouting out her Cock Nazi orders to him: 'Not so hard, Nash. You're driving my ass into the stapler.'"

What did that reflect about Nash's lingering hands on me? I wondered. Was he just being his naturally flirty self with me? Or was he interested in additional office conquests? And what evil thoughts had wiggled their way through Hilary's brain after she had seen me exiting the bar with Nash? I remembered the look of disdain on her face when Nash had congratulated me after the volleyball game. Was it *Hilary* who had barricaded me in the sauna—just for the pleasure of seeing me sweat, so to speak? At the time I'd considered that the sauna incident might be only a prank, but more recently I'd convinced myself it was someone warning me away from investigating Mona's murder. Now I had to rethink things again.

We were almost at Jessie's friend's building, so I let the subject drop. The girl turned out to be a total dingbat, a skinny rich thing with hair bleached the color of sunlight and fake boobs so hard that they looked like they hurt. When she opened her mouth, she made Nicole Richie sound smart. While the chick was rifling through her Birkin bag, I shot Jessie a look of dismay and she offered an expression that said, "You wanted to get in, didn't you?"

I'd certainly heard of Soho House, but I'd never had the chance to go before. It was a hip, exlusive private club on 14th and Ninth, at the very northern end of the meatpacking district. We checked in at a small reception desk on the ground floor and then took the elevator up to the lounge. It was really a series of glass-walled rooms, including a sleek bar decorated in black and gray, and lights with big red lampshades, and then smaller rooms with couches and tables. One had a billiards table.

Jessie's friend tore away from us as soon as we walked in the door, and the two of us grabbed seats at the bar. We let our eyes roam, checking out the smaller adjoining rooms, but there was no sign of Brandon. I hoped I hadn't dragged Jessie down there for nothing.

We were on our second round of drinks when Jessie's amber eyes flickered.

"The eagle's landed," she said, pointing with her chin. "Over there on the couch."

I turned my head discreetly. In one of the smaller rooms just beyond us, Brandon was flopping down on a couch. He was dressed in jeans and a shiny black shirt, surrounded by a posse of six or seven guys, none older than thirty, and one beefy enough to be a bodyguard. The good news was that they didn't look as though they'd be leaving anytime soon. The bad news was that I couldn't imagine how we were going to insinuate ourselves into the group.

"Looks pretty impenetrable," I said, glancing back at Jessie.

"We may be in luck, though," she told me. "See the guy in the red shirt? He plays one of the other FBI guys on the show. He's a friend of a friend, and I think he might remember me."

"Are you just going to walk over to him?"

"No, they won't like that. But hopefully he'll have to hit the head at some point, and I can grab him."

For fifteen minutes we waited. One of the other guys in the posse stood up and headed past us. Jessie tugged at her tank top so more of her boobs were showing and flashed him a coy smile. But he simply checked out her chest and kept on moving.

"That's the kind of guy who doesn't stop for a B cup," she said in disgust.

Finally we saw the red-shirt guy rise from his chair. He stretched, yawned, and then made his way toward the main room. His head swiveled back and forth, and it was pretty clear that he was looking for action.

"*Tom?*" Jessie called out when he was ten feet away from us. "It's me, Jessie."

"Hey, what's happening?" he said, striding toward us and giving her a hug. He was about five ten, cute in a generic way, with one of those supershort haircuts that's peaked in front and teeth that looked as if they had never met a whitening strip they didn't like.

"Not much. This is a friend of mine, Bailey Weggins."

"Hey," he exclaimed again, pumping my hand. "Nice to meet you."

"Congratulations on the show," she said. "You're absolutely *awesome* on it."

"Well, it's not like I'm the star or anything. But like my manager says, it's a start. And the show's a surprise hit, didya hear?"

"I've heard, yes."

"Look, you wanna join us over there? I mean, I'm with Brandon, so you'll have to be cool about it, but I think I can trust you not to ask for the dude's autograph or anything."

"We'd love to join you," Jessie said. "And don't worry. We'll behave."

Tom's face darkened. "Hey, someone told me you went over to one of those rags a while ago. You're not still there, are you?"

"No, no, I'm not with them anymore. I'm doing freelance PR work now, for a men's fashion designer. So is Bailey."

"Wow. Can you get me any shit?"

"Of course. You can come by the showroom."

"Great. So, okay, why don't you come over, then?"

I stood up, in awe of Jessie's lying skills. I fibbed to get my way in the door for stories, but my style didn't hold a candle to hers.

We followed Tom to the little enclave, where, unfortunately, there were now two blond babes seated in the mix. We were introduced around as fashion girls, and as Brandon took my hand to shake it, I was struck again by the disproportional size of his head. It reminded me of those rubber animal heads that you put on the eraser end of a pencil. He stared hard at me. I didn't think he could possibly remember me from the other night because he'd never glanced in my direction. He was probably just naturally wary of strangers edging into his camp.

The guys asked a few perfunctory questions about our jobs, while the other two girls eyed us suspiciously. They were all glammed up in tight bustiers and three-hundred-dollar jeans. Before long the guys were dominating the conversation, swapping stories about shooting the show and the hijinks of all involved. We had to listen to one tale about how a cast mate had put a SMALL PENIS ON BOARD bumper sticker on the producer's car and the fact that no amount of scraping could take the thing off. In addition to Tom, one of the other guys in the group apparently had a small role on the show; another turned out to be Brandon's stunt double. The guy I'd thought might be a bodyguard never said much at all and tossed down Sprites, which seemed to confirm my hunch.

While most of the guys seemed happy as clams to be hanging with a *star,* Brandon himself looked bored and restless. He kept swiping his fingers through his thick, dark hair or scanning the room, and every minute or so he'd blow out his breath in a big blast. He was like a Doberman who'd been tethered to the garage with a seven-foot chain. Only when there was a burst of laughter would he be drawn momentarily back into the conversation.

I felt myself growing restless, too. I needed to talk to Brandon, but I couldn't figure out any easy way to strike up a conversation. He was four bodies away from me, and he wasn't exactly Mr. Inclusive. Suddenly, the guy to his left went off to shoot pool, leaving an empty space on the sofa, but before you could say "star fucker," one of the two blondes secured his spot. She started jabbering away at Brandon, and though he eyed her as if she were a pet monkey husking peanuts on someone's shoulder, she had at least managed to grab his attention.

I whispered to Jessie that I was going to hit the restroom. I didn't really need to pee. I was just hoping that when I returned, I could sit in a different place, a spot closer to Brandon. That was going to be my only shot at talking to him.

As I stood up, two other people broke into our little circle: a woman in a dress so short that you could see her butt crack and a guy dressed in skintight white pants and shoes with the word *Dolce* on one and *Gabbana* on the other.

"Brandon," the guy gushed, thrusting out his hand. "It's Eddie. I did the makeup on that movie you shot in Toronto last year. *Saber Force*, remember?"

In the bathroom, I splashed cool water on my face and reapplied bronzer and gloss. I looked tired and I felt it. While I'd been trying to obtain a read on Eva's husband, I'd also been brooding about the situation with Ryan. What if he had actually stumbled onto some major clue about the murder and was about to go to Nash with it? That would be rich, wouldn't it? *Buzz* hires this hot crime writer named Bailey Weggins, and one of her first major assignments is reporting on the death of the editor in chief. Except the other person on staff, who generally files stories on stuff like the latest wedding of Nick Cage, scoops her.

More important, though, Ryan might be hoarding information that could help clear Robby. If that was true, he was not only keeping Robby in limbo, he was putting himself in danger.

Fueling my foul mood was the Beau situation. As it turned out, I wouldn't have been able to have dinner with him tonight anyway. But it bugged me that he'd blown me off, even with an excuse that might have been legit. I knew I should call him. After all, I'd said I would. But I felt too annoyed to. If he really wanted to see me, he could damn well work a little harder.

I pushed open the door from the ladies' room into the small hallway. Holding up the wall was Brandon's beefy bodyguard. One second later, Brandon blasted out of the restroom, the door swinging wildly behind him.

He nodded to the bodyguard, some private signal that for all I knew meant, "Man, it felt good to whiz." Then he trained his eyes on me.

"You look familiar," he said bluntly. I was standing so close to him that I could see he had an underground mole on his chin that raised the skin like a welt.

"Oh yeah?" I said, a loud *Uh-oh* running through my mind. "We've never met before."

"But I've seen you."

"It might have been at the *Track* party for your wife last week. I was there, too."

"Is that right?" he asked warily.

"Pretty amazing what happened, isn't it? I mean the murder."

"Yeah," he said. "Score one for the good guys."

So Brandon had liked Mona about as much as Kiki had.

With that he nodded again to the beefy guy and walked past me. I followed them with my eyes. To my surprise, they didn't turn in the direction of the table but instead walked briskly through the room and out the front door of the lounge.

Unfortunately, I couldn't score one for *me*. I'd finally snared a chance to talk to Brandon, but I'd learned nothing more than I had when I'd been sitting at the table, watching his boredom swell like a bruise.

As I maneuvered my way back through the chicly dressed crowd toward the table, I saw that neither Jessie nor Tom was there. I heard Jessie's voice call my name, and I turned to see both her and Tom standing at the bar.

"So Brandon split," I said. "I hope we weren't too dull for him."

"Nah, it wasn't you," Tom acknowledged. "It was that makeup guy who barged in. Brandon hates him."

"I know why," Jessie said. "I was one of three people who saw that movie, and it looked like Brandon was wearing false eyelashes in it."

"Nah, that's not it," said Tom. "Gay dudes just creep him out. I like Brandon, but he's sort of a redneck. He's the kind of guy who calls gays pansies."

And then something hit me with the force of a volleyball to the side of my head. As I'd considered Brandon as a suspect, I'd been focused on the idea of him trying to protect Eva's career and thus indirectly his own. But what if his reaction had been even more visceral than that? What if he had only recently learned of Eva's condition? Maybe she'd been forced to reveal it when she knew the information was about to surface. If Brandon hated gays, it meant that he was rigid and intolerant, and therefore discovering Eva's situation—knowing that he'd been making love to someone with ambiguous sexuality— would have thrown him into a tailspin. He wouldn't have wanted the world to know.

Of course, killing Mona wouldn't have stopped the information from coming out, because Jed would have peddled it elsewhere. But killing Mona hadn't been a rational act. It was the end point of a conversation that got out of hand.

With nothing to keep me at Soho House, I decided to split. Jessie announced she was going to wait around for her friend but encouraged me to go ahead. I grabbed a cab in front of the club. Riding uptown, I found two voice messages on my cell phone, which I'd never heard ring over the din in the lounge. The first call was from Nash, saying there was no need for me to come in. The second was from my good friend Jed Crandall, returning my call. It sounded as if he were in a bar packed with people.

I called Nash back immediately, just so he'd know I'd received the message and didn't look as if I were shirking any responsibilities. Then I tried Jed. A song by what sounded like Creedence Clearwater Revival nearly drowned out his voice, making it clear he hadn't moved far since he'd phoned me.

"Thanks for getting back to me," I shouted.

"What's going on? Your boss won't return my calls."

"Where are you, anyway? The Hudson?"

"No, I'm downtown. At the Cedar Tavern." That was on University Place, three blocks from me.

"I'm actually headed that way. Why don't I stop by and we can chat?"

"I'm with a whole bunch of people."

"It won't take long."

He must have pulled the phone away from his ear, because for a few seconds all I heard was a pounding mix of music and people screaming to be heard.

"Okay," he said, returning. "I'm at the bar. But you better be quick because I'm not staying much longer."

I was there within five minutes. As promised, he was standing at the bar, wearing a grubby T-shirt and swigging a beer. The place was mobbed, and it was hard to tell who was with him and who was just packed in nearby.

"So what's the deal?" he yelled, once again not even bothering to ask if I'd like a drink. "Does your boss want the info or not?"

"Well, I spoke to him on your behalf, but there's a hitch."

"Oh yeah?" he asked, pausing midway in the air with his Bud bottle. "And what would that be?"

"We're not the first people you've offered the info to, are we?"

"What are you talking about?" he asked, clearly pissed.

"You talked to other people."

"No way. I haven't offered this to any other publication."

"I didn't mean another publication. You told Kiki about it, didn't you?" It was a long shot, but I figured there was no harm in running with it and seeing how far I got. The worst that could happen was that he'd deny it. But he didn't.

"Yeah, I told her," he admitted. "But so what?"

CHAPTER 16

Even though this was the information I'd been looking for, hearing it still left me stunned.

"So *what?*" I asked. "You made it sound as if you were offering an exclusive, but in truth you've staged a bidding war."

"That's not true," he scoffed. "I figured it was only fair to give Kiki the right of first refusal. I don't know *why.* That chick is the biggest bitch in the universe. But she wasn't interested in it anyway, so I went to Mona."

What I desperately wanted to ask was whether or not he'd tipped Kiki off to the fact that he would be taking the information to Mona next, but I was afraid if I did, Jed would put two and two together. He'd realize that I didn't give a rat's ass about a bidding war, that I was instead trying to figure out if Kiki had had a reason to be enraged with Mona. And he'd waste no time trying to make a buck off *that.*

"Okay, I'm going to take your word for that," I said quickly, trying not to allow him any time to think. "I'll go back to Nash with what you told me and maybe he'll give you a call."

"He's got two more days," Jed said. "Then I'm going else-where."

It was after midnight when I left the bar, and though University Place was still bustling with people, my block on 9th looked deserted, and my building was all the way down at the other end. I told myself to just walk quickly and keep my eyes peeled, but I froze on the sidewalk, unable to budge. After everything that had happened over the past few days, I just didn't feel comfortable trouncing down there alone in the dark. Instead I walked down to 8th, an always busy street, and then north to my building.

There was a note under my door from Landon, asking if I wanted to have a drink tonight, so I wrote him a note back, suggesting coffee in the morning, and slipped it under his door. Feeling ragged, I poured myself a glass of milk and curled up on the couch. I'd come home tonight with one key piece of information and a couple of hunches. The information: Kiki had known there was potentially damaging information about Eva on the open market. The hunches: The argument between Mona and Kiki at the party might very well have involved that information. Kiki may have learned or guessed that Jed was running to Mona with it and tried to pressure Mona into turning down Jed's offer. When Mona didn't acquiesce, Kiki (perhaps even at Eva's insistence) may have followed Mona to her office and tried to bully her—and the bullying turned deadly. Other hunch: It was possible that Brandon only recently learned of Eva's secret, and he would have been desperate to prevent it from surfacing in the press. *He* may have followed Mona to her office, attacked her, and then left the party with the excuse that he was bored. He'd accused Kiki of being missing in action for part of the party, but I recalled that she'd also questioned *his* whereabouts.

So besides Kimberly, there were now two other party guests with excellent motives to have followed Mona to her office.

But a question dogged me. Did any of this relate to the "something big" that Ryan had whispered about to a friend? It was hard for me to figure out how he could have ended up with this. And if this *wasn't* the something big, what was?

As I sat in the half darkness mulling all of this over, my phone rang, making me jump.

"So is this part of the Bailey Weggins summer plan?" Beau asked in amusement. "Have her way with a man and then disappear?"

"What do you mean?" I asked.

"I'm sitting through one of the most boring dinners in my life, listening to this investor explain why he thinks *The Shawshank Redemption* is the greatest film of all time, and I just keep hoping you'll call and tell me you can have dinner tomorrow. But nothing."

"I'm sorry. I was going to call you. I ended up working later than I thought tonight, and then I went out to track down a lead. I actually just got home."

"How's your story?"

"It turned out okay, I think. I wrote it in the first person, and that's sort of weird. I used to work with this great old guy at the *Times Union* in Albany, and he always said that the worst thing a reporter could do with a story—after making it up, of course—was to put himself in it. I'm afraid after the issue comes out that this guy is going to get in his old burgundy Impala, drive down the New York State Thruway, and take me over his knee."

"You better not put ideas like that in my mind. I'll have a hard time falling asleep."

"If you could see this guy, the image would give you nightmares. So other than having to listen to a tribute to *The Shawshank Redemption*, how did the dinner go? Did you come away with any money?"

"I think so. This guy is so loaded he's just looking for

places to park his dough. Of course, I plan to blow his mind with a huge return on his investment."

"Then it's a good thing you went through with the dinner."

"In one sense, yes. So what about tomorrow night?"

I hesitated for a second. Should I hold back just a little? Make him wait until, let's say, Thursday or Saturday so that I'd seem less accessible? But *why*? I'd told myself I wanted a fling, and this was what a fling was all about: fast, fun, no machinations, no overthinking. And I could use another break from pondering Mona's murder and agonizing about who might be stalking me.

"Sure, tomorrow night is fine."

"Great. Seven-thirty okay?"

"Sounds good."

"I'll call you tomorrow. Would you like me to pick you up?"

"No, just leave word about the restaurant and I'll meet you there. I may have a few things to take care of."

That's cute, Bailey. Try throwing in a little mystery *now,* after you've managed to come across as the easiest, most transparent girl in New York City.

Once I climbed into bed, I let my mind drift back to last night with Beau. After he'd blown me off for dinner, I'd forced myself not to go there, but now that he'd redeemed himself, I luxuriated in the memory of our delicious encounter and fantasized what the next one would be like.

In the morning, there was another note from Landon under my door, suggesting breakfast on his terrace whenever I so desired since he wasn't working today. I hadn't dragged myself out of bed until eight-thirty, and when I rapped on his door, I felt ready to mainline caffeine.

"Wow, it smells unbelievable in here," I said as I inhaled an intoxicating blend of French toast and fresh oranges.

"I know how much you need your nourishment when you're tracking down killers. Why don't you head out to the terrace and I'll be right along. There's fresh-squeezed orange juice already out there."

The *Times* had predicted it would hit ninety today, but the morning was surprisingly comfortable. I sat at the table and watched a steady stream of silver jets flying over the city and twinkling in a clear blue sky. A few minutes later, Landon emerged with a tray heaped with breakfast food.

"I thought I heard you come in last night," he said. "It was pretty late, no?"

"Yeah, I was out following leads in bars all over Manhattan. By the time I finished, I was practically crawling on all fours in fatigue."

"So what's happening? Every day there's a different tantalizing headline in the *Post* about the murder, but then they don't seem to *know* anything."

"As far as I can tell, the police don't have a suspect yet. They apparently still have Robby in mind for it, but fortunately they haven't done anything about it yet."

"And what about you? Any ideas?"

"Until this weekend I assumed I was tracking a lot of the same stuff they were, though of course at least a day or two behind them. But I may have stumbled onto something they're not aware of."

I shared what I'd learned about Eva, as well as the fact that Nash had requested that I remain mum about it.

"My God, what a revelation," he exclaimed. "Maybe that explains why *I* find her so attractive. So what are you going to do? You don't want to piss off your boss, do you?"

"No, but I've got a moral dilemma on my hands. I promised Nash that I'd keep the information under my hat when it appeared Kiki probably hadn't known about it. But she *did* know, and even if Jed didn't tell her he was going to Mona with the information, I'm sure she figured he would get to Mona soon enough. The night of the party she may have tested the waters with Mona and somehow learned that Mona was going to be speaking to Jed. She could have slipped out of the party, found Mona's office, and confronted her about it. Mona would have just finished her call with Jed, and if she'd been in the dark before, she wasn't any longer. When Mona refused to assure Kiki that she wasn't going to run the item, Kiki flew into a frenzy and smashed Mona over the head."

"Your money's on Kiki, then?"

"Not necessarily, because there are still some other possibilities."

"Of course. Why am I not surprised?"

"I think Eva's husband is another viable suspect. Now that I've met him, I can see that he's the kind of guy who would have been totally humiliated if this information saw the light of day. He could have gotten wind of what was going on through Kiki and gone down to Mona's office himself."

"What about Eva? She had the *most* to lose."

"She was never out of sight, apparently."

"Well, at least it means you're not working with some psychopath at *Buzz*. There has to be small comfort in that."

"Unfortunately, I *may* be working with a psycho." In between bites of French toast, I told him about what had transpired in Dicker's clubhouse.

"Well then, doesn't that imply the killer is someone you work with and not this Kookie woman or Brandon?"

"So far I haven't found anyone on staff with a motive. As much as people disliked Mona, no one seems to have had reason to be in a rage that night—except Robby, and I'm not buying that one. I'm thinking that the sauna incident may have been a sick prank. There's another writer at *Buzz* named Ryan who's pursuing some big lead on Mona's murder and may have wanted to scare me off the story. And there's another chick who may be involved with Nash and seems to think I'm competition. I keep wondering if it was either of them."

"How dreadful. Is there anything you can do?"

"Just be careful. And of course, I have to keep in mind that it might *not* have been a prank. Who's to say that Kiki or Brandon—or Kimberly, for that matter—didn't hire someone to try to scare me?"

"My head is spinning just trying to keep track of it all."

"I know. And the biggest problem is that I'm stuck in terms of what to do next."

Landon returned to the apartment to fetch more coffee, and I stood up and walked to the railing. I had time for half a mug more, and then I needed to fly.

"I've been thinking about that story you told me about your brother, Cameron," Landon said as he returned.

"You mean the girls in the red coats?"

"Yes. I actually had something similar happen to me yesterday, though it's not nearly as enchanting a story. I was walking across the street from a supermarket. Suddenly I noticed an altercation out front. There were two boys, both Hispanic, and a very handsome older-looking woman, about seventy. She was carrying a plastic shopping bag and the boys were yanking on it. I realized that they were attempting to mug her."

"In broad daylight?"

"It was about seven o'clock. Now I knew better than to attempt a citizen's arrest, but I yelled out, 'Stop! Get away from her!' And then the most amazing thing happened. The boys turned and they were both wearing these big green aprons. And they called out to me that she had shoplifted from their store and they were trying to get the things back."

"Wow, just what your aunt said. An optical confusion."

"I know. And I felt so guilty for having immediately assumed the boys were hooligans."

I gulped the last of my coffee, gave Landon a hug, and tore out of there. I realized as I let myself back into my apartment that I hadn't shared anything with him about Beau. And there was a simple reason for that. So far, it had been nothing more than a one-night stand. Hell, as far as I knew, he might call and try to get out of *this* dinner, too. There was no reason to expend energy describing him at this stage of the game.

My section of the pod was empty when I arrived, though there were other people in the general vicinity. People seemed sluggish from the close, almost moody, as if the revved-up pace of shipping the issue yesterday had distracted them from the funk they were in following the murder, and now they were knee-deep in it again.

As I'd sat on the subway rocketing north, I'd considered how I was going to handle my dilemma with Nash today. I'd toyed with a couple of different options, but I knew there was only one way to proceed. I had to tell Nash what I'd learned about Kiki and urge him to go to the police with the information. I certainly didn't want to imply, "Or I will": My job was important to me, even more so now that the person in charge wasn't a she-devil. I just hoped Nash would realize that he now had no choice but to speak up.

Since Nash wasn't in yet, I used the time to clean up the mess on my desk and race through e-mail, which I was way behind on. One of the deputy editors had sent me a note saying that a female soap star I had never heard of had just learned that her husband was a bigamist and was keeping a wife and child in Virginia, and maybe there was something in it for us. Under the Mona formula, an A-level celebrity committing a B-level crime was worth covering, as was a B-level celeb committing an A-level crime. But a C-level celeb with an infraction that was only a B would never have seen the light of day. I wondered if the formula would change under Nash.

He sauntered in actually just as this question was flashing across my mind. There was none of that hurricane-making-landfall feeling to his arrival that there always had been with Mona. He nodded at people, complimented somebody on a caption from yesterday, and greeted his assistant, Lee, with a smile. He looked confident, even cocky, thrilled to death with his new job. Cat had said he lacked vision as an editor, but he clearly didn't subscribe to that theory.

I gave him a few minutes to get settled and then sauntered into his office. I felt nervous, consumed by that weird free-floating anxiety you experience when you are sitting in your gyno's reception area before your appointment, flipping through a four-month-old copy of *Time* magazine that has a cover story on global warming. But I didn't have a choice. I needed to do this.

"Hey, Nash, have you got a minute?" I asked.

"Yeah, come in. I'm meeting with someone at ten-thirty, but I can spare a few minutes."

"I came across some important information last night, and I wanted to share it."

He'd been multitasking when I first spoke to him, thumbing through pink phone slips, and now he slowly raised his head and eyed me expectantly.

"What have you got?" he said.

"I know Jed led you to believe that Kiki didn't know about his bombshell, but she did," I said. "And my guess is that she knew he'd either told Mona or was about to."

"Who told you that?" he asked, his expression suddenly cross. I had to be careful how I presented my information to Nash. I didn't want him to think I'd been going behind his back, even though I had.

"When I had my talk with Kiki, she made a comment I found interesting and then I confirmed something with Jed and I put a few things together, and it's pretty clear that Kiki knew that Mona would be receiving the hermaphrodite tip," I said.

He eyed me warily, smart enough to be suspicious of a sentence that ran on that long.

"Do you really think Kiki could have killed Mona?" he asked eventually.

"*Someone* killed her, and there's an excellent chance it was someone at the party that night," I said. "So the next question is who had a motive. Kiki had one. So, for that matter, did Eva's husband. When I arrived on the floor that night, Brandon was attempting to bolt the party. Maybe *he* was the one who had the fateful confrontation with Mona. I think we have to consider the two of them as viable suspects."

"Well then, we don't have any choice but to go to the police, do we?"

"Agreed," I said, relieved. "I've been writing about crime long enough to know that there's a real danger in trying to keep important information from the cops. It always comes back to haunt you."

"Tell you what, though," said Nash. "I want to be able to let Dicker know what's going on. Let me try to grab him this morning, and as soon as I've given him the heads-up on all of this, I'll call this guy Tate."

"Fine," I said, smiling. I wasn't completely comfortable with Nash stalling for a few more hours, but I wasn't going to buck it as long as he notified the cops sometime today. I turned, ready to leave.

"You know what this means, then, don't you?" Nash said. I spun back in his direction. "If it's true, it means that Mona died because of her job, because of some stupid gossip item. How fucking insane is that?"

"I know. And Jed will find someone else to give the information to anyway."

"You know—" He caught himself and shook his head, as if he'd just found a good reason to hold off on what he'd been about to say.

"What?" I asked.

"Ryan . . . No, never mind."

"What?" I asked again, feeling a big squirt of adrenaline.

"No, it's nothing. I'm just thinking out loud. I'll catch up with you later, okay?"

Damn! I shouted to myself. Ryan had said something to

him, dropped a hint. Nash wasn't going to spill, though. And I didn't think it would be wise to beg.

I turned around again, and things went from bad to worse: Hilary was standing in the doorway.

"I've got a 'Juice Bar' issue to discuss with you," she said to Nash, ignoring me for the moment.

"Unless it involves a potential lawsuit, it's got to wait," he told her brusquely. Ouch. She tried not to look offended, but I could tell his remark had smarted.

"Cute pants," she said to me as we exited the room side by side.

Except they weren't, and she knew it. They were a pair that poofed out a little too much around the thighs, but they were the only clean thing I had in my closet, other than the dress I would be wearing to dinner.

"Good morning, Hilary," was all I said in reply.

As I returned to my desk, my phone was ringing, and I made a dash for it. To my surprise, Robby was on the other end. As he said my name, I heard levity in his voice.

"What's up?" I asked.

"I've got some great news—I *think*. It looks like I may be in the clear."

"Oh, Robby, that's fantastic," I said, feeling a rush of absolute relief. "Do they have a suspect?" It seemed crass to immediately ask that question, but I couldn't contain myself.

"That I don't know," he said. "But they found me on the film from the security camera in the lobby, and apparently I was exiting the building with the letters in my hand not all that long after Mona was talking on the phone. That doesn't exactly give me time to have gone into her office and killed her. Plus, the weapon is apparently missing and I wasn't wearing a jacket, so it's pretty clear I didn't have it with me. They're still being a little cagey with my lawyer—I think they can't bear to give me up as a suspect—but we hope to learn more details later today."

"I'm just so happy to hear all this. And I'll definitely include it in the follow-up story. The more people who know you've been officially cleared, the better. Then you won't have some cloud hanging over you."

We agreed to meet in person within the next day or two so he could take me up-to-date on everything that had happened. After I hung up, I left a message for Tate to call me so I could hear any "official" statement from him.

I should have been ecstatic as I leaned back in my desk chair. Not only was Robby innocent as I'd always hoped, prayed, and mostly believed, but also the police were now going to be off his back. Yet I felt myself being swallowed up by a weird blue mood. It was due in part, I thought, to the fact that I was stalled as far as the story was concerned. Several possible suspects were staring me in the face, but I had no idea how to jump to the next level and uncover additional information about them.

Of course, on one level there wasn't the same degree of urgency to learn the truth that there had been five minutes ago—before Robby had broken his news to me—yet I still had to discover who the murderer was. I'd found Mona, after all, and I wanted answers. Plus, there was a possibility the murderer was stalking me and wouldn't stop until he or she was apprehended. And after everything that had happened so far, I couldn't stand the thought of Ryan just swooping in and breaking the case wide open with whatever secret he'd dug up. It made me nervous, and more than a little jealous.

I glanced up from my desk. More and more people had drifted in, but Ryan's desk was still empty. From my limited experience, he generally didn't show his face on Tuesday mornings. I wondered if he was still asleep or charging around town chasing down information that would confirm whatever freakin' theory he had.

I reached under my desk for my tote bag and dug out the file with the party invitation list, which I'd been carrying around with me ever since last week. There was a small section at the end that listed the fifteen or so *Track* staffers who had gone to the party. Using the directory on the computer, I found their extensions and jotted them down. With everything on my plate last week there'd been no time to talk to them. What I *could* do now was call them and quiz them about Kiki's and Brandon's whereabouts at the party.

Over the next hour, I managed to speak with most of them. Because I didn't want to shoot off any red flares, I told those I did reach that I was doing a follow-up story that focused on the impact of Mona's death on the celebrity world, and I wanted some additional information about the party. I was looking for color, I told them, tidbits about the night. I backed into questions about Kiki and Brandon by first inquiring about the atmosphere that night, Eva's entourage, and so on. "How did Brandon and Eva seem to be getting along?" "Did he stay by her side?" "Did Kiki do a good job of handling Eva?" One of the people I caught on the phone was a senior editor who seemed so eager to talk that I asked if she wanted to meet at the coffee shop off the lobby rather than talk on the phone.

But my interviews produced little that was news. Several people had witnessed the spat between Mona and Kiki but reiterated that it had been so fast, no one had a clue what it was about. Afterward, Kiki had spoken briefly to Eva and then headed toward the bar. Someone said he'd thought she'd hung there for quite a while, but that was okay because Eva was sitting with people from the record company.

As for Brandon, most people remarked on the fact that he'd looked like a free agent that night, wandering from one spot to the next with all the patience of a hummingbird. What people weren't able to do was attach a time to when they'd seen Kiki and Brandon at various moments and places, so I couldn't determine if there were any gaps in their presence at the party, other than the time I'd seen them in the reception area.

There was one last question I laid on each person, and I

felt like such a pathetic loser doing it. "Have you had a chance to speak to one of my co-workers, Ryan Forster? He's working on another angle." I'd been able to ask the question without Ryan overhearing me because he'd yet to show his face at work.

But he hadn't made contact with anyone on my list.

While I was on the phone doing one of the interviews, Beau had called, leaving an address for a restaurant on Gansevoort Street. Even in my blue mood, I grinned stupidly.

It was four o'clock, and there seemed to be no reason to hang at work. I probably had heard back from all the people at *Track* I was ever going to hear from. I was dying to know if Nash had called Detective Tate yet, but I didn't feel comfortable checking up on him. I was going to have to take him at his word.

"You splitting?" Jessie asked as I slung my purse over my shoulder.

"Yeah," I said. "There's nothing left for me to do here today. By the way, you don't have any idea where our friend Ryan is, do you?"

She glanced back at his desk, as if that might provide an answer. "Looks like he took the day off."

"That doesn't seem likely, with all that's going on."

"Maybe he's working on that big, big angle. I'll ask around, see what I can find out. I'll give you a call later."

"My cell, okay? I won't be home."

She smirked at me in amusement. "Hot date?"

"Hm-hmm. With that guy you saw me talking to at Dicker's."

Before she could pump me for details, my phone rang.

"Bailey?" a vaguely familiar voice inquired. "Please hold for Cat Jones."

"So you have someone place your calls these days?" I asked Cat when she came on. "That doesn't seem very Zen-like."

"Sorry, but I had no idea where you'd be. Look, I've come

into some info you might want. Is it possible for you to stop by?"

"Info?" I said, surprised. "About what?"

"Dicker. But I don't want to go into it on the phone. Can you swing by here on your way home?"

"God, Cat, I appreciate the call, but can we meet someplace else? I just don't feel like stopping by *Gloss*."

She sighed. "Okay. What about Café Jacqueline, the place down the street from here? Could you meet me there in fifteen minutes? I know you're not that far from me."

"Sure, that's perfect." It was the kind of spot that you went to for lunch when you didn't want the tab for two to exceed $40. I was surprised Cat even knew about it.

I waved good-bye to Jessie and told her we'd talk more on the phone later. I was at Café Jacqueline in less than fifteen minutes, and I'd already gone through one cappuccino by the time Cat finally blew through the door. She drew glances from the crowd as she waltzed in, dressed in a pink, off-the-shoulder top and a yellow, pink, and green check pencil-shaped skirt with a row of amazing box ruffles that fishtailed back and forth as she walked, enough to add a draft to the room. I was glad I was sitting down and she couldn't see the pathetic poof in my pants.

"Wow, I'm making a little progress," she said. "You seem happier to see me than you did the last time."

"Cat, come on. You know I'm not mad at you. . . . You seem in a good mood."

"Really? If someone had told me when I was twenty-six that my career would one day consist of planning features on things like the healing power of an organized purse, I would have stuck an ice pick in their heart."

"So what's this news that you've heard?" I asked after she'd had time to order her own cappuccino.

"I know you were interested in the whole Mona/Dicker

dynamic, so I made a few inquiries. I figured it was the least I could do."

"Thanks," I said, though with Cat you were always smart to suspect there was some hidden agenda. "What did you find out?"

"You know how I mentioned to you that she'd been stalling on her contract? Well, she apparently had a huge offer to produce reality TV shows and was about to take it."

"*What?*" I said. This was a total contradiction to what Carl had told me.

"Why seem so surprised? I'd mentioned the other night that it might be a possibility."

"It's just that someone told me the opposite—that she was staying at *Buzz.*"

"I've got this on pretty good authority. What she *did* do, apparently, was dangle her offer in front of Dicker so that he upped his offer to her, and then she used that to finagle even more money for the new job. I hear there was no way he could match the final TV offer. She was going to make a boatload of money."

So Carl had totally misled me. Why? I recalled that schmaltzy, Hallmark-card line he'd tossed out about Dicker, about how he was really a good guy. I wondered if Dicker had offered Carl some kind of payment, one of those death payments that companies occasionally slipped to families when an executive died. That way, he could count on Carl not bad-mouthing him in any way.

Whatever the reason, I was back where I'd started with Dicker. He'd had a very good reason to bop Mona on the head.

CHAPTER 17

I wasn't meeting Beau until seven-thirty, so after I arrived home and before I showered, I sat outside on my terrace, watching the dusk creep up on the city and trying to relax. I'd even made myself a cup of green tea, using a teabag from a gift basket someone had given me ages ago. I felt a little ridiculous sipping it, as if I were suddenly leading my life according to the pages of the new and improved *Gloss* magazine that Cat was busy creating, but I just needed something to help slow down my brain.

I hadn't lingered at my meeting with Cat. I appreciated her trying to help me, and I liked the fact that things were starting to normalize between us again—but I'd been anxious to be on the move. I returned home, then headed for the gym. I told myself that thirty minutes on the treadmill would not only rev up my heartbeat, but might also kick my mind into fast gear, allowing me to determine what I should do with the bombshell about Dicker. But there seemed to be no obvious next step. I certainly wasn't going to show up on the eighteenth floor again and try to grab a few minutes with the guy as I had the other day. Unless, of course, I wanted to end up losing my gig at *Buzz* and being escorted out the building by security.

So my next tactic had been to give my brain a breather—hence the green tea—but unfortunately it wasn't working, either. I couldn't stop thinking about the murder. I had viable suspects—Kiki and Brandon and now Dicker again—but I didn't know how to flush out any more information about them. I also didn't want to lose sight of Kimberly. She claimed to have an alibi but I'd not yet been able to verify it. It seemed that the only thing I could do was wait: to see how the police responded to the information that Nash provided about Jed Crandall's auction, and also, to my chagrin, to learn what Ryan was cognizant of—once he shared it with Nash.

Finally I forced my thoughts away and considered the night ahead with Beau. I'd been looking forward to our encounter all day, but at the same time I was nervous. Ever since my marriage had blown up, I'd been pretty wary with new guys, and more times than not I seemed to fixate on one minor problem, which would eventually lead me to reject a perfectly decent man. It might be something as ridiculous as the fact that he had goofy-looking patch pockets on the jacket he'd chosen to wear one night.

About a year after my divorce, I met this charming and successful architect, and though he didn't exactly make my knees buckle, I found him attractive and incredibly easy to talk to. He took me out to dinner twice, and then, for date three, he suggested we drive north on Saturday afternoon to pick apples and admire the fall foliage. I rendezvoused with him at his place, and when I was using his bathroom before we hit the road, I happened to notice a tube of something called Boil-eze on a shelf—and that was the beginning of the end for me. I began to ruminate about where in the name of God the boil *was*. His back? His leg? Or, worse, his *ass*? And how could anyone even go into a store and buy something called Boil-eze and leave it out on display? The phrase *drain a boil* suddenly forced its way into my mind, nearly making me retch. On the drive up the Taconic State Parkway, I could barely look the guy in the eye, and by the end of the day this little tic I'd acquired had ballooned into a full-blown distaste for the poor man. He sensed something was off, but he had absolutely no idea what it was. In fact, if he'd thought for a hundred years, he still wouldn't have figured it out.

But with Beau, I wasn't being the least bit skittish, and that worried me.

The restaurant he'd suggested had a French-sounding name and was located on Gansevoort Street, just off Ninth Avenue in the middle of the meatpacking district—and only a stone's throw, actually, from Soho House. I was tempted to walk there because it was nearly a straight shot west of my apartment building, but it would take a good half hour and I didn't want to arrive all sweaty and withered looking. I hailed a cab and arrived five minutes early, ahead of Beau.

It turned out to be a Moroccan restaurant: brick walls, banquettes covered with bright red kilim rugs, and those Moroccan lanterns with colored panes of glass. It was dim inside; light came only from the lanterns and little votive candles tucked into notches in the walls where a few bricks had been removed. Because it was hot, the door to the street was open, framed by long, pulled-back drapes, and it created the sensation that I was walking along a street in Marrakech. Except that the view from the door, once you were inside, was more Parisian in feeling—you could see the red awning of the French bistro Pastis and loads of people sauntering across the broad stretch of Ninth Avenue.

I had just opened my mouth to ask for a bottle of sparkling water when Beau strolled through the doorway. He was wearing a moss green–colored polo shirt and black jeans, and his hair was damp, as if he'd stepped out of the shower only moments before. My heart did this kind of crazy thing, like someone in a straitjacket flinging himself around the walls of a padded cell.

"Hi there," he said, smiling as he pulled out the wooden chair from the other side of the table. I half expected he would kiss me, even on the cheek, but he didn't—maybe because I was already sitting down and it would be awkward. "You look fabulous."

Fabulous was too strong a word, but I did think I looked hot. I'd chosen this pale yellow sundress, sort of low cut, and these cool sandals in blue and yellow. As I'd left my building, I'd worried that it might have been a little too F. Scott Fitzgerald for the meatpacking district, but the night was so warm, it was nice not to have anything on my arms or legs.

"Thank you. So do you, I might add."

"I hope this restaurant is okay. I never asked you what kind of food you like—besides pasta with clams, of course."

"Everything. And I love Moroccan food. Have you ever been there?"

"No, but it's high on my list. That's the one drawback of spending so many years in Asia. I'm a little behind on exploring the rest of the world. Have you actually been there?"

"Yes, I spent a wonderful week there. Marrakech, Fez. I even stayed one night in a tent out in the Sahara."

"You didn't go alone, did you?"

"No, I went with another girl, another travel writer. I do these travel pieces sometimes. You don't make much money on them, but the trips get paid for and it's been a cheap way to stay in great accommodations."

"So you're a traveler at heart."

"I don't know what I'd do if I couldn't travel. Besides the fact that I love it, I have to have something to talk about besides corpses."

God, my words sounded clunky, as if I were on a blind date with someone my mother had set me up with as opposed to a man who had already spent half of one night inside me.

The waiter dropped off menus and a wine list, and Beau diverted his attention from me to select a bottle. I watched his gorgeous brown eyes scan the list of wines. He seemed to handle everything with total self-assurance and also an easiness born of not worrying about what others thought. I felt short of breath just looking at him. I just had to find a way to regain the wonderful, effortless rhythm of our conversation the other night.

As the waiter departed, Beau leaned into the table and stared long and hard at me. Then he slid his hand across the table and held the fingers of my right hand lightly in his own fingertips.

"So is this bracelet from one of your many travels?" he asked, gazing at the pale yellow stones.

"Yes," I said, wondering if he could feel how hard my pulse was pounding. "From Ecuador."

"Where's your next trip going to take you?"

"I'm planning to go to Italy this September. Rome and Florence."

"I bet it would be really fun to be off on an adventure somewhere with you—though I fear I might never want to get out of bed."

I felt myself blush.

"Well, we'd have to eat eventually, so we'd be forced to order room service," I said. "That way you'd at least have the opportunity to taste the local cuisine."

"Good point. And perhaps occasionally take a walk, to deal with the kinks in our legs."

"Right."

"You know, I don't think I ever really told you how much I thoroughly enjoyed the other night. It was quite the unique experience."

I could feel even more blood rushing to my cheeks. In a minute it was going to be hard to distinguish me from one of the red kilim rugs in the room.

"Unique? Why? Because generally when you pop in unexpectedly on women you barely know, they don't let you bed them?"

He laughed in this funny, knowing way, and I realized that the opposite was probably true—that women always let him bed them, no matter what the circumstances.

"Not just that," he said. "The whole experience. One minute I was talking to a real estate agent who couldn't stop snapping her gum and the next minute I was eating under the stars with you."

And after that I just relaxed. A tape of haunting Middle Eastern music played in the background, and it almost seemed as if we were in an exotic place light-years away from Manhattan.

We both ordered this lemony chicken dish, with some kind of spice that totally evoked North Africa for me. Over dinner we talked about the plot for his movie, where else I'd traveled over the past few years, Buddhist monks. He asked me about my marriage and I gave a few short general answers: lawyer; went to Brown, too, but ahead of me, and we didn't meet until an alumni event in New York; had no idea where he was at the moment. I left out the "bookies were calling in the middle of the night threatening to set him on fire" details for fear of freaking him out. He said more about his own romantic history this time. He'd ended a pretty serious relationship in December because she had accepted a long-sought-after job in London.

Eventually we found our way to Mona's murder.

"I can't believe I've gone all night and haven't asked you about it," Beau said. "Is there any news?"

"No, except my friend Robby has been cleared."

"Did you get your story filed or whatever the language is?"

"Uh-huh. But now I'm working on the follow-up. It's a little bit tricky for me because generally I don't like to go into the office more than two or three times a week, but during this period I feel I need to be there every day. Can I ask you a totally off-the-wall question?"

"Did *I* do it? No. I'd never even heard of Mona Hodges until last week."

"*Almost* as off the wall as that. Do you think there's any chance Thomas Dicker could have?"

"*Dicker?*"

"Yes, Dicker."

"Wow. I know he's often referred to as a killer, but I never thought it was supposed to be taken literally. But why would he kill this Mona chick? I thought she was helping to revive his media empire."

"She'd apparently been offered a very big job elsewhere and had decided to take it. I'm thinking that in a moment of anger he might have just lashed out at her. You've been with him a couple of times. Do you think he could have done it?"

"He's got a short fuse, that much I know. I didn't experience it directly, but I heard him on the phone with someone and it wasn't very pretty. Sure, I could see it. Not premeditated, but in a flash of rage—like you said. Do you want me to ask him?"

"What do you mean?"

"I'm going to meet with him again this week. I'm not that interested in the project, but I thought I'd hear him out. I'll just come right out and ask him—while he's got a large piece of steak in his mouth—did you kill Mona?"

I laughed. "Actually, if you want to help me out, there *is* one thing you can do."

"Just say it. I'd love to play Dr. Watson to your Sherlock Holmes."

"It would be only normal for you to ask Dicker about the case. After you've made a general inquiry, can you just mention in passing that you heard a rumor that Mona was going to be leaving, that she had accepted this job producing reality television shows? I'd love to know his reaction—whether he looks as if he knew or didn't know."

"Consider it done. My life won't be in danger, will it? They're not going to find me torn limb from limb by the hound of the Baskervilles?"

"Not unless you plan to go traipsing across the moors of Devonshire," I said, smiling.

I liked that he wanted to play Dr. Watson. It meant that he found what I did exciting, that he wanted to be helpful. A little part of me, though, was worried about how fast things were moving. It was feeling less and less like a fling by the minute.

After he'd paid the bill, we walked out into the sultry night. Dozens of people were strolling along the sidewalks, coming in and out of the restaurants that lined Ninth Avenue and Gansevoort. The boisterous noise of diners spilled out onto the streets from the open windows of Pastis.

"Feel like another espresso?" Beau asked. "Or a brandy? We could stop here at Pastis. Or I could serve you either at my place."

Just hearing him say "my place" made my knees weak.

"Sure. I mean, your place sounds great."

His apartment was on the tenth floor of a fairly old building in Chelsea. At one glance I could see that it was nice, really cool, in fact—what you might think would belong to a guy of his age and profession, but you never make that mental leap in advance because there are so many times when you walk into a man's place and discover that he's got an extensive trucker hat collection on display or that the only piece of art is one of those dartboards with the tiny cupboard where darts are stored.

There was only one side-table lamp on in the living room, but I could see well enough because of the city lights that splashed through a row of three big windows. The walls were a soft white and the furniture was mostly black leather, but the rug was a smashing-looking primitive design in blue and black and orange. Lining the walls were black-and-white photographs, mostly, it seemed, scenes from the Far East. Off the living room, behind French doors, was a small, nearly darkened room, which was probably meant to be a dining room; but Beau had set it up as an office, with a round wooden table as a desk.

I liked the fact that his place wasn't neat as a pin. A coffee mug was still sitting on a side table, and the *Times* lay strewn on a huge ottoman that looked as though it functioned as a coffee table. Ah, but his bed was made. At the end of a long white corridor, I could see a door opened to his bedroom and a glimpse of his bed with a smooth gray comforter.

"I can make espresso," he said as he stepped into his kitchen and flicked on the light. "Or rather, I've got this expensive machine that can. A Christmas gift from my mother."

"I might actually take some brandy," I said, "if it's still being offered." I felt jittery, and I feared that if I had another espresso, I might start bouncing off the walls like a squash ball.

"Absolutely," he said. He moved into the living room, pulled a bottle of brandy from a wooden cabinet, and splashed some into a couple of short glasses.

"Did you take these photographs?" I asked, moving closer to one that was of a simple teahouse with a woman alone at a table.

"Um-hmm. Almost all of them are from my time in Japan and Hong Kong."

"Did you ever think of doing that—being a photographer?"

"For some people that's a logical sequence. You start with still photography and then pick up a videocamera and so on. But not for me. I enjoy taking photographs, but I wanted to make movies from the moment I started going to them. I guess I prefer things in motion," he said, laughing.

"Should I start break dancing right now?" I asked.

"Actually, I had something else in mind."

He brought my glass to me. Other than that moment in the

restaurant and then later, holding my hand as we'd made a dash for a cab, he hadn't touched me yet; and now, before I could take a sip of the brandy, he leaned down and kissed me deeply. As I leaned into him, I could tell he already had an erection.

"Even better than I remembered," he said as he finally pulled away.

I took a fast sip of brandy—like a hiker who's just been rescued after two days in the woods—and then he took it out of my hands and set it onto the side table. He kissed me again, pulling down the straps of my dress so that he could kiss every inch of my neck and shoulders. I felt a rush of heat shoot through me and reach all the way to my toes.

I expected that he would suggest a walk down the corridor to the inviting-looking bed, but instead he unzipped my sundress halfway and let the top part fall to my waist. My breasts spilled out. Taking them into his hands, he kissed each one, running his tongue around my nipples.

When he pulled back briefly this time, I frantically yanked his shirt over his head. His chest was more tanned than I'd noticed in the dim light of my bedroom, and his skin was deliciously soft. I ran my hands over the wide expanse of his chest and then reached with my right hand to stroke him between his legs. He moved away slightly.

"I was a little greedy last time," he said softly. "I'd like to take my time with you tonight."

He reached behind me and unzipped my dress the rest of the way, so that it fell in a puddle at my feet. I had only this little yellow thong on, chosen after about an hour's worth of deliberation. Now, I thought, we're going to throw ourselves onto that bed down the hall. But instead he reached behind me and with his right hand swept the newspaper onto the floor and laid me down on the ottoman, face-side up. He slipped a finger under the band of my thong and tore it down my leg. And then he explored every inch of me with his mouth.

By the time we finally dragged ourselves to the bedroom, my legs felt so rubbery that I could barely move them.

I was awake before him in the morning, my internal alarm clock rousing me at seven, because I knew at some point I had to haul myself into *Buzz*. Beau must have sensed I was awake because all of a sudden he opened his eyes halfway and grinned.

"You okay?" he asked sleepily.

"I'll know better when I try to stand up."

"Do you have time for breakfast? I don't have much here, but there's a place around the corner where we could pick something up."

He said he'd come back later to shower, so we were out the door within fifteen minutes, me in my crumpled sundress and unintentional bed head. He didn't seem to mind, though. He led me to this charming little bakery/deli place where they served croissants and coffee in huge bowl-shaped cups. For a moment again, it felt as if I were somewhere far away with him.

As he was flagging down a cab for me, I felt the jitters return. I wanted to know for sure that I'd be with Beau again. Hell, I wanted to be with him again tonight. But he hadn't yet said a word about the next time.

"Thanks for a great night," he said as a taxi lurched to a stop. He leaned down and kissed me lightly on the mouth. Okay, I thought, relaxing just a little. He's finally about to propose something.

"Thank *you*. And for that nice dinner, too."

"I have my assignment, right?"

"Assignment?"

"With Dicker. I'm supposed to be Dr. Watson."

"Oh right, of course."

"I'll call when I have info, okay?"

"Great," I said.

But as the cab shot off, I didn't feel so great. It was nice

that he'd offered to help me in my research—I mean, wasn't
that a way to stay connected?—but at this moment all I wanted
to know was when our next encounter would be. And he'd
said absolutely nothing about it.

I'd turned off my cell phone before showing up at the
restaurant last night, though I'd checked for messages a couple
of times during the early evening just in case there was news.
Now I saw that Jessie had called after Beau and I had arrived
at his place.

"Call me whenever you can," she said, her voice laden with
alarm. "The shit really hit the fan tonight." Her words jolted me,
as if the taxi driver had suddenly slammed on his brakes.

It was only eight-thirty, but I called her cell anyway, too
anxious to wait. Her voice sounded froggy, as if she were up
but hadn't yet spoken today.

"What's going on?" I asked urgently. "It's me, Bailey."

"God, where do I start? Are you on the way to work?"

"Not at the moment. I was thinking of going in around ten.
What's going on, anyway?"

"Well, first of all, something weird is up with Ryan."

"What do you mean?" I demanded. I could only imagine
what he'd done now.

"As you know, he never surfaced yesterday," Jessie said. "I
figured he'd taken the day off or was just out and about,
searching for the story of the century. Well, at around seven I
was hanging around, making a few calls, and that new deputy
managing editor, the one with the lisp, comes over and starts
quizzing me. It seems they finally put two and two together
and realized that Ryan hadn't put in for a vacation day and had
never called in. They start trying his cell phone—that's the only
phone he has, apparently—but don't reach him. Finally at
around eight, they send someone down to his apartment on
the Lower East Side to see if there's any sign of him. And it
turns out he doesn't live there anymore."

"He just up and left?"

"No, no. He apparently moved out weeks ago. I vaguely remember overhearing him saying something on the phone about changing apartments, but I never knew when or where. The problem is he hasn't let anyone know what his new address is."

"That sounds really odd," I said. "When was the last time he was actually seen at work? He wasn't there Monday night when we left for Soho House."

"No, but he apparently came back. He was here late that night. Since then, there's been absolutely no word on him."

"Did anyone talk to the police?"

"Someone said that Nash was going to call one of the detectives on the Mona case because it would expedite matters. There were a few people huddled in his office just before I left, but when I wandered down they shooed me away. I'm planning to head in as soon as I get dressed."

"I'll get in there soon, too."

"Before you do, though, there's one other thing I need to tell you. You know how I've been snooping about the barbecue. Last night I was at the copier, waiting for this assistant from fashion to finish, and we start chatting about the Dicker party and she drops this huge bomb."

She took a breath. "She mentions that just before she got on the bus, she saw Hilary come running across the lawn, drenched. Remember I said that she'd lost her ride—and I thought it was Nash she'd come with? But here's the interesting part. When this girl used the expression *running across the lawn,* it struck me as odd, and I asked which direction Hilary was coming from, and she says—are you ready?—from the area down by the clubhouse."

"Oh God," I said, flooded with dread. In one sense, it was good to finally have a clue as to who had barricaded me in the sauna, but Hilary wasn't going anywhere and this meant I would always have to keep my eye on her.

"Why would she have done that to you, do you think?" Jessie asked.

"I've got a theory, but why don't we wait till we're face-to-face. I'd rather not get into it on a cell phone."

We signed off, promising to see each other in a short while. I realized how good it had been to have Jessie around during the last week; she'd not only given me insight and assistance on my story, but watched my back as well.

At home I hurried through a shower, dressed, and was on the subway toward *Buzz* forty-five minutes later.

You could tell in one glance that something was wrong. Through the glass wall of Nash's office, I saw a small crowd gathered around his desk—the managing editor, one of the deputy editors, and a chick I didn't recognize, but she was wearing one of those bland, tan summer suits people in HR often sport. Jessie may have been shooed away earlier, but I had every right to poke my head in.

After I set down my junk, I walked in that direction and caught Nash's attention through the glass. His hands were at his waist, akimbo, and his legs were apart, in a kind of Captain Magazine stance, and he lifted a hand just long enough to shoot me the five-minute signal. So I wasn't going to be invited into the inner sanctum right then, but it didn't look as if I were going to be denied access indefinitely.

Beating a temporary retreat back to my desk, I saw Jessie standing at her desk with a mug, as if she'd just returned from the kitchenette.

"Has Ryan ever done anything like this before?" I asked.

"Not that I know of. He's flaky, but he's also really ambitious, and he never seemed irresponsible about his job."

I had a weird feeling about him being missing today. Yet I also knew that Ryan had a real sense of entitlement. If he was chasing a story and thought he was close to the prize, he might not feel any need to check in.

"You're probably anxious to get to work," I told Jessie, "but have you got a minute to talk about this thing with Hilary? I need to know everything you do."

"I told you everything I found out," she admitted, lowering her voice even more. "Why do you think she did it? You said you had a theory."

"I think it has to do with Nash."

"*Nash?*"

"It seems from what you say that there might be—or might have been—something going on between them. The other night I had a drink with Nash, just to talk business, and Hilary saw us coming out of the bar. Since then she's made a snarky remark to me every chance she's had. When Nash chose me for his volleyball team Saturday and we beat the crap out of *her* team, there was steam coming out of her nose. At the time, I didn't know why she was taking it all so seriously, but now I think she may have been jealous. She may have decided to make me pay."

Jessie shook her head, but in distaste, not disagreement. "It totally fits with the sneaky Hilary I know, the one who tried to find a college student who needed money so she'd spy on Mary-Kate Olsen. But what are you going to do?"

"I don't know. I doubt if I confront her about it, she'd come clean. Maybe all I can do for now is proceed cautiously."

For the next few minutes, I bided my time by returning e-mails. There was one first thing this morning from Nash, stating that a female stalker had been harassing several New York City–based male celebrities and he wanted me to follow up on it. I suspected that the woman might be suffering from eroticism, a psychological condition in which the person truly believes that someone she's never met is in love with her.

While I made a preliminary call on the matter, I kept my eye on Nash's office. At one point I saw him reach for the phone, say a few words, and then hang up. He spoke to the three women still in his office, and their expressions registered shock and dismay. It appeared he then dispatched them, because as I headed toward his office again, they were leaving, looking distraught.

"What's happened?" I asked anxiously as I barged into Nash's office.

"The police found Ryan in his new apartment," Nash said. "He's dead."

I'd been worried that something was the matter, but the news still thundered through my skull.

"Was he murdered?" I blurted out. All I could think was that Ryan had found out who Mona's killer was—and that the killer had turned on him.

"No," Nash said, his voice flat. "He died of a heroin over-dose."

CHAPTER 18

It was one of those moments when the expression *my jaw hit the floor* didn't seem like outrageous hyperbole. I actually had to force myself to close my mouth.

"So he was an addict?" I asked hoarsely.

"Apparently," Nash said, sweeping back the top of his silver-tinged hair with his hand.

"Do you think anyone here had a clue?"

"I doubt it. That kind of news would have traveled fast. I'm wondering now if he might have made an attempt at rehab before he came here. He was vague about what he'd been up to during the past few years—said he'd been freelancing, but he didn't have a hell of a lot of clips. But his edit test was great, and as you know, the turnover here is outrageous. We'd hire ex-cons if they could write cute heads and decks."

I stood stock still in the middle of his office, letting my mind race.

"Nash, listen," I said finally. "Do you think there's any chance . . . Do you think someone could have killed Ryan? I mean, someone who knew that he was an addict and set it up to appear as if he had died from an overdose by injecting him with the drug?"

"But why . . . ? Are you saying you think this could be related to Mona's death?"

"Yes. Was Ryan on to something? He apparently indicated as much to a friend of his—and you started to say something to me yesterday about him."

He sighed and pulled his glasses off his nose, tossing them onto his desk. "Yes, he might have been on to something. But I have no idea what it was. Monday night, after he finished his profile of Mona, he said he had something that he thought might be big, and that he wanted to keep pursuing it. I said fine, go for it. I started to tell you, but then I realized that it was pointless to get you riled up if he was just blowing smoke up my ass so that he could stay on the story."

"Try to recall verbatim what he said," I pleaded.

"Christ, I can't remember the exact words. It wasn't anything very specific, that much I can tell you. It was just 'I think I may have something good. You gotta let me have a light load this week so I can pursue it.' And anyway, we're making a big leap here, Bailey. As far as we know, he was just a junkie who OD'd."

"I know, but—"

"We can discuss this further as we learn more facts. The cops are headed over here now, so I need to get a move on. Plus, I need to make an announcement to the staff."

"Sure," I said, moving slowly toward the door. "Just one last question. Where was Ryan's new apartment?"

"Way out in Queens. I wonder if he moved because he was running through cash so quickly and couldn't afford Manhattan anymore."

I paused near Lee's desk, trying to lasso my thoughts. If someone had murdered Ryan by giving him a fatal dose of heroin—and I knew it was too soon to jump to any conclusions—that person would have had to travel to Queens. It was hard to imagine Kiki, Brandon, or Dicker—or even Kimberly for that matter—hiking out to one of the outer boroughs, but of course they could have paid someone to do their dirty work, just as they could have recruited someone to try to scare me off. But how would any one of them have figured out where Ryan lived? As we'd discovered, he'd just moved, and there was no record at *Buzz* of his new address. Maybe he'd been followed home—after he stumbled too close to something he shouldn't have.

As soon as I approached my desk, both Jessie and Leo rolled their chairs toward me, anxious for news.

"What's going on?" Leo asked, his voice hushed.

"He's dead, isn't he?" Jessie proclaimed.

"Nash is about to make an announcement," I told them. "It's better that he tell you."

The words were barely out of my mouth when people started to rise from their desks all around us. It was clear an e-mail had just come through. I checked my screen. All the e-mail said was that Nash would like everyone to gather toward the front of the office by the table. People made their way to the exact spot Nash and Dicker had spoken from the day after Mona died.

Nash gave everyone a chance to arrive before he walked somberly into our midst. It reminded me of some old movie, in which a group of aspiring thespians are putting on a play and the director comes in to make an announcement, like the funding came through or it didn't come through or the show's going to Broadway or whatever. Except what Nash had to say was that Ryan had died and his death appeared to be drug related. He never uttered the h-word, but I doubted that anyone was thinking, in between gasps, that Ryan had succumbed to reefer madness. People tried to ask questions, but Nash shook his head and said he had told us all he knew. He mentioned that the police would be arriving shortly and to please cooperate. At one point, I felt someone's eyes on me and turned my head slightly to see Hilary staring coldly at me. As soon as my eyes caught hers, the edges of her mouth turned up ever so slightly in a smile. It gave me the willies.

Nash's remarks ended up taking no more than two minutes, and then we all straggled back to our desks, phones ringing like crazy all around us. As I slid into my seat, Leo and Jessie both looked at me, Leo shaking his head in dismay.

"I don't know about you," he said, "but frankly I'm afraid to come in here anymore. Working for Mona seems like a damn pig roast in comparison."

"Had you ever seen any sign of a drug problem?" I asked the two of them.

"Not me," Jessie said.

"I hadn't *specifically,*" Leo whispered. "But now that this whole thing has happened, I do remember something weird. I was in the bathroom one day a few months ago trying to get pizza sauce off my shirt. I'd been standing at the sink for, like, five minutes and I realized suddenly that there was someone in one of the stalls, quiet as a mouse. I recognized Ryan's shoes. At the time I figured he was just taking care of business, but there was something kind of creepy about how *quiet* he was."

"You need to tell the police about it, okay?" I told him.

And it didn't take long for them to materialize. Tate and McCarthy appeared on the floor a few minutes later, along with two people in crime scene unit jackets, and Nash led them over to Ryan's workstation. They began by combing through papers on top of his desk and then tackled the drawers. People made feeble attempts to pretend to be working, but you could see them following the action, their heads popping up prairie-dog style from their cubes. I positioned my chair at an angle in an effort to glimpse what was transpiring behind me. The cops were working in a tight cluster, though, and I was at a disadvantage. At one point I heard one of the cops mutter, "Bingo."

After ten minutes of exploring Ryan's desk, Tate straightened up and surveyed the pod. Almost instantly his eyes fell on me. He sighed, cocked his head to the left indicating I should follow him, and then nudged his partner. Oh goody. It looked as though I were going to be having another chat with the two of them in the conference room.

Though some people had tried earlier to watch discreetly, every single person in the pod and the greater open area seemed to gawk as I walked with Tate and McCarthy toward the corridor that led to the conference room. I felt as conspicuous as Kimberly Chance the night she wore the outfit *Buzz* had dubbed "the Biker Barbie Look."

"You sure end up near a lot of dead people," McCarthy said as we stepped into the room. It sounded like nothing more than a wisecrack, so I made no attempt to answer it.

"Tell me anything you can about Ryan, will you, Miss Weggins," Tate said. "Were you aware he was a drug user?" To my relief, there was nothing antagonistic about his tone, and I relaxed into the chair I'd taken.

"I had no idea whatsoever," I said. As I spoke the words, I heard anguish in my voice and I realized that the reality of Ryan's death was finally sinking in for me. "He kept to himself, though, and I don't think people here knew him very well."

"According to your boss, Ryan had seemed kind of high-strung lately. Would that be your observation?"

I was surprised that Nash had characterized it that way, because he preferred it when people were pumped, working on all eight cylinders, and I would have assumed he thought Ryan was just busting his tail over the last week.

"I didn't really know him very well, but, yes, he did seem more agitated than usual," I admitted. "One night in fact, he lashed out at me. He was working on a profile of Mona at the same time I was writing up the murder, and he claimed that I was interviewing people who were *his* sources. He'd never been particularly friendly to me, but this was the first time he was out-and-out hostile."

"Was he out of line?"

"I'd have to say so. There was bound to have been a bit of overlap in the people we spoke to. But there's something I need to tell you, in case Nash hasn't had a chance yet. Ryan intimated to a few people that he had discovered a very important piece of information."

"About?"

"The *murder*. He conveyed to Nash that he was on to something, and one of my co-workers overheard him tell a friend on the phone that he had something big."

"Do you have any idea what it might have been?"

"No. Maybe when you look at his phone logs you'll have a clue, but I don't know what it could be. . . . Do you think he might have been *killed*—because of what he knew? I mean, could someone have gone to his apartment and given him a fatal injection?"

I hadn't been able to contain myself from blurting out that question, though I didn't for a second think Tate would answer me. To my surprise, he pursed his lips and stared pensively at me, his eyes enlarged slightly by the lenses of his glasses. It appeared he was deliberating whether or not to share something with me.

"We're talking off the record, right?" he asked finally.

"Yes," I said, almost afraid to breathe.

"When they found Ryan early this morning, they had to break down his door. The dead bolt was on. There was drug paraphernalia at the scene, and it appeared he'd recently shot up. There was no indication of anyone else having been there."

"Wow, I . . ." A thought began to flicker in my brain, fuzzy as a dust bunny. Before it could fully form, Tate articulated it for me in the form of a question.

"Do you think that Ryan might have killed Ms. Hodges?" he asked.

"And then killed himself, you mean?" I asked. "I'll admit I did wonder at times if Ryan's hostility toward me might be because he was covering up his role in the murder. He was one of the last people to see Mona alive. But I never had a clue what his *motive* could be for killing her. He was one of Mona's favorites. But what if Mona found out he was doing drugs? She might have threatened to fire him. Do you think he shot up here at work? Did you find drugs in his desk?"

Tate smiled wanly at me, and I knew then that he'd done all the divulging he was going to.

"Thank you for your help," he said. "I assume you'll be following this story for the magazine, so if you hear anything of significance, please get in touch with me."

"Of course," I said. As they left, McCarthy flashed me a skeptical look. Though Tate seemed to have developed a degree of respect for me, McCarthy clearly wasn't on the same plane.

After they left I sat for a moment, half in shock. *Could* Ryan have been the killer after all? Is that why he'd acted so testy lately? On the night of the party had Mona divulged an awareness of his drug use, prompting him to react violently? Was he the one who trapped me in Dicker's sauna because he thought I was getting way too nosy? Had he then taken his own life in remorse for what he'd done? But why had he bothered arranging all those interviews? What was the "something big," he'd been talking about to people? I couldn't help but think of that moment he'd seemed to have a brainstorm when we'd been discussing his departure for the party.

It just didn't add up. Perhaps his death had only an indirect connection to Mona's. Maybe he'd become too wired up about the story he was working on, which made him up his intake of heroin.

Though Ryan seemed to have few friends on staff, it was possible that someone might know something. Once the police were off the premises, I would interview the staff again. I'd also try to discover the names of any friends he had on the outside. Before leaving the conference room, I used the phone to place a call to my contact in the medical examiner's office. It was too soon for an autopsy to have taken place, but there might be some initial findings of interest. I reached only her voice mail and left a message, asking her to get in touch as soon as possible.

As I walked back to my desk, I wondered if Nash had talked to Tate yet about the Eva angle and the possibility of Kiki and Brandon as suspects. If Ryan *hadn't* killed Mona—and I had no real reason to believe he had—there was still a murderer at large. Surely Nash had said something by now.

Jessie mouthed, "Everything okay?" as I sat down. The cops had departed from Ryan's desk. I nodded quickly to her and wheeled my chair toward Leo, so close, in fact, I could smell the patchouli he was wearing.

"Leo," I whispered, "I need to ask you a question."

"How fast do I think we all can find jobs someplace else?"

"Save that for later. When one of the cops said the word *bingo* a little while ago, could you tell what they were referring to? You've got a better angle than I do."

"There was something stuffed in the back of Ryan's drawer," he whispered back. "I think it was an old plastic bag."

A plastic bag. The word *bingo*. That probably meant it was a bag of smack or an empty bag with just traces of the drug. Leo had been right in his guess that Ryan had sometimes shot up at work. He'd apparently sometimes kept his stash in his desk drawer. That was a pretty reckless thing to do and meant that he was no casual user.

For the next couple of hours I bided my time, waiting for the police to make their rounds and quiz people. I asked Nash's assistant to track down a copy of Ryan's résumé for me so that I could pursue whether he had friends at any of the places he'd worked in the past. I also caught up with the deputy editor about the stalker article I was working on for this week. I did an Internet search on erotomania and made a few calls. There were in-person interviews I needed to conduct, but I could put those off until tomorrow.

Finally, the cops split and I set out to talk to people, following in Tate's tailwind. I explained to my co-workers that in writing a follow-up to my story about Mona's murder, I needed to include the fact that there had been another death of a *Buzz* staff member—and I wanted input from them. I was greeted by a whole range of reactions. Some, like Leo, were freaked about Ryan's death, others appeared numb with shock, and a few actually seemed fascinated, as if they'd just gotten to see a Mack truck jackknife on the opposite side of the meridian.

It turned out that Ryan had zero pals on staff. No one knew much about him, or what he'd been up to, or who his friends on the outside were. And no one claimed to have known he was an addict. But then, without warning, I stumbled on something during one of my last conversations. It was with the assistant beauty editor, of all people, whose tiny office was toward the very back of the floor near the entrance to *Track*. And I had almost skipped her, figuring she'd be clueless.

"Were you friendly at all with Ryan?" I asked routinely. She was very cute and hip looking, with short platinum blond hair, super dark eyebrows, and a tiny silver stud in her nose.

"No," she said glumly. "To be honest, I didn't even know who he was—until last week, that is."

"Why?" I asked. "Did he interview you for his profile of Mona?"

"Yeah, he wanted to know what I thought of her, if I liked working for her, that sort of thing. I told him how Mona used to come into the beauty closet with these huge shopping bags and sweep stuff off the shelves into them. She even took this kit we had that lets you design your pubic hair in a heart. I think just because it was *free*."

"Did you have any contact with him after that? Or notice anything unusual about his behavior?" I'd asked everybody a variation of the last question. Since Ryan had claimed to be on to something, I wondered if anyone had accidentally been afforded a peek at what it was.

"That was my only contact with him . . . except, well, I saw him down here again this week. On Monday, at around five."

"What do you mean?"

"He was sitting in that office over there," she said, pointing to a glass-fronted room that was catty-corner to hers. It was the one reserved for West Coast staff, the one Mary Kay had used to make herself camera ready.

That was odd. I wondered if he might have been using the office to make a private call, the same way I'd used the conference room.

"Was he on the phone?" I inquired.

"The phone? I don't think so. Maybe. Then I saw him talk to one of the cleaning ladies by the service elevator."

Goose bumps rose in waves up each of my arms.

"Katya? The one who was injured the night Mona was killed?"

"I guess. She was blond. She came off the elevator and he called out to her and then said something to her, and she went into the office with him for a minute."

"Did you overhear what they were talking about?" I asked, desperately hoping that she had picked up even a phrase or two.

"No, I was on the phone. We're doing this hair trauma story, and I'd heard this rumor that Kate Bosworth's extensions had caught fire one night on a movie set and I was trying to find out—"

"Yeah, okay," I interrupted. "But could you get any sense of what was going on with the two of them?"

"He was asking her questions, I think, like an interview, but he was doing most of the talking. She didn't seem very happy about it. She kept fidgeting, didn't sit down. I thought it was sort of odd, which is why I noticed them."

I let go of a sigh. Had Ryan simply been pumping her

about the night of the murder, or was it more than that? I'd sensed all along that Katya might be holding back information out of fear. Maybe Ryan had thought so, too. Had his pestering convinced her to confide in him?

"Did you notice anything else?" I asked.

"Not really. They didn't talk that long. She got back on the elevator. He turned out the light in the office and left."

"Did you tell the police about this?" I asked.

"No," she declared, "they didn't ask me anything like that. They just wanted to know if I knew he was an addict and if I'd ever seen him being hostile to Mona."

As I walked back to my area of the floor, my mind was reeling. I had to talk to Katya and find out if she'd held information back, something that she'd divulged to Ryan. Perhaps Ryan's death might jolt her into coming clean. As soon as I sat down I called building maintenance, and after being forced to convince them that I was not a producer for *Access Hollywood, Entertainment Tonight, The Insider,* or *E!* I learned that Katya clocked in at four each day in the basement.

It was time now for one more conversation, with a person I'd put off seeing all day: Hilary. I dreaded the idea of it, but because of what Jessie had learned about Hilary's actions on the day of the barbecue, I had no choice. I would never be able to goad Hilary into admitting that she'd locked me in the sauna, but I could at least put her on warning that I was on to her—and that just might prevent her from trying any other evil tricks in the future.

"What's it about?" she asked when I told her over the phone that I needed to speak to her.

"Just a few quick things," I said. "I'm doing a follow-up story on Mona's death."

"Can you be more specific? I've told you all I know about the party, Bailey, and I'm really very busy."

"Blind items," I said. I'd pulled that out of the air in desperation, since I was hardly going to announce my real agenda. "I'd like to talk to you some more about those."

"I've already been over that ground with you."

"There's been a new development. And it's a very serious matter."

"All right," she said begrudgingly. "Why don't you drop by now."

I wouldn't have minded having Jessie's advice about the best way to handle my imminent discussion, but she'd left the building on a story. I'd be on my own—with the Cock Nazi. When I walked into Hilary's office, she was sitting quietly at her desk, her eyes skimming a page of handwritten notes. But I had the sense that she wasn't reading any of the words, that instead she'd been just sitting there waiting for me to arrive.

"Isn't that terrible news about Ryan?" she said as I sat in the chair across from her desk. "Did you know he was a junkie?"

"No, I didn't. Did *you*?"

"Me?" she asked, laying one of her hands against her breasts in mock surprise. "How would I have known? I didn't sit right near him like you did."

"But you've got your ear close to the ground on everything. No one can keep a secret from you, can they?"

"How sweet of you to say that," she said sarcastically. "Now what can I do for you? As I told you on the phone, I'm extremely busy today."

"Why was Mona so willing to run blind items against the advice of our lawyer?" I didn't really care what she had to say. I was just stalling until I could figure out the best way to broach the party at Dicker's.

She slipped her arms behind her back, grabbed her hands together, and arched her back as if to crack it. Her chest was thrust in my direction. To put it bluntly, I was getting kind of sick of her tits.

"Mona knew readers loved them. They didn't even mind not knowing for sure who we were talking about because they liked the puzzle aspect, trying to figure out who it was. But you said this was *serious*. Why don't you get to the point?"

"I've been wondering if one of the blind items Mona was planning on running may have led to her death."

Her glistening lips parted involuntarily in surprise. "Which item are you talking about?" she demanded.

"I don't have any specific information. I was hoping you did."

"I'm sorry, Bailey," Hilary said. "I know you're our star reporter here these days and that Nash has given you this *verwy, verwy* big assignment—but there are some things involving 'Juice Bar' that I'm just not at liberty to discuss. Unless you're willing to explain what relevance all this possibly has to Mona's death."

"Let me ask you another question, then," I said. "Why is it that you dislike me so much, Hilary? I don't recall doing anything to get on your bad side."

Hilary tucked in her chin and observed me wryly, her eyes raised. "My, aren't we paranoid," she replied. "Have you thought of seeing a shrink for that?"

"Does it have anything to do with Nash?" I asked. "You always seem a little annoyed when you spot me with him." It had been nervy of me to go there, but I realized that you never made any headway with Hilary if you were on tiptoes.

"Maybe it's not paranoia, just pure self-absorption," she replied, hard as a slap. "But I assure you, Bailey, I give as much thought to you during the day as I do my Stayfree panty liner."

"Really?"

"Really."

"Then why play that little prank on me last Saturday, the one with the sauna door?"

"*Sauna?*" she exclaimed, her expression perplexed. "I have no idea what you're talking about."

"Oh come on, Hilary. You weren't down by Dicker's clubhouse, soaking wet?"

"Since you seem so hell-bent on knowing, yes, I was down there. I was trying to find a ride back. Mine fell through and I didn't want to go with everyone else. I get bus sick. But I was not in any sauna. Now would you mind getting out of my office?"

Her expression had been truly confused when I mentioned the sauna. Maybe she was a better liar than I'd realized up until now.

"Fine," I said. "But just know that I've got my eye on you."

I stood to go, my heart pounding. As I walked toward the door, I wondered if she might try to tackle me from behind.

"Oh, Bailey," she said just as I was about to step into the corridor. "Speaking of blind items, did you know that Mona was thinking of running one about Nash?"

I turned back to her.

"What do you mean?" I asked. My mind was having a hard time grappling with what she'd just said.

"We both like working for Nash, don't we? But let's face it, he's a total tomcat. And it turns out that lately he's been enjoying a fling with a certain married talk show host. Once Mona learned about it, she felt she had no choice but to run an item. The woman has a seven-month-old baby, for God's sake. Out of respect for Nash, though, Mona was planning to run it as a *blind* item."

"When did this happen?"

"It came up about a week or so ago," she said, smiling smugly. "Just before Mona died. Nothing's run yet. I think Mona was still mulling over the best time to go with it."

"So—so Nash's name wouldn't have been mentioned?" I asked. I'm sure she took satisfaction in my stammering, but I couldn't help myself. This revelation had taken me too much by surprise.

"No," Hilary replied, still with the cat-who-ate-the-canary grin. "I believe Mona was going to refer to him as the executive editor of a leading celebrity magazine. I don't know about you, but I'd say that might have resulted in another blow to the head with a Kate Spade handbag."

"And Nash was aware of Mona's intentions?"

"Oh sure. At least Mona said she'd told him."

I turned to leave again, but this time she didn't beckon me back. Instead, I could hear her nails clicking on the base of the phone, tapping numbers. Who was she calling—Lucifer? Just to check in and report that she'd been dutifully about his business today?

I passed two people on my way down the hall who both glanced at me curiously, proof that I looked as rattled as I felt. I made my way to the kitchenette and pulled a bottle of water from the fridge. After five gulps, my heart was still thumping. Hilary had given no indication that she was guilty of the sauna incident, but I was still very suspicious of her. She clearly didn't like me, and she seemed obsessed about Nash and me.

Just as disturbing was what I *had* learned from her: the fact that Mona had planned to do dirt to Nash. Why would she have undermined him that way? Was she growing tired of him as her number two and didn't care if he quit in a huff? Or did she think it wouldn't matter to him, that he might even be flattered by the attention?

More important, how had Nash responded? Certainly he would have been livid with Mona. Had he demanded that she not run the item? Even *begged* her not to? Was it possible that he was the one who'd smashed Mona in the head? Nash knew that Ryan had learned something big and that I was uncovering stuff, too. *He* could have locked me in the sauna. *He* could have known I was going to Katya's because I had asked Lee for the address.

As my heart rate slowed down, I saw things suddenly from another angle. What if it was all a lie? Hilary clearly had the hots for Nash, and she seemed infuriated by the fact that his loins lit up for anyone but her. Perhaps she concocted the story about the talk show host on the spur of the moment just to gall me. She'd convinced herself that there was something between me and Nash, and maybe this was her way of making me feel as consumed with jealousy as she was.

I checked the time on my watch. As tempted as I felt to stand there stewing about all of this, I didn't want to miss Katya. It was ten to four and she should be arriving at work any minute.

I took the freight elevator to the basement. Once a few weeks ago when I'd boarded the regular elevator in the lobby, it had taken me to the basement, called by one of the mainte- nance men before I'd had a chance to push the button for six- teen. As the doors parted, I'd been offered a glimpse of the dark, cavernous space down there, but that's as close as I'd ever been to the area.

There wasn't a soul in sight when I stepped off the eleva- tor. In the distance, though, I could hear the faint sound of hip- hop music, and I caught a trace of cigarette smoke in the air. It was against the rules to smoke in an office building in New York City, but they probably didn't pay much attention to that down here.

I glanced around, trying to figure out what direction to head in. There didn't seem to be any rhyme or reason to the design. In front of me was a huge space filled with Dumpsters and boxes and a few hallways branching off. I decided to head toward the music, down a small dark corridor. There was a mouse glue board every ten feet, and I made a point of not looking down for fear of seeing some little rodent still squirm- ing for its life. Before long, I found the place where the music had emanated from. It was a small room with a row of metal lockers and a square table, where two maintenance guys sat drinking cans of Mountain Dew. A table fan on top of the lock- ers swiveled back and forth, making a dull whirring noise. The two men glanced up in surprise when they saw me.

"I'm looking for where the cleaning crew checks in," I said, trying to sound as if I were on an authorized mission.

"Keep going," one of the men told me, "and take a right at the end of the corridor. You'll be in another corridor, and it's all the way at the end of *that*."

But I didn't have to go that far. As I reached the end of the hall, Katya and another woman were just making the turn. Katya looked startled by the sight of me.

"Katya," I said, "may I please speak to you for just a moment?"

She sighed raggedly. "I must get to work," she said.

"One minute. That's all I ask."

Her shoulders sagged in consent, and the other woman moved on, pushing her large rubber trash can on wheels.

"Katya," I said, my voice low, "I don't know if you've heard, but a reporter on our staff—his name is Ryan Forster—died last night of a heroin overdose."

She flinched. "I am very sorry to hear that," she said, finding my eyes for a second and then pulling hers away.

"I know that he spoke to you last week, about Mona's murder. Can you please tell me what you told him?"

She took a deep breath and her eyes flickered in anger. "He asked me what I remembered about that night," she said, trying to keep her voice even. "I told him the same thing I told you. I do not remember anything. Except the long sleeve. Now why won't you leave me alone?"

She gripped the handle of her cart and began to move off.

"Katya," I said softly, causing her to stop in her tracks, "I know there's something else. About Mona's death. I hope you'll change your mind at some point and tell me—or the police."

She said nothing, just started walking again. I gave her time to reach the service elevator, knowing that she wouldn't be pleased to have me on her heels. A few minutes later, I retraced my steps and took the elevator back to sixteen.

My phone was ringing as I neared my desk, and I raced to grab it.

"Now, now, catch your breath," said a voice on the other end. I could tell it was Brandy, the medical investigator I knew with the ME's office.

"What have you got?"

"Something very interesting."

"Well, don't keep me in suspense."

"This is just between you and me, okay? You can't use it in any kind of story right now. Your co-worker died from injecting pure heroin. We haven't run the tox screens on him yet, but we tested the stuff that was in the bag on the table in his apartment."

"So he bought bad stuff?"

"Well, you wouldn't exactly call it bad. If anything, it was too good—uncut, not ready for distribution to the masses."

"Could someone have sold him that by mistake?"

"It's possible. But that's an awfully expensive mistake. I'm wondering if it was purchased intentionally. Maybe he committed suicide. Or . . ."

I knew what she was going to say before she said it. Maybe someone else had bought the pure heroin and substituted it for Ryan's stash. Someone who wanted to make sure that the next time he shot up, he'd be dead within minutes.

CHAPTER 19

When I set down the phone a minute later, my hand was trembling. Though there were several possible explanations for Ryan's death—such as suicide or a drug dealer getting even—there was a chance that he had been murdered because he'd uncovered who the killer was. Brandy hadn't had much more to share, just that the cops were working on the murder angle and that anyone who knew where to buy heroin could probably figure out how to get his or her hands on a pure version, though it would have cost a pretty penny.

Of course, no one on my suspect list probably jumped in a limo and traveled over the 59th Street Bridge to kill Ryan. All they would have done was substitute a bag of pure heroin for the one he hid in his desk drawer. That meant Ryan's killer knew about his addiction. They also had easy access to the floor—or had gained it.

I turned slightly in my chair and let my eyes rove toward Nash's office. My stomach knotted. Was it possible that he was the murderer of both Mona and Ryan? I'd never asked him about who he'd talked to the night of the party, but he certainly could have slipped back over to our offices without anyone noticing. For him Mona's death had turned out to be like winning the Daily Double. Not only had it guaranteed that the blind item about his affair would never run, but he'd also ended up with the number one job at the magazine. It would have been a cinch for him to slip the bad heroin into Ryan's desk.

So what did I do now? One thing I knew for sure: I had no intention of charging into Nash's office to start grilling him about the blind item. Knowing that Ryan probably had died because he'd unearthed a major clue to the killer, I wasn't going to put myself in unnecessary danger. I was already vulnerable simply because I was snooping. What I would have to do was find a way to chat with Nash nonchalantly and learn whatever I could. For the past few days, because of Mona's death, because of the incidents in Brighton Beach and the sauna, I'd played host to a free-floating anxiety. But now it felt more like low-grade fear.

Not expecting to reach him, I tried Detective Tate's cell phone. To my surprise he actually answered, his voice nearly overwhelmed by the clattering sounds of what I assumed was a coffee shop.

"I was getting ready to pack up for the day and I just wondered if there was any news."

"On?"

"Ryan. I mean, any news from the coroner or tox screens or anything like that?"

"Not that I can discuss at this moment," he said. "But I want you to keep your eyes open, you hear me?"

"Absolutely. There's one piece of news I think you should know. Someone on staff told me they saw Ryan talking to Katya the other day—you know, the cleaning lady who was injured by Mona's attacker? He seemed to be trying to extract some information from her."

A pause. Lots of clanging and shouting in the background.

"Maybe he was just interviewing her for his article," he said.

"No, it wouldn't have been necessary for the profile piece he was assigned. Katya's been acting very nervous lately, and I got the sense when I talked to her that she might be holding something back out of fear the murderer would come after her. It's very possible that Ryan pried it out of her and then confronted the killer with the information."

Another pause.

"Okay, thanks, I'll look into it," he said. "Tell me the name of the person who told you this."

I gave him the associate beauty editor's name. I felt a little guilty. If flaming hair extensions could send that chick into a tizzy, a second visit by the cops would *really* freak her.

"Anything else you might want to bring to my attention?" asked Tate.

I realized that I'd better come clean. "Well, I wasn't sure I should bring this up, since it may be totally unrelated to the murder," I began, "but there have been one or two questionable incidents this last week or so."

"Such as?"

"I went to Katya's apartment in Brighton Beach to interview her last Thursday and after I left I was followed by a man who then chased me down the street. I ducked under a parked car and called the police on my cell. The man ran away when some people showed up. The patrol officer I spoke with at the time thought that maybe the interview and the attack were connected."

Tate mumbled a comment to someone in the diner and then said, "And you agree with this assessment?"

"It's possible that it might have been connected. The guy who came after me may have been watching me or watching Katya's apartment. Or he may have just been your average mugger. But then, a few days later, at a party for *Buzz* at Tom Dicker's East Hampton house, there was another incident. I went to chill in the sauna and someone put a log of wood against the door, locking me in. They took it away after I'd screamed myself hoarse."

"Do you have any idea who did it?"

"No, and for all I know, it was just a nasty prank on the part of a co-worker. But coming on the heels of the other attack, it seemed strange—like a warning."

"You need to be extremely careful here, Ms. Weggins. Whether it seems connected or not, if anything else unusual happens, you need to contact me immediately, okay? And I'd suggest you take a few days off on your story."

"I can't do that," I protested. "But I will be cautious, and I will tell you if I run into anything that could have to do with the case."

Well, *almost* anything. I hadn't told Tate what I'd learned about Nash. Until I could be sure Hilary wasn't lying about it, I didn't want to prompt the cops into dragging Nash into the interrogation room. I set down the phone experiencing a smidgen of guilt.

"You okay?" Jessie asked from her side of the bullpen. I had a feeling I looked pretty bewildered.

"Hanging in there," I said. "How about you?"

"I agree with Leo—this is all totally creepy."

"By the way, I had a little chat with Hilary about why she was down by the clubhouse. She said she was running around in the rain in order to try to find a ride."

"Oh *really*? Do you believe her?"

"She was definitely in the area at the *time* I was barricaded in the sauna. But when I pressed her, there was no recognition in her eyes. She may be a very good liar, but I had the vague sense she didn't know what I was talking about."

"I'll keep snooping, okay?"

"Thanks. I'm going to split now. Call me on my cell phone, will you, if anything turns up?"

"You mean if another staffer bites the dust? Sure thing."

It was too late now to try to make contact with any friends

of Ryan's. I hoped that by going home and fixing myself a semidecent meal, I'd be able to see the situation from a more advantageous angle and come up with a few strategies. There was a tiny chance Katya would change her mind and attempt to reach me. Also, now that I had shared my concerns with the police, they might be able to extract any secrets from her that would lead them to Ryan's and Mona's killer.

Before I left I checked the voice mail on my cell, irrationally hoping that while I'd been making calls and scurrying around Beau had left a message. Just something short and sweet, like "Every time I feel the scorch marks on my thighs, I think of you. It is essential that I see you tonight." But there was nothing.

Before departing, I sauntered over toward Nash's office. I wanted just to take a look at him and see if I viewed him differently now that he'd become a potential suspect in my mind. As I parked myself by the book giveaway table, feigning fascination with three or four unauthorized bios of teen stars, I glanced through the glass wall of Nash's office. He was standing by his table with the two deputy editors, in that Captain Magazine stance again—legs astride and arms akimbo—staring at what I assumed were layouts. He looked like a guy who might get wasted sometimes at a party or cheat on his wife. But there was no way to tell if he was also capable of killing in a moment of desperation.

As I stepped onto the elevator a minute later, two navy-suited dudes with briefcases were already on board, their handsome, square-jawed faces completely expressionless. I bet they work for Dicker, I thought. They looked like some of the guys I'd seen at Dicker's party. I imagined them buying and selling Dicker's magazines, crunching the numbers so it all worked out in his favor—even if a few whiny editorial types had to forfeit their jobs in the process.

And then, as if I had conjured him up, there was Dicker himself, shooting off into the lobby from another elevator car the same time our car disgorged us. Today he had on a thickly pin-striped suit that made him look as if he were in the cast of a *Guys and Dolls* revival, though the sight of him hardly inspired me to burst into a show tune. He spotted me immediately, and instead of looking past me, as I would have expected, he jerked to a stop and held my eyes. I had the feeling that in the body language of the filthy rich and frighteningly powerful, it translated as "Stop—I want to talk to you."

"Hi, Mr. Dicker," I said. In just the time it had taken to say those three words, I could feel the adrenaline begin to shoot through me.

"I heard the news," he said brusquely. "This guy who died—what do you know about him?"

"You mean, did I know he was a drug addict?" I said. "No, I wasn't aware of it." I started to add, "*No* one did, apparently," and then caught myself when I realized how absurd that sounded. Of course *someone* did: the person who killed him.

"What do you think happened to him?"

In a split second I had to decide whether to be forthcoming or not. I chose to go for it and see what his reaction was.

"Actually, I just talked to a source of mine," I said, lowering my voice. "It looks as if someone may have killed Ryan."

Dicker's face, which seemed permanently pinched in vexation, sagged briefly and then quickly reset into an expression of alarm. What I couldn't tell was where the alarm came from. Was it because this was all news to him—or because the police knew Ryan's death was *not* an accident?

"I need to know more about this," he said. "What are you doing right now?"

"Uh, nothing in particular," I said as the hairs on the back of my neck launched upward.

"Then come with me," he said. "I'm going to meet a couple of people for a drink. You can ride in the car with me."

"Um, okay," I said.

There was already too much momentum for me to resist—

Dicker was on the move again, striding ahead of me through the lobby. Briefly I wondered if I should be afraid, but I reassured myself with the knowledge that he was not going to kill me in his limo in the middle of midtown with the driver sitting up front. Besides, I'd been racking my brain for a way to speak to Dicker again, and now it was being handed to me by the man himself.

His limo was right in front of the building on Sixth Avenue, and without giving the driver a chance to jump out, Dicker snapped the door open and waited for me to enter, holding his suit jacket closed with the other hand. No sooner were we in the car than his cell phone ringer went off. He obviously knew who the person was from the caller ID because he answered with, "So what are they asking for?" Over the next few minutes, with his face once again hardened into that look of perpetual perturbation, he listened, barked, listened, and barked some more about what seemed to be a crisis at one of his printing plants. I stared out the window, curious and just a little bit fretful about our destination.

While we crawled up Sixth Avenue, I considered the best way to use this opportunity. It would be totally foolhardy to play any kind of cat-and-mouse game with Dicker. My best bet would be to reveal what I knew and observe his response. And at no time would I give even a hint of my suspicions about him. If he was indeed the killer, he was probably interested simply in learning what I knew.

After ten minutes of fighting traffic on Sixth, the driver turned right on 56th Street and we glided toward Park Avenue, where we turned right again and then took another right onto 55th. Dicker was still growling into the phone when we pulled up in front of the St. Regis Hotel.

"Damn," Dicker said, finally snapping the cell phone shut. I wasn't sure if he was commenting on a detail he'd learned during his phone call or the fact that the ride hadn't afforded him the chance to talk to me.

He glanced at his watch. "Look, I'm a little early. Why don't you come in? I'll buy you a drink and then the car can take you home when these people arrive."

I told him fine and he jumped out of the car, surprising me by extending his hand, so that I wouldn't have to struggle out of the limo.

The St. Regis is probably one of the most expensive hotels in New York. Dicker cupped his hand on my elbow as we stepped into the lobby. It's an opulent-looking space, lots of antique brass and gold trim and a ceiling painted sky blue with clouds and fat naked cherubs. At the moment it was bustling with super-rich-looking tourists, and bellboys wearing those round caps that you see in movies from the forties. They fit perfectly with Dicker's suit.

He directed me left, past a small courtyard-style restaurant to the bar. It was dark, mostly wood paneled, with a huge mural above the bar that, according to a legend at the bottom, was of Old King Cole. Dicker pulled out a leather-backed seat for me. The room was nearly empty except for two men next to us at the bar who couldn't have been under ninety and a few women with shopping bags sitting at the small tables that ran along the wall.

"What would you like?" Dicker asked.

"A glass of Pinot Grigio," I said to the bartender, who was sliding two cocktail napkins in front of us. I would have preferred not to drink at all, so I could keep my wits about me, but I knew if I requested a Pellegrino, Dicker would view me as a total wuss. To my surprise, he ordered a Tom Collins for himself.

"Let's get back to business," Dicker said. "What do you mean, this guy was killed?"

"*Might* have been killed," I said. "I don't have anything definitive yet, but this is from a pretty well-connected source of mine. It appears that someone may have substituted pure heroin for his regular stash."

"Jesus," he said, practically spitting the word. "Does Nash know about this?" Again, it was hard to assess his response. He seemed completely agitated about the news, but it could have been because he was just learning that his carefully planned accident wasn't coming across as an accident.

"Uh, not yet. I haven't had a chance to tell him. I really just learned all this moments ago."

"This is a major problem, presswise," he said, shaking his head. "You're gonna have to excuse me while I call our PR person."

Her assistant must have been the one who picked up, because he told the person on the other end to "find Linda and find her fast." While Dicker waited, he took several swigs of his drink and swiveled his chair so that he could scan the room. Behind me, I could hear the two geezers gabbing. They were talking about the old Pan Am Clipper Club and how much they missed it.

"Track her down, then, and have her find me," Dicker said finally. "I need to talk to her—*now*." As he shut his phone, I saw his eye catch something of interest out in the room and he nodded in recognition. The person he was meeting had clearly arrived. Instinctively, I turned my head.

To my complete shock and dismay, Beau Regan was strolling toward us. And by his side was the stick chick who'd been with him at Dicker's party.

Okay, I didn't dry heave, but I came really, really close. My brain flashed back on Beau telling me that he planned to see Dicker again during the week, but when Dicker threw out his invitation, it never crossed my mind that he was meeting Beau tonight. And what was *she* doing with him? How could he stand to be in her company after he'd been with me?

My only consolation was that Beau looked as horrified as I did.

"Let me see now," Dicker said. "It's Weggins, right? Binky Weggins?"

"Bailey," I said, barely remembering myself.

"This is Beau Regan—and Jade, right?"

"That's right," she said. Of course, no guy would have a hard time remembering *that*—especially when connected with a girl who looked like she did. Up close, I could see that her eyes were actually jade colored. She was wearing a white suit with a pink bustier underneath, and she had one of those white Louis Vuitton bags with the colored letters, the kind that cost more than my Jeep. As she shook my hand, she let her eyes run up and down my outfit—my khaki-colored shirt and black pants. I had the feeling she didn't think it was very special.

"Hello, Bailey," Beau said soberly. "I'm surprised to see you here."

"You two know each other?" Dicker asked at the same moment that Jade jerked her head in Beau's direction. She hadn't recognized me up until this moment, but maybe now she was recalling him chatting with me at the barbecue.

"More or less. I'm surprised to see you here, too," I said, addressing Beau. It had suddenly dawned on me that Beau might have thought I knew Dicker was meeting with him tonight and had found a way to tag along.

"We had a little business to discuss," Dicker told him.

"And if that's all, I'll be on my way," I said, looking straight at Dicker.

"Yeah, but I want you to call me if you hear anything else." He tugged a silver pen out of the inside pocket of his jacket and scrawled a number on the cocktail napkin that had been under his drink. The napkin was damp and the numbers blurred around the edges as soon as he wrote them down. "That's my cell number. Call me anytime—day or night."

"Sure," I said, sliding off my leather bar stool. "Have a nice night." That comment would have to work for the group, since I certainly wasn't going to bother with individual farewells. As I walked past the table of lady shoppers, they too eyed my outfit with disapproval, as if I looked dressed to begin a shift at Hooters. I hadn't felt like this much of a loser since my freshman year in high school.

I nearly flew through the lobby, anxious to be anywhere but within a mile radius of Beau Regan and the St. Regis Hotel. I saw Dicker's car outside, the driver paging through a *New York Post* with the window down, but I'd never confirmed with Dicker that I could take the car, and it seemed best to just skip that idea. I spent ten futile minutes looking for a cab and then trudged to 53rd and Fifth Avenue to pick up the E train.

There were so many different emotions churning around inside me that it was hard to know which to light on. I was furious with Beau for how humiliated he'd made me feel in the bar. And I couldn't stop obsessing about how he could be with another woman within the same twenty-four hours that he'd been fucking my brains out. In fact, how could he be with such a snooty chick to begin with? He'd been dismissive of her the other day at Dicker's. Had he just been bullshitting me? Of course he must be sleeping with her. As I'd discovered, the guy made his move before the first date even got off the ground.

Then there was Dicker. If only I'd been granted a few extra minutes alone with him, I might have been able to develop more of a sense of what was going on with him. He seemed fairly freaked about the Ryan news, but I hadn't been able to tell why.

Rather than let myself into my apartment, I banged several times on Landon's door. I was about to give up when I heard him plodding through his foyer. When he opened the door I saw that he was shirtless, wearing what appeared to be bathing trunks.

"Going for a dip?" I asked.

"No, I was enjoying the late afternoon sun on the terrace and I must have dozed off. I'm so glad you knocked. I was probably snoring so loudly they could hear it on Fifth Avenue."

"Can I ask your advice?"

"Of course. Is everything okay?"

"Not really, no. In fact, everything is going to hell."

"Well, well, come in. Sit. Just let me take off my trunks. There's no reason in the world you should have to look at these legs."

While he disappeared into his bedroom, I fidgeted in one of his pale gray armchairs. I couldn't sit still. I felt, in fact, as if I were ready to jump out of my skin.

"Okay, now talk to me," Landon said, returning in a pair of khaki pants and a blue cotton boatneck sweater.

I started by spilling the news of Ryan's death.

"Good God," he exclaimed. "If things keep moving at this pace, they'll have to change the name of the magazine from *Buzz* to *Buzz Kill.* I refuse to allow you to work there one more second."

"I don't think I'm in any imminent danger at the moment. Because I don't *know* anything. You see, Ryan must not only have learned who the killer is—which makes me feel like a total loser, by the way—but the killer clearly figured out that he knew. Ryan may have even *confronted* the killer. As long as I'm in the dark, I'm okay. But it also means that if I want to stay safe, I can't pursue my story."

"Why don't you just switch gears for a few weeks? Won't they let you write gossipy stuff—like 'Is Barbra Streisand's Marriage on the Rocks?'"

"Most of our readers are twenty-four and could care less about Barbra Streisand."

"Seriously, Bailey, you're not going to keep working on this, are you?"

"Even if I wanted to, I'm nearly stalled. I've spoken to most of the people on staff, and I honestly don't know what else to do. My only hope is that I hear from Katya or manage to locate friends of Ryan's. But if you *must* know, I do feel extremely anxious about this, and I promise not to do anything stupid."

"How about joining me for dinner? I'm eating with a friend at a restaurant on Jane Street. He could help me talk some sense into you."

"I'd love to, but I don't know if I have the psychic energy. I'll find something at home."

"This is really getting to you?"

"It's not just that." I told him all about Beau and about what had happened tonight at the St. Regis.

"Okay, which role do you want me to play? Bailey's friend or devil's advocate?"

"Devil's advocate, of course," I said.

"Let this guy off the hook, then. He had no idea that you would be there, so therefore he did nothing wrong."

"I suppose you're right," I conceded, "but it doesn't make it sting any less. It reminds me of the night last year when I spotted that investment banker I was seeing—you know, K.C.—going into a restaurant with another woman. But you know what's really stuck in my craw? The fact that it was *her*—Miss Louis Vuitton. She looks like some shallow, vain fashionista who's had a credit card since she was in the fifth grade. I bet that the only thought that's passed through her brain this week is whether she's overdue for an eyebrow wax."

"So you'd be less indignant if he were dating Madeleine Albright?"

"Absolutely. It's a matter of respect."

"So what you're saying is that you don't mind him dating other people, it's just his choice."

"Right . . . well, I guess. I don't know, exactly."

"Bailey, I've got very bad news for you. I think you may be smitten with this guy."

"Smitten is too strong a word."

"Then what word *would* you use?"

"I just really like the guy."

"And that's not what you were hoping for this summer," he pointed out. "You wanted a fling."

"Those two things aren't diametrically opposed. I wanted a fling with someone fun and smart and sexy—and so it stands to reason that I would *like* him. I guess you're right, though. What I'm feeling is that, no, I *don't* want to share him with another chick, even if it's Madeleine Albright. He's fling enough for me, and it's insulting that I'm not fling enough for him."

"But you don't know all the circumstances about tonight," Landon said, rising from his chair. I could tell he was searching for a polite way to hurry me along so he wouldn't be late for his dinner. "Maybe there's a reason he had to bring her. What I'm trying to say is give the guy at least one more chance."

"If he gives *me* another chance," I said. "I have this very bad feeling he thinks I knew he'd be there tonight—and that I came along on purpose. . . . Well, I guess I have to wait and see how it all plays out. As you always say, there are lots of fish in the sea. I just have to find one without a fanny pack."

I had tried to end on an upbeat, chipper note, so that I didn't cast a pall over Landon's evening or leave him with the sense that being my friend was always going to entail seeing me through an endless series of dating debacles and helping me pick through the shards afterward. But to be honest, I felt like shit when I let myself back into my apartment—and vaguely fearful, too, because now I was finally alone.

And it didn't get any better when I discovered that Beau had called my home phone at around four in the afternoon. There was no word about his thighs being scorched, but he did say he'd enjoyed our evening and would love to get together Friday night if I was in town. He asked that I give him a call. I wasn't sure why he'd called me here at home rather than my cell, but at least now I knew that he'd wanted to see me again.

But did that really change anything? I was still bugged by the fact that he had been out with that vapid-looking fashionista. I wanted to call him back, but I immediately thought better of it. I needed more time to figure out the best way to try to salvage the situation. Right now, less seemed like more.

Since I'd been in too much of a funk to stop at the deli, I was forced to make a dish I resort to when my cupboards are nearly bare: "pasta with practically no ingredients." It's just fusilli mixed with sautéed garlic, oil, Parmesan cheese, and a little bit of dried chili pepper. Hardly fine dining, especially if you have to resort to the Parmesan you buy in the green cardboard shaker, but if you consume it with a couple of glasses of red wine, which I did, you can convince yourself that it's perfectly sublime.

While I ate, I forced Beau from my mind and read through every single note in my composition book and all the interviews I'd taken in several reporters' notebooks. There were no epiphanies. As far as the case went, I was stuck, totally stuck. In all likelihood, I wouldn't be able to gain any more access to Kiki, Brandon, or Kimberly. Tomorrow I'd continue to try to track down some of Ryan's friends and mosey into Nash's office for a "casual" talk. But my only real hope was that Katya would change her mind and tell me what secret she was harboring.

I realized with a start that I had never filled Nash in on what I'd learned from the medical investigator. I'd steered clear of him ever since Hilary's revelation—or lie. But I'd told Dicker. I knew I'd better inform Nash. Knowing he'd probably left work—it was after ten—I called his office number and left the news for him on his voice mail.

I'd barely set the phone down when it rang. Be Beau, I thought. Be Beau begging for mercy. But it was Jessie. As soon as I heard her voice, I knew something was up.

"Tell me," I said.

"New development. After I talked to you and you said Hilary didn't register any guilt, I went back to the person who'd seen her sopping wet near the clubhouse. I asked for more specifics—you know, 'Could she have been leaving the clubhouse?' and that sort of thing. The answer was very weird."

"What?"

"She said that no, Hilary did *not* come out of the clubhouse. But the waiter did."

"The waiter? Which waiter?"

"She couldn't remember much about him. Just that he was
tall, kind of skinny. And that she saw him coming out of the
clubhouse just around the time the rain started. Oh, and he had
a shaved head. Does that mean anything to you?"

My breath quickened and my mind raced. Tall and skinny
fit the description of the guy who had followed me in Brighton
Beach. I thought back on the waitstaff at the barbecue. I'd seen
a tall, skinny bald waiter in the kitchen.

"Maybe," I said. "I mean, I remember someone like that at
the party. But I don't know him. Someone may have paid him
to come after me."

I thanked her for her help and signed off. My stomach was
churning. Ever since last Friday, I'd factored in the idea that the
killer may have paid someone to stalk me, but now there was
evidence that it might be true. It seemed to make everything
even scarier. Someone was after me, but I didn't know who he
was or whom he was working for. Tomorrow I'd try to learn
what I could from the catering company. But I realized that
there was a problem with that tactic. I'd have to ask Nash or
Dicker's office for the number, and if either one was involved,
he might discern I was on to him.

I tried to read for a while, but it was useless. At midnight,
I decided to force myself to fall asleep. I triple-locked my front
door and checked that the terrace door was bolted. I also made
sure that the windows were locked. There'd be no leaving
them open as I'd done the night Beau stayed over.

It was stuffy but not real hot in my bedroom, so I ran the
AC for just a couple of minutes, shut it off after I'd undressed,
and then switched on the table fan on my dresser right before
flopping into bed. Fortunately I was so fatigued, sleep soon
overtook me. I played with a few thoughts in my head, but

they quickly broke apart, the way a sheer, thin sheet of ice might if you held it in your hands. I was asleep within minutes.

When I woke up, I knew instantly it was because a sound had roused me—though I don't know how I knew that. As I forced my eyes open, the only noise I could hear was the hum of the fan and the distant murmur of traffic far below. Perhaps the sound had infiltrated my dream somehow, nudging me awake by its incongruity to the story line. But what was it and where did it come from?

I lay motionless in bed, wide-eyed, listening. The time on my clock radio was two forty-five.

Just as I started to close my eyes again, having convinced myself that what I was contending with was probably the return of the insomnia elf, I heard another sound. It was dull and muffled and otherwise undistinguished. I shot up in bed. I was pretty sure the sound had come from outside, at the far end of my terrace, near the living room.

I quickly slid out of bed and turned off the fan. I froze in place and listened again. Far away someone honked a horn, but that was all.

Quietly, I made my way down the short hallway until I reached my living room—and then I froze again. All the lights were off, but the glow of the city faintly illuminated portions of the terrace and even the edges of my living room. I swung my eyes around the room. Nothing seemed amiss. The noise, I realized, might have been the sound of my patio furniture being rattled by the wind or a plastic bucket being blown over on the roof space adjacent to my terrace—on the opposite side from Landon's terrace.

I walked across the room, practically on tiptoes. This is insane, I thought. Who am I trying to hide from? I peered out the glass door to my terrace. I could see the outlines of my patio table, my small grill, and my flowerpots loaded with red geraniums. Nothing's the matter, I told myself. You're just on pins and needles because of everything that's happened.

I pressed into the glass door and turned my head so that I could see the small section of roof to the left. That appeared empty, too.

But then my eyes found their way to the door in the brick enclosure to the stairwell. It was gaping open, as if someone had just passed through it.

CHAPTER 20

I jerked back from the glass, petrified. Was someone out there now? Or had they been out there and fled already? Or was the door simply agape from an earlier visit by one of the building maintenance staff?

I bolted across the living room and, using the intercom, called down to the front desk. Unfortunately, at this hour there was never a doorman on duty, just one of the porters. The groggy voice that answered belonged to Steve, I thought, who unfortunately had the IQ of a pigeon. I insisted that he send the super up immediately.

I switched on two of the lamps in my living room and waited, my eyes glued to the door and windows to my terrace. I was tempted to call Landon, but I hated to wake him if this was all a false alarm. After twenty minutes—and me calling downstairs twice more—the super, Barry, tapped at my door. He was wearing bagged-out clothes that had obviously been retrieved from the hamper only moments before, and his toupee was slightly askew, giving him the shortest forehead in

Manhattan. I explained that I'd heard noises outside and had discovered the stairwell door open.

He looked across my living room toward the door to my terrace, then back at me. I think he may have felt anxious about going outside to investigate. Finally he sighed, withdrew a flashlight from his deep pants pocket, and crossed the room.

Before opening the door, he turned on the wall light outdoors, his hand reaching instinctively for the spot. His eyes shot around the terrace, and then finally he unbolted the door and stepped outside.

He didn't go very far at first, just hung by the door, letting his flashlight sweep over the roof area to the left of my terrace. After a few seconds, I stepped out behind him. The stairwell door was just as it was when I'd looked out earlier—gaping open to a pitch-black stairway. Shouldn't there be a light on? I wondered for the first time.

A simple, waist-high wrought-iron railing separated my terrace and the roof area. Barry crossed to it, lifted his left leg over, and then hoisted the rest of his body to the other side. The experience seemed to knock the wind out of him, which was no surprise considering his pot belly was so big that he might as well have been hiding a basketball under his shirt. After catching his breath, he proceeded cautiously toward the stairwell door, the beam from the flashlight bobbing nervously over the bricks. When he reached the door, he paused and trained the light inside. Hesitantly, he reached into the darkness and flicked on a light. There was nothing there except the gray walls of the stairwell.

After cocking his head and listening for a minute, he pulled the door closed and retraced his steps toward me, sweeping the flashlight once more around the roof. Then he huffed his way back over the railing and shook his head.

"The door must have blown open," he said.

"Blown open?" I exclaimed. "Barry, there isn't a big enough breeze tonight. And why is the light off in the stairwell?"

"I'm gonna check and see about that. One of the porters probably turned it off, or forgot to turn it on tonight. But there's no way someone could have gotten up here. They would have had to go by one of the porters."

I felt a tiny bit like the boy who cried wolf. There was no real evidence that a prowler had been on my terrace, and Barry was not going to make a mental leap and buy my suspicions. Because, after all, it would only reflect poorly on him. I had a hunch, however, that he would investigate the matter further. I'd seen *some* concern in his eyes, especially about the light being out.

After I'd shown him out, I made a cup of tea, and when that didn't help, I poured a splash of brandy and sucked it down, though it was the cheap kind that stings as you swallow it. For the next few hours I lay on the couch, my eyes glued on the terrace door. At around six, as daylight seeped into my living room, I finally passed out from exhaustion.

At eight, the alarm went off in my bedroom and I woke with a start, my heart beginning to pound again. There was a momentary rush of relief when I realized that it was only my clock radio jarring me awake. But within seconds that relief evaporated as I realized that it might be ages before I felt safe in my home again. I should call Tate, I thought. I'd promised to let him know if anything threatening happened, but I couldn't be sure that my nighttime terror had something to do with Mona's murder. Maybe Barry was right and the door simply had blown open.

Dragging myself to the bathroom, I realized that my head was throbbing, a punishment for buying and drinking cheap brandy. I was just about to step into the shower when my phone rang. Great, I thought. Probably Jessie announcing another dead staffer.

But it was Beau's voice I heard after I'd forced out a weak "Hello."

"Rough night?" he asked, his voice friendly but slightly tentative.

I came very close to lobbing a sarcastic retort—a line like "Yeah, after I left you I had to interview Jason Bateman and he begged me to demonstrate the reverse cowgirl position for him." Instead I muttered something about working late.

"Is this one of those days you go into *Buzz*?"

"It wasn't going to be, but there've been some new developments, so I'm heading in—shortly."

"I'm not all that far from you right now," he said. "Would you have time for a cup of coffee?"

"Uh, I guess," I said. My hesitancy was due to one thing: my sudden fear that he was about to blow me off. Maybe he belonged to that small breed of men whose good manners required that they spell out the bad news to you in person rather than simply never call you again in your lifetime.

"It won't take long," he said, sensing my hesitation. "I just wanted to see you after what happened last night."

I suggested that we meet in half an hour in the coffee shop on the ground floor of my building. That left me time to shower, though not to wash my hair. I had planned to wear only jeans to work today, and I threw them on along with a white T-shirt in an attempt to be blasé. But after surveying myself in the mirror, and realizing that I looked like hell, I tore off the outfit and exchanged it in a frenzy for a slim beige pencil skirt, an off-the-shoulder black sweater that revealed a hint of cleavage, and a pair of leopard-print slingbacks that were more than mere "fuck me" shoes—they screamed, "fuck me hard!" There was no kidding myself. I wanted Beau Regan to eat his heart out.

Before heading down to the coffee shop, I unlocked the door to my terrace and slipped outside. In the early morning light, with the sounds of the city rising from below and my red geraniums grinning at the sun, it was hard to conjure up how scary the place had been the night before.

As Barry had done, I hoisted myself in my pencil skirt over the wrought-iron railing, then crossed to the stairwell door and opened it. The light was on now. The only object I saw in the stairwell was a mop, leaning against the wall on the landing just below. There wasn't a lick of evidence that anyone had ever trespassed. After returning to my apartment, I bolted the door and once again double-checked the locks on the windows in both living room and bedroom. Despite the fact that I had no proof of a prowler, I wasn't going to take any chances.

Beau was in the coffee shop when I arrived, dressed today in a navy suit and crisp blue-and-white-striped shirt—but no tie—and already drinking a cup of coffee. If he'd shagged Miss Louis Vuitton, he obviously hadn't sprung for breakfast. I supposed they could have eaten early, but she seemed like the type who never crawled out of bed before noon.

I put on an easy, carefree smile as Beau pulled out the other chair at the table, though inside my stomach felt like a salad spinner at full speed. Beau looked so sexy today. His skin had that gleaming smoothness from just being shaved. I couldn't believe he liked being in the company of that bimbo.

"You look great," he said. "Big interview today?"

"Oh, thanks," I said breezily. "No, just a few appointments."

"I appreciate you squeezing me in this morning," he said after signaling for the waiter to bring me coffee. "I felt lousy about what happened last night. There was a moment when I actually thought you'd tagged along on purpose, knowing I was going to be there, but then I realized that there'd be no way you'd do that. After you left, Dicker explained that he'd more or less hijacked you."

"Well, you'd mentioned you were going to see him this week, but when Dicker asked me to join him, I never guessed you'd be there."

"I'm sorry if that was awkward for you. If it's any consolation, I felt ridiculous."

"No problem," I said, as if he'd volunteered to go for a tub of buttered popcorn at the movies and had forgotten to bring napkins back with him.

Yet I had to admit, it *was* a problem for me. It wasn't rational. As Landon pointed out, I had no legitimate reason to be annoyed. We were hardly going steady, and Beau hadn't known I'd be there. But regardless, I didn't like the idea of sharing him.

"You're not pissed?"

"Look, I probably seemed discombobulated, but it was mostly because I was finally alone with Dicker and I was hoping I had at least a few minutes to talk to him."

"Do you still think he might be the murderer? I never had the opportunity to ask him that question about Mona."

"I don't know what to think anymore." I told him quickly about Ryan's death and how he may have learned the truth.

"That's horrible," he exclaimed. "And now you're trying to figure out what you missed?"

"Yeah. And I'm not coming up with a single thing. . . . Any ideas as a filmmaker? I mean about looking at a situation from a fresh angle?"

He thought, his fingers splayed against his full mouth. I noticed that his lips were even more chapped than they'd been the other night. Probably, I thought in disgust, from a night of endless sex with *her.*

"This doesn't really help, but one of the trickiest parts when you're doing documentaries is the continuity," Beau said. "You don't shoot scenes in sequence, so when you stitch them together later, you need to make certain they flow the right way and everything makes sense. On big-budget films you have someone who does that for you. They make sure when you shoot a scene that the guy is still wearing a red shirt, the way he was when you worked on that scene four days before. And that the clock says the right time. But on low-budget films like mine, I have to watch out for that myself. Along with my editor. I have to constantly step back and pretend I'm a stranger watching the film for the first time."

He smiled. "That's probably not what you were hoping for," he said.

"That's not true," I said. "Maybe I should try that—stepping back a bit. I certainly need to do *something*." After deliberating for a second, I told him about the noises on my terrace last night.

"Christ, Bailey, that's scary. Did you call the police?"

"No. Maybe I should have, but in the end all I was dealing with was an open door. What does that prove?"

"You don't have real great security up there, right?" he asked. "Isn't the door to your terrace just glass?"

"Hm-hmm. I've always felt pretty safe because it's not easy for someone to get access to the roof. But now I'm wondering if someone did."

He did that cocking-of-the-one-eyebrow trick. "Do you want to stay at my place tonight?"

I was sipping my coffee as he said it, and I almost choked. God, the guy really liked having his cake and eating it, too. As much as I wanted to take him up on his offer, I didn't think I could do it. I'd already been too easy, too available, too transparent. It was time for heart hardball.

"I appreciate the offer, but let me see how it goes. I may be working late tonight."

He smiled at me with sly amusement. I was playing with him because of the St. Regis incident and he knew it.

"I better get going," I said after peeking at my watch. "Who knows who's dead today on the sixteenth floor."

The check was already on the table, and he threw down a few bills to cover it rather than pay the cashier. Out on the sidewalk, he put his arm around me and gave me a squeeze.

"Well, if you decide to tough it out alone tonight, at least call me, will you? I want to know what's going on."

"Sure," I said. "Have a good day, okay?"

I offered him a fast peck on the cheek and took off, mincing toward the subway in my tight skirt. I could feel his eyes watching me, and I smiled to myself. Game, Weggins.

My smugness evaporated, though, as soon as I descended the subway steps. The oppressive heat in the station and the newspaper inserts grimly plastered along the stairs seemed to bring back all my anxiety. Someone was watching me, perhaps had even paid me a visit last night. Someone who was worried that I knew too much. And the last Scooby Doo on the case—Ryan—most likely had been murdered. I could throw in the towel as Landon suggested. I could run home, call Nash, and quit my job at *Buzz*. No one, given all that had happened, would blame me for it. Except myself. I would have to live with the knowledge that I'd come close to unmasking the killer and then had walked away, leaving others in danger, because I was afraid. The train pulled up and the doors opened. I hesitated on the platform for a second and then jumped on the train.

A few reporters were hanging outside the building when I arrived, including a nice guy from the *Daily News* whom I'd known for years. He tried to pump me for info, but I just shrugged helplessly and hurried past.

I filled my coffee mug in the kitchenette and dived into my work. The story on the stalker with erotomania wasn't going to be long, but I needed more details. I made a bunch of calls and also arranged two in-person interviews for the next day. The mood at *Buzz* couldn't have been more somber.

In between working on my *Buzz* assignments, I focused on Ryan. I phoned for the official updates from the police and the ME's office, but they amounted to nothing more than what I knew already. Then I went to work trying to track down friends of his—I was particularly looking for the one he'd been speaking with when Jessie overheard him. Perhaps Ryan had hinted to the person what information he had in his possession. According to his résumé, he had worked at *People* at one point and also *Entertainment Weekly*. I phoned around to several people I knew at each magazine and also made cold calls, running through various phone extensions. I found a few people familiar with him but no one who had considered him a friend.

At one point, I strolled over to the book giveaway table again, in order to check out Nash's office. He was punching at his computer, apparently editing copy. Just looking at him was disconcerting.

Shortly after two it began to thunder and rain, casting even more of a pall over the place. People traipsed in from lunch, their clothes soaked through. I felt not only wiped out from my nearly sleepless night, but also morose. Mona was dead, Ryan was dead. A tall, skinny man with a bald head was apparently stalking me, and though I could watch out for *him,* I couldn't watch out for whoever had hired him—because I had no freakin' idea who it was!

I also felt glum about Beau. I'd left the coffee shop so triumphant, so convinced that I had been the victor. Beau was sorry he'd embarrassed me, and he was apparently eager to see me again. Yet here was the problem: He'd never once explained the circumstances of being with the fashionista or volunteered that he wasn't going to be spending another minute in her company. I'd been with the guy only twice, so I could hardly expect him to ask me to go steady. But deep down I knew what I had wanted him to say: "Bailey, I did have a date with that woman, and until I met you I had every intention of playing the field; but after being with you this week, I realize I don't want to be with anyone else." Yeah, right.

As I ruminated about Beau, I recalled what he had said about the need to step back, to be sure of the continuity. I flipped open my notebook and thumbed back to the page where I'd jotted down Ryan's remarks the day he'd had the lightbulb go off. What I had wasn't verbatim because I'd scribbled the comments *after* our testy conversation in the kitch-

enette. But I was pretty sure I had the gist right. I'd asked him
if he'd seen anyone. He'd said that he'd spoken to Mona and
then walked down the corridor. He'd passed Katya on her way
toward the bullpen. He'd said that as far as he could see there
was no one else around, that the place was empty. Then he
had started to say something else, and at that moment he'd had
a revelation.

With my expectations low, I stood up from my desk and
headed toward the corridor that led to the back door to *Track*.
I walked slowly, letting my mind loose. Had Ryan seen something after he'd passed Katya, something that he later realized
was significant? Had one of the editors with an office in the
back still been around when he'd walked by? By the time I
reached the door to *Track,* no lightbulbs had gone off for me.

I had my eyes cast down in thought as I returned to the
pod, and it was a second before I realized that Nash was standing outside his office, signaling for me to hightail it over there.
He flicked his hand open and closed a couple of times, as
though he were trying to help me back into a parking space.
Oh boy.

"Got your message last night, of course," Nash said, closing
the door behind me. "About Ryan. And the police intimated as
much when I spoke to them this morning."

"So what do you think?" I asked.

"About the fact that he was probably murdered?"

"And the fact that someone here might have done it."

"What do you mean?" he asked brusquely.

"Well, that Ryan, you know, kept a supply of drugs here . . .
at work," I said haltingly. "I mean, I assume he did since the
police found a plastic bag in his drawer. So my guess would
be that someone who knew he did drugs substituted the pure
heroin Monday night—or thereabouts—counting on it to kill
him."

He studied me, his face hard. "Because they didn't like the
way he wrote a lead?" he asked sarcastically.

"No, because he knew he or she had killed Mona."

"Wow, that's quite a theory," he said after wiping his open palm down along his face. "I suppose my next question should be, do you have any suspects in mind?"

"No, no, I don't," I said quietly. "What about you? Any guesses?"

I cocked my head like an eager beaver, trying to look like a devoted employee anxious to hear her boss's wisdom. But really I was holding my breath, watching his reaction with trepidation.

"No, not at the moment. But what about your theory that Mona was killed by an outsider? Earlier you were all charged up thinking it was tied to Eva Anderson somehow."

"I know. I know. There's some evidence pointing in that direction, and it's quite possible there's still a connection—and that someone from the outside gained access to Ryan's desk."

He wagged his head in frustration. "Well, I'd suggest you think this latest theory through before you go off half-cocked on this. We're certainly not going to run anything in the magazine stating that Ryan's death is linked to Mona's—unless we have absolute proof."

My cheeks reddened from the slight. "Of course," I said. "Well, if that's all, I better get back to work."

"There's one more thing," he said. He sounded stern. "Hilary told me you've been asking a lot of questions about blind items. I thought we'd agreed that we were going to keep that stuff under our hat."

That little brat. I wondered what else she had told him. Had she mentioned that she'd shared the news about the blind item concerning *him*? But that would only backfire on her, right?

"I never told her anything about Eva," I said. "If she's implying that, then she's just trolling, trying to figure out what we know that she doesn't."

I was nearly squirming at this point and was relieved when

he shrugged and turned back to his table, indicating that our little chat was over.

I'd thought the day couldn't get any worse, but it just had.

Back at my desk I rooted around in my purse for a bag of M&Ms, a stash I keep for days like this one, and tore it open. I was just about to pop a handful of them in my mouth when the phone rang.

"Bailey Weggins," I announced.

"This is Katya," a voice said.

I fought off a gasp in my throat.

"Yes, Katya, hello," I said nearly in a whisper. "How can I help you?"

"I would like to talk to you. If you still would like."

"Of course. Are you all right? You sound frightened."

I lifted my eyes and glanced around the room, just to be certain no one was watching me.

"Yes, very frightened," she admitted. "You were right. There is one thing I have not told you."

My breathing quickened. "But what about the police? If there's something important, we'll need to let them know."

"No, no," she said, her voice suddenly desperate. "There is a reason that I cannot speak to them. You will understand when I tell you."

"All right," I said hesitantly. "When shall we meet? Are you in the building now?"

"No, I have not yet arrived. Nine o'clock. That is when I can meet."

"*Nine?* I thought you arrived at four. Can't you do it then?"

"No," she said. "I must start some of my other floors. I cannot take any chance with my job. At ten we have a break, but I am able to meet you sooner if I am very quick about it."

"Where shall we meet?"

"There is a room in the basement for the cleaning persons. We can speak alone there. The others do not come for their break until ten."

"Um, okay," I said. "The room is just down the hall from where I saw you?"

"Yes, just down the hall. And you must promise me you will tell no one."

"Of course."

"Please. My life—it is in danger already. And yours may be, too."

I set down the phone, and let my hands drop to the desk. I felt chilled by her words. Out of the corner of my eye I became aware of Jessie, poised, watching me.

"*What?*" she asked, rolling toward me. "Is everything okay?"

"I'm going to be getting some information that may tell me everything. I can't believe it may all be coming to a head."

"Who just called you? Was it news about the waiter?"

"No, it was the cleaning lady. But you can't breathe a word to anyone, okay?"

"Absolutely."

For the next few hours, I tried to concentrate on my work, but it was hard. I downloaded information from the Internet on erotomania, but my eyes found little traction on the words. At six-thirty, seeing that the rain had finally stopped, I ran out to a touristy Italian restaurant in the neighborhood and asked for a table, where I ordered chicken piccata in a sauce the consistency of mud. But at least it was a diversion.

The office was still packed when I returned. From overhearing Leo all day, I had a clue that the tentative cover story this week was on Britney Spears. In focus groups, people apparently claimed that they'd sooner buy a magazine with Sandra Day O'Connor on the cover than one featuring Britney, but when we slapped her on the front, the issue invariably flew off the stands. Jessie called it train wreck journalism.

By eight-thirty, things were quieting down. Jessie's desk light was still on, but she was nowhere in sight and I wondered if she'd gone for the night without bidding farewell. Some of the junior people in the pod were still toiling away, though it was dark in most of the offices rimming the open area. Nash was holed up in *his* office. And at one point I saw Hilary stick her head in his door and say something. She'd probably popped in to tell him that she suspected me of stealing all the shoes from the fashion closet.

At eight forty-five, I slipped out of my seat and headed for the freight elevator. Before I pushed the button, I glanced up and down the hall, making certain no one saw me, and I did that again as I waited. The empty elevator finally arrived with a groan, and as I stepped inside, it felt as if my heart were in my mouth.

The elevator made no stops, but it moved very slowly. Finally it reached the basement level, rocking slightly as it settled in place. The door slid open. There was no one in sight, just rows of canvas Dumpsters and a huge pile of discarded furniture that had appeared since my previous visit.

I set off toward the small room for the cleaning crew. This time I heard no music, just the loud, discordant hum of the fluorescent lights overhead and a motor sound—perhaps a generator—far off in another part of the basement. I rounded one corner and passed the small room where I'd seen the maintenance men the other day. It was empty now except for the fan, which swiveled back and forth in a futile attempt to cool the air.

I reached the corner where I'd encountered Katya. I glanced once behind me, then turned in the direction of the room for the cleaning crew. Everything down here seemed to be in a time warp. The rotary fans, the fluorescent lights. There were even red metal buckets hanging on nails along the walls, each of them emblazoned with the word FIRE—and filled with sand.

A doorway came into view, up on the left. As I stepped inside the room, I saw that there was a table, a row of ancient-looking gray metal lockers similar to the ones I'd seen in the other room, and a small mirror hung lopsidedly on the wall.

It was a moment before I spotted Katya. She was standing at the far end of the room, at the edge of the table. Her shoulders sagged in her blue uniform, and I could see, even from the doorway, that there were still dark half-moons under her eyes.

"Hello," she said somberly.

"I'm glad you called," I said. "I was hoping you'd get in touch with me." My pulse quickened as I crossed the room to her. I knew that what she was about to reveal might point me toward the person who'd killed both Mona and Ryan.

"Well, you asked me to, is that not correct?" she said snappishly.

"Yes," I said. "I had a feeling there was something you might want to tell me."

"Tell you?"

Why the curt tone and the skittishness? I wondered. Were they just a reflection of the fear she was experiencing?

"About the murder," I said.

"So you didn't believe me the other evening when I told you I saw nothing?"

Gosh, this was maddening. She'd called me down here because she supposedly had information to divulge, and now she was being cagey again. I decided my only strategy was to urge her on by letting her think I knew more than I did.

"Katya, I know what's going on," I said evenly. "Ryan and I worked together, and we exchanged information regularly. I know he spoke to you. Now, please, tell me in your own words. I can help you if you'll only tell me."

She took a deep breath, straightening her body, and her lips parted, as if she were about to speak. But instead her mouth formed into a snarl. Rows of goose bumps raced up my arms. I didn't like the way she was acting.

"So you know, do you?" she asked, her voice filled suddenly with confidence and disdain. "You are what they call a smarty pants, then. And so why should I not kill you just like I killed your lady boss?"

CHAPTER 21

I stared at her dumbly, trying to grasp what she'd said with the difficulty of someone grabbing on to a doorknob slathered in grease. I played her words back in my head. She had just confessed to killing Mona. And she had wrongfully assumed that I had come to the basement knowing the truth.

"Why?" I asked weakly. "Why would you do that to her?"

I caught a glimmer in her eyes. She had just realized her mistake, probably because of the stupefied expression on my face.

"So," she said, smiling ruefully. "You trick me. You did *not* know, but you talk to me to find out what you can. Everyone at your *Buzz* magazine is just alike."

I reached back slowly with my hand and gripped the edge of the table for support. With one ear I listened for sounds emanating from the rest of the basement. I was in big trouble, and my whole body was pulsing with fear.

"Katya, I didn't try to trick you, really," I said as gently as possible. "I approached you because I thought you were afraid, that something was troubling you."

She snickered again. "Oh, something was troubling me, that is true. I don't want to go to one of your American prisons."

"Why did you do it?"

"Your boss was an evil woman, a witch. She wanted to take my job away."

"Your job—*why*?"

She snorted with disdain. "She didn't like the way I dust in her office. And she say that I don't remove the drinking glasses from her table and they cause rings on her tabletop. She had the woman who worked for her call my boss."

"And so you hit her out of anger?"

"Is that what you think? No, I was *protecting* myself. She attacked me first."

I flashed back to the wound on Katya's head.

"Why?"

"I saw her come down the hallway—from that party, I think. I went to talk to her, to ask her not to make trouble for me. I thought she would be a kind person and listen, but she said she did not want me on her floor anymore—even in the building. I give her push, just a little push, but not to harm her. When I turned around, she hit me—on the head with that trophy of hers. I picked up the trophy and I hit her back. It was what you call self-defense."

Hardly self-defense. Whereas Katya's wound hadn't appeared life-threatening, Mona had taken a brutal pounding. It seemed more than likely that Katya had worked herself into a rage that night, had pushed Mona, and then had snapped when Mona struck her. In fact, I was being given a glimpse of that mercurial, unstable side of her personality now. But I knew I had to do my best to appear sympathetic and find a way to escape.

"The police will understand," I told her. "They understand about self-defense."

She rolled her eyes incredulously and then, shifting moods

again, smiled at me. "You know, you helped me so much that night."

"What do you mean?" I asked. But I knew what she was about to say. It was about how I had played into the whole charade.

"You asked me about my attacker," Katya said. "That gave me the idea. And then I just play along with it, for you and the police. I even give that one special detail about the long-sleeve shirt. I don't want to come back to work here, but André say that I have to or it would look funny."

"How did Ryan learn the truth?" I asked, my thoughts now rushing ahead.

She shook her head dismissively. "He called my company. He found out that there had been a complaint by your boss. So then he calls me and tells me to come to his floor and asks lots of questions, sticking his nose where it doesn't belong— just like you."

"But how did he suspect you in the first place?"

"He saw me in the big office."

"He saw you hit Mona?"

"No, no," she said in frustration. "He said he saw me earlier, emptying the wastebasket in her office. And he knew that there was no reason why I should be back there later."

So that had been Ryan's revelation, the lightbulb that had gone off when I questioned him. He had been describing Katya coming down the hall. He knew from the press reports that Katya had been attacked outside Mona's office, but why would she be there if, as he'd witnessed, she'd already cleaned that part of the floor? He must have realized that Katya had been following Mona back to the office.

"Had you seen the drugs in his drawer? Is that how you knew he used them?"

"I look in all your drawers," she said, her lips curled. "And I know your secrets."

"And so you substituted the pure heroin. Is that something André obtained for you?"

She smiled proudly. "Let's just say we have our connections. I call André after this man talks to me and he brings the drugs. I did not think the man would return that night, but he did. He was doing drugs a long time. He would have died soon anyway."

"You had me followed from your apartment that night, didn't you. But it wasn't André—he was too tall."

"That is André's cousin. A very good man. He paid you a visit at your building one night, too."

"And in the sauna. How did he manage to work at the party?"

"That wasn't hard. I have connections on other floors. I am getting tired of your questions. You ask too many."

"Katya," I said, trying to keep my voice even, "the police are closing in on you. You need to come upstairs now so we can call them."

She laughed harshly. "Oh, I don't think so," she said. "I think you are like the man Ryan. You keep it all to yourself so you can write a big story. Besides, I have nothing to worry about. The police have no proof."

That might be the case, but it was clear she wasn't going to be taking any chances. I had to get out of there and get out fast. From somewhere off in the basement, I thought I heard the sound of footsteps. This was the time to go. I jumped back from the table, spun around, and sprang across the room.

I felt her reach for me, try to grab my arm, but I was too quick. She didn't attempt to come after me, though. I reached the door and threw myself out and to the right. Ten feet away, André was standing in the corridor with another man—the tall, skinny waiter with the shaved head whom I'd seen in the kitchen at Dicker's.

I backed up, fear gushing through me.

"Stop her," Katya called out, aware obviously from my retreating steps that I'd spotted André. From the pocket of his black leather jacket, André drew something silver and held it toward me. For a second I stared at it stupidly, as if he were holding out a tool of some kind, expecting me to take it. And then I saw that it was really a knife. A short, fat one that gleamed momentarily as he cocked his hand to the right.

I turned and heaved myself in the opposite direction, running as fast as I could in my slingbacks.

"Help!" I called as I plunged down the hall, hiking up my skirt with one hand. My cry emerged with all the force of someone summoning a waiter. I tried again, and this time it was louder, but there was no response from any direction.

About fifty feet ahead of me the corridor dead-ended, but it looked as if it branched off to both the left and the right. All of a sudden the lights went out, and I was running in total darkness. One of the men must have flicked a switch. Disoriented, I stumbled, reached out for support, and felt my purse slip off my shoulder. Before I could catch myself, I slammed into the wall with the right side of my body and fell to the ground.

I could hear the men panting as they ran behind me and the sound of someone's hand skimming along the wall as he moved. Frantically I struggled to my feet, picturing the knife in André's hands, and started to run again. The two men were nearly on top of me now, and an arm suddenly swept the air, just grazing my body. It felt massive and I sensed it must be André's. I jumped away, but the arm swiped again and this time he managed to grab the back of my stretchy black top. In one swift movement, he knotted his hand around the fabric and used it as a pivot to ram me hard into the wall. The first thing that hit was my head, and I groaned from the blow. I reached out for something to hold on to so I wouldn't fall again, and my hands found a hard metal object protruding from the wall. I realized, even in the darkness, that it was one of the red buckets I'd seen earlier, the ones filled with sand that

said FIRE on them. I moved both hands up to the rim and
yanked so that the bucket came off the nail. I aimed without
seeing and flung the bucket as hard as I could. It hit someone
in the face, I thought, making a sound that was a cross between a clang and a crunch. He growled and spat out a few
words in what must have been Russian as the bucket bounced
several times on the cement floor.

With my palm against the wall, I began to run again. Far-
ther up, I could see light bleeding into the corridor—the lights
were clearly on someplace up ahead. I ran faster. The corridor
ended, but there were two others, both lit, branching off to the
right and the left. I chose the one to the right, because instinct
told me that it led back in the general direction of the elevator.
After a short distance, the corridor opened onto another wide
expanse of basement, this area filled with dozens of huge cardboard boxes and a few dollies leaning against the wall. I hadn't
a clue where the elevator was or even a stairwell, for that matter—and I could hear footsteps behind me.

I took off in the direction that I sensed must be north, hoping that I was running parallel to the corridor I'd originally
come down and that I'd wind up back near the elevator. Suddenly, on one of the support posts, I spotted a fire alarm and
an extinguisher just below it. I pulled down hard on the alarm,
and instantly the clanging began. I looked behind me. No sign
of the men. I yanked the extinguisher off the post, and with it
tucked beneath my arm I began to run again.

Within a minute, I found myself in territory that seemed familiar—the herd of Dumpsters and the stacks of office furniture. I knew that the elevator was just ahead. I raced in that
direction, and when I reached it I jammed the button with my
finger—but I could see by the pointer above that the elevator
was on the twelfth floor. Over the clanging I could hear shouts,
in Russian. André and his cousin would be here any second.
Just down the hall was the room where I'd seen the maintenance men that day. I raced down there, ducked into the room,

and almost without thinking flung open the door of one of the metal lockers. Quickly I climbed inside.

There were several slits in the door, nearly at my eye level; as I gripped the extinguisher in my hands, I peered out into the room. No sign of anyone, though they couldn't be far behind. The only sound I could hear was the deafening clanging of the alarm, only slightly muffled inside the locker.

And then the cousin burst into the room. My body felt liquefied by fear. I commanded my fingers to locate the little pin on the extinguisher. It was too dark and I was too crammed in to be able to see if I'd found it, but I was pretty sure I had.

After glancing up and down the length of the room, the cousin turned to go. But then he lurched to a stop in the doorway, and I could almost see his mind working. *Go, go, go!* I wanted to scream. He spun around, took one long stride, and flung open the locker closest to him.

After he found it empty, he kept going, one locker after another. He flung open each door so hard that the whole unit shook. As he drew closer to mine, he entered a blind spot in my peripheral vision and I could no longer see him. With adrenaline pumping through my veins, I gripped the extinguisher tightly, my foot poised to kick in case he tried to close the door once he saw what I had in my arms.

Finally my time was up. The locker door flung open, light filled my eyes, and I pulled out the pin then squeezed the trigger. A huge explosion of white spray spewed forth directly into the cousin's eyes. He shouted, first in surprise and then in pain, and stumbled backward into a crouch. I tried to jump past him, but as one of his hands sought his eyes, the other reached for me. He grabbed my ankle and yanked. In one swift motion I belly-flopped onto the floor with a smack. The fire extinguisher went sailing across the room.

The fall knocked the wind out of me, and for a second all I could do was kick feebly in the cousin's direction. I craned my head around. He clawed with both hands at his eyes now.

I struggled to my feet and lumbered out into the hall, in the direction of the elevator. The elevator must have come and gone since I was first in the corridor because the dial indicated that it was now on six. For the first time I noticed, farther down the hall, an EXIT sign. That must be the damn stairwell, I realized. As I took a step toward it, a movement caught my eye and I turned to the left. André and Katya were standing just behind me.

They lunged toward me, each grabbing hold of me. I felt André reach into his pocket, and I knew he was going for the knife.

Above the clanging, I could suddenly hear clattering. The stairwell door burst open and Tate and two patrol cops charged through. One of the patrol cops had his gun drawn.

André released me and took off. Before Katya could do the same, I kicked her as hard as I could in the knee. Her legs buckled and I slid out of her grasp.

One of the two cops took off after André. Tate and the other hurried over to Katya and me.

"She killed Mona," I said, out of breath. "There's another guy, down there, in that room to the right. I squirted a fire extinguisher at him."

Tate reached under the back of his sports jacket and yanked out a set of handcuffs. As he cuffed Katya, he told the patrol cop to check out the room.

"You have no proof," Katya spat at him. "I do nothing wrong."

The stairwell door sprang open again and this time there were not only four cops, but also three New York City firefighters. Tate, with Katya in tow, conferred quickly with them, pointing as he talked. One cop headed down toward the room with the lockers, two took off through the basement, and the last escorted Katya through the stairwell. Around this time, someone finally turned off the goddamn alarm. Silence seemed to sweep through the basement like a wave of water.

"Sit there for a minute," Tate said, gesturing toward a box. "You're bleeding and you need to see someone. And I need to talk to you."

I glanced down at my legs. One knee was oozing blood. I touched my head where it had hit the wall. I could feel a large egg there and a smear of blood.

"How did you know to come?" I asked weakly.

"I dropped by the office tonight to talk to your boss—and follow up with you about our conversation. It took a while, but I got your office buddy—Ms. Pendergrass—to spill where you were. We've had plenty of concerns about Katya, and I didn't like that you'd gone down here. Just as we were about to try to find you, the alarm went off."

A minute or so later, Evil Cousin was led off and I was transferred to the small locker room. Tate disappeared somewhere, doing his job. I waited for about ten minutes with a uniformed police officer standing right by the door. I could hear lots of commotion echoing through the basement, which I figured had to do with the search for André. At one point, the voices and footsteps faded away completely, and I wondered if the hunt had taken them far, far back to the other side of the basement.

After about ten minutes, EMS workers arrived with a collapsible stretcher.

"You don't have to put me on that," I said. "I'm really okay. I'm just banged up a little. And there's a doozy of a bruise on my head."

"Well, let's take a look at it, shall we?" said one of them, a chunky woman with her hair pulled back in a tight ponytail. She inspected my scalp and offered me one of those instant ice packs. She took my pulse and blood pressure and dressed the cut on my knee.

"Why don't you let us bring you in for observation?" she asked. "You might have a head injury."

"Thanks, but I feel okay, really. I just need some sleep—and maybe a margarita."

"Make it a cup of tea, okay?"

Through her radio, she announced to a dispatcher or driver that she and her partner were leaving empty and then told me to call a doctor if I experienced any headaches.

It was another fifteen minutes before Tate returned, carrying my purse. He pulled up a chair at the table and sat across from me.

"You know for sure that Katya did it, don't you?" I asked.

"Yes. André's cousin volunteered plenty of information, including where Katya supposedly hid the paperweight that she used as a weapon. Without that, we might not have a case."

"What about André?"

"He's not so lucky," he said. "He fled the building and ran in front of a car. He's on his way to the ER. Now tell me what you were doing down here. You had no business pursuing this on your own."

"Look, I apologize, but I wasn't really trying to play police. As I said when I called you, I had this sense that Katya knew something. She seemed anxious, almost afraid. What I didn't realize was that she was simply concerned that someone was going to learn the truth about what had happened. She suspected I might be on to her, and she asked me to come down here. I suggested that she go to the police, but she stressed that there was a good reason she couldn't. My plan was to find out what she knew and report it to you. When I got down here, I said some things that made her think that I *did* know the truth and she admitted to committing the murder, and to killing Ryan. She obviously had André and her cousin around in case they decided I posed a threat."

I recapped for Tate, to the best of my ability, every word Katya had said and my subsequent pursuit by André and his cousin.

"You'll need to come down tomorrow and make a full statement," Tate said.

One of the police officers was given the job of escorting me to find a taxi. I deliberated going back to sixteen, but I didn't have the energy. The cop kept his hand cupped under my elbow as I limped along beside him, in part because of how bruised I was and partly because the heel had come partially unglued from one of my leopard slingbacks at one point. He hailed a cab for me and even opened the door.

"Where you headed?" he asked me, obviously planning to give the driver the address for me.

"I'm not sure yet. I need to think about it."

Unexpectedly, I felt tears well in my eyes. I was overcome by a mixture of sadness and anger and guilt. I sank back into the leather seat and fished my cell phone out of my purse to phone Landon. Nobody home. Then I called Beau.

"Does your offer still hold?" I asked. "It's Bailey, by the way."

"Of course. Are you all right?"

"No. I mean, I'm all right now. But I was attacked tonight."

"By who? Where?"

I told him in a few broad strokes what had happened and said I would provide all the details when I saw him.

"What's the exact address again?"

He gave it to me and then asked how far away I was, explaining that he was out at the moment, but just ten minutes away. He would have no trouble beating me back to his place.

The taxi encountered one of those inexplicable pockets of traffic you can find in New York at any time, and I cursed out loud each time the driver would inch ahead two feet and then tap his brakes. All I wanted was to be out of the cab, someplace where I could flop onto a sofa or bed. Was I stupid to have called Beau? I knew I didn't want to be alone, but it may have been best to wait for Landon to surface, or to give Jessie a call. Well, it was too late now.

There were so many thoughts colliding in my mind. I was furious at Katya—for killing Mona and Ryan, for tricking me, for luring me down to the basement so that André could shut me up for good. I was angry with Ryan, too. Tate had accused me of playing cop, but that's what Ryan had done. He'd followed his hunch to his death—and put me in danger, too. If he hadn't been so hell-bent on competing with me, he might have shared the information and I could have talked some sense into him.

And then there was the guilt that had drilled its way into my system. Just over a week ago, I had walked in on a crime scene and made a completely erroneous assumption—the way my brother, Cameron, had years ago with the red paint on the seesaw. It was another case of what Landon's sister had called an optical confusion. The police, at least initially, had not seen things any more clearly than I had. As Katya had revealed, I'd given her the damn idea. I could still hear the words I'd used when I'd called 911: "Two women have been attacked."

There was classical guitar music playing when Beau answered the door, meaning he'd probably been home for a few minutes. He was wearing blue jeans and a pink dress shirt, a different color from the one he'd had on earlier, and some back corner of my brain went to work analyzing what this selection of clothes meant. Had he been dressed up only minutes ago and then thrown on his jeans when he returned home? Where had he been? Who had he been with?

But the front and center part of my brain could deal only with the insanity of everything that had transpired tonight. Beau hugged me and then quickly pulled back to look at me.

"God, you've got a huge egg on the side of your head."

I touched it gingerly. "I had an ice pack for it, but I lost it somewhere along the way."

"Let me make another for you, then. Do you need to see a doctor?"

As I trailed him to the kitchen, limping from my bruised

knee and broken slingback, I explained that an EMS worker had treated me. After Beau had fabricated an ice pack out of ice cubes and a bright red dish towel, we transferred to the living room, where I kicked off my shoes and began to pour out every detail of the night's events. Beau offered me a glass of white wine, which I gulped greedily despite orders, and he sat near me on the couch. Every few sentences he would ask questions to help him clarify the story in his mind. And more than once he asked for reassurance that I was really feeling okay.

When I was finally finished with the story, he expelled a loud sigh.

"What do you think of Katya's claim of self-defense?" he asked.

"Not much. I think Mona *did* hit her with the paperweight—Katya's injuries support that. But maybe she shoved Mona harder than she says and *Mona* reacted in self-defense. At the very least, Katya could have just gotten out of the office and then sued Mona's ass. But she obviously flew into a rage and walloped Mona."

"What did she do with the paperweight, just drop it in her trash cart?"

"No, the cousin told the police where it was so she must have taken it with her, maybe in one of the pockets of her apron. She would have had to be careful at the hospital. But they generally give you some kind of plastic bag for your belongings, so she could have hidden it in there, inside her clothes."

"It just all seems so ironic," he said. "Mona apparently angered tons of people in the magazine world and the entertainment business—but it was the cleaning woman who killed her."

"And I was so dumb not to have seen it."

"You shouldn't beat yourself up over it, Bailey. Like so many things, it's only obvious in hindsight."

"But it *should* have been obvious. One of the rules of police work is that you focus first on the last person to have seen a homicide victim alive. And just because she was the cleaning lady didn't mean she couldn't have had some issue with Mona. In the cab down here I remembered something Robby said when he was first encouraging me to go to work at *Buzz*. He said he'd once overheard Mona verbally bitch-slap the mailman. No one was really safe from her meanness."

"But even the cops didn't put two and two together," Beau acknowledged.

"That doesn't make me feel any better," I said. "It was really like this bizarre optical illusion. Or what my friend calls an optical confusion. And it colored everything that happened *afterwards*. For instance, when Katya seemed so sullen and worried after the attack, I assumed she was afraid the killer was coming after her. But she was simply fearful of getting caught."

"So how did this guy Ryan figure it all out?"

"He had an advantage. He saw Katya that night, more than once. Ryan knew from all the press coverage that Katya had been injured when she'd gone in to clean Mona's office. But when he was answering my questions about Mona, it seems he suddenly remembered that he'd seen Katya in Mona's office earlier in the evening. He wondered why she would have gone back there. Katya told me that she saw Mona return from the party and followed her back to that end of the floor. Ryan figured that out. Then he apparently called the cleaning company and found out that Mona had been making complaints about Katya."

"And then he confronted Katya?"

"Yes. He called her and asked her to come to the floor before she started her shift. He may not have come right out and accused her, but he obviously implied as much or asked enough questions for her to realize that he was going to keep pursuing it. André had connections in the drug world that allowed him to quickly obtain the pure heroin. Sometime on Monday evening, when Ryan was out for a while, Katya managed to make the substitution with the heroin Ryan had in his desk. He came back and took it home. The police found a bag in his drawer, but that must have been an old one. It was reckless of him to store drugs at work but it seems he had a severe habit. I just wish I'd figured out what he was up to."

"You can't blame yourself. The guy was a fool to have baited someone he thought might be a killer."

"I know. But I still feel awful that he's dead."

After I took a long sip of my wine, Beau pulled me over and laid my head in his lap. He stroked my hair softly and I lay there, quietly, attempting to focus on the smell of him—that exotic scent he wore—and not how big of a mess the night had been. After a little while I felt myself drifting off, and I just let go.

"Hey, why don't we go to bed?" Beau said. I stirred awake, not certain of how long I'd been asleep.

"Have I stopped the blood flow to your thighs?" I muttered.

"No, but I can see you're exhausted."

It was clear when we crawled into bed that Beau had no expectations that we'd have sex, but I felt suddenly so needy for the release. Under the sheet I stroked his chest and let my hand find its way to between his legs. The sex was less intense than before—my body was almost too achy to move—but it was the release I craved.

In the morning, I woke to the sound of the shower shutting off, and Beau strolled out of the bathroom with a big white towel around his waist.

"You can sleep longer if you want," he announced. "I'm in no rush this morning. I even have bagels here."

I squinted at my watch. "No, I better get moving. I now have another huge story to write—and Nash is probably furious that I haven't called yet."

While I dressed, Beau fixed coffee and toasted the bagels. His kitchen had a counter and we sat on the stools to eat the breakfast. Though I knew this might not be the best time for the discussion I was about to have, I also knew I couldn't leave without having it.

"Thanks for providing such great company last night. It would have been tough to be alone."

"Glad you were able to reach me. I was sorry you hadn't called earlier."

"Speaking of earlier, I have a follow-up question from our breakfast yesterday."

He cocked his eyebrow and eyed me expectantly.

"We talked about how awkward Wednesday night was, but I realize there's something I need to know," I said. "It's not about putting any pressure on you, but I just have to know for my own sake. How serious is your relationship with that woman?"

He stretched his neck in discomfort. "Not serious," he said. "The date that night was something we'd set up even before I took her to Dicker's barbecue. She'd asked me to a club to see a friend of hers sing. When Dicker wanted to change the meeting with me to Wednesday, he just told me to bring her along. Frankly, I think he might have his eye on her."

"And you wouldn't care?" I asked. I felt like such a loser begging for details, but I had to know the truth.

"No," he said, laughing. "In fact, I don't have any plans to see her again."

I smiled politely, trying not to look insanely giddy.

Beau picked up his coffee spoon and studied it. There was something on his mind. Suddenly I had a bad feeling.

"Look, Bailey," he said quietly. "There *is* something—someone I'm sleeping with."

"Oh really?" I said. It came out stupidly, as if he'd just told me he'd found a place where you could find good fresh mozzarella.

"I'm sorry I didn't say anything before—but based on what you said that day in East Hampton, I thought you were looking for something with no strings attached."

"Do you mind if I ask how serious it is?"

"Not very serious. She's another filmmaker, and she travels

a lot. For the time being, at least, she wants something fairly casual. And that works for me, too. The relationship I told you about the other night was fairly intense, and after she moved to London I promised myself I wasn't going to get into anything serious for a while."

"And so that's what you want with me—just something casual?"

He laughed, tossing his head back. "I haven't even had a chance to think about what I want with you. It feels like I got hit by a bus when I saw you in East Hampton. Then I found myself walking towards your apartment one day like someone out of *The Manchurian Candidate*."

"Should I take that as a compliment?"

"Absolutely. But I'll be honest. As attracted as I am, I guess I don't feel ready for anything steady or serious. Or exclusive. I always thought you were on the same page."

"I don't want anything serious," I said, my voice embarrassingly high. "And I'm not just saying that. When I broke up with someone in January, it was because he was ready to move in together and the mere thought of it gave me a panic attack. But the nonexclusive thing . . . Well, let me think about it, okay?"

"Of course."

I glanced at my watch again. "Yikes," I said, "I better dash." I was trying to break into the light and breezy Bailey, but I felt as though my heart were being squeezed. I hobbled to the door in my busted slingback.

"So call me later, will you?" Beau said. "I want to know how you're feeling—and what happens today with the police."

"Sure. . . ." My voice trailed off as I gathered my thoughts.

"Listen, Beau. Maybe I'm being impetuous for saying this now and I should wait until my head wound heals, but . . . What I'm trying to say is that I don't need to do any more thinking. True, I was looking for something very casual this summer. But I realize that's not what I want from *you*. I really like being with you, and though I'm not looking for some big commitment, I'd like to get to know you without always wondering how I measure up to the competition."

I smiled, afraid I was sounding like some district attorney in her closing arguments.

"So you're blowing me off, is that it?" he asked. There was a trace of bittersweet in his voice. As miserable as I felt, I found some reserve of cockiness before I opened my mouth again.

"Under the current conditions, yes."

"Let me think about what you said," he told me. "I don't want it to just end right here and now."

"All right," I replied.

He started to smile, a rueful smile, perhaps, but before he could say anything else, I kissed him on the mouth and slipped out the door.

It took me forever to find a cab. In my wrinkled clothes and broken shoe, I probably looked like a hooker who'd been sideswiped by a car while working Ninth Avenue. Once I was finally settled in the backseat, I called Nash on his cell phone.

"God, Bailey, where the hell have you been?"

"Sorry, I went to a friend's and turned my ringer off. I was just feeling miserable."

"You're okay, right?"

"Yeah. Slightly bloodied and bowed but basically fine."

"I was still in the office last night when everything was happening, but the police wouldn't let me go into the basement. The next thing I knew, you were gone. Tate filled me in on most of it. But you've got to come in and write this up. And I want you to do press as well. This thing is huge."

"I'll be there in about an hour," I told him. "I'll tell you everything then."

I leaned back and pressed my hands to my forehead. My head was throbbing again, and I felt the beginning stages of a weird mental hangover—from the stress and guilt and fear and anger.

I would just have to suck it up and cope because I had a boatload of stuff to tackle today, not the least of which was my article on the arrest of Mona's murderer and my own involvement in it. I needed to take Nash blow by blow through what had happened to me last night, as well as ask him what he meant by *press*. (Did he expect me to sit across from Larry King one night this week? Was I supposed to get my hair highlighted or anything?) It would be nice to be in Nash's company and not be nursing those nasty suspicions about him (I just hoped the egg on my head wouldn't be an excuse for him to paw me.)

I also couldn't wait to talk to Jessie and thank her. Based on what Tate had told me, she'd still been around last night after all, and had directed my rescuers to me. I had even more respect for her nosiness now. I also wanted to sit down, face-to-face with Robby, now that he was totally in the clear. There would be other people to fill in, too—Landon and Cat, for instance. And I knew I had better touch base with my mother. I'd been less than forthcoming with her about my ups and downs through the case, but she was bound to hear something now.

And then there was Beau to think about. I didn't regret my ultimatum to him. I'd read enough articles in *Gloss* to know that men liked them as much as they enjoyed hearing you talk about vaginal itch. But I also knew that I couldn't go to bed with Beau again if he was sleeping with someone else. If he wasn't interested in being exclusive, I would get over it sooner or later, but I knew it would be hard not to wince whenever I thought of him and how good it could have been. And I would probably have to have Landon make his famous blues-banishing brisket and spoon-feed it to me with half a bottle of Cabernet.

But for now I was going to remain optimistic. I could sense Beau's strong attraction to me, and maybe that attraction would be enough to make him forgo his sometime girlfriend. I was just going to pray to the gods of love and lust that he couldn't tell me no.

More
Kate White!

Please turn this page
for a preview of

How to Set His Thighs on Fire: 86 Red-Hot Lessons on Love, Life, Men, and (Especially) Sex

---

Available in hardcover.

I love writing Bailey Weggins mysteries, but I also have a day job that I'm crazy about—being editor in chief of *Cosmopolitan* magazine. I took over almost eight years ago, following in the footsteps of Helen Gurley Brown. Young women consider *Cosmo* their bible, and each month we now sell over two million copies on newsstands alone, making it the most successful monthly magazine in the U.S.

My job is to shape the direction of *Cosmo*, generating lots of ideas for the magazine. But I have learned a ton from being here—about men and love and sex and life in general. And so I thought it might be fun to bundle some of the fascinating things I've discovered into a book. It's out right now and it's called *How to Set His Thighs on Fire*. Here's a sampling for you to check out.

ONE

The Eye Makeup Technique That Will Make Him Gaga

I've heard people say that women wear makeup for other women, and to some extent that may be true. We want to walk into a party or an event or even into work and have other females decide that we look damn *good*. I also think we wear makeup for ourselves, for the sheer joy and pleasure of it. When you try out a new teal eyeliner pencil or shimmery gold lip gloss, it's really fun.

Plenty of times, though, we apply makeup with men in mind—because we want to snag one, seduce one, enchant one, reinforce the decision of one who has already chosen us, or make one who has ditched us eat his bloody heart out. So in those instances the question becomes, what kind of makeup do *men* really dig? If you are clearly on a man mission, what should you go for?

Well, it depends a little bit on the man. But I feel safe making some broad statements based on what I've learned.

1. Guys hate too much makeup, especially foundation that makes your skin look like the shade of a Band-Aid and anything goopy on your lips that suggests they will become stuck to your mouth if they attempt to kiss you.
2. They also hate too *little* makeup. Despite how much they rave about the natural look, most guys want you to make a fuss with your appearance. It shows you care.

3. And if there is one makeup effect they really go bonkers over, it's what makeup artists call smoky eyes—eyes that are lined with black and covered with deep gray shadow.

Why do smoky eyes fire up guys? I think it's in large part because they're so mysterious. Helen Fisher, research professor and member of the Center for Evolutionary Studies in the Department of Anthropology at Rutgers University, says that we humans are programmed to mate outside of the family group and thus it's the unfamiliar and the mysterious that really turns us on. Also, distinctive eye makeup draws attention to the eyes, which, according to Fisher, are the only feature that actually gives insight into what's going on in the brain.

To create a smoky eye, first apply concealer or an eye shadow primer so the color will stay put and not get blotchy. Rim the area along your upper lashes with a black pencil that you've sharpened the heck out of so it doesn't go on too thickly. Start from the inner eye and work outward, pulling each lid tautly as you work so that you can come as close to the lashes—even *into* the lashes—as possible. Now line the lower lid, too. Then smudge the liner ever so gently with your fingertips. This will prevent the line from appearing harsh and also create a "bedroom eye" feel. Next apply a charcoal or deep gray shadow to your lids, going just slightly above the crease (otherwise you'll risk looking like a raccoon). You may have to experiment with eye shadows because some grays can smear and look messy. For an extra special touch, you can add a pearlized gray highlighting shadow to the area along your brow bone. Finish by curling your lashes and applying very black mascara.

The rest of your face needs to be nicely balanced so you don't look Goth. Pick a soft color for your cheeks and then try a matte lipstick or gloss in nude or a brownish pink. For the right occasion, red lips can look pretty dramatic with smoky eyes, but for a basic date or party, that effect is probably going to be too overpowering. Keep your lips more neutral.

Now, you are ready to enchant.

TWO

How to Find the Time to Do the Things You Really, Really Want

Despite how thrilling it was to land the *Cosmo* job, there was one aspect of it that broke my heart. About half a year before I was offered the position, I'd begun writing my first murder mystery, and as I was accepting the job, one of the thoughts flashing through my brain like a security alarm was, *Oh damn, there goes the mystery.* I knew I would have to abandon it.

In my previous position—as editor of *Redbook*—writing a book on the side hadn't posed a problem. I had my job pretty much under control and I only had to lug work home a couple of nights a week. I was able to snatch time here and there to work on my mystery, and I loved it. I had developed a soupçon of career malaise, and I found that imagining corpses and killers was shaking me out of my slump.

But *Cosmo* was a much bigger fish to fry than *Redbook,* and I knew I would be a fool not to give it my undivided attention from the start. I could just imagine what my boss would have said if I announced during our interview that I also planned to write a mystery that year. She would have probably murdered *me.*

During my first months at *Cosmo,* I would occasionally think of my gutsy, irreverent, amateur sleuth, Bailey Weggins, and feel a twinge of sadness as I pictured her stuck in a drawer, cooling her heels. I was thrilled with my new opportunity but I hated sidelining Bailey.

Why did I have such a big yearning to write a mystery? Partly because the fabulous, fearless Nancy Drew was one of my first role models and she inspired me to want to create my own detective. Plus, I'm in such a precarious business that I've always liked the notion of having a Plan B in case I am given the boot. While plotting out how I was going to shape *Cosmo*'s future and picking out sexy bustiers for the cover, I promised myself that someday I'd find my way back to Bailey Weggins.

Then a funny thing happened. It was Christmastime, about six months after I started, and since I had a few vacation days, I decided to drag my four chapters out of the drawer. As I reread what I'd written, I discovered that I'd had Bailey find the dead nanny sprawled on a copy of *Cosmo*, something I'd completely forgotten doing. I couldn't even recall *Cosmo* being much on my radar back then. So you know what? I took it as a clear sign that I was meant to combine editing *Cosmo* and writing mysteries. Since that day I have published four Bailey Weggins murder mysteries: *If Looks Could Kill, A Body to Die For, 'Til Death Do Us Part,* and *Over Her Dead Body.*

The challenge, of course, was figuring out how to accomplish both without doing a lousy job at either one. In fact, the question I get asked most when I give a speech or an interview is, "How do you *do* it?" I know why that question is so popular. Most of us who dream of writing a book, starting a jewelry line, or creating awe-inspiring sculptures can't afford to leave our jobs (at least initially), and so we're desperate for any advice on how to juggle successfully. For me, mystery writing hasn't exactly been a breeze, but it's been *doable* and that's because of two little strategies I've relied on. Here's what they are. If you try them, I swear they'll work for you, too.

Strategy 1: To find the time, you must *make* the time.
It sounds obvious but in order to tackle a major goal—whether it's writing your first novel or *finally* putting all the pictures in your photo albums—you have to block out the time to do it and view that time as sacred. It's easy to believe that if you feel passionate

enough about something, the time for it will magically present it-self during the course of the day. But that doesn't just happen. You must designate a certain period when you're going to do the job—and you may have to experiment a bit to figure out what works best for you. Despite the fact that I had written two non-fiction books in the evening (with one eye on *Law and Order* or *ER* most of the time), I realized that fiction came most easily to me in the mornings. So after trial and error, I began blocking off time on weekends when my kids were sleeping (they're teenagers so they don't raise a head off the pillow until at least eleven) and on weekdays before my staff arrived.

Once you designate a block of time for a goal, you will prob-ably wonder how you're supposed to do what *used* to happen in that time period. Interestingly, when you organize your time, you become more efficient at accomplishing your to-do list. You putter less, end phone calls earlier, etc., and what you used to do in that slot probably will gravitate to your "found time." But if your sched-ule is impossibly packed and you're already an efficient machine, it may not be possible to shoehorn a project into your life without letting something else go. Then you have to throw a few things overboard. In order to write my mysteries, I gave up tennis (I was pathetic anyway), leisurely shopping excursions (I do miss that), and sleeping late on Saturday and Sunday mornings (miss that, too!). But for me, the trade-off was worth it.

Strategy 2: To actually be productive in your time slot, you have to learn to *slice the salami*.
As we all know, just because you block off time doesn't mean you will accomplish anything constructive in it. I was a pro at telling myself that I would write in the morning and then *not doing it*. That's because writing often seemed so tough. I dreaded the notion of sitting there for hours trying to put words to computer.

I was saved by a technique called "slice the salami." When I was a young writer, I interviewed a time management expert named Edwin Bliss (one of his books is called *Getting It Done*) who had devised this particular approach. His point was that if you make a project too big, it seems like a huge hunk of salami. Now, there's nothing very appetizing about *that*. But if you carve it into thin slices, it's much more appealing.

Bliss says we have to do this with projects, too—in other words, slice them down into appealing pieces. For instance, don't promise yourself you're going to put your entire photo album together on Saturday. Just say that you are going to spend one hour getting started by sorting as many photos as possible by *date*.

You'll have to figure out for yourself how thin your slices need to be in order to seem manageable for you. I knew, because I'd always tended to put off writing, that mine had to be very, very skinny. So for the first few months, I told myself I would only write for fifteen minutes a day.

Well, fifteen minutes turned out to be the secret for me. And something interesting happened. After fifteen minutes, I'd usually keep at it, because I had a nice flow going. Eventually I extended my salami slice. It's up to two hours now (and I also discovered that it helped to aim for a certain number of *pages* during that period). But I know that it's smart not to take it beyond that or I just won't want to dig in. I frequently write for four hours, but if I set myself a goal of four hours, I'd never sit down at my desk.

Admittedly it's been nutty at times to do *two* jobs. But overall it's been a good thing. The book writing has given my brain a chance to refuel for *Cosmo,* and working at *Cosmo* has given me killer ideas for my books.

THREE

How to *Double* a Man's Pleasure in Bed

Earlier I mentioned that guys like a firmer touch in bed than women may imagine. But there's another touching technique that can really captivate, as well. You could call it double delight.

The basic idea is that you stimulate *two* body parts at the same time—kind of a stereo effect. For instance, as you trace your tongue around the rim of your guy's ear, you can run your fingers seductively along the inside of his thigh. This technique is ultrapleasureable not only because you're in contact with more flesh but also because you're triggering twice the erotic anticipation.

There's a twist that makes it even more delicious. Use the *identical* stroke on each body part. You could, for example, make circles with your tongue on his nipples at the same time that you stroke his testicles in a circular motion. There's something about experiencing the same exact movement in two places simultaneously that is truly mind-blowing.

FOUR

You Really Should Take What a Guy Says Literally

As women, we sometimes choose to load what we say with meaning that isn't totally apparent in the words we use. For instance, a friend asks how you're feeling and you respond, "Good—I guess." She knows, in part because she's a girl, too, not to be misled by the word *good*. The correct translation? "I'm not so good but I need you to keep probing because it's hard for me to spit it out." (Or perhaps, "I'm not so good but I need you to keep probing because you're part of the problem.")

Because *we* do this, we assume men do it, too, and when we have the slightest feeling that a man is being less than direct, we push him to cough up what he *really* thinks or feels.

I've known from the research I've seen that guys are very literal when they speak. But I don't think I was totally convinced until I read the mail at *Cosmo* and saw how baffled guys are by women's failure to take them literally and by our unrelenting desire to read things into both their words and their tone of voice. One guy asked in an interview, "Why do women always assume something is *wrong*? I was on the phone with this girl, and I guess my tone was a little off. She kept asking 'Are you okay? Why did you say that?'"

Oh sure, on occasion some guys are cagey as hell—or totally duplicitous. And sometimes a guy who's in a funk will sulk and force you to use a crowbar to uncover why he's acting crabby toward you all of a sudden. But for the most part, guys mean what they say. And because of that, you generally should take what a guy says at face value and not go crazy trying to analyze it—or probing for more info.

When he tells you he's fine, for example, chances are he is (unless there's real evidence to the contrary). When you ask him if he wants Italian or Mexican and he answers "Mexican," he really, really wants Mexican. He's not just saying that to be polite, or in the hopes you'll dig deeper for the truth.

So don't ask, "Are you sure?" "Really?" or "You're not just saying that, are you?" It drives a guy nuts.